Courting
the Countess

by

Donna Hatch

This is a work of fiction. Names, characters, places, and incidents are either the product of the author's imagination or are used fictitiously, and any resemblance to actual persons living or dead, business establishments, events, or locales, is entirely coincidental.

Courting the Countess

Cover Art by *Debbie Taylor*

The Wild Rose Press, Inc.
PO Box 708
Adams Basin, NY 14410-0708
Visit us at www.thewildrosepress.com

Publishing History
First Tea Rose Edition, 2016
Print ISBN 978-1-5092-0948-4
Digital ISBN 978-1-5092-0949-1

Published in the United States of America

"Get your hands off my sister!" a voice snarled.

Tristan snapped his head back and stepped away. Alone, Elizabeth wobbled on her feet. Her half-brother, Martindale, stalked into view, bristling like an angry dog.

With his hands held out, Tristan faced Martindale. "My lord, we were merely—"

"None of your lies, Barrett."

Other voices made exclamations of delighted horror. Elizabeth faced a nightmare; most of the houseguests stared at her, including some of London's worst gossips. Naturally, they would assume the worst. Heat crawled up Elizabeth's neck and burned her cheeks. She'd never live down the humiliation. Closing her eyes, she clamped her mouth shut to avoid screaming at the injustice of it all. She'd only desired a few moments alone with the man she loved. Instead, she'd been caught in an intimate embrace in a dark garden. Gossipers would spread an exaggeratedly sordid tale all over England. She'd be utterly ruined.

Dedication

To my husband,
who never stopped courting me,
even after twenty years of marriage.

Chapter One

England 1813

Lady Elizabeth had never dared hope she would find the kind of joy that inspired poets and musicians...until she met the incomparable Tristan Barrett. She sat rooted in a wingback chair, fighting the impulse to rush outside to the garden where he'd invited her to meet him tonight. In the garden. Unchaperoned. Tristan was like no other, worth any risk, even defy social conventions and her parents, the Duke and Duchess of Pemberton.

Elizabeth glanced at the clock over the mantel in the drawing room, her nerves stretched to a snapping point. When would the gentlemen end their after-dinner conversation and join the ladies? Time lengthened into eternity. If she survived the waiting, she and Tristan would steal away together for a few precious moments. She trembled in anticipation.

Finally, the host of the house party led the gentlemen into the room. Tristan sauntered in last. Elizabeth's heart leaped. From across the drawing room, his dark-eyed gaze fastened on her with an intensity that sent heat to her cheeks. He smiled at her, a smile filled with promise.

Tristan. Elizabeth barely managed to suppress a sigh. Perhaps tomorrow Tristan would approach her father and declare his intention. He would marry her and rescue her from Duchess's dominion. Elizabeth ached to build a new life of love and safety with him.

One of the gentlemen launched into a terrifying account of his neighbor getting burglarized. "Servants discovered the burglars, but before they could raise the alarm, the burglars held them at gunpoint."

Several guests exclaimed. While sympathy for the ordeal the servants must have suffered touched Elizabeth, her focus remained so tightly on Tristan that she couldn't summon true alarm.

Elizabeth's father, the duke, scowled down into his glass. "Dark days, indeed, when burglars get so brazen."

"I've heard similar stories." Tristan's brother, the Earl of Averston, spoke as solemnly as Father. "Bow Street is linking all such break-ins to the so-called King of Crime."

Tristan stood next to the earl near the French doors. Their dark superfine frockcoats and waistcoats, and crisp, white shirts contrasted with the blue and gold wallpaper and white woodwork. The Barrett brothers made a stunning pair—raven-haired, tall, and beautifully proportioned like two Greek gods, yet so opposite in temperament. Tristan, charming and gregarious, had caught her eye the moment she'd seen him. Though she'd pretended to be disapproving and unaffected by his flirtations, he'd wormed through her defenses. His grin banished the gloom in her thoughts, the gloom in her life, the gloom in her heart.

Other guests took up the topic of crime in London, a subject Elizabeth thought best not to discuss in front of young ladies with delicate sensibilities like her younger sister.

Tristan whispered to the earl, who nodded in reply, and he eased toward the open French door leading to the garden. Pausing, he glanced back at Elizabeth, a secretive smile tugging at his expressive mouth, before slipping outside.

Excitement exploded in a shower of color. She was about to take a walk in a moonlit garden with the charming Tristan Barrett. If only for a moment, she would bask in the warmth of his affection.

Her parents would think her foolish for forming a *tendré* for a younger son with a tainted reputation. They'd be furious if they suspected she agreed to meet him without a chaperone. Elizabeth smoothed her ivory silk gown with her gloved hands and shot a nervous glance at Duchess, the woman who condescended to call herself Elizabeth's mother.

Elizabeth arose and spoke under her breath. "I'm retiring for the evening, Mother." Her face heated at her lie.

Duchess waved her away without taking her eyes off the hostess. A brief flash of anger shot through Elizabeth that Duchess made so little effort to pretend she cared, even in the presence of others. Elizabeth murmured, "Good night," in the unlikely chance anyone might hear. Or care. She slipped into a dimly lit adjoining room and headed to the French doors leading to the terrace, her shoes tapping on the hardwood floor. Moonlight cast long shadows on the floor, and illuminated a pathway. After opening the door, she paused at the threshold. Her stomach fluttered.

Meeting Tristan tonight was dangerous.

Yet, how could she not? Yes, she'd only known

Tristan a week; however, Romeo and Juliet met mere hours before they were willing to smash the barriers separating them. If Elizabeth wanted to secure her Romeo, she needed Juliet's boldness.

She frowned. Perhaps Romeo and Juliet were the wrong role models. She certainly didn't want a disastrous end. Perhaps she ought to emulate her favorite heroine, the courageous and devoted Lady Enide, to be worthy of her own knight.

The memory of Tristan's kiss that afternoon when he'd invited her to meet him tonight emboldened her. She would seize this opportunity for happiness. After taking a steadying breath, she stepped onto the terrace.

A full moon cast near-midday illumination over the gardens. The balmy night air wore a sultry breeze, slipping over her skin, carrying the scent of roses, jasmine, and honeysuckle. Stepping softly, she crossed the stone terrace, descended the steps, and all but raced out into the garden where Tristan awaited. Her footsteps crunched on the gravel as she followed the melody of tinkling water through hedgerows and ornamental trees. A tall figure waited by the fountain.

"Tristan?" she called.

"I'm here, my darling." Infused in moonlight, he was a black-haired Apollo come to life. As his hand closed over hers, she marveled again at his masculine perfection. His teeth flashed, his impenetrable dark eyes fixed upon her. "Shall we take a turn about the garden?"

"That would be lovely."

His gaze rested upon her as they strolled, arm in arm. "I enjoyed your poetry rendition this afternoon in the library before the others arrived. It was exquisite."

She glanced up, basking in his praise. Though she once viewed flattery with suspicion, she'd learned to trust Tristan. His eyes always softened when he complimented her and his voice rang with sincerity. "Truly?"

"Indeed. I'd hoped to hear more of it," he added. "Pity we were interrupted before you could continue. I understand your shyness, and I was honored you gave me a glimpse into your heart through the way you read."

She turned over his words in her thoughts, "a glimpse into your heart." Tristan did indeed have a poetic side, allowing him to feel the spoken word as deeply as she. "Do you think Keats had it aright, then?"

"He is brilliant."

"I agree. I find Byron a bit dark at times, nevertheless, he has poignantly beautiful poems, as well."

Tristan quoted, his voice rich and resonant:
> *"She walks in beauty, like the night*
> *Of cloudless climes and starry skies,*
> *And all that's best of dark and bright*
> *Meets in her aspect and her eyes..."*

He gazed at her. "You do walk in beauty, Elizabeth. You *are* beauty. I am fortunate to have found you."

She moistened her lips, her pulse racing at his nearness. "I, too, feel fortunate."

He drew her close. She went willingly into his arms and rested a hand on his chest. His heart beat strong under her palm. With gentle fingers, he traced circles on her cheek, then bent his head toward hers. Tingles of nervous exhilaration raced down her back.

He kissed her with warm, soft lips. Her heart thudded in her ears. At that moment, she fully understood what had driven Romeo and Juliet to such drastic measures and why Lady Enid and her Prince Eric fought so hard for one another.

Tristan's first kiss this afternoon had been a promise of more. Tonight, he grew passionate. She'd never been kissed by anyone before Tristan, but he clearly knew how.

Tristan's kiss enfolded her in a cushion of joy. Then his hands began a slow exploration of her body. Startled, she froze. All daring drained out of her.

She let out a strangled breath, and pulled away. "Tristan, I'm not a strumpet."

"No, beloved." He touched her cheek. "You are a lovely and desirable lady."

He enfolded her in his embrace and kissed her again, but disappointment that he would take such liberties cooled her ardor. She stiffened, pulled away, and captured his hands with hers. He was supposed to be the perfect storybook hero. They weren't even married yet. Was he so sure her father would give permission that he considered them already betrothed?

"Get your hands off my sister!" a voice snarled.

Tristan snapped his head back and stepped away. Alone, Elizabeth wobbled on her feet. Her half-brother, Martindale, stalked into view, bristling like an angry dog.

With his hands held out, Tristan faced Martindale. "My lord, we were merely—"

"None of your lies, Barrett."

Other voices made exclamations of delighted horror. Elizabeth faced a nightmare; most of the houseguests stared at her, including some of London's worst gossips. Naturally, they would assume the worst. Heat crawled up Elizabeth's neck and burned her cheeks. She'd never live down the humiliation. Closing her eyes, she clamped her mouth shut to avoid screaming at the injustice of it all. She'd only desired a few moments alone with the man she loved. Instead, she'd been caught in an intimate embrace in a dark garden. Gossipers would spread an exaggeratedly sordid tale all over England. She'd be utterly ruined.

Immersed in his role of haughty marquis, Martindale snarled, "Consider your second, Barrett. Tomorrow you shall receive my challenge."

Elizabeth's heart stalled. "No! You can't do this." Elizabeth's protest died on her lips as her brother rounded on her.

"Silence! You've behaved like a common whore."

Elizabeth recoiled as if he'd slapped her.

Tristan stiffened. "Hear now, that's no way to speak to the lady. I give you my word, it was merely a kiss."

Martindale let out a scoff. "I should trust the word of a known rake?" He turned to Elizabeth, his eyes boring into hers. "You've brought disgrace upon the family."

Tears burned Elizabeth's eyes. Her brother was right. Only Tristan could save her from shame. She turned to him, silently pleading for rescue.

Tristan glanced at her, his expression unreadable, before returning his attention to Martindale. He lowered his voice. "Let us go inside and discuss this in private."

"You've compromised my sister," her brother practically shouted. "There's nothing to discuss.

Choose your weapon."

Elizabeth hugged herself while her knees threatened to fold. Her voice collapsed to a whisper. "You cannot mean to duel."

"My formal challenge will be delivered at dawn." Martindale marched away.

"Elizabeth! What have you done?" Duchess's strident voice broke through the buzzing in Elizabeth's head as her mother arrived upon the scene.

Oh, heaven help her. She'd probably be bedridden for a month. Elizabeth choked back the bile in her throat and grappled with the idea of running away, simply disappearing.

Tristan started to reach for her but dropped his arm. "I'm sorry. I never meant for this to happen." He strode away.

Stunned, she stared after his retreating back. He hadn't declared his intentions—no words of love, no vow to marry her and rescue her from her ruined state.

She'd been abandoned.

Chapter Two

While other houseguests retired for the evening, Richard Barrett, the Twelfth Earl of Averston, paced Lord Einsburgh's library. Though the hour crept past midnight, sleep fled in the face of Tristan's stupidity and all the consequences that must follow. Richard wanted to slam a fist through the wall. Or through his brother. When word reached him that Tristan had dallied with one of the duke's daughters, he'd stared in open-mouthed shock that his reckless brother had sunk to a new level of stupidity. Word spread like a contagious disease until all the guests knew of the couple's folly. By tomorrow, half the county would chew on the gossip.

Richard swung back to Tristan slumped in an overstuffed armchair, nursing a brandy "You half wit! What were you thinking? The daughter of a duke? How could you be so irresponsible?"

He couldn't remember being so angry. He swept a hand through his hair. Of all the thoughtless inanities Tristan had committed, this eclipsed them all. He clenched his hands unable to determine if he were more angry or more afraid. Afraid the duel would take place. Afraid Tristan would get hurt. Afraid he'd fail his family. Richard stuffed down fear and fed anger.

Tristan never lifted his head nor offered a word in defense, just endured anything Richard saw fit to mete out. Which was a good thing, because Richard wasn't finished.

"I've warned you your debauchery would get you into trouble, but I never dreamed you'd be so idiotic as to try to seduce an eighteen-year-old girl, who, might I remind you, is a daughter of one of the most powerful dukes in England!"

Tristan finished his brandy, set the glass on a Chippendale table, and proceeded to drink from the bottle. He remained silent.

Richard itched to snatch the bottle from Tristan's hand and smash it against the paneled wall. Struggling to think amid his roiling emotions, he continued, "Perhaps the girl's brother will have a cooler head tomorrow and will reconsider delivering the written challenge, but I doubt the Duke of Pemberton will simply let the matter drop."

Tristan mumbled something unintelligible and took another long drink of brandy.

Richard rubbed his hands over his face. Tristan had always been wild. His devil-may-care attitude had gotten him into constant trouble, but with Tristan's smooth tongue and famous charm, not to mention a great deal of work on Richard's part, Tristan usually evaded deserving consequences.

Unless Richard acted, his brother could face an enemy's sword or pistol. He could die. The thought froze Richard's heart into a solid block of ice. He'd lost his parents. His sister, Selina, painted somewhere in Italy—far out of reach. He couldn't bear it if he lost Tristan, too.

Dragging in a ragged breath, he ordered his thoughts. As head of the Barrett family, he could negotiate with the Duke of Pemberton and his son, the Marquis of Martindale. If they reached a concession, Pemberton could influence Martindale to refrain from delivering the formal written challenge to duel.

Pemberton's price would probably be marriage to his daughter. Few dukes would settle on a second son, and an irresponsible lad of twenty-two at that, but under the circumstances, marriage between Tristan and Lady Elizabeth would be the best recourse. It was time his wayward brother faced the consequences for his actions. He must take responsibility.

Yet, who would have thought such a timid creature as Lady Elizabeth would fall for the charms of a rake? In what little Richard had seen of her, Lady Elizabeth had seemed a sensible, if painfully shy, girl. Nevertheless, Tristan's powers of seduction were legendary, and apparently, even young ladies of good breeding were not immune to his charm.

Or perhaps Lady Elizabeth possessed dubious morals. Too many women had such a failing, as his mother had proved, and as he feared his sister, Selina, may yet demonstrate.

Richard stopped pacing. "I'll speak to Pemberton in the morning before matters get further out of hand."

Tristan finally looked up. "What do you mean?"

"I shall convince him to intercede."

"No." Tristan straightened, and a determined glint entered his eyes. "If Martindale wishes to issue the challenge, I will accept."

"Don't be an idiot. This is no time for misplaced heroism."

"This is my problem. I'll duel him."

"Absolutely not. I don't mean to stand by and

watch you get shot, or stabbed by a rapier. Even though you deserve it."

Tristan arose and stood remarkably erect considering the amount of brandy he'd just consumed. "You will not interfere. You've done that my entire life and I refuse to allow you to do it again. I can look after myself."

"You aren't responsible enough to look after yourself. This incident is further proof."

"I'm not a child. I am fully capable of fighting—and winning—a duel. Stop meddling in my affairs."

Meddling? Interfere? A dark and ugly force took hold of Richard. He cursed. How could his own brother turn on him? He'd looked after his brother all his life, bloodying noses of boys who bullied Tristan, taking the blame—and often the whippings—for Tristan's pranks, and protecting his younger brother from himself. That Tristan viewed his protection as meddling twisted in Richard's gut.

Richard made a sharp gesture. "Fine. Fight your duel. Get yourself killed. I'll be rid of the headache of pulling you out of a new scrape every week." Despite his angry words, the thought of his only brother facing such danger left him cold. Dark panic welled up.

Tristan's eyes took on that cocky, invincible gleam Richard knew all too well. "I'm the best fencer in Angelo's and I shoot better than the Duke of Suttenberg. I'll win."

"Then what? Are you prepared to *kill her brother*?"

Tristan's gaze wavered and he wetted his lips. "Neither of us would risk being caught dueling. If we simply fight to first-blood, the authorities will never know, and no one will die."

"Do you have any idea how many minor wounds can turn fatal? Father's wound wasn't much worse than what one might receive from first blood."

Tristan strode to the dark windows. After resting his hand on the panes a moment, he turned back, his shoulders squared. "I refuse to live in fear of what might be. Do not speak to the duke, do not speak to the marquis, do not intervene in any way. I mean to see this through."

At least Tristan was taking this seriously. For a change. A part of Richard admired the pup's willingness to take the consequences of his actions—but this was not the time. The stakes were too high. Richard rubbed the space between his eyes where a headache throbbed.

He ground his teeth and delivered the killing blow. "Fight this duel and I will cut off your funds. Completely."

Tristan swung back around, his jaw dropping. "You wouldn't!"

Richard folded his arms and glared back, openly daring Tristan to challenge the ultimatum. Though the ruthless tactic made him feel a beast, Richard said nothing. If he opened his mouth, he would tell Tristan just how terrified he was at the thought of losing him.

Fury rippled off Tristan in tangible waves and Richard fisted his hands, bracing himself against his brother's rage.

After letting out a stream of expletives that would have impressed a sailor and condemning Richard to Hades, Tristan let out a growl. "You win. You always do." Tristan wrenched the door open and left Richard alone.

Donna Hatch

Richard's victory tasted bitter as he stalked the corridor toward his room, cursing his brother, cursing the house party, and cursing women in general. Normally, he avoided house parties. They always proved to be excuses for debauchery or a prelude to the parson's trap. However, Lord Einsburgh hosted outstanding foxhunts, and hunting was one of the few indulgences Richard allowed himself.

"Richard?" Leticia Wentworth's familiar voice halted his footsteps.

As he waited for her to catch up, he tried to get his breathing under control.

Still wearing her silk evening gown, she approached. "Goodness, what a frightful scowl." She briefly brushed her fingers along his forehead in a comfortable, intimate gesture. "Do you fear the worst, then?"

The knots in his chest eased at her touch. "I do. I only hope Pemberton can be coaxed to intervene. I doubt he wishes to see his son duel any more than I wish that for Tristan."

Leticia nodded with a slight frown. "The grievance is serious, however. Much is at stake." She let out a sigh. "I have to admit; I'm not terribly surprised. Tristan rarely thinks through the consequences of his actions. I'd always feared his impulsive nature would get him into more trouble than you could get him out of."

"The duke will probably demand marriage." Despite Tristan acting like a randy youth, he had reached his majority, so age wasn't a barrier, though Tristan wasn't a peer, being born the son of an earl certainly didn't make him beneath Lady Elizabeth's status.

Concern etched Leticia's face. "Will Tristan agree to marry her?"

"He'll have little choice," Richard said darkly. "I'll thrash him, else."

She squeezed his arm, soothing him the way she had in childhood. Due to Leticia's height, their eyes met easily. He'd never been presumptuous enough to kiss her. He'd always planned to marry her but hadn't found the right time. She smiled, and the edges of the ice in his chest thawed.

She tightened her grip on his arm. "You're worried."

"Do not concern yourself, Tish. All will be well. I won't allow my brother to be harmed."

"I know you won't. I have faith in you. Good night." She kissed his cheek before gliding away.

His tension faded as he watched her retreating form. She'd grown from a freckle-faced girl with skinned knees into a lovely, poised, and gracious lady. Yes, she would make a fine countess. He'd see to that before the Season's end. Now if only he could beat some sense into his brother and marry him off to the promiscuous chit who no doubt deserved him.

In his room, Richard paced, trying to find words to convince the Duke of Pemberton to prevent a duel.

Chapter Three

Head bowed, Elizabeth sat in a straight-backed chair in the sitting room of her parents' guest suite. She wanted to raise her head and stand up to her parents but she deserved their scorn after her actions tonight. No one who lived upon the mercy of others had any right to make demands.

The candles sputtered, casting an eerie, fitful light over the room. The scarlet fabric of the furniture appeared blood red, as if foreshadowing the duel.

In a rage, Father stood over her. "How could you have been so stupid? We've taught you better."

Elizabeth slumped. Disappointing Father pained her more than Tristan's apparent abandonment. After all, if it weren't for Father, she'd be a penniless, fatherless orphan.

Duchess sat, grim-faced, opposite her. Disapproval radiated off her. Her white knuckles and heaving chest foretold of Elizabeth's looming punishment. Waves of dizziness encompassed Elizabeth. No doubt, she would have to take to her bed and pretend another illness while she recovered from the lashing that would surely come the moment they returned home. Worse than the looming punishment, the pain of Tristan's abandonment eclipsed all else. The memory of his retreating back twisted her stomach into knots upon knots.

A single ray of hope edged into her heart; perhaps

he had retreated to afford them time to find a solution. She clung to that idea. She loved him. She'd be a poor wife if she doubted him at the first test of their love.

Elizabeth glanced at her brother, searching for signs of his thoughts. Glowering, Martindale stood gripping the back of a settee but Elizabeth could not discern whether he was angrier at Tristan or at her.

Duchess made a sound of disgust. "Your sisters never acted with such a lack of sense."

The unspoken reminder, because they were *her* daughters, and not children of an actress, echoed in Elizabeth's head. Those same words lashed her ears each time Elizabeth knelt, bared and trembling, while the duchess punished her. Duchess always repeated her warnings to Elizabeth not to be a fallen woman like her mother, to be more grateful to the ducal family for their kindness in taking her in and presenting her as a legitimate daughter, castigating her for failing to be more like her sisters, and threatening her if she failed.

Father continued to rail. "Your rashness has led to your ruin!"

Elizabeth lifted her head. "We didn't—"

Father turned with clenched fists. Elizabeth flinched and clamped her mouth shut. He stood over her, his face mottled and purple. She'd never feared he would strike her until now.

"You were caught in the arms of a known libertine," Father raged. "It doesn't matter what you didn't do."

"Perhaps, if Tris—ah, Mr. Barrett, will marry me—"

"Never! No daughter of mine shall marry a disreputable rake, much less a second son." He turned and resumed pacing. Whether he spoke out of pride, or a desire to punish her, or some other plan he had not yet announced, she could not say, but she wouldn't so easily give up Tristan. Somehow, she and Tristan must convince Father love was more important than social standing. Besides, a girl could do worse than the brother of a wealthy, powerful earl.

Duchess made a sharp gesture. "You've shamed the whole family and you've placed Joanna's future at risk."

Fighting tears, Elizabeth fell silent. It always came back to her sisters, how she ought to think of them, how they were so wonderful and she was such a failure at everything she did. The only thing she succeeded in doing was bringing continuous disappointment to the family name. Tonight, she brought scandal. If only they understood how wonderful Tristan truly was.

Recalling Tristan's tenderness gave her courage. If he loved her, she must be worthwhile. She raised her head and squared her shoulders, she appealed to her father. "He's a good man, Father, honorable, gentle, kind. I love him and he loves me."

"He's a rake!" her father shouted. "He's famous for his love-affairs. I'll not have our name associated with his."

"Use your head," said Duchess. "You've known him for five days. He cannot possibly love you. Even if marriage is on his mind, it's only for your dowry. No respectable man will have you now."

The words "because you have nothing else to offer" went unspoken, but Elizabeth heard them all too well; words they'd hurled at her each time she'd perform poorly on her harp, and when she couldn't overcome her shyness enough to make witty conversation, and too many other instances she refused to face at that moment. She should be used to it, yet her heart broke a little more each time she failed to find approval. She wondered why she tried.

Father made a sound of disgust. "I can't believe you would be so foolish. If you had to set your cap at someone, you should have chosen the elder brother. Not only is he an earl, but his moral character is spotless. Lord Averston is a great deal like his late father. The younger brother has absolutely nothing to recommend him." He growled and turned away.

Elizabeth seldom cried in front of her parents but tonight, all her strength went to holding her tears at bay. They didn't know Tristan at all. Underneath that flirtatious exterior was a warm and intelligent man. He, of all people, saw in her a person of worth.

Re-gathering her courage, she moistened her lips and steadied her voice. "I acted with exceedingly poor judgment. What I did was inexcusable. I shall, of course, do what I must to rectify the situation, to save our family honor. If, as you say, no respectable man will have me, then it stands to reason that my only choice is to marry the man who will have me, even if he's a younger son."

"Be silent," Duchess snapped, "and leave the thinking to those whose judgment is sound."

"No daughter of mine shall make such a poor match." Father made a gesture toward her brother. "It's in Martindale's hands now."

Elizabeth risked a look at Martindale who'd been silent through the entire interchange. He stood scowling darkly, his posture stiff. They'd never been close, but the thought of her brother crossing swords or pistols with an armed opponent made her blood chill. He could be hurt, even killed. As could Tristan. Fear squeezed her heart.

She rose and went to her brother, steeling herself against his look of censure. "I'm sorry." Despite her best efforts, tears filled her eyes. "I'm so sorry."

Martindale looked at her without expression for a long moment. Disheartened at the realization that she'd find no forgiveness from any quarter, she dropped her gaze.

"I know," he finally replied quietly. "Are you all right? Did he hurt you?"

What had remained of her control melted at his unexpected concern, and her tears flowed in earnest. "No, of course he didn't." She put her hand over her mouth to stifle a sob. "Please don't duel. If you should be harmed…"

Martindale stiffened and drew himself up. "I won't recant. As promised, I will follow the gentleman's code and deliver the formal challenge in the morning. Our family has settled sensitive matters such as this successfully for generations. I will uphold tradition." He patted her awkwardly on her shoulder. "All will be well."

Nothing would be well. A niggling fear whispered all chance at happiness had perished.

Chapter Four

Richard awoke when his valet Wesley entered his bedroom and pulled open the bed curtains. Surprised he'd slept despite hours of tossing, Richard rubbed his eyes.

"My lord, the duke's valet brought his master's breakfast tray to him a moment ago."

Richard sat up. "Thank you, Wesley. Did you request an audience with the duke?"

"It's done, my lord."

Outside, pink and lavender glimmered at the far eastern horizon, leaving the rest of the sky blanketed in blackness. Richard washed and dressed with care, then stood clenching and unclenching his hands. Unable to eat, he drank a cup of tea without tasting it as he awaited a reply from the duke.

Morning did not diminish his concern over the grave situation between his family and the Pembertons. Nor did it soothe his ire toward his idiotic brother.

Part of the blame lay upon the duke's daughter. Empty-headed chit. She should have known better than to go off alone with a man, especially a known rake. If she'd had an ounce of sense, she would have refused and they would all have been spared that charming little scene in the garden.

Richard jumped at a scratching at his door. Scrabbling at his self-control, he took several deep

21

breaths and pressed opened palms against his thighs.

Wesley answered the door, and returned. "The Duke of Pemberton has agreed to see you now, my lord."

"Excellent." Nerves turned Richard's stomach to stone as he strode to the duke's suite.

An elderly valet admitted him into the sitting room decorated in crimson and gold, and bid him wait to be announced. Richard caught himself drumming his fingers on his thigh, and forced his hands to remain still. It would not do to reveal his unease to the Duke of Pemberton. Surely, the duke would be reasonable. However, Richard had dealt with Pemberton during sessions of House of the Lords. While His Grace had always been affable to Richard, he'd also shown a disturbing ability to deal with his opponents with ruthlessness. The thought of failing both Tristan and his family honor left a ragged hole in his chest.

He drew a breath and let it out slowly. Facing his own duel surely would not be as alarming.

The valet returned. "His Grace will see you now."

Richard drew himself up. He would not fail.

The duke entered from an adjoining bedroom. An imposing man, despite his casual attire in Cossack trousers and a banyan draped stylishly around his frame and tied at the waist, Pemberton eyed Richard without a trace of emotion.

Pemberton's sandy brown hair had grayed at the temples but his fit form belonged to a younger man. Richard stood a few inches taller than the duke, just above eye level. At least there would be no intimidation on that front.

Richard bowed, and stood unflinching, returning a

frank stare of his own. "Your Grace, thank you for seeing me at such an early hour."

"I presume you're here in response to last night's debacle, Lord Averston."

It wasn't a question, but Richard nodded once.

"I also presume you have come to resolve the difficulty without a duel."

Richard tried to quiet the fluttering in his stomach. "Your Grace, my brother acted impulsively and he shall be strongly reprimanded. He is prepared to do anything you ask: a public apology, or whatever you and the marquis see fit to remedy the situation."

The duke sat on a gold brocade settee facing him and crossed one leg over the other. "My daughter has been compromised and her reputation is sullied. An apology will not suffice."

Richard's stomach dropped. Barely holding on to his composure, he raised a brow. "He merely kissed her, sir. Her virtue is still intact." Providing she hadn't already given it away to someone else, that is.

Pemberton's face darkened. "She was caught alone with an infamous libertine by some of the biggest gossips in London. And according to the marquis, your brother was touching her in a most intimate manner."

Richard winced. Stupid, stupid Tristan!

Pemberton held out his hand. "Still, I do not wish for any harm to befall my son, and I respected your father, God rest his soul. For their sake, I am willing to negotiate an alternative."

Relief trickled through Richard. "Thank you, Your Grace."

"I will prevent the challenge from being issued. My price is marriage."

Richard nodded, unsurprised. "Of course. My brother's follies are merely the foolishness of youth. He'll rise to the responsibility and shall be a good husband to your daughter. He has a substantial allowance, and a number of profitable investments. She will lack for nothing."

Pemberton frowned. "You are mistaken. I refuse to allow any daughter of mine to wed a man with such unacceptably flawed character, and a mere second son at that. The only husband I will accept for her is you."

The floor gave way beneath Richard's feet. He gripped the back of the nearest chair. In silence, he wrestled with the enormity of the duke's demands. Marry the chit himself? A girl who either lacked sense or fancied herself in love with his brother? "Sir, I did not compromise her."

"Your brother is responsible for her difficulties, therefore your family honor is at stake. Clearly, your duty as head of the family is to make amends in the only way acceptable. As a man of unimpeachable character, and a peer, you are the only member of your family suitable to marry a duke's daughter."

Numb, Richard paused, searching for an escape. "Miss Leticia Wentworth and I have an understanding." His voice sounded faint to his own ears. Or perhaps the roaring in his head drowned out his voice.

"Are you officially engaged to be married?" the duke demanded with an imperious tone.

Richard searched for a way out of this trap. In the end, he could only confess, "No, sir, I have not yet formally sought her father's permission, but it's always been understood—"

"Then there's no reason why you cannot marry my

daughter. She'll bring you a substantial dowry, and she has been schooled in everything expected of a young lady of her standing. She was raised to marry a peer of the realm."

Gripping the seat, Richard tried to draw in a breath but failed. Give up Leticia? He'd always planned to marry her. She was perfect for him—gracious, witty, intelligent, loyal, strong enough to assume the role of countess, and he'd loved her since he was a child. Best of all, he trusted her. It had never occurred to him to marry anyone else.

Besides, failing to marry a girl when everyone of their acquaintance expected a proposal was decidedly bad form, even for a peer. More importantly, he'd raised her expectations. She had made her affection clear. If he failed to come up to snuff, he'd break her heart. How could he hurt a childhood friend in such a callous way?

No. It was unthinkable. The idea of striking such a mortal blow to Leticia twisted his gut as if someone drove a blade straight through him.

The duke frowned. "Do you not find my daughter desirable?"

"She's lovely," Richard managed, though at the moment, he had trouble remembering her face. "But Miss Wentworth's expectations, not to mention her feelings—"

With a growl, the duke leaped to his feet. "Very well, if you refuse to marry my daughter, I see no reason to prevent my son from issuing a written challenge. I warn you, he is an excellent shot, and is undefeated at fencing."

Aghast, Richard stared. "You wouldn't risk your

son's safety, nor encourage him in such illegal activity."

"Oh, I assure you, affaires of honor have a long-standing tradition in our family. Honor is everything. If you refuse to correct your brother's mistake, he shall correct it with his blood."

Alarm flashed through Richard. He could not bear to risk his only brother in a duel. Even superficial wounds could prove debilitating…or fatal.

Richard peeled his fingers off the chair back, turned away, and paced to the windows, desperate to find another answer. But another answer failed to present itself. He was condemned to marry a girl with no sense of propriety, doomed to repeat his father's fate of betrayal and heartache and loneliness. Such a future filled him with ice. Worse, hurting Leticia in such a deeply personal way would leave scars on his soul time would never heal. She may never recover from the heartbreak. Would this decision sentence her to the prison of spinsterhood, alone and broken?

Regardless, he could not stand by and allow his brother to face almost certain death. Fighting back the dark panic that arose at the thought of losing Tristan, Richard took several deep breaths before he could steady his voice enough to speak without losing his dignity. He steeled himself and squared his shoulders. Duty always came first. "Very well, sir. I will wed your daughter."

Pemberton cursed. "You make it sound as though you find the task unpleasant."

Richard tempered his rising ire. "Your Grace. I would be *honored*"—he almost choked on the word— "to marry your daughter. Joining our houses would be advantageous to us both. In many ways." He offered a respectful bow.

Satisfaction glinted in the duke's shrewd eyes. "Excellent. Then we are agreed."

They finalized the arrangements, all the while Richard keeping a tight rein on his building sense of entrapment, and the dread at having to break the news to Leticia. They agreed to notify their solicitors to draw up papers for a marriage settlement.

Sick at heart and exhausted from the effort of controlling his inner turmoil, Richard all but rushed outside to the gardens. His restlessness drove him to the site of the fiasco last night. Now that he'd saved Tristan from being shot or stabbed, he wanted to wring his neck.

A figure stood in his path. Scowling, he looked up at Leticia. Her smile faltered at the thunderous look he no doubt wore. He wasn't prepared for this encounter. Not yet. Shoring up what was left of his tattered composure, he forced himself to approach her.

She eyed him. "How fared negotiations with the duke?"

"Just grand," he said.

She stiffened at his tone. Or perhaps his expression. "He agreed to a compromise?"

He nodded grimly and drummed his fingers on his leg, pacing back and forth by the fountain. Wishing for a gentle way to reveal the awful truth, he hedged, "He agreed to prevent the marquis from issuing the challenge."

She waited, her expression grave. "Then what is it?"

He braced himself as if awaiting a blow. "He

demands marriage."

"Oh." She let out a sound of relief. "'Tis not so bad. Expected, even. Perhaps once he marries, Tristan will reform—"

"Not Tristan." A weighted silence settled over them. "I am to be the sacrificial lamb."

Her mouth parted. "The duke wants you to marry his daughter?"

"Yes. Otherwise, he will allow—no, encourage— the marquis to demand satisfaction."

Her clothes rustled as she sank onto a bench. "I see." Her shoulders slumped and her bottom lip quivered.

His heart writhed at her obvious pain. "I'm so sorry, Tish. I would not have courted you had I known that we would not be...er...oh, hang it all. I had planned on approaching your father this Season to ask for your hand."

Her voice grew faint. "I suspected you would. I hoped." As if finding strength from some inner source, she raised her head to look him in the eye. "Of course, I understand you're obligated to marry Lady Elizabeth, given the circumstances. Besides, a duke's daughter is the ideal match for you; she has a generous dowry and powerful connections. Much more than I."

He sat beside her. "Surely you know those have nothing to do with this union."

Her eyes grew moist. "I know. It's just..." She swallowed and looked away. "I've loved you forever. But now, it doesn't matter." Pain etched lines in her face and poured off her body like a blood from a mortal wound. Before he could form a response, she stood and hurried away.

Richard fought back his impulse to run after her, draw her into an embrace, and declare he'd find another way. He cursed. There was no other way.

He'd broken Leticia's heart like a merciless beast, choosing Tristan's life over Leticia's. If he'd married Leticia when he had the chance, the duke could not have issued his ultimatum, and he and Leticia would be wed. Perhaps he was unworthy of Leticia, but she was perfect for him and she didn't deserve to have her heart so brutally wounded. Worse, being dismissed by a man everyone expected would marry her would call into question her reputation.

Then again, if Richard were already married, the marquis would be delivering his formal challenge for a duel at this moment, and Tristan could very well die.

Richard walked without seeing his surroundings. An arranged marriage. To a girl of questionable judgment. Questionable morals. Questionable fidelity. How could he ever trust her?

Lady Elizabeth would likely cuckold him at her first available opportunity. Probably with his own brother.

He hardened inside. Never. He'd take her in hand and inform her that he would not tolerate such disgraceful behavior. He would not be made a fool. Perhaps it would do to be a bit heavy-handed at first.

It was time to leave the house party and return home. He had arrangements to make. He'd pay his respects to his future wife—the brainless twit—and then go home, dragging his errant brother with him by his ear. Insolent whelp, thinking with his nether regions instead of his brain!

Richard returned to the house and rang for Wesley.

"Prepare to leave today. Where's Tristan?"

Wesley paused. "I believe he's still abed, my lord."

With rising irritation, Richard strode into Tristan's room and threw open the door. "Tristan, you irresponsible pup, get up. We're leaving."

Still wearing his evening clothes, Tristan groaned, rolled over, and pushed himself to a seated position. An empty bottle of brandy sat on the nightstand.

Richard wanted to slap him. "Pull yourself together. We leave within the hour."

Tristan held on to his head as if he feared it might roll off his shoulders. He staggered to the washstand and splashed his face. After washing, he turned back and studied Richard through bloodshot eyes. "What happened?"

"I met with Pemberton."

Tristan slumped in the nearest armchair. "And?"

Richard pinned him with a cold stare. "No challenge will be forthcoming."

Tristan closed his eyes, but instead of his shoulder sagging with relief, his hands fisted. "And his price?"

"He demands I marry his *ruined* daughter."

Tristan's eyes popped open. His mouth worked for a moment before he stated, "You agreed."

"Of course I agreed!" Richard exploded. "I didn't have much choice."

Tristan turned away, the muscles of his jaw working. "I'm not surprised he wouldn't settle on a second son...nor one of my questionable reputation."

"No one questions your reputation. You're undoubtedly the most dissipated libertine in England. Now *I* must pay for your sins."

In a rare flash of temper, Tristan leaned in, eyes

sparking and fists clenched. "You don't have to pay for my sins, you pompous boor. *You* decided to get involved, not I. If you'd get out of my business and let me teach that hotheaded brother of hers a lesson—"

"You'd what?" Richard took a step toward him. "Shoot her brother? Do you think she'd want you with her own brother's blood on your hands?"

That checked Tristan. He slouched and pressed a hand to his head. "I can fight my own battles." Despite his brave words, the fire had left his voice, leaving only the sullenness of a thwarted child.

"Fight your battles, but not on the dueling field." Richard threw open the draperies and raised a window.

From behind him, Tristan hissed in his breath as light flooded the room. Unsympathetic, Richard rested his hands on the windowsill and stared outside, wishing the breeze would cool his boiling anger.

Behind him, Tristan asked. "Does Tish know?"

"Yes." Richard glared at the clouds flitting across the sky.

Tristan's voice hushed. "How did she take it?"

"With the grace of a lady," Richard ground out.

Tristan let out a long breath. "Poor Tish."

Leticia's visible pain haunted him. Richard's anger bubbled up all over again that Tristan had backed Richard into such a corner that he'd been forced to break the heart of a childhood friend and a true lady, not to mention the girl he'd planned to wed for as long as he could remember. "If I hadn't gone to such trouble saving your miserable skin, I'd shoot you myself."

With a scoff, Tristan said sarcastically, "Maybe you should ship me off to Italy like you did Selina."

"I didn't ship her off; I agreed to let her go."

31

Perhaps Richard should have tried harder to be involved in his sister's life, but he'd been so busy rescuing Tristan that he'd all but ignored Selina until she'd started getting into trouble, too. Hopefully when she returned from Italy where she was painting to her heart's content, she'd be more manageable. With any luck, the maiden aunt he'd sent as a chaperone would imbed her with better sense. The weight of all Richard's roles bore down on him.

He turned back to face his brother. "I have arrangements to make for my upcoming nuptials. Ready yourself to return home. Clearly, I cannot trust you to remain here. No telling what else you might do." He strode to the door where he paused and turned. "Before we leave, I require something of you."

Tristan eyed him, his mouth set in a mulish line.

The pup's obstinacy only fueled Richard's determination. "Go to Lady Elizabeth and apologize for everything—toying with her heart, compromising her, and forcing her to marry a virtual stranger."

Tristan stood to do battle but winced at the motion.

"Then make your apologies to Pemberton and Martindale."

His brother blanched as if he'd been handed a death sentence. Facing the girl's father and brother might help heal relations between the families. If nothing, else, it would be good penance for Tristan. Richard wrenched open the door. Tristan's valet hovered in the doorway, eying Richard fearfully.

Richard ordered, "See that he's prepared to leave within the hour—make that two hours."

"Of course, my lord."

Shaking in barely suppressed fury, Richard walked

the corridor clenching and unclenching his fists. There was only one way to truly let go of his anger. He had to run. After warning his valet to have a change of clothes and a bath ready, he strode as quickly as he dared through the gardens to the wide-open fields beyond. Once safe in the protective anonymity of nature, he tore off his cravat and frockcoat, tossed them over a nearby hedgerow, and broke into a run. Focusing only on keeping his footing on uneven ground, and the hiss of his breathing, he ran. He ran until his lungs burned and his legs turned to liquid.

The sun had reached its zenith by the time he slowed. He turned back to the house and walked. A breeze cooled the perspiration-damped hair on his brow. He let his anger and frustration dissipate with each breath. He could do his duty. He would do his duty.

Refocused and in control of his emotions, he strode back to Lord Einsburgh's house. Careful to avoid any areas where he might encounter guests, he recovered his abandoned articles of clothing and returned to the ministrations of his valet. Without comment, the aged, trusted valet transformed a sweaty runner into an earl. Back in the persona, Richard made arrangements to have his hunting horses returned home, his belongings packed, his carriage made ready. Most of all, he must prepare himself for his doomed wedding.

Chapter Five

Nervous perspiration trickled between Elizabeth's shoulder blades, but she didn't dare move; her parents had no tolerance for fidgeting. Instead, she sat near a window of Lord Einsburgh's library with her hands clasped together, her head bowed, praying she appeared appropriately contrite. Her inevitable punishment loomed over her. She must find the strength to endure what was to come, and to survive the separation from Tristan.

Father had wasted no time informing her of her betrothal…to the cold and stern earl.

Tristan was forever out of her reach—unless he found a way to rescue her.

Voices murmured at the door to the library. Elizabeth raised her head. One of the voices resonated like Tristan's. Hope flared. He'd come to declare himself and demand to be allowed to marry her!

The tension in her shoulders lifted, yet still mindful of her parents, she resisted the urge to raise her head.

"Very well, but make it quick," came her father's voice.

She watched out of the corner of her eye as a pair of gleaming Hessian boots approached. The cushion next to her sank under the weight of a body. She finally allowed her gaze to move upward, passing over a pair of buff-colored breeches hugging muscular legs, a chocolate brown frockcoat embracing a broad chest and shoulders, a scarlet and gold waistcoat, a crisp cravat, then to Tristan's handsome face. His gaze drew her. She clenched her hands together to prevent herself from touching him. Faint circles under his eyes suggested he'd suffered the same tortuous thoughts that had haunted her last night.

His lips, the same lips that had kissed her so sweetly only hours ago, were fixed into a straight line.

"Lady Elizabeth." His rich baritone rippled over her and her heart swelled in response. "I have come to apologize. I lured you outside alone and into a compromised position. My behavior was unbecoming of a gentleman and I regret the difficulty in which my actions have placed you."

The formality of his tone arrested all movement. Even her heart stilled.

He continued, "I hope someday you will forgive me, and that you and my brother will be content. He is a far better match than I and will make you an honorable husband."

She stared in disbelief. Rather than a declaration of love, he was giving her away to another—without any sign of regret. How could he do that if he loved her? Surely more lay behind his words than what appeared.

His voice lowered. "Please give me some hope that you will not hate me all of your days."

"No, of course I won't." She glanced at Father and Duchess as hope took seed in her heart. He'd been speaking just loud enough that her hovering parents would hear his words. Was this defeated apology only a ruse so her parents would not suspect his true plans?

She adopted his formality, speaking so her voice

would carry. "I could never hate you, Mr. Barrett. I will always hold you in high regard. I am not faultless. I knew better than to meet with you without a chaperone but I wished to have a few moments where I might speak openly." And kiss him again, but she knew better than to voice that. "I was foolish. I do not place all the blame on your shoulders."

He touched her hand and raised it to his lips. "You are a true lady in every way. You will make an ideal wife."

She tightened her fingers around his, reluctant to release him, and searched his face for any confirmation that he meant more than he said.

He caressed her fingers, his smile turning soft, and hope leaped within her breast. He wasn't saying goodbye, she could feel it in his touch, in the affection in his eyes. He planned to still make her his, she was sure of it. Perhaps he planned to elope.

His voice hushed. "I shall never forget our diverting conversations. Or you."

Her heart fluttered. He did love her and would come for her. She would do whatever was required to be his wife. She dropped her voice to a whisper. "You will always have a place in my heart."

He squeezed her hand, then stood and walked away, his back straight, his shoulders square. He stopped in front of Duchess and Father. "Your Grace, I wish to apologize for the difficulty and embarrassment I caused you and your family. Please know I hold you in the highest respect and I hope you will forgive a foolish young man whose heart got the better of his sense."

His heart got the better of his sense. That was a declaration! Joy bubbled up inside her. He truly cared.

He would never step aside and allow another to marry the girl he loved.

Tristan said something Elizabeth did not quite catch and bowed low to her parents. Duchess glowered at Tristan as if he were a dead rodent, but Father looked thoughtful. As Tristan straightened, he glanced back at her, inclined his head in a brief bow, promise glimmering in his eyes, and left the room.

Dearest Tristan! With the empowering strength of his love, she could become courageous and strong. She would survive Duchess's punishment knowing the man of her heart would soon come for her and she'd never be forced to submit to another beating. She would suffer any scandal, even that of eloping, if it meant she would be his wife.

Mrs. Tristan Barrett would be the best wife ever; loving, faithful, and above reproach. In return, she, at last, would be loved and safe.

Chapter Six

Richard stared unseeing over the landscape near the front steps of Lord Einsburgh's manor house where he'd been, well perhaps not enjoying the house party, exactly, considering his uneasy truce with Einsburgh, but at least enjoying the prospect of a good hunt…until last night's disaster. Behind him, the voices of the servants mingled with the horses' stamping feet and the jingle of harnesses attached to the coach waiting to take him home.

Then a thought struck him; he'd been so absorbed in his own irritation and in finding ways to pound some responsibility into Tristan, his horror at having to inflict pain on Leticia, as well as all the arrangements he had yet to make, he'd failed to consider Lady Elizabeth's feelings. She might have all the sense of a half-wit, but she'd no doubt be distressed by last night's events. As her betrothed, however reluctantly, he should, at the very least, have a conversation with her.

Tristan appeared, grim-faced from his encounter with the Pemberton family and said nothing as he climbed into the carriage.

Richard turned to him and put a hand on Tristan's shoulder in an attempt at reconciliation. "I'll join you shortly, Tristan. I need to take care of one last detail."

He returned to the house and found the ducal family cloistered in the library. The very air thickened with tension.

At Richard's arrival, Pemberton tossed down the day's newspaper. The headline caught Richard's eye; another story about the supposed King of Crime. At the moment, crime in London seemed trivial compared to Richard's personal crisis.

Pemberton made a gesture at two girls seated on a settee. "Joanna. Leave us."

Obediently, the younger and more beautiful of the two arose and slipped out of the room. Richard rested his gaze upon his intended. From a nearby window, sunlight fell upon her bowed head, tinting her brown hair dark red, almost mahogany. Her demure gown of pale pink accented her slender figure. She sat with her hands clasped in front of her.

Richard bowed to the Duke and Duchess of Pemberton. "Your Grace. I request permission to speak with your daughter."

"Of course." The duke and duchess moved to the far side of the room.

Richard approached Lady Elizabeth. Though the settee had room for two, Richard went down on his knees in front of her and placed a hand on either side of her legs, leaning on the edge of the cushion. She tensed.

Lady Elizabeth's thick hair had been pulled back into a loose knot at the crown of her head, with a few wayward tendrils escaping to frame her face. Her lowered eyes were thickly lashed, fringed by a pair of high, arched brows. Her fair, unblemished skin bore no hint of a freckle. Her lips, though thinner than he would have liked, still had a pleasing shape. Her slightly pointed chin exactly like her father's led the eye down to a slender, graceful neck.

Perhaps he'd been so focused on Leticia that he'd simply not taken the time to really look at Lady Elizabeth. Furthermore, her younger sister, Lady Joanna, a beauty of stunning proportions, outshone everyone within miles. Now that he gave Lady Elizabeth his full attention, he discovered her own quiet beauty.

At his silence, she glanced at him before her eyes darted away. Then, perhaps because she'd seen something reassuring, or unexpected, she met his gaze. Her clear, gray-green eyes danced back and forth between his as if to divine his thoughts.

The seductress of last night had vanished, and in her place sat a young, innocent, vulnerable girl. His future wife. He'd best begin things well.

"Lady Elizabeth," he said. "I know the circumstances of our betrothal are somewhat unique, but I feel it necessary to ask you; do you agree to marry me?"

Her eyes opened wide and her mouth parted. He realized she'd been pressing her lips together in a tight line. Now that they had relaxed, they were much more shapely. Lovely. Kissable. No wonder Tristan had been tempted. Any man would.

She seemed to take a thorough measure of him, her eyes continuing to dart between his. He waited for her reply. Her vulnerability evoked a protective instinct inside Richard. Her fragrance, a blend of roses and violets and some other fragrance he could not identify curled around his senses in an intoxicating blend of innocence and sensuality.

The thought took him aback. He shouldn't be looking at another woman thusly, even a woman he must marry. Surely, his heart could not be so inconstant as to forget Leticia this soon.

She moistened her lips, making them even more tempting, and shot a glance at the duke and duchess. "Yes, my lord. I agree to marry you." The soft tones were flat, unemotional.

"Willingly?" he pressed.

She blinked and appeared to choose her words with care. In that moment, his estimation of her rose. Perhaps she would not always be rash. Faint hope glimmered that she'd prove faithful.

She lowered her eyes. "I will not have Martindale's blood on my hands. Or Tristan's. I must marry you."

Stung, he drew back. "Of course."

He didn't know what he'd hoped she would say. If she'd gushed about all his fine qualities, he might have suspected her of spinning a tale. Nonetheless, hearing her blatant declaration that she'd only marry him to prevent bloodshed smote his pride.

So be it. Neither of them wanted this marriage, but he would do anything to protect his brother and his family honor. He and his father had worked too hard to repair the scandal to the Barrett name and the Averston title caused by his disloyal mother. Lady Elizabeth's flaws could again smear his family's name. An errant brother was one thing. An errant wife was another completely. He'd better lay down the law.

He stood. "I will, of course, require of you at least two sons—the proverbial heir and spare." She seemed to fold in on herself. He didn't know what she found repulsive: him or the idea of sharing a bed with a stranger. "Eventually," he added. "No need to rush it. Beyond that, I ask little of you." Remembering his resolve, he hardened his voice. "Except this; do not make the mistake of thinking I will allow any indiscretions. If I even suspect you to be unfaithful, I will take swift action. Is that clear?"

She paled, and her lips pressed into such a hard line that they almost disappeared. "I understand, my lord."

Grimly satisfied he'd accomplished the unpleasant task of taking a firm stand with his betrothed, he turned, nodded to the duke, and took his leave.

The enormity of his impending marriage weighed upon him until he could hardly keep his head up. Though Lady Elizabeth might not be the immoral strumpet he'd first supposed, he didn't dare trust her with his heart or she would make a fool of him. He'd refused to repeat his father's suffering.

Regardless of her beauty, the thought of being bound to a faithless and indiscreet wife left him sick with dread.

Chapter Seven

Immersed in her song, Elizabeth sat in the music room of the Pemberton London House, miles away from the Einsburgh house party and the setting of her greatest joy as well as her darkest disappointment. In a moment of serenity, she plucked the strings of her harp, moving her fingers in familiar shapes and patterns. Though Duchess often snipped at her to stop wasting time on an activity for which she had no talent, Elizabeth loved the harp. Music brought her peace. It brought as much comfort as poetry.

A voice cleared. Startled out of her reverie, she paused, her fingers stilling over the strings, and glanced up.

A footman hovered in the doorway of the drawing room.

Elizabeth lowered her hand, the motion sending twinges of pain through her shoulders that had not yet healed from Duchess' riding crop. "Yes?"

The footman bowed. "Forgive me, Lady Elizabeth. His Grace wishes to see you in his study."

Elizabeth rocked the harp back onto its feet and stood, careful not to move her newly healing back overmuch. At the looking glass, she tucked in the fichu more securely around her neckline.

Her attention drifted back to her hair. Perhaps she should take the time to put it all the way up. As it was, only the sides had been caught up in a ribbon, leaving the rest to hang loose down her back. She lifted the brown curls to get a look at the back of her neck, but a dark bruise showed underneath her hair above the fichu. She'd have to leave her hair down to keep her disgrace concealed—thank goodness its thickness provided the covering she needed. After taking a moment to smooth her hair, she went to Father's study.

As she entered, he stood and came to her, holding out his arm for her to take. "It's a fine day; do take a turn about the garden with me."

She nodded at the signal that he wanted to speak in private. A rare, sunny day greeted them as they stepped outside and strolled along the terrace to gardens more proportional to a country estate than a Townhouse. When the Pembertons constructed the manor house two hundred years ago, London's city limits had not yet reached the area. Elizabeth breathed in the scent of herbs and flowers, and lifted her face to the sunshine.

Father broke the silence. "I wanted to express my pleasure with your decision to marry Lord Averston."

Elizabeth allowed a rueful smile to turn up her lips. "I had a choice?" she teased gently.

The corners of his eyes crinkled. "To be honest, my dear, I almost expected you to elope."

Elizabeth looked down, hoping he didn't see the guilty hope in her eyes. "That would be a fine show of gratitude to you and Duchess for all you've done for me." She woodenly repeated the duchess's words that had dogged her every failing.

"I'm sure you fancy yourself violently in love with Mr. Barrett." Father patted her hand and smiled. "Young people often make rash decisions. I must say

I'm gratified you see the wisdom in marrying the man I chose for you. I didn't forbid you to marry Mr. Barrett because I wanted to remove your happiness; I wanted to ensure it."

Elizabeth visually traced the contours of Father's dear face. Though his ducal duties often limited her time with him, which often left her at the mercy of Duchess, she cherished unguarded moments such as these with Father.

Before she could speak, he continued. "My choice in young Lord Averston was not made in haste. He is a fine man—honorable, dependable, levelheaded. He's very much like his father, a man I respected and admired. I grieved when he passed. His son has exceeded his father's reputation and I am confident he will be a good husband to you."

Elizabeth almost groaned out loud. Father's description of Averston's qualities sounded as joyful as a dry river stone.

Father awarded her one of his rare smiles. "I know that doesn't sound exciting or romantic, but I trust you'll understand later."

"If you say so, Father."

"You won't believe this, but... I almost eloped."

Elizabeth halted, staring at her father. "With Duchess?"

"Oh, no." He smiled sadly. "With your mother—your real mother."

Elizabeth's jaw dropped. "You almost eloped with your mistress?"

"Hard to believe, isn't it?"

"Very hard to believe."

A faraway look shimmered in his eyes. "I was

young and more guided by my heart then. Fortunately, I knew my duty; my father was in poor health and I had four sisters who depended on me to add to the family empire. So I gave up your mother and married Duchess, to whom I had been betrothed since her birth. She was the daughter of a marquis and had a substantial dowry of both lands and ready capital."

He fell silent and only the murmur of trees broke the silence. A moment later, he turned and began walking.

Elizabeth fell in step with him. Gathering her courage, she asked the question that had only begun to take seed in her heart a moment ago. "Did you love my mother, then?"

"Oh, yes. Very much. She had a sassy tongue and a generous heart. She found joy in even mundane activities."

Elizabeth reeled at the revelation. Duchess's reminders of Elizabeth's murky parentage and that she relied upon the ducal family's charity and mercy had always forced Elizabeth into submitting to Duchess's discipline. As a child, Elizabeth hadn't known any better; like most children, she'd meekly submitted to the authority figure. Later, when she balked at being singled out for such pain, she had felt so unworthy and terrified at the prospect of being turned out and 'fed to the wild dogs as she deserved' that she'd obediently lifted her skirts with trembling hands and bent over to submit to Duchess's cane. Later, as Elizabeth grew closer to womanhood, Duchess changed tactics and forced her victim to bare her back to receive the lashing of a riding crop. Sufficiently cowed and convinced that she deserved nothing more, Elizabeth had always cooperated. The few times she'd resisted, the punishment had been doubly painful, as had her recovery.

Of course, all of it paled compared to the lashing she'd received after getting caught kissing Tristan. That one had been so bad Elizabeth had feared she'd broken a rib.

If she'd known she'd been loved and wanted, she might not have submitted to Duchess's cruelty.

Father's voice drew her thoughts back. "You have your mother's miniature?"

"Yes. She was very beautiful."

"Indeed she was. One of the most beautiful actresses of her generation." He drew a breath. "When no warmth developed between Duchess and me, even after Martindale was born, I again took your mother as my mistress."

If Elizabeth watched him any less closely, she might have missed the wistful longing that softened the lines of his face.

His voice hushed. "She never wanted another protector; she knew I'd one day return to her. I almost ran off to the continent with her then." A quick, wry smile touched his mouth. "I couldn't, of course. I'd never abandon my tenants and my responsibilities. Duchess didn't seem to mind that I had a mistress as long as I was discreet and kept up public appearances of marital accord. Later, we had Mary."

Their footsteps took them along the garden paths but Elizabeth hardly noticed the fountains or statues or foliage. Images of her younger father loving an auburn-haired beauty almost enough to abandon his duty filled her head.

"You probably know the rest," he said, "how your mother died three days after you were born, and that Duchess gave birth to a third child—a stillborn—a week later. It seemed a sign from God. So I brought you home and claimed you as the daughter of the Duke and Duchess of Pemberton. I wanted to make sure you had every advantage that your mother did not."

Elizabeth nodded as hazy details now became clear. Knowing Father had loved her mother swept away a lifetime of anguish. All those years, she'd thought she was merely a penniless illegitimate waif without anyone to mourn her if she died. To learn her father took her home because he'd loved her mother, because he loved the child they'd created together, changed everything. She wasn't the by-blow of a village lightskirt, a child that her father raised out of pity; she was the child of two people from different worlds who loved each other. The knowledge raised her value in her own eyes. Thanks to Father's revelation, she knew she was the product of love. She cradled that truth close to her heart.

Aching to throw her arms around him, she resisted; he'd always discouraged such displays of affection. Instead, she settled for slipping her hand into his and squeezing it. "Thank you for telling me, Father."

He squeezed it back, then removed his hand as he always did when he got uncomfortable with too much physical demonstrativeness. "I trust you'll keep my secret, just as you've kept the secret of your true birth."

"Of course, Father. I'd never shame you in such a way."

Smiling with affection, he turned back toward the house. "I must bring this pleasant interlude to a close.

48

Duty calls. Always duty."

With her head filled with her father's revelations, she walked with him back to the house and curtseyed. After Father took his leave of her, a servant approached.

"My lady, are you at home to the Earl of Averston?"

Her heart thudded. She hadn't seen her betrothed in nearly three weeks. He'd called upon her last week, but she hadn't yet recovered from Duchess's punishment enough to arise from her bed, let alone receive visitors, and he'd left no message. Perhaps he had a plan to convince Father to let her marry Tristan instead of him.

If Tristan planned to send for her and carry her off to Gretna Green, surely he would have come for her by now. Or maybe Lord Averston had mentioned her supposed illness and Tristan was waiting for her to recover before he took her away. And yet, recalling her father's commitment to honor, eloping seemed less palatable than it had at first. Must people always be torn between duty and love?

Shoring up her courage to face the formidable earl, she nodded. "Of course. Please show him into the front parlor."

He hesitated. "The Duchess is out making calls. Shall I send for—"

"Not necessary. Lord Averston is my betrothed."

"Of course, my lady."

With head high in an attempt to appear composed, she entered the parlor. Lord Averston stood at her approach. She paused. In the three weeks since she'd seen him, she'd forgotten his strong resemblance to Tristan. Somehow, in her memory, she'd painted him as a younger version of her father—powerful, dignified, often stern—not at all the handsome, black-haired young man before her.

She gestured to the sitting area. "Pray sit down, Lord Averston."

He took a seat in a blue and white striped armchair. Elizabeth sat across from him on a settee.

As they exchanged pleasantries, he remained polite and self-possessed but his fingers drummed on his thigh, his one sign of unease. He never smiled. No, he was nowhere near as attractive as Tristan who wore a perpetual grin and whose eyes glimmered with joy, and at times, mischief.

"Shall I ring for tea?" she offered.

"Thank you but no." He looked her over as if remembering something. "Are you well?"

"Yes, thank you."

"You have sufficiently recovered from your illness?"

Oh, that. "I am much better, thank you."

He nodded absently. "The unhealthy London air, no doubt."

"No doubt," she agreed with a hoarse edge to her voice. Unfortunately, her so-called illness struck in any clime whenever the duchess flew into a rage over Elizabeth's failings. Father thought she had delicate health. Her eldest sister, Mary, suspected the truth, but Elizabeth concealed all traces and learned to evade direct questions. Now that Mary had married Lord Brinton, Elizabeth no longer had to hide from her sister's questioning gaze. Joanna, of course, remained blissfully ignorant in her own little world of perfection. Only Elizabeth's ladies' maid knew the truth, and

Elizabeth had sworn her to secrecy. No, her shameful secret would remain forever hidden.

Lord Averston cleared his throat. "Lady Elizabeth, I hope you know as your betrothed, I have your best interest at heart."

"Of course," she replied, uncertain of his meaning.

"And as your future husband, I am honor-bound to protect you from harm and scandal."

"Thank you." She waited, wondering, but a cloud of doubt chilled her.

He moistened his lips. "Is there any reason why we should marry in haste?"

She blinked. "My lord?"

He drew a breath and appeared to brace himself. "You haven't engaged in behavior—with anyone—that might have the potential to put you into a...delicate condition?"

She stilled. Indignation welled up. "Delicate condition? Are you asking me if there's any possibility that I am—" she lowered her voice even though they were alone, "*enceinte*?"

He nodded, his dark eyes sober.

Her face burned in a mixture of outrage and embarrassment. He thought she'd given her virtue to Tristan. Or someone else. And now he thought she might be carrying a child...because he thought her loose. It took all her will to keep from bolting from the room or giving in to the temptation to rail at him for making such a crass assumption.

Stiffly she replied, "My virtue is intact, Lord Averston, and there is no child. It makes no difference if we marry in three days or three years."

He let out a breath of clear relief. "Forgive me. I

had to make certain—for your own protection and that of our future children."

She gritted her teeth. "Of course."

Regardless of his explanation, anger and embarrassment twisted her insides into a series of knots. She clamped her mouth closed and took a bracing breath through her nose lest she throw something at his arrogant, judgmental head. Instead, she forced herself to form the words, "I apologize for giving you reason to believe I might need such...*protection*, my lord."

"Shall we marry at the end of the Season in my family seat?"

She stared at the floor so he wouldn't see her boiling. "If that pleases you."

She almost blurted out the truth of her parentage just for the pleasure of ruffling his stuffy composure, and in the hope that he'd view her as beneath him and reject her, but that would dishonor Father.

"Excellent." He arose. "Thank you for seeing me and putting my mind at ease in this matter."

She stood, still unable to look him in the face. His clothing rustled as he bowed and bade her good day. In reply, she sank into a curtsy, her fists curled at her sides.

After he left, she remained standing. Humiliation brought tears to her eyes. Just because she'd made the mistake of getting caught kissing the one man who loved her, all of society painted her as 'fast.'

Careful not to slam any doors, though sorely tempted to do so, she stalked to her bedroom and threw herself onto the window seat to stare out of the widow. As she struggled against the whirlwind of thoughts, guilt crept in. After all, she had given Lord Averston good reason to believe the worst of her. Everyone else did. Why should he be any different?

She had to admit that her actions had been rash, and the timing of the guests who had found her with Tristan had been the worst. She might have thought the same of anyone else caught in such circumstances.

As she sat trying to take deep breaths, her cheeks cooled, the knots in her stomach loosened. If Lord Averston were truly as honorable as her father believed, perhaps he merely wished to protect her from wagging tongues. It also said something about his character that he would marry her with the intent to legitimize another man's by-blow without making her humiliation known—unnecessary, of course, but honorable and kind, nonetheless. It was exactly what Father would have done. Tristan, too, would have been as kind.

Perhaps the Barrett brothers were not so unlike after all. In fact, before she met Tristan, the prospect of marrying a man like Lord Averston wouldn't have been so bad, even if it were devoid of true love. Nonetheless, loving Tristan changed everything. She could never be happy married to the brother of the man she loved.

Chapter Eight

In the Pemberton family London house, Elizabeth sat at her dressing table while her lady's maid, Maggie, arranged her hair. Without even the faintest anticipation of tonight's ball, Elizabeth stared glumly at the mirror, her thoughts drifting.

She touched her lips with her fingers, reliving Tristan's glorious kiss. She remembered their connection as they'd discussed shared interests. With him, she'd felt valued. Beautiful. Safe. She should have known nothing that wondrous would last.

In the month since the house party, Tristan had made no contact with her. Her hope that he planned to rescue her faded. No doubt he was too much a man of honor to make romantic overtures to a lady about to marry another man. Especially his own brother.

At the moment, she wanted him to love her enough to break the rules, not honorable enough to keep them. How else would they be together?

She let out her breath. If Tristan didn't marry her, and instead became her brother-in-law, could she successfully conceal the feelings of her heart and be a proper wife? Worse, her intended did not want her. He probably never would. His disapproval had been all too clear.

When Duchess entered, Elizabeth flinched. Hating her own cowardice, she battled to keep her head up, her posture straight. Duchess's very proximity made Elizabeth break out in cold perspiration.

Duchess stood over her, watching her with a critical eye. "Tonight your behavior must be above reproach."

"Yes, Mother," Elizabeth said to Duchess for the maid's sake.

She almost welcomed marriage—even to Lord Averston—anything to escape constant displeasure, constant ridicule, constant fear of punishment. At least living at the earl's estate, several days' journey from her ancestral home, would spare her all that...unless her husband was as stern and displeased as he seemed. Would he beat a wife who disappointed him?

Duchess put her hands on her hips. "If Lord Averston's brother has the bad form to attend the ball tonight, you must greet him as if nothing has happened between you. Be courteous, but give him no more than a glance. The rumors are quieting. Be sure you do nothing to reawaken them."

"Yes, Mother." Elizabeth's heart quickened at the thought of seeing Tristan again. If only he would climb her balcony and spirit her away!

"Keep your head raised as if you have nothing of which to be ashamed. And for heaven's sake, smile. Look as if you're pleased by your upcoming nuptials."

Elizabeth attempted to obey.

Duchess made a sound of disgust. "You look as if you've eaten something that's soured your stomach." She shook her head. "If only you didn't have that crooked tooth."

Elizabeth turned with resigned disappointment to the mirror that revealed that lower front tooth folded over the tooth next to it. She reminded herself to smile only enough to show her top row of teeth and not the bottom row. At least Tristan hadn't seemed to mind her less-than-perfect-tooth.

Dear Tristan! He'd been so contrite, so courteous when he'd apologized for placing her in a compromising situation. His smile had been warm and soft, full of longing and of regret. She'd frankly forgiven him. And fallen in love with him all over again.

He wouldn't have intimidated her with expectations of a wife's behavior the way his hateful brother had.

"Elizabeth! Attend me!"

Elizabeth snapped her attention back to Duchess as beads of sweat dampened her forehead. "Forgive me. What did you say?"

"Stay in my sight at all times."

"Of course."

Maggie finished Elizabeth's hair and helped her step into her ball gown. While the maid fastened the buttons down the back, Elizabeth glanced down to admire her gown. Seed pearls had been sewn into the center of each silk rosebud adorning the sweetheart neckline and the tops of each capped sleeve. Creamy lace peeped out of the parted skirt. The bodice was low enough to suggest a *décolletage* without actually revealing her diminutive cleavage. She felt feminine and lovely. When Duchess had been absorbed in a gown for Joanna, Elizabeth had requested a few personal touches making it a little less austere than Duchess's usual taste.

Duchess continued perusing Elizabeth's

appearance. "In this case, it's fortunate you don't have your sisters' well-endowed figure. At least you don't *appear* a hoyden."

Elizabeth found it ironic her non-voluptuous figure, which had drawn criticism from the beginning of her first Season, now drew the opposite.

Duchess frowned at Elizabeth's gown, pursed her lips. "I don't recall asking the modiste to add both rosebuds and seed pearls."

Elizabeth flushed guiltily and pretended to look at the gown so as to avoid Duchess's critical gaze. "I think it's lovely."

"It borders on ostentatious." Duchess sighed. "There's no time to change now."

Moments later, Elizabeth followed the duke and duchess into the ballroom, walking next to Joanna, who naturally looked glorious with her cheeks flushed and her mahogany hair in an intricate upsweep. Her figure drew admiring stares from every male she passed. Elizabeth wanted to put a bag over her head every time she appeared in public with her perfect sister.

Her oldest sister, Mary, and her husband, Lord Brinton, joined them in the reception line where they would greet their guests. Mary kissed Elizabeth's cheek in greeting, her eyes shining in anticipation of the ball.

As they waited for Duchess to give the signal to open the ballroom doors and admit the guests, Elizabeth admired the latest chalk drawing on the ballroom floor, the family coat of arms embellished with flowers and cherubim. It was a shame, really, that within the first set of dances, all that art representing days of work would be smudged beyond recognition.

"You look lovely, Lizzie." Mary squeezed her

hand.

Elizabeth squeezed back, warming at the praise. She tried to quiet her fluttering nerves.

With a nod from Duchess, the servants opened the double ballroom doors to admit the guests who eagerly eyed the dazzling white chalk art and lined up to be announced and greet the hosts.

Gentlemen fell all over themselves for the opportunity to speak with Mary and Joanna. With Father's dark hair and vivid green eyes, Mary still reigned as the *ton* beauty, a fact not lessened by her marriage, but many others flocked to Joanna.

Mary tightened her grip on Elizabeth's hand. "There's your betrothed. Wasn't it kind of him to arrive ahead of the crush?"

Elizabeth followed her sister's gaze to the ballroom doors. Lord Averston stopped to speak with a group of gentlemen as he waited to be announced.

"Lord Averston is very handsome, isn't he?" Joanna watched him dreamily.

He did indeed look exceptional in an immaculate black superfine. He chuckled, a silky rumble filled with true delight that filtered to Elizabeth despite the conversation rippling around them. Everyone in his circle joined his contagious laughter.

Elizabeth stared. This was the stern Lord Averston? Though she'd observed the close family resemblance between Tristan and his brother, tonight he was stunning. With his expression filled with mirth, it revealed his beautifully formed features, his expressive mouth. The lights cast an almost bluish tint to his shining black hair. He stood a few inches taller than the circle of gentlemen who'd gathered around him. The breadth of his chest and the dignified, regal set of his shoulders proclaimed him a powerful man.

He laughed again, affected a brief bow, and made his way toward Elizabeth and her family. Her heart thudded as he neared, and when his gaze landed upon her, her mouth dried. She hadn't expected this level of nervousness at seeing him again. His chiseled face was composed, but his mouth still curved in merriment. The Lord Averston of the Einsburgh's house party had seemed incapable of smiling. Yet the Lord Averston of tonight was the picture of conviviality. Was it possible he was more like Tristan than she'd formerly believed?

"I envy you, Lizzie," whispered Joanna. "Who would've imagined one evening of folly would place you in the position of Lord Averston's wife?"

Elizabeth glanced at Joanna, but there was no reprimand in her sister's expression. Joanna's expression reflected no other emotion but admiration as she watched Lord Averston.

"Only his brother can rival him in beauty," Joanna added. "Pity his brother is so dissipated."

Heat rushed to Elizabeth's face. "Tristan is flirtatious, but I don't believe all the rumors about him. He and I connected at a deeply emotional level."

Mary spoke with lowered voice as Lord Averston neared. "Well, you'd better disconnect with Tristan and connect with Lord Averston."

How could she? Tristan had confided in her things he'd never revealed to others. They shared such a love of poetry and views of the world. He was eloquent, intelligent, and caring, and he'd said such lovely words of endearment, the kind of words she'd longed to hear but had never dared hope.

Elizabeth doubted Lord Averston would ever utter the tender words Tristan had. No doubt, he was incapable of it despite his smiling countenance tonight. She'd do well to guard herself against disappointment.

With polite reserve, Lord Averston greeted her parents, and Mary and her husband, Lord Brinton.

At last, he turned to her. "Lady Elizabeth. You look especially lovely this evening."

No warmth came from his voice. He bent over her hand, and for the brief moment his hand grasped hers, no warmth came from his touch. His eyes drew her in, so dark, she could hardly separate iris from pupil, yet no warmth came from his expression.

This was the stern man who'd so warned her against infidelity, the man who'd asked her if she might be with child because he thought her an immoral hussy.

She must remember however cheerful he appeared to his peers, he was unyielding.

"Lord Averston." She curtsied.

"Lady Elizabeth, I would be pleased if you'd do me the honor of standing up with me for the first dance."

Moistening her lips, Elizabeth inclined her head and found her voice. "Of course, Lord Averston. It would be my pleasure."

As he turned to her sister, the corners of his eyes crinkled just a little. "Lady Joanna. Be sure you inform me if you require assistance fending off the dozens of admirers that will no doubt hound you at every turn."

Joanna laughed gaily. "I will indeed, my lord."

Clearly, he found her sister more charming than she—just like every other gentleman. Tristan alone hadn't shared that opinion.

But as it is, I live and die unheard...

Lord Byron seemed to know.

As Lord Averston's gaze shifted back to Elizabeth, he inclined his head. "Until later, my lady."

Before she could further consider his words, Lord and Lady Einsburgh approached. His wife, half his age, glided next to him, her features as set and hard as they were beautiful.

Elizabeth greeted an endless sea of faces, until the string quartet struck up a lively country dance and a tall form appeared beside her.

"May I claim my dance?" Lord Averston stood with a hand extended.

Breathless with trepidation, she placed her trembling hand in his. He led her out to the dance floor and stood tall and straight as other couples lined up next to them, leaving them as head couple. Elizabeth twisted her shoes against the floor to spread around the chalk on her soles and refrained from fidgeting with her gloves.

Lord Averston leaned into her, causing the light to ripple over his black hair. "Are you cold?"

"N-no."

"You're trembling."

She pressed her lips together and studied the shoe flower on her dancing slipper. As the music began, they waited for their cue to begin the dance.

He leaned in. "You look lovely."

"You're too kind," she replied.

"I was sincere."

She faltered, unnerved by his focused stare. She didn't for a moment believe his flattery, nor did she care for his opinion overmuch. "Thank you, my lord.

I'm gratified to have earned your approval."

Oh dear. The sarcasm in her heart made it into her voice. Perhaps he hadn't detected it. She made a point of adjusting one of her gloves and glanced at him.

His face was utterly void of expression. "Are you mocking me?"

The blood drained from her face, leaving her cold. "Never, my lord."

"Don't look so alarmed. I won't take you to task." His mouth quirked at the corners briefly and his expression thawed. At last.

The musicians struck up the number and her feet automatically began the dance steps. With his hand touching hers, he moved with confidence through the dancers, his steps light and fluid. Naturally, a man like him with such discipline and exacting standards would excel at everything, including dancing.

Each time they joined hands, he held hers firmly, guiding her through the sequence and placing her in the correct position to take the next dancer's hand. They reached the end of the line and had a moment to rest before they would be drawn into the formation again.

"You dance very well," he said.

She shrugged off the praise since he was only making small talk. "As do you, my lord."

"Yes, well, I am to be your husband soon. Let's leave off all this 'my lord' business."

She blinked in surprise. "That seems inappropriate."

His head tilted to one side. "Why? We are to marry, after all. No one can accuse us of becoming too familiar."

"My parents always call each other by their titles

when they converse."

"Even in private?"

"I do not recall them ever addressing each other by their Christian names."

"Mine did, but only in the comfort of our home. Still, you needn't use 'my lord' with every sentence you speak."

"If that is your wish."

The next repetition drew them back into the pattern and all conversation stopped. As they danced, he moved with precision and grace, weaving in among the other dancers, returning to her.

"What is that fragrance you wear?" he asked as they touched hands and danced in a small circle. "I smell rose and violet, but there's something else."

"It's called angelica, my lord—er…" She trailed off.

"It's a unique combination."

She couldn't resist teasing him just a bit. "Uniquely unpleasant or uniquely good?"

His eyebrows rose as if her pert question surprised him, but his eyes took on what appeared to be a twinkle. Was that a sign of humor?

"Quite pleasant, I assure you," he said.

When the set ended, she smiled up at him, breathless from vigorous dancing. He returned a smile that transformed him into an approachable, warm human instead of the statue he so often appeared. Her pulse quivered.

Unless Tristan came through for her, this handsome man would be her husband, a man whom she'd thought was as cold and unfeeling as granite. Until now. Had she been altogether wrong about the earl?

He lifted her hand to his lips. "Thank you, Elizabeth."

She found her tongue but not her voice, and her words came out as a croaked whisper. "My pleasure."

He escorted her back to Mary who stood in a circle of other ladies, affected a bow, and moved away.

Mary squeezed her hand, her eyes shining. "See? All will be well."

Elizabeth's trepidation regarding her upcoming marriage to Lord Averston must have been obvious. Then again, Mary could often read Elizabeth, sometimes uncomfortably so.

The next few dances passed in a blur. To her surprise and delight, Elizabeth danced many sets. She'd never exactly been a wallflower, but tonight she seemed to have more offers than normal. Caught up in the pleasure of dancing, her fears lifted and she enjoyed herself. Lord Averston also stood up with many ladies, some pretty, others plain, and he treated them all with equal courtesy. His smile, though less unrestrained than Tristan's, was dashing and often warm.

As she and Mary stood together sipping lemonade, a waltz was announced. Mary's husband arrived. "My lady, do stand up with me now, I beg you."

Mary grinned. "How could I refuse?"

Lord Brinton drew Mary out onto the floor and into his arms. Gazing into each other's eyes, they swept out of view.

Elizabeth sighed at the happiness shining in Mary's face.

Lord Averston appeared next to Elizabeth. "If I may have this pleasure." His low voice rippled over her.

She looked up at him, visually measuring the distance between her head and his chin. He was a little taller than Tristan. "Of course."

Without breaking eye contact, he led her out to the dance floor. His hand encircled her waist. There was something keenly sensual about that simple gesture. She shivered as he led her through the waltz.

After a moment of silence, he said, "Your younger sister appears to have made a splash."

Elizabeth glanced at Joanna who had a dozen hopeful suitors following her around like so many lovesick puppies.

"Of course. She and Mary always do." Then fearing she might sound jealous, added, "I'm pleased for them both."

One corner of his mouth twitched. "Finding yourself in the middle must be difficult."

His observation drew her attention to his onyx eyes. She moistened her lips. "I don't enjoy attention as they do."

"Oh?" He raised a brow.

"I'm uncomfortable with so many eyes on me."

"Are you? That surprises me. You carry yourself with poise."

"You're too kind, but in truth, crowds make me a bit unsettled. I prefer smaller groups, providing I'm not called upon to perform, that is."

"Perform? Do you play an instrument?"

"I play the harp, and every time I must do so for others, I fear I'm going to be ill. At my last musicale, my hands shook so badly I could hardly find the correct strings. It was humiliating. Duchess was outraged I'd disgraced her." Elizabeth shuddered at the memory of Duchess's wrath.

"Then I must do what I can to shield you from unwanted attention."

The concern in his voice captivated her. She could not draw her gaze from his. Stunned by his unexpected show of compassion, she managed, "I would be in your debt."

His mouth curved and his eyes softened. "Not at all. It's my duty as your future husband to protect you."

She looked away. He may yet prove honorable. Kind even. But he would never be Tristan.

His voice slipped around her. "My sister Selina played the harp for a time, but she has a preference for art over music."

"She's in France, I hear?"

"Italy, actually. She's with my aunt painting to her heart's content. Tell me, Elizabeth, what else interests you? Do you also sew? Ride?"

She faltered. Then, deciding to throw out caution, answered truthfully instead of how she ought. "I do ride. I also love to read—poetry especially, but also novels and the newspaper, and even scientific periodicals."

That brow shot up again. "Really? You're a bluestocking?"

She sniffed. "No, of course not. Of late, I've been following the work of reformers and their efforts to help those who wish to better themselves by finding honest work. I've also read a great number of discussions concerning the railroad."

His mouth curved. "I have as well. Tell me, what do you think of the railroad?"

He was teasing her, but she looked him full in the face. "If we can keep out the charlatans who created false canal ventures, one day the railroad will be a preferred way to travel, as well as transport merchandise."

"Most people think it a passing craze at best, and a fraud at worst."

"Most people resist new ideas."

He chuckled softly, his eyes crinkling at the corners and banishing the last of his sternness. How handsome he looked when he smiled. "True."

"What do you think about it?" she asked.

"I am persuaded, as you say, that with the right people in charge, it could be a profitable venture."

"Then perhaps as a member of parliament, you could find the right people to put in charge."

He grinned and she almost missed her step at the beautiful sight. "I could. Perhaps I will."

She couldn't resist smiling in return.

"Pray tell," he said, "what other news has caught your attention?"

Taking a moment to consider, she paused, enamored with the unique position of a man actually asking for, and listening to, her opinion. "I've been following the mysterious Mr. Black whom they are calling the King of Crime."

He nodded. "That story has caught my attention, as well."

"Did you read about the series of thefts in Mayfair? They robbed four houses all next door to each other. They even attacked the servants." The article in the paper had outlined how the thieves had terrorized the servants as they'd stolen jewelry and art. She shivered at the thieves' violence.

He nodded grimly. "All credited to this Mr. Black. I've hired extra hands to help guard my house in London until the law can catch him." At what must have been a worried expression of her face, he squeezed her hand. "Bow Street is leading the investigation. I'm sure they'll find him soon, not to worry."

Until they caught this King of Crime, he would only grow in power. Elizabeth missed her step and turned her mind back onto the music's rhythm and her step. As she focused on dance and music, and on her attractive partner, her tension faded.

The music ended. As he led her off the dance floor, he drew her aside and bent his head close to hers. Her heart thudded and her gaze strayed to his lips. Would he kiss her? Surely not. They were in a crowded ballroom, and she doubted her very proper husband-to-be would engage in a public display. Could she bear to kiss him when her heart belonged to another?

"Thank you for the dance, Elizabeth. I enjoyed it very much."

"I did as well…Richard."

He bade her good evening and moved away, his back straight and strong. As she cooled her heated face with her fan, she squashed her burgeoning admiration for Richard Barrett, Earl of Averston. There should only be room in her heart for Tristan.

Chapter Nine

With Elizabeth's hand still warm from the gentle pressure of Richard's touch during the waltz, she watched him thread through the crowd. He stopped, his head turned toward the balcony. Curious, she followed his line of sight. Leticia Wentworth stood at a balcony overlooking the ballroom from an upper story. Miss Wentworth's head lowered, clearly looking down at Richard. Even at that distance, her expression filled with such yearning that a sympathy pain pierced Elizabeth's heart.

"Ah, a lover's gaze," came a voice from behind her. "Impossible love is so romantic."

Elizabeth turned to see two ladies standing together, watching Lord Averston, their gazes so focused on the romantic tragedy that they seemed unaware of Elizabeth's presence.

The elder frowned at the younger. "Don't make it sound so idyllic. They're victims of circumstance and are doomed to live with broken hearts."

"Always longing for one another, forbidden to touch." The younger lady sighed.

"They'd be married, they say, if it weren't for the duke's promiscuous daughter."

The blood drained from Elizabeth's face, leaving her cold. Through her actions with Tristan, she had caused heartache for others. She'd been so consumed with her own disappointment, she hadn't spared a thought for the lovers who'd been torn apart.

The elder woman continued, "She succumbed to one of the most dissipated young bucks in England. Now look how her foolishness has destroyed the happiness of this would-be couple."

"Well, you must admit," said the younger lady, "Tristan Barrett is very charming, and even more handsome than the earl. Difficult to resist, indeed."

The older lady let out a snort. "She should have more sense than to be led astray by a rascal. Lord Averston is a man of honor and will no doubt marry her quickly since she may be with child—his brother's child. I doubt he'll ever love her." She nodded to punctuate her statement, sending her ostrich feathers bobbing on her headdress.

"Of course he won't love her; his heart belongs to another."

Unable to hear more, Elizabeth turned away. She'd hurt Lord Averston in a profound way. To have brought such heartache and disappointment upon Miss Wentworth, who'd always seemed so kind, made Elizabeth want to crawl under a rock. How they both must despise her!

What a bitter marriage she and Lord Averston were doomed to have, both longing for another. It wouldn't be merely a marriage of convenience; it would be a marriage of loneliness.

Thus far, Tristan had failed to make his intentions known. Had she imagined his unspoken promise?

With weighted heart, Elizabeth left the ballroom, seeking refuge through the doors opened to the cool night air. Couples strolled by arm in arm, their voices low and intimate. She looked away at the reminder of her moments with Tristan and how horribly wrong it had all gone. After finally reaching a place of privacy, she sank onto a stone bench below an arbor of climbing roses; she let out a strained breath.

She'd brought grief to the man she had agreed to marry. Lord Avertston had been gallant to hide it. If Tristan failed to elope with her, she could cry off, of course, which would free Lord Averston to marry Miss Wentworth. No doubt, he prayed she would.

Duchess would be furious if another scandal tainted the family. The familiar sickening fear clutched her stomach like a fist at the thought of Duchess's fury. Besides, Martindale might go forth with the duel with Father's blessing. That she could not abide. Worse, she would disappoint Father.

No. Unless Tristan came for her quickly, she would have little choice but to marry Lord Averston. In time, they would grow to care for one another. In time, he'd stop wishing she were Miss Wentworth. In time, she'd stop wishing he were Tristan.

Perhaps she was the greatest fool ever.

"Oh, Tristan, where are you?"

Another horrifying thought struck her with such force that she nearly fell off the bench. Richard's kindness on the dance floor could have been merely some kind of act to quiet the gossips. He might not feel any tenderness for her at all. In fact, he might despise her. What if he turned out as bad-tempered and disapproving as Duchess? That image certainly fit with the earl of the house party.

She must not think of that. Instead, she recited innocuous lines of poetry about birds and flowers, visualizing each image. A few moments in the garden breathing the scented air and focusing on poetry restored her spirits. Though reluctant to leave her solitude, her duties as host's daughter required that she mingle with the guests. Wishing she could return to the haven of her room, she headed back through the open doors and into the crowd.

A soft, feminine voice called her. "Lady Elizabeth." Leticia Wentworth stood behind her.

Oh, no. Not her, of all people.

Miss Wentworth gestured to the hem of her ball gown where a torn length of lace dragged the floor. "I wonder if you might direct me to the retiring room. My gown is in need of repair."

"Of course. This way." Elizabeth led her to the room where a maid waited inside with a sewing basket for just such a purpose. After ensuring her guest was receiving adequate care, Elizabeth turned to leave.

"Lady Elizabeth," Miss Wentworth said, stopping her. "May I speak with you?"

Elizabeth cast a glance at the maid, but as a long-time servant of the family, she'd proven herself discreet in all matters. Swallowing hard, Elizabeth turned back to take whatever Miss Wentworth saw fit to deal her, and allowed all her guilt and sorrow to show in her expression. "You must despise me."

Miss Wentworth made an attempt to smile but sorrow shone through. "No, of course I don't despise you."

"But you and Lord Averston…"

Miss Wentworth shrugged delicately and lowered her gaze. "It is all in the past."

Her words only served to deepen Elizabeth's guilt.

"I cannot account for your calm."

"I admit I was a bit overset. After all, I'd dreamed of marrying Richard all my life." Miss Wentworth swallowed. "However, Tristan flirted with you outrageously at the house party. I doubt any lady alive could have withstood him."

"It was more than flirtation. We found much common ground and grew to enjoy each other's company."

"Of course. He is very charming. I'm sure he found you equally fascinating." Though she spoke her words with just the right amount of sincerity, something about them felt forced. At least she was trying to be amiable when she could easily have been a shrew.

Elizabeth fidgeted with her gloves. "If I'd known how things would turn out, how many people would be affected, I would have acted differently." Been more careful not to get caught, for one thing.

"Retrospect gives one a clearer vision." Miss Wentworth's face clouded and for a moment, pain twisted her mouth, pain so profound that Elizabeth put her hand over her heart aching in response.

The maid finished repairing the lace. "There now, Miss. Good as new."

Miss Wentworth paid the maid a vail to thank her for her help. With the aid of a mirror, she smoothed her hair. "I hope you will make him happy. A man like Richard does not give his heart lightly." She shot a meaningful glance at Elizabeth and left.

Did she mean that as some kind of warning that if Elizabeth failed to make Richard happy that she would have to reckon with Leticia? Or did she mean Richard had already given his heart to Leticia, so Elizabeth had little chance of earning his love?

The maid put away her sewing supplies, reminding Elizabeth of her presence. She fixed a stern stare upon the maid.

"I can count on your silence, I hope?"

The maid looked hurt. "Of course, milady."

"Thank you." Elizabeth fished a coin out of her reticule and handed it to her.

The maid's pout turned to a smile and she nodded once more. Reassured, Elizabeth went in search of lemonade. She spotted Lord Averston escorting Duchess off the dance floor at the close of a dance set, their heads close together in intent conversation.

As Duchess spoke, Lord Averston's expression showed first puzzlement and then disapproval. With a nod, Duchess left his side. His eyes narrowed and his mouth pressed into a flat, angry line.

What could Duchess have said to anger him?

Unwilling to go near him while he was angry, she halted. Sipping her lemonade, Elizabeth rested a shoulder against a column.

The music stopped. Father, in his role of host, called everyone to attention. "Welcome, honored guests."

"Smile," came a low, nearby voice.

Elizabeth jumped. Lord Averston appeared at her side. All traces of anger had left his expression but something intensely focused entered his eyes and he looked her over as if searching for something. He held out a gloved hand. "Your father has decided to make our betrothal public."

Elizabeth studied him, but his onyx eyes remained unreadable. No sign of anger or bitterness revealed itself in his enigmatic gaze, only that probing stare. She moistened her lips. "Isn't our engagement already well known?"

"Only in gossip. Now it will be confirmed—with our own version of the story."

Father raised his voice, "I'm very pleased to announce that my beloved daughter, Lady Elizabeth, has received and accepted a marriage proposal with my blessing."

The crowd murmured, but Elizabeth was only aware of Lord Averston's presence beside her. He rested a hand at the small of her back, an intimate and possessive gesture at odds with his unfathomable expression.

"The lucky gentleman who has turned her head is a man of integrity and honor. A gentleman I have grown to respect and admire in the years that I have known him as he shouldered the responsibility of his title at a young age." He paused for dramatic effect. "I bring you Lady Elizabeth and her betrothed, Richard Barrett, the Earl of Averston."

While applause broke out, Richard escorted her to Father's side. He made a gesture indicating he expected a verbal response from the earl.

Lord Averston stood with regal bearing as he faced the crowd. "I appreciate the warm welcome I've received into this noble family." When he looked at Elizabeth, his broad smile lit his face and made him even more handsome and approachable. Could it be possible he might come to care for her in time? "The first time I conversed with this lovely lady, I knew she would become my countess."

Elizabeth noted his play on words as he spoke the

truth couched in what appeared words of love.

"I hope to be worthy of her. I vow to bring as much happiness to her as I'm certain she will bring to me." He emphasized the last few words in a way that made her wonder at his true meaning.

Elizabeth's smile faltered before she forced it back into place. Was that a warning? A threat? Or did he speak the words he knew the listeners hoped to hear from a couple about to wed? Though she watched him carefully, nothing in his expression revealed his intentions, or his feelings, or the significance behind his words. He probably felt nothing for her but resentment for her role in placing a barrier between him and the gracious Miss Wentworth whom he loved. He'd been kind to Elizabeth during their dance, but clearly, it was all a ruse.

Lord Averston stood poised and handsome, every inch a gentleman. He lifted her hand to his lips while applause broke out. At least he played the part well. On the other hand, he could reveal a different side once they married. Would he treat her with indifference? Disdain? Hatred? Violence? His true character would reveal itself to her in private. He might be no different than Duchess. The idea left her with the urge to flee.

After all, people's image often bore little likeness to their true characters. Duchess played the epitome of a poised and gracious lady in public, but transformed into something different in private.

Standing beside the stranger who would soon be her husband, unless Tristan came for her, Elizabeth turned to accept congratulations from well-wishers who exclaimed how delightful it was to see two people so obviously in love. She kept a happy *façade* in place as she spoke to the guests but fear twisted until her insides felt jagged and bleeding.

Chapter Ten

Richard stood next to Elizabeth, trying to look lighthearted when his fists itched to smash something. He hadn't indulged in such a release of anger in years, not since he'd broken one of his mother's figurines when he was a child, but the urge never quite left him. Usually such fierce passion drove him to run until he nearly collapsed. Unfortunately, he couldn't do that now.

He kept his focus either on his betrothed or on the well-wishers who congratulated them. He avoided looking at the duchess. Her words moments ago as they'd danced rang in his ears, confirming his fears for Elizabeth's treatment at home.

"Many husbands find it necessary to be a bit heavy handed with their wives, Lord Averston," the duchess had said. "Especially at first. Young girls can be so flighty until a strong parent—or husband—uses a firm hand. I'm sure she'll be a satisfactory bride someday, but don't hesitate to use physical punishment to ensure her obedience. She's surprisingly willful unless I remind her of her place."

Richard had choked and missed his step. Only after taking several breaths did he dare speak. "I assure you, Duchess, I will be the kind of husband she both needs and deserves, and physical punishment will have no place in our marriage."

She'd only smiled smugly and admonished him to keep her words in mind. He'd wanted to carry Elizabeth off that very night just to protect her from her mother. However, the wedding must proceed on schedule to protect everyone's reputation.

He bade the ducal family good night, and offered Elizabeth a gentle smile after he kissed her hand in farewell.

Outrage still burned in his gut over the proof of the duchess's abuse as the evening arrived for the Jenison's musicale. Determined to try harder to win Elizabeth's trust and to stop comparing her to Leticia, Richard entered the drawing room that had been converted to a theater. Rows of chairs faced a low platform to be used as a stage that evening for Lord Jenison's new tenor he sponsored. Crystal chandeliers blazed with light. Laughter and conversation echoed in the soaring ballroom. Though Richard didn't consider himself a music expert, he'd accepted the invitation out of a sense of duty, and because Elizabeth would be there.

After helping himself to some punch, Richard glanced about the room in search of a place to sit. Lord Einsburgh stood speaking with Mr. Drummell, a companionship that did nothing to improve his opinion of either man. Ever since Mr. Drummell had been accused of treason—though he'd been acquitted due to a lack of evidence—Richard still viewed him with suspicion. Whatever Drummell and Einsburgh had to say to one another, the subject couldn't entirely be above the board. There were times when Richard suspected the man was as powerful in the world of crime as the notorious King of Crime, Mr. Black—not that Richard could do anything about it at the moment.

He'd hired servants to act as guards and armed them, as much to protect his property as to protect his faithful staff from the thieves who sometimes brutalized servants. Hopefully, it would be enough.

Nearby, Tristan flirted with a lady whose face Richard couldn't see—no doubt a widow who had already invited Tristan home. At times, Richard almost envied the way women threw themselves at Tristan. Clearly, Tristan hadn't really loved Elizabeth, despite the risks with her reputation he'd taken, or he wouldn't have moved on to other prey so quickly. Disappointing, really. Yet it simplified a few matters.

Tristan stepped to one side allowing the lady's face to come into view. Richard nearly choked on his punch. The prey was his own betrothed.

Irritation sprang to life. Had Tristan no propriety? Richard set down his glass and stalked toward them, battling the conflicting admiration for Tristan's tenacity and the urge to throttle him for his audaciousness.

Tristan greeted him with his usual jovial charm. "Good evening, o' brother of mine."

Richard wasn't impressed. "I didn't expect to see you here."

"What, and miss the season's brightest new star? You know how I adore the opera." His eyes glittered with mischief, a look Richard knew all too well. The pup was up to no good again.

Richard glowered before turning to Elizabeth. How had he failed to notice how lovely she was? With a willowy figure ladies probably envied, and blessed with delicate features, she truly was a sight to behold. His chest swelled in pride that she would soon enter ballrooms on his arm.

"Lady Elizabeth. A pleasure to see you again." He bent over her hand.

"My lord." She lowered her eyes.

Did he imagine a sudden pallor in her cheeks? He touched her arm. "Are you well?"

"Yes, my lord. And you?"

"Very well."

The awkward small talk came to a grinding halt and Richard became all too aware that she and Tristan had been comfortably conversing only a moment before. Irritation at Tristan for making him feel inadequate brought his blood to a simmer. Tristan looked at him as if wishing he'd go away. Richard gritted his teeth and refused to give them the privacy they clearly both wanted. It would be improper considering the hovering scandal. He crushed the thought that his irritation sprang from jealousy.

He cast about for a topic to address with Elizabeth. "Would you care to sit with me during the performance?"

"I…" She glanced first at Tristan and then over her shoulder. "My sisters are saving me a place."

He followed her line of gaze and spotted her elder sister, Lady Brinton, sitting with the younger, Joanna. "Of course."

"We'd be delighted if you'd join us," she added. "Both of you." Her gaze rested long enough on Tristan that her affection shone through.

Poor chit was still in raptures over his brother. She obviously didn't want this marriage any more than he. Maybe Tristan would save the day and elope with her. That would solve everyone's problems. However, Lord Pemberton would probably kill Tristan for bringing such scandal upon his daughter and his name, not to mention the smear upon the Averston family honor.

Underneath it all, annoyance flared at her obvious preference for Tristan. Women flocked to Tristan with little effort on his part. They always had. The dog.

Richard stifled a growl. If he made the attempt, he could win the hearts of the fair sex as easily as his gregarious brother. Richard had simply never bothered. He'd been too busy learning his future role as earl, and then when the title passed to him in his youth, he'd been too absorbed in all his duties. Besides, he'd always planned to marry Leticia, who'd made her affection clear, so there hadn't been a need to perfect the art of courting.

Lady Mary motioned to Elizabeth who then turned to him, her gaze darting to Tristan. "Please excuse me; I believe my sister wants me. Will you join us?"

"We'll be there shortly," Richard said.

She offered him a tentative smile, but when she turned to Tristan, her expression took on the delight of a child presented with a gift. Richard ground his teeth as she moved to join her sisters.

"Methinks thou art peeved, o' brother of mine," Tristan quipped. "How can that be possible, with so many beauteous maidens afoot?"

Richard glared. "I can't imagine. Oh, wait, perhaps it's because you are playing for my intended."

Tristan's eyes glinted. "Afraid of a little friendly competition?"

"There's no competition. She's marrying me."

"Against her will."

Tristan's words stung. They made him sound like a beast that ravished unwilling maidens. "Circumstances which you forced," Richard shot back.

Tristan's eyes narrowed. "The competition, brother dear, comes with wooing her. I doubt very much you are capable of winning her heart."

"She's a person, not a prize."

"Ah, but her affection would be a prize, would it not?"

"One which you do not deserve."

Tristan snorted. "And you do?"

"I will be her husband."

"No one is disputing that fact. But can you win her heart?"

Richard faltered. Would Elizabeth think of his brother when Richard took her into his arms? His hands curled into fists as a dark and primal urge overcame him. "You go too far."

"Then court her, you idiot, and try to make her happy." Tristan turned on his heel and strode toward her.

Richard cast a longing look outside the drawing room doors leading to the garden and freedom outside, wishing to escape and run until his lungs burned. After taking several long breaths, he calmed his simmering anger, and focused his thoughts.

Perhaps spending extra time with Lady Elizabeth would serve the dual purpose of giving the *ton* the impression that they were well and truly in love, which would quell any lingering rumors about her being compromised by a known rake. It would also prevent Elizabeth and him from entering the marriage as total strangers who viewed each other with caution, or worse, resentment.

Very well, he'd court Lady Elizabeth. He squared

his shoulders and formulated plans to woo his betrothed. After making a mental note to send her flowers in the morning, he stopped by the refreshment table and picked up two glasses of lemonade.

No doubt for the sake of propriety, she'd saved him a seat next to her in the rows of chairs facing the makeshift stage. He put on his most charming smile. "My lady." He held out the glass of lemonade, only to realize, too late, she already had one.

She blinked but recovered and accepted the one he offered. "Thank you. Mine had grown warm."

At least she was gracious. As a footman passed by, she hailed him and set her discarded glass on the tray. Richard sat next to her as the host welcomed the guests and introduced his *protégé*. Elizabeth's fragrance tickled his senses. Richard admired the curve of her face, and his fingers itched to touch those little curls that skimmed her shoulders and brushed against her cheeks.

The host introduced the young tenor who all but preened. An Italian newly arrived in London, he no doubt considered himself worthy of his benefactor's efforts. Richard had to agree when, as the music began, the tenor's smooth voice swept him away into a world of beauty and tragedy.

Aware of the lady at his side and her feminine fragrance, Richard reached for her hand. She stiffened, but allowed him to hold it. She sat rigidly, her breathing making little catches. Richard peered into her face. Was that fear in her expression? He traced tiny circles with his thumb on the back of her hand, taken aback by how much he wished he could feel the texture of her skin rather than the fabric of her evening gloves. He willed her to relax. What was it about him that frightened her? Or did she cringe from him by virtue of the fact that he wasn't Tristan, and she wanted no one but him? The thought stiffened Richard's spine.

Regardless of the source of her stiffness, she eventually relaxed into his touch. He enfolded her hand into his, surprised by how much it mattered that he'd won this small victory.

The next musical piece began with the same passion and brilliance as the first. Most of the women, including Elizabeth, and a few of the men, were left in tears at the close of the stirring performance. As the audience leaped to their feet to show their appreciation, Richard caught Tristan casting glances Elizabeth's way. With her head turned toward Tristan, Richard couldn't see her expression but imagined her longing.

Richard took a calming breath. After all, if she were truly smitten, he could hardly expect her to disown all her affections for his brother overnight. Very well, he'd wrest them away from Tristan. "My lady, would you like to meet the singer?"

"Oh!" Dragging her attention from Tristan, she lifted her gaze to Richard. She blushed and her expression turned decidedly guilty.

Anxiety rippled over him like rings in a pond caused by thrown stones. Her guilt didn't bode well for their future or his chance of being spared the same fate as his father. Richard purposely opened his free hand from the fist into which it had curled, and pressed it against the side of his leg, trying to calm his rising panic.

Elizabeth faced him. "I, er, yes, of course I'd like to meet the singer."

Casting a withering glare Tristan's way, who grinned with overt smugness, Richard placed a hand under Elizabeth's elbow and guided her toward the host. Though he seldom used his rank to achieve his motives, tonight he made an exception.

Mr. Jenison's face lit up at their approach. "Lord Averston, I'm so happy you could attend. Did you enjoy my new *ingénue*?"

Richard inclined his head. "Most assuredly. Lady Elizabeth and I would very much like to meet him."

"Of course, Lord Averston. Always happy to assist a friend." He led them to the front of the line waiting to meet the tenor. "May I present Alonzo Puccini. *Signor* Puccini, may I present Richard Barrett, the Earl of Averston, and his betrothed, Lady Elizabeth, daughter of the Duke of Pemberton."

The tenor bowed. "A pleasure, I am sure. Are you musicians?" He cast an appreciative gaze over Elizabeth.

"Not I, but Lady Elizabeth plays the harp," Richard said.

"Ah, the harp!" The tenor kissed his fingers. "How beautiful."

Elizabeth shook her head apologetically. "I only play for my own enjoyment. I'm not good enough to perform."

The tenor's eyes shone. "Music for one's own enjoyment is music in its purist form."

The smile that overcame Elizabeth was pure joy. "I think so, too, but others seem to think the only reason one learns music is to impress others."

Signor Puccini shook his head. "Not so. When I perform, I close my eyes and the audience disappears, leaving me alone with the passion of the music. I enjoy sharing it with others because it makes them happy, and"—he winked—"they pay me well. But I sing when I am alone, as well."

"I do love to play. It soothes me."

"Then you must never stop."

"Thank you. I won't."

As she spoke to the tenor, Elizabeth became animated, her eyes sparkling with enthusiasm. Richard stared at the transformation. *Signor* Puccini clearly noticed, too, but she seemed completely unaware of the musician's obvious admiration. Richard had been wrong about Elizabeth; she was innocent of the ways of men—including flattering rakes—and of her effect upon them.

He wanted to shield her from lechers and protect her from heartbreak, including that of his brother. From what source did that protectiveness spring? He wound her arm through his in a clear message of ownership. "Thank you for speaking with us, *Signor*. We should allow others the honor of meeting you as well."

The Italian bowed. "Farewell, my friends."

As they moved toward the center of the room, Richard kept a firm hold on Elizabeth's arm, reluctant to let her go. "Do you sing as well as play the harp?"

Her enthusiasm dimmed and Richard felt as if he'd lost something valuable. What had he said?

"I can carry a tune, but I don't have a truly fine voice."

"Perhaps you will sing or play for me."

"Oh, no, I… Perhaps." Her brow puckered.

He placed a hand over hers. "Only if you feel comfortable doing so, Elizabeth."

She looked up at him with a searching gaze, part hopeful, part fearful. He wanted to drop down on one knee and beg her to trust him, vowing to protect her from all those who would do her harm.

Tristan appeared next to him and raised a brow. "Rank certainly has its advantages."

Richard ignored the barb. "Was the evening all you'd hoped?"

"Most diverting, indeed. In many ways." He tugged at his cuff as he glanced at Elizabeth.

She quickly looked down at her hands but not before Richard caught the hope glimmering in her eyes.

Richard silently cursed Tristan and strengthened his own resolve to snatch her affection from his brother who didn't deserve her. "Shall I escort you back to your sisters, Lady Elizabeth?"

"Thank you." She kept her eyes fixed on a point in front of them.

As he walked with her, he cast about for other ways to reach that spark he'd seen in her. "Have you seen the new exhibits at the Royal Academy of Art?"

"Yes. There were some promising new artists this year, don't you agree?"

"Indeed." He hoped she wouldn't ask him for specifics since he hadn't actually been there in years.

He couldn't help but consider how his relationship with Leticia had always been so effortless. There'd never been awkward moments where he'd tried to say something clever.

He halted that line of thought. Thinking of Leticia and what might have been would not serve his commitment to do his duty and to attempt a satisfactory marriage with Elizabeth.

They reached her sisters and they all bade each other a good evening. After the ducal daughters left, Tristan looked too happy for a man robbed of a conquest. No doubt, he viewed tonight as some sort of success, if only because Richard had failed to cause Elizabeth to fall into his arms. At the moment, all he wanted to do was wring Tristan's neck.

He took a steadying breath. There was time. Richard would prove himself to Lady Elizabeth and purge his brother from her thoughts.

Chapter Eleven

Elizabeth ignored the impressive arrangement of hothouse flowers the maid carried to the marble table in the foyer. No doubt, they were for Joanna from one of her many admirers.

"For you, Lady Elizabeth," the maid said.

"For me?"

Of course. Tristan. He'd been so attentive last night that hope had bloomed in her heart. He clearly had planned some way for them to be together despite her father's decision.

Smiling, Elizabeth took the card and read the inscription.

> *To my betrothed.*
> *Kindest Regards,*
> *Richard*

Richard? She tried to quell her disappointment that the flowers hadn't come from Tristan. Then she chastised herself. Richard had been attentive and was clearly attempting to make the best of an uncomfortable situation. 'Kindest regards' wasn't glowing with poetry or adoration but the gesture was both thoughtful and unexpected. He'd even signed it with his Christian name. Marriage to the handsome and kind Lord Averston wouldn't be a prison sentence.

Yet how could she think about Richard when so much of her heart belonged to Tristan? To distract herself, she picked up her father's cast off newspaper and curled up in an armchair. She found nothing about the railroad, but an article describing the work of reformers immediately drew her in. One reformer in particular, Mrs. Goodfellow, had made enormous strides in helping a number of unfortunates leave the street, receive training, and procure honest employment. The problem was, she needed individuals willing to hire those she'd helped reform.

"When I am the lady of my own house, I'll hire, them," Elizabeth said. "Everyone deserves a second chance."

The next article that caught her eye was a follow up on the ongoing search for the "King of Crime," Mr. Black. The article outlined a few arrests of criminals employed by him, but they could not, or would not, give information regarding their leader's identity or whereabouts.

London would be much safer if and when the authorities caught the illusive criminal. He seemed to be behind a number of crimes including thefts of both houses and businesses, and even the horrific act of the spiriting away of orphans and selling them to brothels. She rubbed her arms and glanced nervously at the window. But that was silly. No one would come near her inside her own home, and father had hired guards with guns and dogs.

She tossed aside the paper and opened the newest issue of, *La Belle Assemblé*. Examining the newest fashion illustrations, she made notes of changes in adornments and styles and dreamed of having the freedom to wear the styles she liked. Duchess kept tight control over Elizabeth's choice of clothing, but one day

Donna Hatch

she'd be her own mistress and could dress as she pleased. She smiled at the thought.

Since today was not an 'at home' day for the ducal family, Duchess and Joanna had gone shopping. Elizabeth whiled away the day reading, playing her harp, and daydreaming.

After tea, a footman approached. "Are you at home to Lord Averston, Lady Elizabeth?"

She blinked. "Lord Averston? Of course. Show him in."

She took a moment to smooth her hair before relocating to the front parlor to greet him.

"Lord Averston." She allowed the surprise to show in her voice.

"Lady Elizabeth. How well you look." His hand closed over hers and he actually touched his lips to the back of her ungloved hand. A current zinged through her at the skin-to-skin contact. A sensual glint appeared in his eyes that seemed at odds with his customary formal demeanor. It was rather unsettling, truth be told.

"Y-you look well, also," she stammered.

"I hope you'll forgive me for being somewhat spontaneous, but I've come to ask you if you'd do me the honor of driving with me in the park."

She glanced at the clock. Half past five. Precisely the most fashionable time to join the promenade. No doubt, he tried to prove to the world they were well and truly betrothed, thus avoiding scandal. Very well. She'd play along with his charade and try to convince the gossipers she and Lord Averston were a couple in love.

She inclined her head. "Thank you, my lord. I'd be delighted to join you for a ride." She looked down at her afternoon gown. "Shall I change into a carriage gown, first?"

"No need. You look lovely."

She sent a servant to fetch her hat and favorite blue pelisse to protect her day gown from the dirt and soot of London. Richard helped her into the outer garment, his hand resting perhaps a bit longer than necessary on her shoulder.

Searching for clues to his motive, she looked up at him, but he only smiled faintly. Perplexed, she donned her straw hat with a wide blue ribbon and kid gloves. She rested her hand on his arm as he led her across the great hall.

Duchess and Joanna entered through the front door, followed by her usual retinue of servants, many carrying parcels from their shopping expedition. Elizabeth paused, her mouth drying, as Duchess's critical gaze landed on her. Surely, she wouldn't find fault with her today, not in front of a guest. In the presence of others, Duchess always behaved with serenity, unlike the rage she displayed in private whenever Elizabeth displeased her.

"Lovely day shopping," Joanna sang out. "My, how I'm tired. I believe I shall rest until tea, Mother."

"Of course, darling," Duchess said.

Joanna sailed passed Elizabeth with only a brief smile at her, and a mysterious tightness around her eyes. She glided up the stairs like a swan taking flight.

With a flick of her eyelashes, Duchess dismissed Elizabeth and focused on Lord Averston. "My lord. What a pleasure."

"Duchess." He inclined his head. "I have come to ask Lady Elizabeth for the honor of her company while we ride at Hyde Park."

"How kind." Her gaze raked over Elizabeth and all but shouted 'don't disappoint me.' "I presume she has accepted."

Elizabeth rasped out, "Y-yes, Mother."

Duchess nodded at Richard. "My lord." She turned away in clear dismissal.

"Good day, Your Grace." Lord Averston called after her, his voice belying a tension Elizabeth could not explain. He put his hand under her elbow and led her to his curricle waiting in the street.

A smartly liveried tiger, a lad wearing the telling orange-and-white-striped waistcoat and white knee breeches, tended the horses. The boy exchanged a word with Lord Averston, then sprang onto his place behind the seat.

Lord Averston held her steady while she climbed on and settled herself. He leaped like a dancer into the driver's seat beside her. Then they were off. Richard guiding the team through the crowded streets in the direction of Hyde Park.

"Elizabeth, if I ask you a direct question, will you give me a direct answer?"

She hesitated. "If that is your wish."

"You're afraid of your mother, aren't you?"

"N-no. No, of course not." Fear coiled in her stomach and shame heated her neck and ears. How did he know?

"You're a different person around her." His gaze slid to hers.

"I don't know what you mean." She fidgeted with her hands and kept her gaze fixed on the horses' ears.

He gentled his voice. "Lady Elizabeth, as your husband to be, I can be trusted with your secrets."

She hurried to deny it. "I have no secrets." She tried not to think of her illegitimacy, her Father's lie to the world, the many forms of Duchess's disapproval.

"Everyone has secrets."

Oh, heaven help her, what had given her away? He couldn't know, could he? She couldn't bear it if he, or anyone, knew. She'd tried so hard to keep her secrets safe, even from Mary. She'd never survive the shame if anyone learned of them. She snuck a glance at him.

Lord Averston's unreadable dark eyes nearly pierced her resistance. "The duchess told me at the ball that I should keep you in line using physical punishment."

A tremor ran through her backbone but she held perfectly still, hoping it didn't show. "I'm sure a great many husbands would agree." The tremor in her voice betrayed her.

"I'm sure many would disagree," he said vehemently.

Hoping he spoke in earnest, she searched his face. "Do you?"

He looked her straight in the eye. "I do most wholeheartedly disagree. No woman should ever have reason to fear her mother. Or husband." He returned his gaze to the road. A moment passed before he added softly, but with conviction, "I will never strike you, Elizabeth."

Tears sprang to her eyes. Looking at her lap, she refrained from speaking, lest the emotion in her voice give her away. Resisting the urge to curl up into a miserable ball that he had discovered the truth, and wanting to throw her arms around him for his sweet words, she sat ramrod straight, her hands folded in her lap as she'd been taught from her youth.

His voice brushed over her senses, soothing her. "I won't press you for details; just know you can tell me what abuses you've suffered if you wish to unburden yourself."

She held her breath, not daring to believe him. She'd never hoped to find such safety until she met Tristan. Perhaps she might find the same safe harbor with Richard. Then again, it could be a pretty lie to gain her confidence. He often leaped from cold and dictatorial to warm and soft, and then back again. Such a changeable man should not be trusted. But oh, how the warm side of him beckoned to her so enticingly.

As if suspecting her inner struggle, Richard changed the subject and they chatted of small matters while he drove. He turned into Rotten Row, the place to see and be seen, and fell in with the parade, obliged to keep to a pace set by the others.

Passers-by flirted and greeted friends. Some gazed at others in open envy, either for their beautiful driving clothes or equipage or mount. Gentlemen wearing the telltale ankle length drab coat and yellow striped blue waistcoat of the Four-in-Hand Club passed. Carriages bearing family crests of the *ton* decorated with liveried servants rolled by in immaculate splendor. Others passed in equal glory, the cavalcade a blaze of grandeur that could be found nowhere else. Riding next to the handsome and stylish Lord Averston, she sat a little taller, proud to be seen with him.

The elegant Duchess of Suttenberg, the mother of the incomparable Duke of Suttenberg, nodded to them both with all the condescension of the queen as she passed in her gilded landau. Next to her sat a dalmatian, freshly washed for the occasion and sitting with as much dignity as his mistress. Her coachman was turned out in perfect style with an old-fashioned flaxen wig and a bunch of lace at his throat. Even his gloves were spotlessly white.

"Lord Averston," greeted the Duchess of Suttenberg.

"Your Grace. May I present my betrothed, Lady Elizabeth."

The duchess's assessing gaze passed over Elizabeth. "Yes, yes, we've met. I like you, girl, you're sweet. However, you need backbone."

Elizabeth gave a little start at her unexpected words. "Your Grace?"

"Being reticent is all very well, but to be the wife of a lord, you must be equal to him, not his doormat." Her face was stern but her eyes twinkled. "Not that I'm suggesting you'd treat your wife as a doormat, of course, Averston."

Richard inclined his head and said dryly, "I appreciate your confidence in me, Duchess."

Elizabeth warmed at his show of humor. She'd like to see that side of the serious Lord Averston more often. Cheekily, Elizabeth said, "I will endeavor to avoid becoming his doormat, Madam."

The duchess laughed. "See that you do. Good day." Her Grace offered a regal wave and nodded to her coachman to move on.

Smiling, Elizabeth glanced at Richard whose lips curved up at the corners. "Well, Lord Averston, there you have it. I'm under orders from Her Grace to be anything but a biddable wife."

He took on an exaggeratedly mournful tone. "I

predict I'm going to regret today's encounter with the duchess."

She tapped her lip with her finger, pretending to be deep in thought. "Yes, I shall be a woman who knows her own mind. I think I'll begin by inviting all your tenants to our country home and throwing nitrous oxide parties."

He choked. "Just don't invite Lord Byron."

"Then indeed I shall. Not being your doormat must include doing everything you beg me not to do."

"In that case, I absolutely forbid you to meet my tenants, manage my staff, and charm all my neighbors."

She laughed at his exaggeratedly stern tone.

Their banter was cut short when Lord and Lady Einsburgh passed by, slowing to greet them. "Lord Averston. Lady Elizabeth. Congratulations on your upcoming nuptials." Lord Einsburgh's eyes made a thoughtful perusal of Richard's carriage and horses, as if calculating their worth.

Elizabeth inclined her head. "My lord. My lady."

Richard said, "Lord Einsburgh. That was a stirring speech you made in the House today."

"Thank you, my boy."

Tension touched Richard's posture. Whether he disliked the condescending tone or the misplaced use of the term of endearment instead of using the appropriate honorific, she could not say.

"No doubt you won a number of people to your side of the issue," Richard added.

"I certainly hope so. Although I am persuaded that you are not yet one of them." He studied Richard through narrowed eyes.

"We shall see."

"Indeed we shall."

No one would have missed that look of challenge. Richard stared him down and the tension between the two men mounted to proportions approaching a thunderclap.

Richard broke the spell. "Good day, Lord Einsburgh. Lady Einsburgh."

The lady inclined her head with barely a glance while she petted a fluffy dog that reminded Elizabeth of something the maids sweep out from underneath a settee.

Next to her, Richard sat rigidly and let out a sound of annoyance.

She studied his strong profile. "Not your dearest friends, I gather?"

He chose his words carefully. "We are often on opposing sides of issues."

"That's not why you dislike him."

He let out his breath, then glanced at her with a sardonic smile she found charming. "It's not that I dislike him, but his scruples seem to be lacking."

"In what way?"

He paused, his expression turning thoughtful. "According to rumor, he's often on the edge of what most consider outside the pale. Not exactly illegal activity, but certainly not things a lord should endorse, in my opinion." He paused. "I can't put my finger on it but something about him feels…shady. I simply cannot trust the man."

"Then why were you at the house party of a man you mistrust?"

He smiled ruefully. "He is one of the few people who offer a fine hunt that time of year. Not to have accepted would have been something of a snub, and I don't need to make an enemy of him over nothing." He glanced at her. "'Tis nothing with which you ought to worry."

If he'd patted her hand and told her not to worry her pretty little head about it, she wouldn't have been more disappointed. Why did most men think they couldn't have an intelligent conversation with a lady?

Emboldened by the new side he was revealing to her, she tossed her head and said saucily, "Her Grace the Duchess of Suttenberg surely would not approve of such a statement, Lord Averston. As the woman who is not your doormat, I must remind you that I have a brain underneath this bonnet."

He grinned, an unexpected response. "*Touché*. In fact, I made some inquiries regarding your railroad. I know some gentlemen who have found a competent team of engineers and planners. I am persuaded they are honest and diligent. I've agreed to help finance their enterprise."

"You have?" she asked in surprise.

His eyes sparkled. "I am not above a gentle nudge now and again."

"How glad I am to hear that."

His mouth twisted to one side. "I suppose now you will be reminding me of it."

She almost laughed. "Only when I see the need."

Again that rare smile appeared. "Did I understand that you're in support of the reformers?"

"You remembered." Again, she looked at him in amazement.

"I remember everything you tell me."

She pressed her lips into a bow. "Then I shall have

to watch what I say."

He chuckled and Elizabeth could not resist smiling at the surprisingly personable and likeable person she discovered in Richard Barrett, the Earl of Averston.

Glancing at him from underneath her lashes, she admired his features softened by humor. "Pray, why do you ask about the reformers?"

"I want to know what you think about their efforts."

"I applaud them. I hope to be a notable supporter."

"A worthy goal, to be sure." He nodded.

"Do you approve, then?"

"Anything we can do to help the poor who wish to better themselves and find honest work will benefit us all."

Delighted with his attitude, she beamed. "You're very liberal for a peer, you know."

He shrugged. "There are worse things."

"Mrs. Goodfellow has founded a house where she brings people to rehabilitate and train for employment. I believe it lies somewhere between London and your estate. Are you acquainted with her?"

"No, but if you wish to help her, then you should. As my future wife, you'll have the freedom to take such actions."

She gaped at him. "Truly?"

"Yes, indeed."

She touched his sleeve, touched by the rare gift he'd just handed her. "I can't tell you how much that means to me."

As the wife of a peer, she'd have the power to make real change, to help people in a profound way. He wouldn't keep her under his thumb, and his vow that he'd never hit her seemed more and more believable. Marriage to Richard began to sound truly appealing.

In the distance, a group of young gentlemen raced their horses, calling to one another. One pulled out into the lead. His fine form seemed at one with his mount, both moving as if defying gravity. Her heart quickened. It was Tristan.

Then, as a group, they were gone. He never saw her. Never even glanced her way.

"…poetry?"

She realized Richard had been speaking. "I beg your pardon?"

"I understand you have a fondness for poetry?" he repeated.

"I…yes." Discussing poetry with anyone other than Tristan seemed unfaithful somehow. A moment ago, she'd been contemplating how pleasant marriage to Richard would be, and now here she was, all aflutter over Tristan again…who apparently didn't want her or he would have made his intentions known by now.

Richard's voice scattered her thoughts. "I presume I shall see you at the poetry reading at the Smythe's tomorrow evening?"

She turned away from the sorrow of Tristan's rejection. "I wasn't aware of it. Duchess decides which functions we are to attend."

He paused. "I see. Then may I offer myself as an escort to you if she has decided not to accept?"

She hesitated. "I do not know."

"Appropriately chaperoned, of course," he added.

"I didn't mean that. I mean, of course I assumed that's what you intended, but I'm not certain if Duch— er, my mother will allow it." With a little luck, he wouldn't notice she'd referred to the woman she called *Mother* in public by her title.

He raised a brow in what was becoming a very familiar motion. "She won't allow you to attend a social function with your betrothed?"

"I…" Truth be told, she seldom could predict Duchess's reaction. "I suppose I could ask permission." The idea of approaching Duchess with any request, and risk bringing down her displeasure, made Elizabeth's stomach turn over. Ever since the debacle with Tristan, Duchess's temper had become more easily roused and Elizabeth had earned a number of unprovoked displays. Elizabeth had begun avoiding Duchess as much as possible.

"Allow me to ask her permission," Richard said. "I'll come tomorrow during your 'at home' hours and present my case."

She studied his face. That was kindness she saw in his expression, right? Or was he merely another person who thought to dictate her every move? No, his earlier vow to allow her freedom to follow her own interests disproved that fear. And he had vowed never to strike her, a vow she believed he would keep if they did, in fact, marry.

When her answer was not forthcoming, he tilted his head. "You hesitate. Do you not wish to attend?"

She paused. Though poetry without Tristan held little appeal, she ought to be polite to her betrothed. He was trying so hard to court her, even though they both wished to be with another.

She wanted to throw up her hands in frustration. Why, oh why had Tristan not come to her? His affections had seemed clear at the recital, but she had heard nothing from him since. Disappointment greeted her every night when he failed to contact her. Surely, she hadn't misread his intentions at their last meeting. Yet, each day he failed her gave her less hope that he wanted her. Perhaps he'd changed his mind...or never really cared.

Aware that Lord Averston waited, she looked away. "Of course I'll attend if it would please you, my lord."

The carriage in front of them halted, and he was obligated to pull the team to a stop. He released the reins and slowly enveloped her hand in both of his.

"Elizabeth." His voice, low and husky, had an odd effect on her heart rate.

She found herself unable to resist meeting his gaze. "My lord?"

His mouth curved. "Didn't we agree to call each other by our Christian names in private?"

"Of course...Richard." Speaking his name aloud seemed uncomfortably intimate.

His eyes lowered to her mouth. Her lips tingled under his focused stare while her heart tripped and her cheeks heated.

"Elizabeth, please be forthcoming with your thoughts, and I will do what I can to give you everything you desire."

Oh my. It wasn't poetic, but the sentiment moved her in a way no line of poetry ever had.

The line of carriages began moving again, drawing Richard's attention away from her. He picked up the reins and they made unremarkable small talk as they completed the promenade. Upon reaching the end of the row, he turned the carriage toward her home.

As they left the park and wound through traffic on the busy London streets, a cry of alarm arose. Amid the clattering of carriages, carts, and hoof steps, someone wailed. "Ye've ruined me purty flow'rs ye 'ave." A ragged flower girl stooped to hug a few crushed blossoms to her chest, her basket in ruins beside her.

Three young men galloped by oblivious to the flower girl. The rider in the rear glanced back, and laughed at the girl's distress before joining his friends pounding through the streets at break-neck speed. Elizabeth stared, recognizing them as the young men in Tristan's company only moments ago. Of Tristan she saw no sign.

Richard stared after them through narrowed eyes. He pulled the carriage to a stop, leaped out and dashed to the distressed girl, kneeling at her side. "Here now. Allow me. They didn't mean any harm, miss." He gently scooped up the rest of the crushed blossoms.

The ragged girl gaped at such a well-heeled gentleman speaking to her. "Milor'…" She spoke as if uttering a prayer.

Richard took a deep breath of the flowers he held in his hand like a small bouquet. "Ah. Posies. I have a friend who likes to make scented pillows out of crushed blossoms. This will make a fine pillow. How much for the lot?"

"Eh?"

"All the flowers. How much?"

"Bu' they're all broke, milor'."

"That makes no difference when one desires crushed blooms. How much?"

"Tuppence, milor'?" She said it in a question as if fearing her price impertinent.

He reached into his pocket. "I'm afraid I only have half a crown, but buy yourself a new basket and blooms, and maybe something sweet?"

She let out a squeak. "Thank ye, milor'."

He nodded to her, gathered his flowers as if they were precious and returned to Elizabeth's side. "I apologize for leaving you in the streets."

"'Tis of no consequence. That was a very thoughtful gesture you made to that flower girl."

A slow grin overcame him and Elizabeth blinked again at the resemblance to Tristan that appeared whenever he smiled…which, truly, was too infrequent, for it profoundly changed his countenance.

His smile turned self-deprecating. "I'm delighted to have met with your approval in something at last."

Elizabeth winced at the unintentional words of censure. "Forgive me if I've been ungracious. You have, of course, a great deal to recommend you and I apologize if I've failed to be more receptive."

His dark gaze held her as if by tangible threads. "Admittedly, ours are awkward circumstances under which a marriage is made. Notwithstanding, I hope we can reach common ground and have a union that is not unpleasant to us both."

Not exactly a declaration of love, but it was an honorable attempt from a kind and honorable man.

Still cradling the blooms in his hands, he held out the flowers. "Perhaps you'd like these…for making those little pillows ladies like to put in drawers? My sister liked to do that."

She accepted them, still almost speechless at his kindness to the flower girl. "Thank you."

He retrieved the reins and they left behind the more

congested part of town, traffic thinned, allowing them to travel with more ease. In front of the Ducal family estate, he pulled his team to a halt. After throwing his reins to his tiger, he helped her down, his hands strong and steady. As her feet touched the sidewalk, he offered his arm and escorted her to the front door.

He pressed his lips to her gloved hand. "Tomorrow, sweet Elizabeth."

Sweet Elizabeth. A thrill went through her at the endearment and at his touch. The words were pretty, and his touch gentle.

Hoarsely, she said, "Thank you for the ride."

With a sheepish smile, he bowed. "It was a pleasure in many ways."

They bade a farewell, and Elizabeth went into her room to press the flowers between the pages of a book. A piece of her heart wished the flowers had been from Tristan.

Tristan would have stopped his horse if he'd been with his friends when they'd caused trouble for the flower girl. He would never be so thoughtless; he'd always been kind and attentive.

Richard, too, had been a gallant, thoughtful gentleman. Any girl should consider herself fortunate to marry him. Richard had been charming today, and his wit had endeared him to her, as did his concern over her welfare and his vow never to hurt her. He'd rescued even a flower girl, someone most men of his station ignored. He was a true gentleman to everyone with whom he came in contact.

While Tristan still invaded her thoughts on a regular basis, a burgeoning sense of obligation, and yes, attraction—even genuine admiration—grew a little more each day for Richard.

Did that mean she had an inconstant heart?

She pressed her hand to her head in an attempt to ward off the rising confusion concerning the Barrett brothers, and to whom she owed her loyalty.

Chapter Twelve

With unexpected anticipation at the pleasure of seeing Elizabeth, Richard arrived the moment the Duchess of Pemberton began her 'at home' hours when she opened her drawing room to visitors, of which Richard was one of dozens that day. The moment he stepped foot into the drawing room, a vague unease stifled his expectancy. Perhaps it was due to the fact that Elizabeth had been so nervous and hesitant about attending the poetry reading with him. Either Elizabeth was reluctant to spend time in his company or her mother so brutal that her daughters feared asking any favors of her. Richard's stomach tightened each time he considered that the duchess kept her daughters in line using force. The thought of forcing her to spend time with him offended his honor, not to mention his pride. If only he could prove his intent to be a good husband, that she was safe with him.

Earning her trust would be the key to getting her to enjoy his company, perhaps even in wresting her loyalty from Tristan. As an innocent, she might still be prey to Tristan's flirtations, but at least the fears that she'd betray Richard had faded. Hopefully in time, they'd evaporate.

He had not yet successfully prevented his thoughts from occasionally returning to Leticia and what might have been, nor stopped imagining the torture she must be enduring not only at the hands of gossips, but of her wounded heart. However, surely in time he and Elizabeth would turn their thoughts and attention toward one another.

Shoring up his resolution to earn Elizabeth's trust, as well as her affection, Richard threaded through a mixture of ladies who wished to visit the influential duchess, and young bucks hoping to catch a glimpse of Lady Joanna. Lady Einsburgh caught his eye, conjuring up a sour taste in his mouth by virtue of her marriage to Lord Einsburgh. Focusing his thoughts, Richard continued his search for his intended. He found Elizabeth sitting by herself on a divan, her hands clasped together, her head lowered, tense and alone. His heart gave a tiny leap at the sight of her and he had to slow his pace lest he give into the mad urge to dash to her side.

"Good day, Lady Elizabeth."

She gave a tiny start, her gaze darting up to his face. "Good day, my lord."

Tender protectiveness overcame him as he bowed. He lowered himself onto the divan next to her and took her hand. Her breath caught. She lowered her eyes and withdrew her hand.

He swallowed his wounded sensibilities. Elizabeth was proving more complex than he'd first supposed. He would do well to tread softly with her. Keeping his voice gentle, he asked, "Shall I speak with the duchess regarding the plans this evening?"

"I already asked her at breakfast. She has a previous engagement but Joanna will attend the poetry reading with my sister Mary—you know her as Lady Brinton."

"And you?"

She hesitated. "I've decided to attend as well."

He couldn't account for the edge to her voice so he chose to ignore it for now. "Splendid. Shall I come for you in my carriage tonight?"

Her gaze flickered. "That's not necessary. I'll go with my sisters."

Another blow to his pride. Carefully keeping his disappointment out of his expression, he lifted her hand to his lips. "Until tonight, then, my dear."

"My lord." She removed her hand from his perhaps more quickly than necessary.

Richard remained a few minutes longer, trying to draw a smile out of her, but with Duchess occasionally throwing hawkish glances her way, he could hardly coax a word out of her. The sooner they married the better.

Of course, she might still be in love with Tristan. The thought pierced him like a barb. Eying the girl next to him, he reminded himself to uncurl his fists. He'd known all along that Tristan had her preference, but he'd hoped that infatuation would fade in time, especially as Richard began courting her in earnest.

What if he had competition? Was it possible that Tristan continued to pursue her? He might plan to take advantage of her affection and seduce her right under Richard's nose. She would be too innocent to realize what Tristan's intentions were until it was too late. The thought chilled him.

Uncertain if he could maintain his composure, he inclined his head to Elizabeth. "I bid you good day. I look forward to seeing you tonight."

"Until then, my lord."

He escaped as quickly as possible. Finding himself alone outside, he pressed his hands to his face. Dash it all, he'd just gotten used to the idea of marrying her. Looking forward to it, even. She was kind and witty and gracious. If he were to be honest with himself, he wanted to marry Elizabeth.

The thought brought him up short. He didn't just desire Elizabeth; he wanted to spend his life with her. He wanted to smile at her across the dinner table, walk with her hand in his in the gardens, wake up every morning with her in his arms.

Very well, he'd confront Tristan and discover his intentions now before he risked his heart on a doomed relationship.

After leaving Pemberton House, Richard drove to Tristan's bachelor's rooms. His brother lounged on a chair, his hair mussed and his clothing in a dreadful state of disarray that would no doubt leave his valet weeping.

Richard took a seat opposite Tristan. "You look as if you've slept in your clothes."

Tristan yawned but looked unnaturally pleased. "Not a lot of sleeping, actually."

"I really don't want to hear about your exploits."

"Jealous?"

Richard snorted and let sarcasm drip from every word. "Insanely, because you are in possession of every quality I so much admire."

Tristan grinned without apology. "More so than you'd ever admit, I'd wager."

Richard folded his arms and stared him down. "Are you or are you not planning to continue courting, or even seducing, Lady Elizabeth?"

Tristan's surprise could not have been feigned. "What? Are you barking mad?"

Richard nodded, satisfied. "Just making sure I'm not wooing my wife-to-be while my brother is plotting against me."

"Not making any headway with her?" Challenge glittered in Tristan's eyes.

"I admit she's a bit shy, but she's been receptive to me."

"Then why do you accuse me of such low behavior?"

Richard fixed a look upon his brother that he normally reserved for slow-witted children. "Oh, I don't know, perhaps because it'd be just like you to wish to embarrass me in front of the whole of society."

"Really, Richard, give me a little credit." Tristan arose and poured himself a drink, then held up the decanter. "Brandy?"

Richard shook his head and folded his hands together behind his back.

"So she isn't falling into your arms and you've come for advice, eh?"

Richard nearly choked. "I'd rather run naked in the park than ask you for advice."

Tristan shook his head. "Tsk, tsk. Your pride will get you in trouble someday."

"For your information, our courtship is progressing in a satisfactory manner."

"Uh huh. Have you kissed her?"

"I am not discussing my courtship with you. I merely came to ask if you are making my betrothal a sham by stealing away with Lady Elizabeth's heart behind my back."

"If that were true, it would be your own fault and not mine. I have no intention of stepping on your toes in such a way."

"In spite of your earlier challenge?"

Tristan let out a snort of disgust. "You are so easy to manipulate, you know that? How else was I going to get you to try to woo the poor lass rather than just showing up at the altar at the last possible moment?"

Richard opened his mouth and then closed it. Of course. Tristan had been playing him. He should have seen that.

Tristan leaned back in his seat and stretched out his legs. "I'm not after your bride, Richard. She was a flirtation, never a serious pursuit. I know my place." Yet something in his eyes made Richard wonder.

"Truly?"

Tristan let out his breath. "Very well. I'll be honest with you."

"That'd be refreshing," Richard said dryly.

Tristan ignored the jab and grew more solemn than usual. "At first, I viewed her as a challenge. She so obviously disapproved of me and seemed completely immune to my flattery. So I did everything in my power to get her to smile at me. Later, we found we had much in common. She's a romantic, she loves poetry, and she revealed remarkable wit once I got her away from her mother and sisters. I admit I truly liked her. I actually entertained the idea of reforming for her." He got up and went to the window.

Richard stared at his brother's back. At least Tristan hadn't been using Elizabeth like a callous rake.

Tristan swung back around. "I'm not for her. Obviously. And I'm not ready to settle down. I might

114

not ever be."

"Then you won't try to win her from me."

"I vow it." Tristan held his gaze steady.

"Do you give me your word that you won't seduce her?"

Tristan let out a sound of outrage. "What kind of a scoundrel do you take me for? I have never seduced an innocent nor a married woman, and I certainly won't start with yours!"

The relief that washed over Richard left him a bit weak and he realized just how important it had been to hear that. Tristan might be a lot of things, but a liar was never one of them. As far as Richard knew, all Tristan's affaires had been with widows and divorcees. In fact, Tristan seldom openly pursued women; they always seemed to throw themselves at him. A part of Richard envied that about Tristan.

Richard stood. "Thank you. Forgive me, but I had to make sure." He made a gesture to Tristan's clothes. "I'll leave you to clean up. Good day."

His mouth still clenched in anger, Tristan turned away, scorn lacing every word. "Do visit anytime."

Richard left vowing to make his future wife so pleased with him that she'd never again look at Tristan. Yet a seed of doubt lingered, a haunting fear that she'd be unfaithful, if not in body, in her heart.

Chapter Thirteen

Warm with excitement, Elizabeth handed her wrap to a footman and smoothed her hair. She searched the crowd for Tristan but failed to locate him. Mary and Joanna chatted beside her, Joanna receiving admiring looks from all the gentlemen present, both wed and unwed, and she preened under their attention. Mary also received a number of lingering looks, but didn't appear to notice. In fact, an unusual tightness touched her mouth.

"Is anything amiss?" Elizabeth asked her.

"Nothing worth mentioning. Shall we find our seats?" Mary linked her arm through Elizabeth's.

"Indeed." Since Duchess had more illustrious plans for the evening, Elizabeth predicted a pleasant interlude without her. She walked with her sisters through the rows of chairs in the drawing room.

They found a seat in the third row. Elizabeth cast a longing glance at the empty chair next to her. She ought to save a seat for Richard since he'd gone to all the trouble to ask her to be here. Yet, she'd rather Tristan took the seat instead. It would be like him to anticipate her presence at a poetry reading and attend in order to be with her…provided his feelings were genuine and hadn't changed.

As she chatted with her sisters, she glanced frequently at the door. Other guests arrived, Miss

Leticia Wentworth and her parents among them.

Leticia Wentworth paused as she passed by. "Good evening, ladies."

"Miss Wentworth."

As they exchanged the usual pleasantries, Elizabeth searched for signs of grief over losing her love, or hidden signs of animosity like her warning about making Richard happy, but Miss Wentworth's expression remained, if not exactly friendly, then neutral. She must be expert at disguising her emotions. As Miss Wentworth bade them a good evening and joined her parents on the front row, the usual guilt that accompanied seeing Richard's lost love arose within Elizabeth with glaring accusation. If Elizabeth eloped with Tristan, Miss Wentworth could marry Richard. They'd all be happily married to the ones they loved.

"I admire Miss Wentworth a great deal," Mary said.

Elizabeth twisted her hands in her lap. "I do, as well. I cannot account for how she can be so civil to me. At least, to my face."

"Elizabeth," Mary said in gentle reproach. "I'm sure she doesn't view you in an unflattering light."

Joanna sniffed. "How can she not when Elizabeth effectively stole Miss Wentworth's beau?"

"Joanna," Mary said sharply, "if you cannot be polite, you should at least be quiet."

Joanna flushed but kept her peace. An underlying sadness weighed Miss Wentworth's posture as she conversed with her parents and other guests. Joanna was right; Elizabeth deserved Miss Wentworth's hatred.

Nearby, a group of gentlemen stood in a circle, discussing the growing threat to London by the King of

Crime, Mr. Black, and the increasingly urgent need to stop him and his notorious ring of criminals. Elizabeth shuddered.

Next to Elizabeth, Mary tensed, her breathing becoming irregular, her complexion turning pallid.

Elizabeth put an arm around her. "Whatever is the matter, dear? Are you unwell?"

Mary offered a quivering smile. "No, no, nothing like that." She glanced around and lowered her voice. "We had a burglary last night."

"What?"

"Two men broke in. One held a couple of footmen at gunpoint while the other made off with some crystal and a couple of vases. They tried to force them to unlock the butlery and hand over the silver, but they didn't have the key. One of the footman tried to fight back but they...hurt him."

Elizabeth let out a gasp. "How terrible. Such brazen burglars."

"Bow Street thinks they were in the employ of that terrible Mr. Black. That seems to be their style, to welcome confrontation instead of operating under stealth."

Elizabeth shivered. To have had such a thing happen to her own sister made the world of crime so much more immediate.

A young gentleman stopped next to Elizabeth and gestured to the empty chair. "May I have this seat?"

Elizabeth offered an apologetic smile. "I'm sorry, but I'm saving it for someone."

"Of course." He bowed and moved on.

Elizabeth glanced to the doorway again and her heart jolted. Tristan had arrived, stunning in an immaculate superfine suit, with a cravat tied in a perfect mathematical knot that seemed incongruous with Tristan's jovial personality, and a green and blue brocade waistcoat. Really, he could wear an old flour sack and look dashing.

He worked his way through the crowd stopping to speak to everyone he passed. Elizabeth shifted so her body would not block the empty seat next to her. With any luck, he'd see that as an invitation.

Not even glancing Elizabeth's way, he took an empty seat next to Leticia Wentworth. Elizabeth's heart stuttered. He hadn't come to her. Had he really given up on her? The air seemed too thick to draw into her lungs. Was it possible Tristan never really loved her? Were all his sweet declarations actually the insincere words of a flatterer looking for a flirtation or even an indecent affair?

Mary's hand closed over hers and she whispered, "It's just as well, Lizzie."

Disappointment filled her, but she nodded and fought to keep her head up. "Of course."

If Tristan didn't want her, she would be doomed to spend the rest of her life with a man she didn't love. Surely, Tristan's love for her hadn't changed and he would make his intensions known, but the thought failed to inspire confidence. It had been weeks with no contact. Now today, not even a glimmer of the love she thought they shared at the house party revealed itself in his eyes. Could he truly be so inconstant? A chilling thought struck her. Did he deserve his rakish reputation? Was she merely one in a long line of broken hearts?

Tristan and Leticia spoke in a comfortable manner,

their postures relaxed, intimate even. Grinning, Tristan leaned in and whispered something in her ear. Laughing, Leticia swatted him with her fan and shook her head as if amazed by his audacity.

Elizabeth had to fight to refrain from slouching in her seat, and almost suggested that they leave. Tristan showed no signs of heartache, no signs even of a man desperate to find a way to be with his true love. How could she bear to sit through a poetry reading while the man in possession of her heart flirted with another?

"How could he?" she whispered. Her eyes burned with unshed tears.

Mary whispered, "They've known each other all their lives, Lizzie. They're practically brother and sister."

Startled that Mary had heard, Elizabeth turned her head away to hide the guilty flush creeping into her face. "I know." However, his conversation with Leticia seemed flirtatious rather than brotherly. Hurt, she looked away.

"Besides, he's to be your brother-in-law; you'd best stop thinking of him in any other way."

Elizabeth nodded, and tried to swallow back the bitterness in her throat. Elizabeth turned her attention back to Mary, and to her terrifying news. "Do you think those burglars might return?"

"We hired armed guards to patrol the grounds with their dogs. That should discourage any future criminals." Mary smiled bravely. "I'm sure that's the last our family will see of such men."

"Would it be presumptuous to hope that you've saved this seat for me?" A deep voice rumbled nearby.

Richard materialized next to the seat Elizabeth had

saved for Tristan. For a moment, she could not speak as a confusing maelstrom of disappointment over Tristan, and admiration for Richard, whirled through her.

Richard's midnight hair shone in the lamplight and his eyes glittered with some unspoken pleasure. His snowy cravat lay in a perfect waterfall that would have impressed Beau Brummell himself, and his burgundy frockcoat hugged his fine form to perfection. It was his smile, however, that kept her rooted in her seat. Partly soft, partly amused, it transformed his normally stern visage into the approachable face of the man who'd shown a humorous side, helped a flower girl, and promised Elizabeth freedom to support her causes. She suspected he possessed more sensibilities than she'd previously supposed. He never spoke the pretty words Tristan had, never made declarations of love, but he was genuine, complex, and alluring. Any girl should be pleased to wed the Earl of Averston. Any girl, that is, who wasn't already in love with another.

Richard raised a brow, his smile broadening as if teasing her or perhaps enjoying her scrutiny. "May I join you, Lady Elizabeth?"

She swallowed and gestured to the chair. "Of course, my lord. I'd been saving it for the man I am to marry."

Mary made a tiny coughing sound as if understanding the double meaning in her words, but Elizabeth ignored her. Richard broke into a full grin. She blinked in the warmth of Lord Averston's rare display and basked in its warmth. As he took the seat next to her, the hostess greeted the audience and introduced those who would render the readings.

As each reading began, Elizabeth mouthed the

words of well-known poems and absorbed ones new to her, immersing herself in verse and emotion, weeping over some, laughing over others. At the end, she sprang to her feet and applauded along with the others in the crowded room.

She glanced at Richard sitting next to her. He discreetly stifled a yawn. A yawn! Only a man with no heart, nor good taste, would yawn after such heart-stirring recitations. All her earlier tenderness for him evaporated in the face of his callous disregard of such beauty she held so dear.

"Ah, a veritable bevy of beauteous maidens," came a familiar voice that immediately set her pulse racing.

Tristan grinned at Elizabeth and her sisters, his gaze resting longest on her. Everything inside warmed under his attention.

His smile faded into one of regret. Was he telling her he wouldn't be eloping with her? An apology lurked under his expression and for a moment, sadness.

That was it, then. With a single look, he'd conveyed to her what she'd begun to fear; they would never be together. Either he never loved her, or he'd chosen to step aside and let his brother marry her. In that instant, all her hopes of a future with Tristan withered.

Tristan returned his focus to Richard and raised a brow in a fair imitation of an expression she'd often seen on Richard, a ready grin raising the corners of his mouth. He nudged Richard playfully with an elbow. "I'm surprised to see you here, given your usual impatience for anything so impractical as poetry."

Richard's eyebrow rose. "I will go to many lengths to please a family member or friend."

Burying her disappointment until she could fully suffer through it in private, Elizabeth tried to catch up with the conversation. She glanced at Richard but only briefly, lest he see her crushing disappointment. "You don't enjoy poetry, yet you came to tonight's reading anyway?"

Richard lifted one shoulder in a half shrug. "If it's important to you, it's important to me."

Elizabeth blinked, uncertain as to whether she felt annoyance with the man who didn't share her enthusiasm of poetry as Tristan clearly did, or touched that he'd chosen to encourage her to attend and spend the evening with her even though he found the whole thing a terrible bore.

Richard kissed the back of her hand and tucked her hand into the crook of his arm. Briefly, vulnerability touched his eyes, as if he were concerned his offering might not be enough, and uncertain as to whether she would grow to care for him or hurt him. She didn't want to hurt him—she wanted to wrap him in comfort. The realization left her momentarily stunned.

Eloping with Tristan would hurt Richard deeply, and her regard for him had grown to the point that she could not drive a proverbial dagger through his heart in repayment for his kindness—not even to marry Tristan.

She drew herself up, resolute. Her feelings no longer mattered. Marrying Richard would be the honorable path to take—to please her father, to avoid scandal, but most importantly, to protect both Richard's character and his heart, even if she didn't possess much of it. In addition, Tristan had made his position clear, so her options narrowed.

Elizabeth stepped closer to Richard and tightened

her grasp on his arm. "It was kind of you to come for my benefit, my lord."

His actions had been both kind and thoughtful. It was one thing to attend a poetry reading because one loved it; attending to spend time with another was an offering.

His eyes softened and he rested his hand on top of hers. "Your company made attending tonight a pleasure, my lady."

Richard seemed to need her in some way, or at least he needed her not to reject him. Yes, she'd marry Richard and try to be a good and faithful wife to him.

"Good evening, all." Tristan bowed and moved to speak with another group.

Richard turned to Elizabeth. "May I bring you a glass of lemonade?"

"That would be lovely, thank you."

As Richard moved away, Mary watched Elizabeth narrowly. "You must admit he's a delightful gentleman, Lizzie. You're fortunate to be betrothed to such a man, especially considering the circumstances."

"Why do I sense a word of censure there?" Elizabeth said.

"A man of his caliber lays his heart at your feet, and you're dancing around it as if you aren't sure you wish to pick it up."

Elizabeth studied her fingers. If only she could transfer her love from Tristan to Richard. At the very least, she'd transfer her loyalty, her full loyalty.

Joanna's court came to pay her homage, and the young bucks surrounded them, leaving the sisters unable, to Elizabeth's relief, to converse further.

Richard arrived with enough glasses of lemonade

for Elizabeth and her sisters.

She smiled at him. "Thank you." His attentiveness filled her with warmth.

"Truly, it's my pleasure." Sincerity wove into every word. He held out an arm and she took it, allowing him to lead her around the room to mingle with the other guests. Three matrons clustered together, oblivious to the rest of the crowd, their faces twisted in anger and their voices carrying to Elizabeth.

"…if we encouraged our daughters to act with such outrageous behavior, we'd all have lords for sons-in-law. All they have to do is be caught alone with an earl's rakish brother and have a family member threaten a duel and"—she snapped her fingers—"countess in an instant."

A chill ran through Elizabeth's veins. "The gossip is never going to end," she whispered.

Richard halted, then with his mouth fixed in stern determination, he broke into the ladies' circle. "Mrs. Hampton, I don't believe I've had the honor of presenting to you my charming betrothed, Lady Elizabeth."

The matrons turned, their mouths agape, and blanched. If Elizabeth hadn't been frozen with humiliation, she might have found the view comical.

One of the women wearing a peacock feather in her hair began stammering, "Oh, Lord Averston. Er, no, I don't believe we've had…the…er…pleasure."

Richard spoke smoothly, his voice quiet, yet riddled with warning. "Since my wife-to-be is rather shy, I trust you will make her feel welcome any time you find yourself in the same gathering, Mrs. Hampton." He fixed a piercing stare upon each of them in turn. "But then, since you aren't exactly in the same social circle as a ducal family, I don't suppose that it will happen often."

Elizabeth almost gasped at the veiled insult.

Mrs. Hampton managed, "Of course, my lord."

He nodded as if satisfied, began to leave, then turned back. "Oh, one more thing; I trust you don't believe those ridiculous rumors about her and my brother. No one who knows her would ever believe it. No true Christian would spread such rumors."

Mrs. Hampton shook her head, her feathers madly waving. "No, my lord. I mean, of course we don't believe that, my lord."

"Very good. Do give my best to your husband."

The color in her face faded into the color of an old dust rag. "Yes, my lord."

He gave the gossips a last stern look before he led Elizabeth away. Elizabeth let out a breath she didn't realize she'd been holding. He'd defended her. He'd stood up to the gossips and rebuked them with a firmness they wouldn't soon forget. He'd protected her from their hurtful words, and possibly even stilled their venomous tongues.

Richard lowered his head to hers. "I'm sorry you heard that. I'd hoped after the ball and our public carriage ride in Hyde Park, those wagging tongues would have tired." He awarded her an intimate smile.

Her humiliation faded as gratitude and growing affection warmed her.

He added under his breath, "Apparently the lower circles still delight in demeaning their betters." A self-deprecating lilt touched his mouth that let her know his snobbery was all in fun.

She couldn't help but return his smile. "That was a terrible dressing-down."

"They deserved worse. I'll not have anyone criticize you."

She hesitated, fearing the truth. "Because you don't want your name stained by association?"

He faced her. "Because I don't want your name stained. You don't deserve it."

For a moment, Elizabeth couldn't formulate a reply. She'd never expected to find a staunch defender in the man who knew the full truth, who'd agreed to marry her only to save his brother from a duel, who probably still loved another. Despite all this, his honor and chivalry won.

She managed, "Thank you."

He placed his hand over hers where it rested on his sleeve, and resumed walking. Elizabeth relaxed. She was safe with him. Safer than she'd felt in a long time. With anyone. Richard would not hurt her; he would protect her. Under his protection, she might find the courage to become her own woman rather than a frightened mouse that cowered at every shadow. Gratitude and admiration filled her entire body with the light of hope.

Looking into his eyes, she smiled, hoping he saw her optimism. "What did you mean when you mentioned that lady's husband?"

A sheepish smile curved his lips. "He's our family physician. It was a reminder that my displeasure with him—or his wife—might result in losing our family as patients, along with any friends with whom we choose to disclose our discontentment."

"Ah. How very ruthless of you, my lord," she

teased.

His eyes crinkled. "Thank you. I've worked very hard to build a reputation of ruthlessness."

Richard came to a standstill and all mirth vanished from his expression. Elizabeth followed his gaze. Leticia Wentworth stood in their path. Her gaze locked with Richard's. The bloom in her cheeks faded and her mouth went slack. She looked absolutely shattered. Elizabeth's breath froze.

Miss Wentworth drew an audible breath and inclined her head. "My lord."

"Miss Wentworth." A faint hoarseness roughened Richard's voice and tension rippled in the air.

Elizabeth wanted to disappear. She tried to look away but couldn't make her eyes cooperate. It was like watching a terrible carriage accident unfolding slowly, dream-like.

He drummed his fingers on his thigh. "How…is your family?"

"Well, thank you." Leticia folded one arm over her chest as if trying to protect her wounded heart.

An awkward moment passed.

Richard inclined his head. "Well, good evening, then." He'd managed to steady his voice.

"Good evening, my lord. Lady Elizabeth."

"Miss Wentworth," Elizabeth managed through looming tears. *I'll be good to him*, she wanted to tell her, but she couldn't speak another word.

Leticia nodded to them and moved away with her head high. Only the fist clenched at her side gave away signs of emotion.

A weighted silence pressed down on Elizabeth and she refused to look at Richard, terrified at what she might see in his expression.

After a few nearly unbearably tense moments, Richard's voice broke in. "Come, Elizabeth, your sisters await. I'll escort you to your carriage."

Almost afraid of what he must be thinking, Elizabeth looked up at him. She found gentleness. Sorrow. But no anger. No resentment. No blame. He laid a hand over hers where it rested on her arm and gave it a tiny squeeze. Amazed, she turned her hand over and returned the pressure, making another silent vow of loyalty to him.

After he guided her to her sisters, he waited as they retrieved their wraps, then escorted them to their waiting carriage. Without a word, he handed them in. After helping Elizabeth in, he held her gloved hand a moment longer than necessary, pressed her hand to his lips and kissed it. She had the insane desire to tear off her gloves and ask him to do it again on her skin.

He finally broke his silence. "Until we meet again, dear lady."

"My lord." Her voice quivered.

He stepped back while the footman closed the door. As the carriage pulled away, Elizabeth sank against the cushions.

Richard Barrett was an uncommonly good man. No gentleman such as he deserved to be hurt or humiliated. Though a part of her heart might always belong to Tristan, she vowed to be a countess who would honor Richard and do all within her power to heal his wounded heart.

Chapter Fourteen

Standing in the main hall of Averston Castle in the middle of the country, Richard linked his fingers together behind his back, hoping to appear calm as the carriages of his wedding guests neared. He'd spent part of the morning sketching an old barn at the edge of his property, a soothing act that helped settle his nerves and fortify him for his next role—host and bridegroom.

He eyed the great hall appreciatively. Though understaffed due to his own neglect as a bachelor, his servants had done an admirable job on the main floor and guest rooms. Windows sparkled, the floor shone like a mirror, and woodwork gleamed. His mother would have been pleased.

He remembered as a child peeking through the stairway railings watching Mother, so lovely in her evening gown, greeting her guests in the main hall. Yet on the heels of his fond memories of his mother followed the stark reality of her betrayal. His shoulders tensed as the memory of her riding away assailed his thoughts. Mingled sorrow, loss, and anger arose from deep inside. In moments like this, Richard reverted back to a bewildered, abandoned child. That same loss and fear continuously haunted him like a merciless monster, waiting to catch him unawares, whispering that he wasn't loved, that he didn't deserve such affection, and that no one could be trusted with his heart.

He shoved the lurking monster back to a dark corner but could never completely banish it, no matter how many times he tried. It always returned another day to wound him.

Voices from outside announced his guests' arrival. The ducal family disembarked from their carriages and swept inside surrounded by dozens of servants, and enough trunks and baggage to supply an army. Richard spotted his betrothed standing quietly among the bustle, the one spot of calm amidst the chaos. He waded through the crowd to her.

She brightened as her gaze fell on him. "Good afternoon, Richard."

He smiled at her use of his Christian name and raised her hand to his lips. "Welcome, Elizabeth. I hope your journey was pleasant."

The corners of her pale eyes crinkled in mirth. "Less raucous than our arrival here. I hope your home will survive the upheaval."

Her good humor eased his tension. "You'd be surprised what my home has survived."

Her eyes warmed and a true smile touched her lips, transforming her from merely pretty to truly lovely. Her serenity eased the tension in his shoulders. He'd expected her to be nervous, but she seemed calm, even happy. Perhaps she welcomed their union after all.

He turned to the others and raised his voice to an authoritative tone. "Welcome, esteemed guests." He scrambled for a way to sound gracious to the ducal family despite his conflicting emotions that tempted him to make it clear he wanted nothing to do with them based on their treatment of his betrothed.

When the noise died down, and all eyes turned to him, he fell into the voice and posture he used when addressing the House of Lords. "I hope you will all be comfortable during this joyous occasion. I am honored to join our houses." There. He'd said that without any tremor.

"The honor is ours, Lord Averston," the duke replied. Was that a warning light in his eyes?

Richard led Elizabeth to the servants standing in a line. "Lady Elizabeth, this is Mrs. Brown, the head housekeeper. This is the butler, Handley. They have both been with the family for years and you may depend on them for anything you require."

Elizabeth nodded to Mrs. Brown, who dropped into a respectful curtsy.

Richard turned to the others and gestured to Elizabeth. "My intended bride, the future Countess Averston."

The servants all bowed and curtseyed. Mrs. Brown organized servants to lead guests to their rooms, while the butler ordered footmen to relocate trunks and hatboxes. Lady Elizabeth made an elegant farewell curtsey to Richard before she followed a maid up the stairs. She paused, glancing over her shoulder, and offered a smile bordering on flirtatiousness.

Cheeky girl. The prospect of marriage to her began to sound more and more appealing. Yet, he reminded himself not to get too attached. She'd proved herself an innocent rather than the immoral hussy he'd originally feared, but she may still become as untrustworthy as his mother. He must remember to shield his heart.

Throughout the day, a steady stream of guests arrived. Lady Elizabeth made no further appearance;

most likely, she rested after her long journey. Richard missed her smile.

Rhys Kensington, his oldest and closest friend, appeared late that afternoon. Richard nearly threw his arms around his friend's shoulders. Instead, he settled for a strong handshake.

"Kensington. Thank you for coming."

Kensington drew him into a hug and heartily slapped his back. "You didn't think I'd miss your wedding, did you?"

"I wasn't certain if you'd returned to England yet."

Kensington grinned. "A duke's daughter, eh? Couldn't you have done better than that?"

Richard followed his lead into the absurd. "Unfortunately, the princess refused my suit."

"Hmm. Should have gone after foreign princesses, then."

"You know how I despise travel by sea."

"They wouldn't come to you?" Rhys opened his eyes wide in mock surprise.

"It seemed rude to ask."

"Ever the gentleman."

Grinning, Richard shook his head at their ridiculous exchange. He'd missed his friend. "Do you reside in London now?"

Kensington shrugged. "When I'm not imposing on distant relatives."

"Do stay here when you need to escape London in the summer."

"Won't having me underfoot be inconvenient while you and your new wife become…acquainted?" His eyes glinted wickedly.

Richard punched him lightly in the arm.

Sobering, Kensington studied him. "No regrets?"

"Regrets?"

"I thought you and Leticia Wentworth…"

Richard gave a firm shake of his head. "I am persuaded Lady Elizabeth is a better match."

Kensington's piercing gaze left Richard with the urge to squirm. "There's more to it."

"Don't believe every rumor you hear. I have no regrets."

"The rumors lately are all about Pemberton's daughter marrying *one of the most eligible and elusive young bachelors in England.*"

Richard shook his head at the thought of such a romantic description of himself. "You must be weary from your journey. No doubt you'd like to bathe and change."

"I would like to get out of my dirt."

Richard waved over a footman. "Show Captain Kensington to his room."

They parted, Richard's spirits lifted by the arrival of his friend. As the dinner hour approached, Richard met with his guests in the drawing room and saw to it that everyone had something to drink while they waited for the others to arrive. Tristan had failed to make an appearance yet, but Richard refused to indulge in taunting visions of Tristan lying wounded on the side of the road. He would be here.

When Elizabeth entered the drawing room, Richard mentally patted himself on the back for his good fortune. Not only did she look beautiful in her cream lace evening gown and pearls, but her welcoming smile reassured him.

He tucked her hand into the crook of his arm and

led her to Kensington. "May I present Captain Kensington formerly of His Majesty's Cavalry? My betrothed, Lady Elizabeth."

Kensington awarded her a wide, toothy grin. "It is, indeed, an unprecedented delight to finally meet you, Lady Elizabeth." He bowed low over her hand. "I shall have to speak with you later and warn you all about Richard's failings so they don't come as a shock after you marry him."

A sparkle entered Elizabeth's eye. "I look forward to that discussion, Captain Kensington. No doubt the perfect image could use a bit of ruffling." She glanced up at Richard, the corners of her mouth curving, a coyness in her smile he'd never seen before.

Richard leaned toward her ear, but spoke loud enough for Kensington to hear. "You would do well to remember that half of what Kensington tells you is a twisted version of the truth."

Kensington laughed. "Except when I say what a lovely and gracious lady you are, and how lucky Richard is that you've agreed to marry him."

Elizabeth tilted her head to one side, and lightly tapped a long slender finger against her lower lip, a movement clearly not lost on Kensington. "I suspect you leave a long line of broken hearts everywhere you go, Captain."

Kensington sighed gustily. "I certainly hope so." That wicked glint returned. "I might give up my ways for one as beautiful as you. Shall I carry you off and save you from Lord Stuffed Shirt?"

She laughed softly. "Certainly not, Captain Flirt. However, I will appreciate any illumination you can shed on his character, especially if it proves less than sterling."

Kensington laughed and Richard joined in. Dinner was announced. Richard congratulated himself for having the sense to direct Mrs. Brown to hire more help and especially for finding the new French chef.

At dinner, he sat at the head of the long table with Elizabeth at his right. The guests' voices ranged from a murmur to a crescendo, punctuated by occasional laughter, all underscored by the clinking of silver on china. A snowy tablecloth highlighted dozens of dishes in an impressive array of delectables.

Lady Elizabeth drew his attention. Bathed by candlelight from crystal chandeliers and silver candlesticks, and accented by her demure gown, her skin took on a golden glow. Each movement of her mouth seemed designed to draw his gaze. He had to consciously transfer his attention onto his other guests. As he ate, he found himself the object of an uncomfortably honest scrutiny by Elizabeth who held her lip between her teeth each time her searching gaze fell upon him.

While the other guests sat absorbed in discussions of two's and three's, Richard raised a brow at Elizabeth. "Have you come to a conclusion?"

Her eyes opened wide. "Regarding?"

"Me, apparently, since I've been the object of your rather unabashed stare."

She blushed and one corner of her mouth lifted. "No. I suspect there is more to you than I previously supposed."

"Oh? In what way?"

"You seem to go to a great deal of trouble to appear serious, even stern. Yet, you have a softer side that you seldom reveal."

"My dear Lady Elizabeth, I assure you there is nothing soft about me." If she only knew how hard he worked at being taken seriously at House of the Lords by peers twice his age.

Kensington flirted with the lady at his right, and nearby, several guests laughed, completely unaware of Richard's conversation with Elizabeth.

She sipped her wine, her lips lingering on the glass, and smiled as if she knew a secret. "You are kind to servants and flower girls. You are also thoughtful. The vase of violets in my bedroom, for example."

He waved it off. "Courtesy to servants inspires loyalty. The violets were a mere gesture. I was taught manners, after all."

"You took the trouble to find out my favorite flower."

He lifted a shoulder in a slight shrug. "'Twas nothing. A trifle. Besides, their scent reminds me of you. I couldn't find angelica."

Uncommon softness entered her expression and she dropped her voice to just above a whisper. "You showed me that you were concerned about protecting me when you asked if we ought to marry in haste."

"I wouldn't want our marriage to begin amid scandal." Uncomfortable, Richard shifted.

The light in her eyes dimmed and she lowered her gaze, hurt showing on her face. "Of course. You mustn't taint your own good name."

Richard silently cursed, realizing how his words must have sounded to her, as if he cared nothing for her reputation—only his family's. It was true, of course, but suddenly sounded very self-serving. He reached for her hand. She startled, her gaze flying to his face.

"That's not what I meant, Elizabeth. My family name will be yours, and I want you to feel safe and welcomed into any circle."

Solemnly, she studied him before whispering, "I haven't felt safe in a very long time."

Something fierce and protective overcame Richard as he squeezed her hand when he ached to take her into his arms. "'Tis my pleasure, and my duty, to ensure your safety."

She nodded, studying his face as if she wanted very much to believe him. "I trust you."

Trust. How rare. How precious. She'd handed him a priceless gift. If only he could hand her his trust as well. In time perhaps.

Throughout the remainder of the meal, she bestowed ready smiles upon him, and he stopped searching for signs of her nervousness about their upcoming marriage. Instead, he searched for new ways to earn more of those priceless smiles.

After the last of the dessert had been consumed, Richard stood and expressed his appreciation for his guests' presence at his wedding on the morrow. He raised his glass to Elizabeth. "To my future wife; the most beautiful lady in all of England. May we share much joy together."

As her pale, gray-green gaze locked with his, he thought of everything he found desirable about her, hoping she could see his sincerity.

Her eyes shone with unshed tears. With his chest swelling, Richard raised her hand to his lips as guests made other toasts and offered well wishes.

The ladies retired to the drawing room to allow the

men their habitual male-only conversation around the dinner table, which he suspected would be full of innuendos about the wedding night and unsolicited advice on how to keep a female under his thumb. He was not mistaken. Fortunately, Rhys Kensington managed to steer the conversation away whenever Richard's embarrassment became painful. Interesting, that, since Kensington usually delighted in needling Richard himself. Soon, more comfortable subjects arose such as crop and tenant issues, as well as the latest *on dits* of horseracing and whose hounds were considered the finest for hunting. Drinks flowed freely and snuffboxes appeared.

Richard's attention drifted until the term "illegal market" caught his attention.

Lord Jenison said, "Some claim there's an organized crime ring run by someone named Mr. Black which is fueling the alarming increase of theft in London."

Richard became alert. "Yes, the 'King of Crime.' I've heard a great deal about him."

Lord Jenison tapped his snuffbox. "If it's truth, this Mr. Black is very secretive. Not even his employees seem to know who he is."

The Duke of Pemberton scowled. "A couple of burglars believed to be associates of Mr. Black broke into my son-in-law's house in London and roughed up a couple of servants. Dreadful. I'm grateful my daughter wasn't home at the time. I increased security around my London properties. I hope you'll do the same." He leveled a meaningful look at Richard.

"A precaution I've already taken," Richard agreed.

Jenison added, "In addition to his link to several

burglaries, some violent, he allegedly owns a number of brothels and flash houses."

Richard sipped his drink, considering. "I assume Bow Street has investigated?"

"Only those crimes committed in their jurisdiction. A few constables have tried to infiltrate the organization but all have gone missing, some of whom later turned up dead."

A chill went down Richard's spine. Silence settled over the dining room.

Pemberton arose. "Come now. This is supposed to be a happy occasion. Let us retire to the drawing room to join the ladies, shall we?"

Amid a chorus of agreement, the others arose and headed toward the drawing room.

Elizabeth's brother, the Marquis of Martindale, matched paces with Richard. "I'm impressed with how well you've handled the idea of marriage to Elizabeth, Lord Averston. You seem genuinely fond of my sister."

"The more time I spend with her, the more fond of her I become."

"Elizabeth and I have never been close, but I do have her best interests at heart. I hope you do as well."

Richard met his gaze. "I give you my word I will be good to her."

Martindale raked Richard with a piercing stare before nodding. "See that you do." He quickened his steps to catch up to Pemberton.

Richard slowed his pace as the weight of his marriage, and the added responsibilities that accompanied such a large step, pressed on him.

In the corridor outside the drawing room, Kensington gripped his shoulder. "You look as jittery as a youth plotting to steal his first kiss."

Richard laughed weakly. Leave it to Kensington to find a way to shock him out of his protective wall. "You're as bad as Tristan."

Kensington grinned and Richard could not resist grinning back. He didn't know what he would have done without Kensington and Tristan in those early days when he'd lost his father and had to shoulder the responsibilities of a title at such a young age.

"Where is your prodigal brother?" Kensington asked.

"I'm sure he's on his way, as soon as he can pry himself out of the arms of whatever woman with whom he happens to be at the moment."

Richard shook his head. "He makes me look like a prudish old maid."

"He makes everyone look that way."

Kensington sobered. "Your betrothed is lovely. Really. Your father would have approved."

"I believe he would." The thought gave Richard no small amount of pride.

In the drawing room, as his gaze met Elizabeth's, a pleased smile touched her mouth. Richard puffed out his chest.

Kensington's voice broke in. "I envy you."

"Definitely no regrets," Richard said with conviction.

Chapter Fifteen

While waiting for the gentlemen to join the ladies in the drawing room, turmoil swirled in Elizabeth's heart each time she considered her burgeoning affection for Richard when her feelings for Tristan were still so poignant. Throughout their courtship, Lord Averston had been a delightful surprise in many ways. How different he was from her first impression of the stern, unemotional man she'd previously supposed.

In the morning, she would be his wife. She had faith marriage to him would be as pleasant as their courtship, regardless of its origin. With trembling fingers, Elizabeth touched her white and silver gown laying over a large chair, pressed and ready for tomorrow's ceremony. All day, serenity had settled into her heart and she'd been certain marrying Richard would bring her happiness. Yet tonight, nervousness plagued her. Silly. Richard was a good man. This coming marriage, while not to the man in her heart, would bind her to a man of honor and kindness. It would be enough. She gathered the serenity that had settled in her heart the moment she'd arrived at Averston Castle and tucked it in firmly around her. Emboldened, she left the safety of her room for the crowded drawing room.

With Captain Kensington at his side, Richard awaited her in the drawing room. From the opposite side of the room, he gazed at her through eyes that had once seemed as impenetrable and cold as onyx, but now held promise. He wasn't cold; he was cautious, careful. While he lacked the overt charm of his brother, his thoughtfulness touched a tender place in her heart.

How had she missed what a handsome man he was? Only Captain Kensington came near him in height and breadth, and no one in the room could compare to Richard's masculine allure. More importantly, she could not have found a man of more integrity and decency.

She should wait for Richard to come to her, but could not resist his pull. She moved toward him, unable to keep her gaze off him.

A hand grabbed Elizabeth's arm and Duchess's voice hissed into her ear, "A lady never approaches a gentleman."

Elizabeth halted and her breath froze. "Of course. I was...merely moving to the window where I might feel the breeze." Although why it mattered that she approached her husband-to-be, she could not guess.

The guests' soft murmur of voices continued uninterrupted, unaware of the private drama.

Duchess's fingers dug into Elizabeth's arm. "Everyone is watching you. See that you give them no reason to gossip further about you or our family."

"Yes, Duchess," she whispered.

"Do not fail this time."

"Duchess." Richard's warm bass rumbled sweeter than any music as he appeared next to her as if conjured by magic.

Elizabeth wanted to weep in relief that he had come to her rescue. Duchess straightened and put on a practiced smile as she turned to Richard.

Richard's gaze lowered to Duchess's grip on her arm. Quietly, but with intensity, he murmured, "I would ask that you not leave bruises upon my intended bride, nor touch her in such a rough manner again. If she's damaged, the wedding is off."

Duchess let out a huff and said *sotto voce*, "You know perfectly well she's already damaged, thanks to your brother."

"Only her reputation, which I am attempting to repair." His gaze flicked to Elizabeth. "I would speak with you, Lady Elizabeth." Again, that icy gaze moved to Duchess and a dark brow lifted.

Duchess let out a laugh of cold humor, a sound Elizabeth knew all too well. She opened her hand and released Elizabeth's arm. "Of course, Lord Averston. I'll give you that pleasure. As long as you marry her on the morrow, I don't care what you do to her tonight." She gave him a meaningful look and turned away.

Trembling, Elizabeth clenched her jaw to keep her teeth from chattering and stared at the floor. Moving slowly, as if trying not to frighten off a wild bird, he held out a hand and waited for her to take it. He stepped closer, enfolding her hand inside both of his.

"Come." He led her to an adjoining room and closed the door.

Stillness enveloped them. Richard brought one of Elizabeth's hands into his chest and smiled down at her with tenderness shining in his eyes. With slow, deliberate movements, he tugged at each fingertip to loosen her evening glove and slid it off her arm. He lowered his head and kissed the back of her hand. His breath, warm and moist, caressed her skin. And his lips.

Oh, his lips were so soft. So gentle. The last of her fears scattered as he kissed first her hand, then each finger. He turned over her hand and pressed his lips to her fingers, her palm, her wrist. Pleasure glided along her skin in unexpected sensuality. Her heart thumped. Heat built inside. She inhaled his masculine scent and stepped closer. He kissed her palm again before wrapping his fingers around it. Warmth shone in his eyes as he raised his other hand to her face. He traced the curve of her jaw and brushed the back of his fingers across her cheek, up and down.

"Soft. Beautiful." Tenderness was joined by intensity. "I will never give you cause to fear me, sweet Elizabeth. I count myself fortunate that we shall wed on the morrow. Any man would be proud to have you as his bride."

She'd only ever dreamed of a man saying such lovely words to her and touching her with such gentleness. Light filled the dark places inside, bringing hope and belonging. Tears rose up and spilled down her cheeks.

He carefully wiped the moisture away with the pad of his thumb, tracing her cheek again. "I hope those aren't tears of sadness."

She let out a half sob, half laugh. "No, indeed. Your words mean much to me, my lor…Richard."

He kissed her hand again. "Ah. A good sign. You give me hope. I'd like to enjoy the pleasure of your company more, but I suppose, sadly, we ought to return to our guests now."

Speechless at the warmth tumbling over her, she nodded.

Richard. A knight in a gentleman's clothing.

In dream-like bliss, she returned to the drawing room with her hand on his arm. During that fateful house party, she thought she had found the man of her dreams in Tristan. Perhaps it was always that way with first loves, but she'd felt such a connection with him. She'd hoped—foolishly—that Tristan would convince Father that love was more important than peerage. It had seemed a doomed dream.

After Richard's tenderness a moment ago, that dream came alive in vivid color that at long last, she'd found safety and contentment, seeds that might bloom into true love.

Chapter Sixteen

Inside his private study, Richard cast a baleful eye at the clock, wondering how his guests expected him to play the host until the wee hours of the morning, and then appear clear-eyed at his wedding on the morrow.

The ladies had long since retired. Sometimes he suspected they were the only ones with any sense. At last, one by one, the men thanked him for his hospitality, complimented him on his exceptional punch—a concoction designed to put any man under the table after only a few glasses—and staggered off to their beds. Martindale ended up in the wrong room, but eventually everyone settled down for the night.

Richard sat alone in his study, sketching a nearby vase of flowers. The subject wasn't of particular interest, but sketching helped him order his thoughts, and tonight his thoughts centered around his imminent wedding. His bride was gracious and kind. Her vulnerability, especially with regards to her boorish mother, touched a soft place inside he'd not known existed. He again recalled the abject terror in her face as her mother had threatened her only hours ago. Something fierce had arisen inside Richard, demanding action, and when Elizabeth had turned to him, so frightened and trapped, his heart had filled with protectiveness.

Despite being overshadowed by her sisters' classic

beauty, Elizabeth was lovely. Her skin had been softer than a flower petal. She'd shivered at his touch, hinting at untapped passion and innocence. Yes, the thought of wedding Elizabeth held tremendous appeal.

Approaching footsteps caught his attention. The door opened, admitting his brother.

"Evening, Richard." Tristan lounged against the door. "You look far too serious for a man about to wed and bed a comely wench tomorrow."

Richard shot a glare at the irreverent quip and set down his pencil. "I should take you to task for calling my betrothed a wench."

"Instead, you're just too happy to see me." Tristan grinned.

"Insolent pup." Yet he could not deny his pleasure that Tristan had arrived.

Tristan chuckled. "My apologies for my delay. I had five hundred pounds to win and a lass to woo."

"Did you succeed?"

"At both."

Richard let out a huff of mingled pride and disgust, and shook his head.

Tristan crossed the room and picked up a decanter and glass. "Do you want one?"

"I had some punch earlier."

"You're still standing? You've clearly not had enough."

"I don't want to arrive at the ceremony three sheets to the wind."

"Or unconscious?"

They shared a laugh. Sobering, Richard added, "I'm glad you've come."

Tristan leveled a surprisingly intense gaze upon

him. "I wouldn't miss it." His irrepressible grin returned. "Let's go swim in the lake."

"You're mad."

"You're tempted."

"Almost." Richard pushed himself to a stand. "I'm going to bed."

Tristan raised a brow. "With whom?"

Straight-faced, Richard said, "Doesn't matter. I'm not sharing."

Tristan laughed. "You're playing the part well for the moment. Except I know better."

"You don't know anything."

Tristan smirked.

Sobering, Richard gripped Tristan's shoulder. "Thank you for coming."

Tristan's expression grew solemn. "I hope you'll be happy."

Richard nodded. "I know you do. I shall, never fear."

"No hard feelings, then, about how it all started?"

"No. You didn't mean to involve me. Besides, she's been a truly pleasant surprise."

Tristan's expression closed over; he sipped his drink. "Glad to hear it."

Richard paused. In all his irritation at how Tristan's folly had affected Richard, and what his intentions were toward Elizabeth, he'd given little thought to Tristan's feelings regarding, well, anything—Elizabeth and the prospect of losing her, and the object of his desire marrying his brother. He eyed Tristan. "You aren't bothered by this marriage, are you? I mean you didn't really have true feelings for Elizabeth—"

"Of course not. I told you, mere flirtation.

Interesting diversion." Tristan made a dismissive gesture.

Richard watched him through narrowed eyes but Tristan's expression remained too tightly protected. That, alone, spoke volumes. Richard paused. If Elizabeth and Tristan were still infatuated with one another, what did that spell for his marriage? However, Tristan had vowed he had no designs upon Elizabeth. Twice. That should be enough. Tristan was honorable enough to be trusted. Wasn't he?

"Good night." Richard went upstairs alone to wrestle with his doubts and fears.

Chapter Seventeen

The wedding day dawned gloomy, with intermittent rain spattering against the windows. Richard scowled out of his bedroom window, wondering if this were some sort of ill omen for his marriage. Gritting his teeth, he chided himself for thinking like an old nursemaid.

Yet he couldn't shake the gloom creeping over him. Did he have the mettle to rise to the challenge of husband and, eventually, father? He had witnessed the fallacies and vulnerabilities of love. His own parents hadn't had the best marriage. His father couldn't keep his mother happy. Or perhaps her character had simply been too flawed to create a faithful union with anyone. How could Richard hope to do better?

Wesley, his aged valet entered, and Richard subjected himself to Wesley's meticulous ministrations. Wesley washed his hair twice, shaved him with more care than he had in months, and helped him dress in an immaculate superfine suit. By then, sunlight slanted down in gossamer rays through parted clouds, and Richard's spirits lifted.

Wesley tied and retied the cravat, each time fretting that it wasn't quite right. After removing the cravat and replacing it with a freshly ironed one, he tried again. Then, after stepping back to examine his handiwork, let out a moan of dismay and reached to re-tie it.

Richard pushed away the valet's hands. "It will do. I'm not entertaining the royal family."

"'Tis your marriage, my lord. Just as important."

Richard bit his lip to hold back a smile. "Indeed, but I doubt my bride will change her mind on account of my cravat." He turned to the mirror. "It looks perfect."

Tristan entered and stared in horror at Richard's necktie. "Good grief, you aren't going out with your cravat in such a state, are you?"

As Wesley stammered, Richard laughed. "He's quizzing you, Wesley. No doubt he overheard our conversation before he came in." With a glance at his brother, added, "You oughtn't tease him so. You know how he likes to fuss."

Wesley looked indignant. "'Tis my duty to see you always dressed and groomed as befitting your station, my lord."

"Indeed it is, and you are most committed to your duty," Richard soothed. "I could never do it without you."

"Just so." Mollified, Wesley held his frockcoat while Richard slipped his arms into the sleeves. Wesley brushed Richard's coat again.

"You missed a spot." Tristan gestured to an imaginary speck.

As Wesley brushed Richard's shoulder blade raw, Richard shot his brother a warning look.

Tristan only grinned. "So the banns were read in both parishes and no one dared to raise a challenge, huh?" His eyes glinted.

"Apparently no one has yet learned about my other twelve wives," Richard rejoined.

"Or our nine drooling half-wit brothers and sisters."

"One of whom is in my bedroom quizzing my valet."

"The other of whom is getting married today."

"Thus saving her from a more gruesome fate of marrying the village idiot." He made a sweeping gesture toward Tristan.

"By the way, has she seen you in daylight, yet?"

Richard drew himself up. "She could hardly keep her eyes off me yesterday. Last night she threw herself into my arms."

"Clearly she has no sense."

He snapped his mouth closed as the unkind remark *You are proof of that* nearly escaped his mouth. Was his bride in love with his brother? He firmly slammed the door shut on such thoughts. He cleared his throat. "Have you seen Rhys Kensington yet?"

Tristan nodded. "At breakfast. A right likeable fellow, that. Cavalry didn't ruin him as much as I'd feared. A trifle serious these days but perhaps that can be remedied. I invited him to join the Four Horse Club."

"I thought you found that club had gotten too respectable."

"It is. But it's still a lark with the right bunch of reprobates. Perhaps with Kensington's aid, I can return it to its former disreputable glory."

Amused, Richard shook his head in mock disapproval.

"Sir." Wesley held out the velvet pouch containing the Averston rubies, the traditional wedding gift to each new countess in the family. Soon Elizabeth would own the rubies and join the ranks of proud countesses in the family. He prayed she would wear them more faithfully than his mother had.

The rest of the morning passed in a flurry of excitement, and at ten o'clock in the morning, Richard found himself by the altar of the parish church, next to a great uncle who served as the vicar. A sudden onslaught of nerves attacked Richard, like a hundred tiny bugs crawling over him. Richard drew a breath to steady himself. It didn't help.

Tristan gripped his shoulder. "Steady, ol' man."

Why his irresponsible younger brother could be a source of strength, Richard could not say, but his nervousness faded.

Then his bride entered the chapel, lightly resting a hand on the arm of her father. Lady Elizabeth was radiant. Her head high, her bearing regal, she glided toward him. In a few moments, she would be his. A level of joy he had never experienced overcame him, but he checked it. Best not care too much too soon. Courtesy and respect, not affection, should lead their marriage. He must not allow his heart to become too deeply involved until he knew for sure he could trust her.

The Duke of Pemberton looked solemn but pleased, and as he placed Elizabeth's hand in Richard's, Pemberton gave a discreet nod. Somehow, the gesture of approval from such an esteemed peer warmed Richard. He inclined his head briefly, hoping the duke knew Richard understood the trust placed literally in his hands. He met his future brother-in-law's gaze. Without Lord Martindale's threat to duel Tristan, Richard would never have come to this point with Elizabeth. He had the urge to shake Lord Martindale's hand.

Richard looked down at Elizabeth's uplifted face shining with radiant joy. At the moment, marrying Elizabeth felt so *right*. The thought caused vague panic to build up in his chest at the level of vulnerability such thoughts left him. Notwithstanding, he couldn't deny the soft reassurance that he was doing the right thing.

Aware only of Elizabeth by his side with her warm hand in his, and her taunting fragrance caressing his senses, Richard heard little of the ceremony taken from the Book of Common Prayer. The vicar pronounced them husband and wife. Murmurs of approval came from the guests witnessing the wedding, but Richard barely heard them.

As they signed the register, Richard leaned down and whispered, "Have I ever told you how lovely you are?"

She blinked, and the happy smile she'd worn earlier transformed into one of pure adoration. Richard made a mental note to pay her compliments more often, especially if such would be his reward. Keeping a firm grip on her hand, he led her to his family coach for the short ride back to his home for the wedding breakfast.

She turned to him with an intensity he'd never seen in her eyes. "Richard, I want you to know that despite the reasons for our marriage, I have every intention of being a good wife to you." Her words rang with a sincerity that begged to be believed.

"I will endeavor to be a good husband to you." Could he be a good husband without giving her his whole heart right away?

As the coach pulled to a stop he stepped out and offered a hand to steady her. The servants had outdone themselves. Swags of flowers lined the front entry, and bouquets and baskets led the path to the dining room where crystal sparkled, silver shimmered, and atop crisp linens sat an intricate ice sculpture of a swan. The French menu for the wedding breakfast included *Jambon de York*, *patés*, hot and cold roasts, *viands*, *salades a la russe*, and fruits.

He made a note to add an additional few pounds to Mrs. Brown's wages the next time he paid her. She'd done a brilliant job of putting together the celebration, and she'd done it without having a lady of the house to consult.

After the guests consumed the meal, they mingled, some indoors and others in the gardens, laughing and enjoying themselves. While Elizabeth conversed with guests on the lawn, Richard stood on the terrace and spoke with each person who wished them well.

Kensington approached. "You must visit soon. I purchased a small place in the lake country. Nothing grand, mind you, but pleasant."

"I'd be delighted," Richard said. "Are you giving up your bachelor apartment in London?"

"No, I'll still spend enough time there to give it some use. Let me know when you come into Town."

They made their farewells and Kensington strolled toward his waiting coach. Smiling, Richard looked around for Elizabeth. When he spotted her, his heart dropped. Next to a tall hedgerow, and apart from the guests, Elizabeth and Tristan stood close together—intimate, even. Everything inside Richard went still.

Tristan handed her a package. What it was, Richard could not see clearly, but after opening it, Elizabeth hugged it to herself as if it were precious, and rewarded

Tristan with a dazzling smile visible even from a distance. Tristan touched her cheek. The pure adoration shining in her expression as she gazed at Tristan could not be misunderstood.

Aghast, Richard stared. Loss and betrayal slammed into him. Jealousy, dark and ugly, coiled inside.

She was still in love with his brother.

He curled his hands into fists. He wanted to throw something. Preferably his fists. Through his brother. After he shook his bride until her teeth rattled. She had seemed genuinely to like Richard. She'd even pledged to be a good wife less than an hour ago. All along, she'd been toying with him, lying to him! The dark and ugly place inside Richard festered like a sore. He'd been a fool to hope. No doubt, Tristan would seduce her at his first opportunity and she clearly would accept him. Closing off all the growing affection he'd held for his wife of only an hour, Richard donned his cool façade and vowed to protect his family reputation, his honor, and especially his heart.

Chapter Eighteen

Elizabeth stood in the garden apart from the others, exhausted from greeting so many guests during the wedding breakfast. Guests lingered, enjoying the weather and each other's company, but Elizabeth needed a moment to collect herself.

Tristan found her then and greeted her. "Welcome to the family, Elizabeth." Though he smiled, that unrestrained manner he once had with her had become visibly tense.

"Thank you." Elizabeth tried to smile but so much history between them left her off-balance. He was her brother-in-law now and could never be anything else.

She'd vowed to be a good wife to Richard and she fully intended to keep her vow. Richard was capable of such charm and tenderness, and she was attracted to him. She owed it to him to be a worthy wife—warm, comforting, and above all, loyal. Her wedding band burned her finger as if mocking her marriage vow and taunting her lingering affection for Tristan. Did one ever stop loving one's first love? Perhaps a tiny part of that new flame would always burn in a secret place in her heart. Regardless, she would not let it interfere with her duty to her husband.

"I wanted to give you a gift." Tristan slipped a package tied with string into her hand.

Elizabeth unwrapped Tristan's package to reveal a

small, leather-bound book, and ran her hand reverently over the embossed title. "Shakespeare's Sonnets. It's lovely. Thank you." She opened the book to find a message written on the first page.

To Elizabeth,

May your heart be filled with poetry and love, now and always.

Tristan

She swallowed the lump forming in her throat. "I…don't know what to say."

He touched her cheek. "I hope you'll be very happy." He smiled sadly and said in a clear attempt to be light-hearted, "Richard's not so bad once you get to know him. Doesn't have an ounce of fun in him, of course, and obviously missed out on both good looks and charm, but I'm sure he makes up for the deficit with his, er…responsible nature."

Elizabeth tried to laugh, but sounded forced. "It must be difficult to have walked away with all the best qualities." Still, she had to admit, her heart didn't pound with quite the force it once had while in his presence. Her burgeoning affection for Richard had nudged aside her once-focused love for Tristan.

Tristan shrugged. "It's a heavy burden, but one I bear just as he must bear the weight of the title."

Richard appeared at her side, took her hand, and wound it through his arm, glaring at Tristan. "Just as you bear the burden of entertaining parlor maids and widows."

Elizabeth stared at Richard, surprised at his harsh words.

Tristan's grin faded. "As you say." He inclined his head and strode toward a group of guests where women's laughter rang out.

Fighting to keep her countenance serene, Elizabeth pulled her gaze from Tristan's retreating back and prayed her expression didn't betray her still conflicting emotions. Before Elizabeth fully recovered her composure, Leticia Wentworth and her parents came to pay their respects.

As Leticia's gaze rested upon Richard, her tortured love shone through. "I wish you all the happiness in the world."

Richard's expression remained neutral, but his tension clearly revealed that he still harbored tender feelings toward Leticia. "Thank you."

Leticia smiled, but sadness touched her eyes.

Elizabeth almost mouthed Thomas Moore,

...And such is the fate of our life's early promise...

Still, the prospect of life with Richard had become a welcome union with potential for a measure of happiness. He appeared to have feelings for Elizabeth, at least on some level, but probably nothing approaching what he must feel for Leticia.

As if fearing her love might be showing, Leticia quickly turned away from Richard to Elizabeth. "You simply must come for tea, Countess. I would consider it a favor if you would allow me to acquaint you with everyone in the parish."

Giving a little start of surprise at her new title, Elizabeth's gaze flicked uncertainly between Leticia and Richard, but she smiled warmly—at least, she hoped it appeared warm. "Gladly. Thank you for coming today."

When Leticia had gone, Richard's dark eyes turned to her. She faltered at the lack of expression there. His mouth pressed into a hard line. Gone was his former tenderness. Without a word, he turned and stalked toward the gardens, his footsteps pounding the walkway.

Stunned by the change, Elizabeth stared after him. No doubt, he'd made a quick comparison between her and Leticia and found Elizabeth lacking. Richard must despise her! Perhaps it was no less than she deserved, after her confusion about who had the greater possession of her heart.

As she twisted her wedding band around her finger, she drew a breath and reminded herself of all Richard's fine qualities. He did indeed have much to recommend him. More importantly, he was her husband. She might not be Leticia, and he might not be Tristan, but Elizabeth would do everything in her power to ensure his happiness. Somehow, she'd banish her lingering affections for Tristan and focus her energy on building a life with Richard. With time, perhaps, Richard might transfer his love from Leticia to Elizabeth. She must be patient and understanding until that day.

Father stepped up to her while Duchess lagged behind speaking to another guest. He put a hand on Elizabeth's arm, and in a rare display of affection, kissed her brow. "Be happy, daughter."

Emboldened by his tenderness, she rose up on tiptoe and kissed his cheek. "Thank you, Father, for everything." If they had been alone, she would have thanked him out loud for raising her as a legitimate daughter, for educating her, for providing a place for her in the world, and for caring enough to arrange a marriage with a good and honorable man. She had grown to share his opinion of Richard. However, she couldn't speak so openly with others nearby. Instead, she poured all her affection and gratitude into her smile.

By the answering quirk of his mouth and the way he tapped her chin, he seemed to understand. After one last nod of approval, Father turned to give instructions to the coachman.

Duchess approached. "Well, I didn't think you'd ever amount to anything, but thanks to your father, you've managed to make a brilliant match. Try not to disappoint your husband."

A lifetime of criticism, pain, ridicule, shame rose up in flash of hot anger. Just last night, Elizabeth had examined her back to assure herself years of beatings hadn't scarred her skin—she didn't wish to repulse Richard on their wedding night. Now, she would no longer live in that kind of fear and pain and indignity.

With her heart practically leaping out of her chest and her whole body trembling in barely controlled rage, Elizabeth hissed, "I hate you. I will never forgive you for the way you've treated me. You are cruel and vicious. I hope someday you get what you deserve."

Duchess's face went from slack-jawed shock to red-faced fury. She spoke in a low voice but every word lashed at Elizabeth. "How dare you! You ungrateful little tart! After all I've done for you—"

"Done for me?" Elizabeth echoed in disbelief, barely managing not to scream the words at her. "You treated me like a…"

As Elizabeth searched for a word to adequately describe her treatment, Duchess's smile turned poisonous. "Like the by-blow of my husband's whore?"

Elizabeth's anger overshadowed the shock at such vulgar words. All her life, she'd allowed Duchess to abuse her because of the shameful truth of her birth. She'd actually begun to believe she was as stupid and clumsy and worthless as Duchess had always told her.

No more. Elizabeth didn't deserve such cruelty. No one did. Furthermore, Elizabeth was a married woman, a countess, the mistress of her own home, and no longer subject to Duchess's tyranny.

Elizabeth drew herself up. Scorn rose off her words like steam. "Stay away from me. Never speak to me again. When you die, I will dance on your grave." She turned and walked, head high, back straight, around the side of the house toward the back lawn where a few last guests remained to celebrate and enjoy the sunshine.

She drew several deep breaths, letting her rage dissipate. As calm overcame her, on it came the heels of triumph. She'd done it! She'd actually stood up to her tormentor and walked away unscathed. She truly was free.

Chapter Nineteen

Richard's guests departed, all smiling, winking, and offering last minute marital advice and well wishes.

Tristan left first, making some reference to a widowed viscountess. Then, to Richard's surprise, Tristan hugged him. As Tristan pulled back, he fixed a searching stare upon Richard.

He lowered his voice. "Exercise your famous self-control and rid yourself of whatever is bothering you. Go make your bride happy."

Richard stiffened. "I don't need advice from a pup."

Tristan looked disappointed. Sad even. "Do you want to go have a drink?"

Though tempted to tell Tristan everything, and thrash him while he was at it, Richard shook his head. It would do no good. Tristan would not change his nature. Elizabeth would not change her affections. Their path seemed fixed toward destruction. For this, he'd broken Leticia's heart. For this, he'd given up a safe, happy marriage with a loyal woman. "Have a safe journey back to London."

Tristan nodded glumly as if recognizing something lost between them. "Goodbye." He turned at Elizabeth's approach and attempted to lighten the mood. "Try to keep him out of trouble. I tire of always coming to his aid."

She offered a pained smile at the jest. "Goodbye, Tristan."

His grin flashed and then he was gone. Elizabeth's brows drew together in a troubled frown and she watched Tristan until he disappeared. The dark and ugly place inside Richard grew. He recalled all too clearly his mother's duplicity, her dishonor, his overarching sense of abandonment.

As they bid farewell to the other guests, Elizabeth glanced up at him again and again, her gaze searching, but Richard refused to look her in the eye. He would protect her from anyone who might harm or frighten her, especially the duchess. But how could he ever love—or trust—a woman whose heart could not be true?

Lord and Lady Brinton were the last to leave. Elizabeth and her sister hugged as if they feared they'd forever be apart, Lady Brinton murmuring in Elizabeth's ear. They were both teary-eyed by the time they parted.

Elizabeth stood on the front steps next to Richard, waving until the carriage disappeared down the drive.

Once they were alone, Richard turned to his bride of a few hours and tried to hold back the compassion creeping over him at the sight of her tears. He remembered all too well the scene with his brother only an hour ago. At least there hadn't been a painful exchange between Leticia and him. She'd been sensible enough to greet him only long enough to pay her respects—deliberately in her parents' presence—which had made him wish he could have married her as planned instead of the mess to which he'd bound himself.

Elizabeth wiped her eyes with her handkerchief. "Perhaps I should rest before we dine this evening."

He nodded, grateful to have a few hours alone. Giving into his desires, he changed into some old work clothes and ran until his legs gave out.

****

Dinner was a formal affair. Richard sat at the head of the table in the formal dining room, which had been restored after the wedding feast. Elizabeth, wearing a soft pink gown with a scooped neckline, sat at his right. Remembering the longing in her eyes as she gazed at Tristan quelled any desire that might have arisen at the sight of her.

Elizabeth made small talk, mostly commenting on the fine weather and the guests who'd come to celebrate their union. Richard toyed with his food.

At last, Elizabeth set down her fork and knife and eyed him solemnly. "Is something amiss?"

He steeled himself. "Why do you ask?"

"You've said very little and you haven't eaten a bite."

"I ate a great deal at the wedding breakfast."

"You're holding your fork so tight that your fingers are white. Why are you unhappy?"

He set down his utensils. "I've just been wed. Today is the happiest day of my life." His tone implied exactly the opposite but he couldn't seem to help it.

She whispered. "You don't look happy."

"Which only proves you hardly know me, madam."

She was silent for a moment. "We aren't the first couple to be a bit unfamiliar with one another. I'm sure in time…"

"In time, perhaps. Good night."

He made a curt bow, left the table, and went to his study. The hurt in her expression at his coldness haunted him and caused a sting of guilt, but dash it all, he'd never experienced such jealousy, such painful betrayal…not since his mother left.

After loosening his cravat, he took a long drink of port, wondering how he'd ever have the stomach for the wedding night. He finally gave in to his desire to throw something and hurled his goblet against the wall. The crystal shattered and liquid ran down the wall.

Out of his pocket, he removed a velvet pouch containing the ruby necklace. He gripped it until the edges bit into his hand. Tonight he would break tradition in many, many ways.

At his summons, the head housekeeper appeared. "My lord?"

"Mrs. Brown, see to it that this is returned to the family safe."

"Of course, my lord." She accepted the jewels without even a raised brow at the break in tradition and left to do his bidding.

He cursed Tristan, cursed Elizabeth, and cursed the duel that had forced him to marry a woman who would prove faithless.

Chapter Twenty

Wearing only her shift underneath her leaf green dressing gown, Elizabeth brushed her hair even though Maggie had already done so.

Richard clearly regretted marrying her.

She'd seen the shielded expression with which he'd looked at Leticia, and his irritation each time he looked at Elizabeth. By marrying, she'd hoped she would escape constant criticism. Instead, she'd come to a new home with a different set of reminders of failure. He'd forever compare her to Leticia and find her a disappointment.

One minute Richard could be so warm, and another he turned cold. His signs of tenderness and his vow in the carriage had convinced her that he would be a good husband and perhaps would even grow to care for her. How could she have been so wrong? So foolish?

Instead of enjoying the pleasures Mary had told her she'd find with her husband, Elizabeth threw down her hairbrush and curled up in the middle of a cold and empty bed.

The idea of star-crossed lovers was certainly more romantic in stories than in reality. The emptiness of a loveless marriage was more painful than she'd ever dreamed. She blew out the candle and wept in the darkness. The words of Thomas Moore's *Weep On, Weep On* taunted her.

Weep on, weep on, your hour is past,
Your dreams of pride are o'er...

In the morning, Elizabeth went into the breakfast room and found a sideboard filled with a delicious array of food. Except for a servant, she was alone.

"Where is Lord Averston?" she asked the footman.

"He has already broken his fast, my lady, and is taking care of estate business."

Her heart shriveled. So this is how it would be. She sat fingering her wedding band as disappointment spread through her.

She raised her chin. So be it. He may not want her as his wife, but his estate needed a countess and she would be the best one possible. After breakfast, she wandered about the house, exploring rooms. One doorway led to a ballroom as grand as the queen's drawing room with gold and blue Georgian decor. At the far end of the room, a Louis XIV pianoforte stood in all its glory. No harp resided in the room, unfortunately. Elizabeth hadn't dared to ask to bring the family harp; it had been a member of the music room for three generations and Duchess had made it clear it would remain where Joanna made better use of it.

She left the darkened room and moved down the corridor examining paintings. One particularly queenly-looking woman caught her eye. The Ninth Countess Averston had such a faraway look that Elizabeth imagined her as a princess in a fairy tale. The countess rested her fingertips upon an exquisite ruby and diamond necklace. Later, as Elizabeth paused to peruse other paintings, she noticed a number of former countesses all wearing the same necklace.

Mrs. Brown, the housekeeper who had been with

the Barrett household for years, passed by, her keys jingling.

"A moment, Mrs. Brown," Elizabeth called.

The thin, intimidating woman halted and turned, looking at Elizabeth as if she thought her not good enough for her young lord. "Madam?"

Elizabeth refused to flinch under the judgmental stare, and rallied her courage. "A number of former Countesses Averston are wearing the necklace in this portrait. What is its significance?"

Did she imagine a touch of malice in the woman's eyes? "A prized family heirloom dating back to the fourteenth century. It's a long-standing tradition for each earl or heir-apparent to give to his bride on their wedding night."

A gift Richard evidently did not see fit to give Elizabeth. She could not ignore the implications. "I see," Elizabeth managed despite her sinking heart.

"Of course, most of the Averston matches were love matches, not..." Mrs. Brown's gaze slid over Elizabeth. "Well...like yours."

Elizabeth's face heated. No doubt, the servants knew their master and new mistress had not consummated their union, and they probably knew full well why not.

Before Elizabeth had managed to form a reply, Mrs. Brown murmured a "by your leave" and strode away with swishing skirts and jingling keys.

Elizabeth sank into a chair and rested her head in her hands. That a man so steeped in family honor and tradition would slight his new bride loudly proclaimed his disappointment in her. What could she do to earn Richard's respect? His approval?

Refusing to wallow in misery, Elizabeth stood. Obviously they might never love each other, not with his heart otherwise occupied, and hers torn, but they should be courteous to one another. Courtesy required that they dine together at the very least.

After whiling away the morning, Elizabeth had luncheon alone. Half expecting one of the servants to snicker as they served their new mistress, Elizabeth choked down a few bites of her meal before going in search of Richard. Even a confrontation would be better than being ignored. She found his study empty. His desk nearly overflowed with correspondence and unopened letters. She marveled over the untidiness of such a seemingly orderly person. Really, a good secretary should be controlling the paperwork.

She found a discarded newspaper and read it, finding mention of her wedding and the columnists' musings as to what kind of countess the new Countess Averston would prove herself to be. Elizabeth grimaced. Hopefully, she would manage to stay out of the papers except for only the briefest and blandest of mentions.

Another article about a series of London burglaries linked to the King of Crime, Mr. Black, set her imagination spinning tales of horror at being victimized by the blackguard. Ever since the break-in at Mary's house, Father had private security complete with dogs patrolling their London house. She hoped Richard did the same. If not, she'd suggest that he begin.

After reassuring herself she was safe from the reaches of a villain like Mr. Black, she turned her attention to one last article, another mention of Mrs. Goodfellow and her reform efforts, stating how badly she needed donations to help fund her reform house.

Elizabeth lowered the newspaper, her mind working. Reform house. Now that she was her own lady, she could help the reformers as she'd been planning ever since she first read of their efforts. Maybe even her loveless marriage could provide a way to make a difference in people's lives.

Prior to dinner, Elizabeth dressed with care in the ridiculous hope that she could get back Richard's esteem. Surely, he wouldn't have treated her so tenderly during their courtship unless he felt some regard for her. She would just have to discover how to find that part of him again.

Richard arrived in the dining room, looking resplendent in his evening attire and bowed to her. "My lady." He held out her chair and took a seat, but barely glanced her way.

"Did you have an enjoyable day?" she ventured.

"Tolerable. Busy and productive." He attacked his chicken. Then, as an afterthought, added, "You?"

"I explored the house. With your permission, I'd like to hire more help. This is a very large house for such a small staff—they do an admirable job, but I wouldn't want them overworked."

He waved negligibly without looking at her. "Of course. Instruct Mrs. Brown to hire whomever you and she see fit."

"Thank you." She watched him eat, wondering how she might break through the ice yet feeling a small victory that she could hire servants as she wished—including reformed workers.

She cleared her throat. "I noticed that your desk is rather overwhelmed. Don't you have a secretary?"

He grimaced. "Not at the moment. My last one left due to his wife's poor health; he had to take her to a warmer climate. I interviewed one in London, but he didn't suit." He met her gaze, offered a tight smile, and returned his attention back upon his dinner. Tiny lines formed at his brow, and his eyes were shadowed.

"You look tired," she ventured. "You're working too hard. Is there anything I can do to help?"

"It's nothing."

Perhaps he merely forgot about the necklace. It might all be an oversight. Even his non-appearance last night in her bedchamber might have been a noble intent to allow them to get to know one another better before consummation.

She cleared her throat, willing to give him the benefit of the doubt. "I perused the family portraits in the gallery. I noticed many of the former countesses wearing a ruby necklace. Has that some historical significance?"

He took a bite and chewed thoroughly. An avoidance tactic? "I believe it started as the gift of a doting husband."

"Whatever happened to it?"

"It's in the family vault." His tone suggested he had no further wish to discuss it.

"Oh." She'd almost hoped to hear it had disappeared. At least that would have been a less painful explanation than that he'd not seen fit to give it to her.

He finished his meal, stood, and offered her a formal bow. As he turned away and began striding toward the door, she raced through her options. Desperate for an opportunity to try to find the soft

Richard hidden so carefully away, she called to him. "Would you care to spend the evening in the library? With me? You might, er…show me around and I could…read aloud to you?" It came out as a rather tentative question.

His expression went completely blank. At last, he replied, "If that is your wish."

They walked side by side without touching to the library. He pushed open the door and stood aside to allow her to enter first. The unique scent of old books greeted her like a friend—the glue, the ink and the lignin of the paper, as well as ancient parchment that reminded her of vanilla blended together in a promise adventure and romance. The lamplight illuminated a two-story room boasting of hundreds, perhaps thousands of books. A painting rivaling the great works of Michelangelo graced the domed ceiling.

Richard guided her to one section and made a loose gesture toward the shelf. "Obviously you're welcome to anything here. This section has poetry, most of it quite old. I haven't kept up with the contemporary poets the way my ancestors did. Over here are our oldest tomes dating back to the fourteenth century. You'll find a lot of medieval minstrels' songs and poems there."

Intrigued, she drew closer to look at the titles. "Ah…*Tales of King Arthur*. I love such stories. Dashing knights committing acts of valor and chivalry, fair ladies who love and honor them, star-crossed lovers, true love. These stories would be fun to read aloud." She touched one old tome. "This is a different book than the one I know, so there may be some new tales in here."

Drawing in a dreamy sigh, she carefully pulled out

the old volume and held it reverently in her hands. She turned around and smiled up at him, bursting to share it with him. Her voice left her. He stood so near that the warmth of his body spread through her. His lips hovered within inches of hers. Heat tightened in her stomach and her breathing grew unsteady. With his dark eyes focused on her lips, his expression grew so intense that her heart skipped and tripped. His mouth parted. He bent his head toward her. She lifted her chin, craving the touch of his lips.

Something shifted in his expression and he let out an unsteady breath. He stepped back, lowered his head, and put his hands behind his back. Something precious, something vital, had passed them by, never to be recaptured.

Disappointment sent a chill through her. She couldn't account for what had happened that made him suddenly so unwilling to touch her when he'd seemed to desire her only days ago. Obviously, she'd failed him in some way. Elizabeth swallowed but couldn't dissolve the lump in her throat.

He indicated the book in her hands. "Do you wish to read that one to me?" His voice took on a vacant tone that probably meant he had no desire to have her read it to him and was merely being polite.

Needing a moment to compose herself, she moved to a group of chairs drawn up together next to a table where a lamp shone. She put the book on her lap. All excitement to read the tales of King Arthur and his knights of the round table withered and died in the face of Richard's coolness. Trying to calm the burning in her eyes and dispel the lump in her throat, she swallowed again. The shuffling of papers came from behind her but she kept her gaze focused on her hands pressed on the cover of the book.

"Read to me about King Arthur and his knights," he prompted.

His clothing rustled as he took a seat near enough to converse, but not near enough to touch. She glanced at him. He sat with a closed book on one knee, papers lying on the cover, and an artist's pencil in one hand. Using the book as a small writing desk, he began writing or perhaps drawing. His lashes concealed his eyes and his expression remained neutral.

"Are you sure you want this one?" she asked. "I could choose another book, if you like."

"I've never read that story, but I enjoy tales of the old knights." He glanced at her. Something cautious, almost hesitant, flickered in his eyes. He returned his focus to his paper. That brief moment of vulnerability in his eyes gave her courage. He might not be as far beyond her reach as she had feared.

Moistening her lips, she opened the book and read. As she spoke, his pencil made tiny scratching sounds. Once she craned her neck to see what he was writing. Not words but a drawing spread across his paper. Satisfied he was listening, she continued. The tales drew her in and buoyed her spirit, but her awareness of Richard permeated every word. If only he loved her as deeply as those chivalrous knights, she would welcome the years with him.

She let the book fall into her lap, stunned at the realization. She wanted Richard to love her—not just offer her a home away from Duchess. Was it possible her feelings for him had grown more than she'd realized? Unable to discern the answer, she picked up her book, seeking answers in the pages. She read until her throat dried. She paused, glancing at the clock.

"Oh my," she said. "I didn't realize how late it had grown."

He stopped writing and followed her gaze. "You're right. I need to meet with the crofter about some roof repairs early tomorrow. I believe I'll retire now." He stood.

Before he turned to leave, she asked, "Who is your favorite knight so far?"

He paused, his eyes moving to some far off sight. "Either Prince Erec or Sir Galahad, I think."

If only she were a fitting Lady Enide, perhaps he would be more like Prince Erec to her. How could she be more worthy of him?

He added as if an afterthought, "Thank you for reading. I enjoyed that." Surprise touched his tone as if he'd suspected he'd be bored by her reading. His lips curved but no joy touched his eyes. Again came that impression of caution, as if he held himself distant, not out of repulsion or condemnation but out of a hesitancy to get too close.

If he held onto his love for Leticia, he would never love Elizabeth the way the knights of old loved their ladies. The thought brought a sting to her eyes.

"Good night, my lady."

She managed around her disappointment, "Good night, my lord."

He didn't remind her to call him Richard. Elizabeth sat in the library long after he'd gone with her head resting in her hands. Tristan was lost to her. Now, apparently, so was Richard. It appeared that she'd live out her life alone.

Chapter Twenty-One

Refusing to succumb to self-pity, Elizabeth arose early in the morning and squared her shoulders. At least Richard had given her leave to hire whomever she saw fit. She might not be an acceptable wife, but she'd be a passable countess. She'd help the less fortunate striving to better themselves.

Elizabeth summoned the head housekeeper. When Mrs. Brown arrived, Elizabeth stepped back at the cold hostility radiating from the woman. Though she shrank from the housekeeper's animosity, Elizabeth reminded herself that she was the mistress of the house. Now was the time to assert her authority.

Mrs. Brown stood at attention, her gaze straight ahead, disapproval etched in the lines in her face. "You rang for me, my lady?"

"I understand the house is still a bit understaffed."

Mrs. Brown sniffed. "I assure you, we will see to your every convenience, my lady."

"I have no doubt of that, but I do not wish for you to overwork yourself or the servants. I plan to hire additional help."

Her tone turned almost condescending. "Oh, my lady, I assure you, there's no need for you to get involved in staffing concerns. The butler and I will see to that."

"Where do you usually hire new servants?"

"Often from Town or from an agency. I admit, we're still looking to fill a few positions but I will handle the matter."

"I realize that's normally how it's done, but I wish to help the cause of the reformers. In particular, I've been following Mrs. Goodfellow's efforts. I plan to aid her endeavors by hiring as many of those she has reformed as possible."

Mrs. Brown's eyes bulged. "Fill the house with pickpockets and prostitutes? Unthinkable!"

Patiently, Elizabeth explained, "Mrs. Goodfellow trains those who are ready to make a change. She helps them start a new life."

The housekeeper hesitated. "Yes, but—"

"I understand her institution is nearby."

"My lady, that place is filled with the very lowest of reprobates from London."

"They have left the streets and are seeking to improve themselves, are they not?"

Mrs. Brown hesitated. "So they say, but—"

"I believe everyone deserves a second chance. As the new countess, I wish to do all I can to aid the downtrodden."

"But surely—"

"They are reformed, Mrs. Brown. If enterprises such as Mrs. Goodfellow's are to succeed, people must offer honest employment to those who wish to find it."

"We cannot trust them! Why, they might run off with the silver, or engage in"—the housekeeper dropped her voice to a whisper—"in immoral behavior."

Elizabeth drew herself up. "I will take full responsibility of that. What I need from you is a list of staff we lack."

Mrs. Brown raised her nose. "May I ask as to whether you've received permission from his lordship?"

Ah, the crux of the matter. Winning over servants was not always a simple matter, but if she allowed the housekeeper to intimidate her, she'd never earn the woman's respect.

Elizabeth fixed a stern gaze at the housekeeper. "Mrs. Brown. You may have been with this family for years, but I am your new mistress now and you will not question my authority again, is that clear?"

Mrs. Brown's lips pressed into a thin line. Then, "Yes, my lady. I understand perfectly."

"Good. I can put your mind at rest that I have indeed received my lord's blessing on hiring any new staff I see fit. Now, either you give me a list of the positions needed, or I will simply bring home as many reformed pickpockets and prostitutes as Mrs. Goodfellow has available for hire."

"Very well." The housekeeper scribbled a list and handed it to Elizabeth, her gaze mutinous. "Will there be anything further...my lady?" Her tone bordered on insolent.

"Make sure my carriage is ready first thing in the morning so I may pay a call on Mrs. Goodfellow."

The housekeeper sank into a sullen curtsey. "Yes, my lady."

Elizabeth let out a breath, savoring her satisfaction for having the backbone to stand up to the formidable woman and assert her authority as the lady of the home. However, she suspected that would not be their last battle.

Early the following morning after eating breakfast alone, Elizabeth arrived at the Goodfellow manor house situated in a charming glen. Ivy clung to the stone walls and flowers grew in glorious disarray along the walkway.

A young girl with her hair pulled back into a tidy knot opened the front door and stared at Elizabeth. In the thick accent of those raised in the alleys of London, she asked, "May I 'elp ye, miss?"

"I am Lady Averston and I wish to speak with Mrs. Goodfellow." She held out her calling card, which still read Lady Elizabeth Pemberton. She made a mental note to order cards with her new title.

"Al'righ', I'll go an' get 'er for ye." Leaving her standing in the doorway, and without taking the card, the girl strode away.

Elizabeth glanced back at the coachman and nodded, then let herself inside. She stood in a small foyer until a rotund, middle-aged woman hurried to her.

"I'm Mrs. Goodfellow. I'm honored by your presence. Do come in, Lady Averston, I pray you. I apologize if Nan left you standing. She's still learning."

The lady curtsied respectfully and led Elizabeth into a tiny, threadbare parlor and gestured to a seat. After Elizabeth settled upon a settee, Mrs. Goodfellow perched on the edge of an armchair. "How may I help you, my lady?"

"I wish to aid you in your cause," Elizabeth replied. "I have been reading about your work and I wish to hire those who are ready to accept honest employment."

Mrs. Goodfellow's eyes opened wide. "Are you? How lovely! Please, do take some refreshment and we can discuss the particulars."

"Thank you."

A reed-thin little girl, probably eight or nine years old, with limp brown hair entered carrying a tray that seemed too big for her. Her gaze never strayed from the floor as she set down the tray.

Mrs. Goodfellow touched the girl's hand. "Thank you, Janey, dear."

The child shied away as if burned, then flicked a hurried glance at Mrs. Goodfellow before scurrying out of the room. Elizabeth's heart squeezed in compassion.

Mrs. Goodfellow shook her head sadly. "Poor lamb. We rescued her from a brothel."

Elizabeth gasped. "How awful!" The thought of a child forced to prostitute herself made Elizabeth lose her appetite.

"It is a heinous crime," Mrs. Goodfellow agreed. "According to rumor, that terrible Mr. Black owns that place. The poor child has yet to have spoken a word." She smiled. "Now, however, she has a future, and in time I hope she can heal from the terrible abuses she must have suffered, thanks to people with generous hearts like you."

Mrs. Goodfellow poured the tea and offered scones, Devonshire cream, and jam. "Pray, how many servants are you looking to employ?"

"I have a list." Elizabeth handed it over.

Mrs. Goodfellow nodded as she looked over the note. "Splendid. We can fill all those positions. I have two or three for each position who I'll send for your head housekeeper or butler to interview. They can have the final say in which person receives the position."

"My head housekeeper is less than enthusiastic at

my proposal to hire people from your establishment," Elizabeth said. "She has some…concerns."

Mrs. Goodfellow nodded, unperturbed. "Naturally. Most people do. However, I can personally vouch for everyone here. By giving her the final say, she may be more inclined to manage them fairly."

"Very well. I will leave the matter in your capable hands. I also wish to make a donation." Elizabeth handed her some of her pin money she'd begun saving from the first moment she'd read of Mrs. Goodfellow's endeavor.

The gesture brought tears to Mrs. Goodfellow's eyes. "How very kind of you, my lady."

Elizabeth inclined her head as her heart swelled. "I applaud your efforts. Please let me know when your next charity event is and I'll offer you my support."

"Thank you, my lady. I shall."

Elizabeth paused. "The child who does not speak…I want to help her. What can I do?"

"Much as I'd like to keep her here, I think a change of scenery would be good for her, although she's not ready for employment yet; she's fairly untrained."

"I wouldn't require much of her."

Mrs. Goodfellow tapped her fingers on the arm of her chair. "I supposed she could work as a 'tween stairs maid. She's stronger than she looks and very willing to do whatever we ask of her."

"I would instruct my housekeeper to ensure that her duties are light."

Mrs. Goodfellow hesitated. "I would ask that you do whatever you can to protect her from molestation."

"I give you my word. I know what it's like to be afraid." The sickening terror returned at merely the thought of Duchess's wrath.

Mrs. Goodfellow nodded, her gaze penetrating, and Elizabeth turned her head away before the lady saw more secrets than Elizabeth was willing to reveal. She couldn't bear disgust and pity in the eyes of anyone who guessed the truth.

They bid farewell, and Elizabeth left the ivy-covered manor house with a light heart and a happy smile. Even if she weren't loved, she was safe and could turn her attention toward rescuing others who longed for safety.

She stopped at the printer's and ordered new cards. Her next stop was at the shop of a modiste who'd come highly recommended. As countess, it would be her duty to throw a ball and invite all the locals. Such an event required a new ball gown, something that proclaimed her lady of the house and not a shadow that quaked at Duchess's voice.

As Elizabeth stood amid swatches of fabric and dress drawings, Madame Prideux dutifully gushed over her "delightful figure" and "lovely coloring" before settling into the business of style and design, all the while, the modiste cooing over her every order as if Elizabeth were some kind of fashion genius.

The modiste clasped her hands. "My lady, soon everyone will follow your style."

Elizabeth laughed softly. "I'm not trying to revolutionize fashion, merely show that my figure is not entirely a loss."

Madame Prideux made all the expected protestations and they again returned to drawings and fabrics. Elizabeth ordered evening gowns and a ball gown in bold colors—scarlet, Cambridge blue, and forest green, so unlike the pastels she'd always worn.

Madame Prideux served biscuits and tea as they completed the measurements and settled on a price.

"I will come to you for the first fittings soon." Madame Prideux bid Elizabeth goodbye, visibly gloating over her profitable morning.

Delighted with the morning's events, Elizabeth visited the tailor to get fitted for a new riding habit. Afterwards, she stopped at the milliner and ordered a new bonnet to go with her riding habit. Excitement about wearing her own creations warmed her. How delightful to wear something of her choice instead of Duchess's. It was liberating.

Chapter Twenty-Two

Several weeks after his wedding ceremony, Richard strode up the stairs toward the house, stripping off his riding gloves. A new footman opened the door, grinning. Richard paused mid-stride, and raised a brow.

The footman's grin only widened. "'ave a nice ride, milor'?"

"Er, yes." Richard eyed him, unsure whether a footman ought to look so happy, and fairly certain he shouldn't be addressing his master in such a way, but he let the matter go. It seemed bad form to reprimand a servant for unnecessary cheer, especially in the country where manners could relax. "Are you new?"

"That I am, milor' an' 'appy I am to be 'ere." The man's accent gave him away immediately.

"You are from London, I take it?"

"That I am. Mrs. Goodfellow said I'd like it 'ere, an' she was righ'."

Richard didn't question the identity of this Mrs. Goodfellow but nodded as if he did. "Very good. Carry on."

The footman touched his forelock, his grin still in place, and returned to his post. Shaking his head in amusement, Richard strode to his room and rang for his valet.

Wesley came in, a little more bent than usual. "Your bath is already prepared, my lord."

"I'm still convinced you're clairvoyant."

"As any good valet should be."

Richard stared. "Wesley, did you just crack a joke?"

"I'd never be so presumptuous, my lord." He kept a straight face.

Richard smiled. "Your sister sends her best—through her husband."

"Met with your steward today, sir?"

"If I didn't need him so badly, I'd tell him it's time to retire. I feel the same way about you."

Wesley looked decidedly smug. "Being needed is my specialty, my lord." He tugged until Richard's boots came off but he moved a bit stiffly.

"Is your rheumatism acting up again?"

"'Tis of no consequence."

"Doesn't cook have a special liniment for that?"

"The stable master does. I have already requested more."

"I'm meeting with my solicitor in the morning so I'll need your skills with the cravat."

"A mathematical knot would be in order, I believe."

Smiling over the valet's logic, or perhaps his subtle humor, Richard worked the buttons of his waistcoat.

A diminutive 'tween stairs maid tiptoed into the room carrying a box of coal. She took one look at Richard, her face transforming into terror, and with a squeak, fled the room.

Richard looked at Wesley with a raised brow. "Good heavens, I've frightened the poor child. Am I so terrifying?"

"Servants are meant to be invisible. Being caught

by the master in a room is bad form for any servant."

"Yes, but really, her reaction seemed overly dramatic. Are you spreading rumors that I eat every maid I see?"

Richard was sure Wesley's mouth almost twitched. "She's new. Hasn't spoken a word."

"Ah. Mrs. Brown is finally hiring more staff?"

"Under the direction of Lady Averston."

"Excellent." At least Elizabeth was taking her role as lady of the house seriously. At Wesley's dubious expression, Richard eyed him. "What?"

"I'm sure her heart is in the right place, my lord, but if you don't mind me saying so, hiring those sorts of folks seems just asking for trouble."

"I trust Mrs. Brown."

"Not Mrs. Brown, my lord. It's the new countess."

Richard allowed a touch of reprimand into his voice at the man's boldness. "My lady is the daughter of a duke. I am certain she's well prepared to manage a household."

"Indeed my lord." Instantly contrite, Wesley kept his peace.

Richard stripped and bathed, wondering what Elizabeth had done to ruffle Wesley's feathers and what "those sorts of folks" meant. He made a mental note to ask her about it at dinner.

As he dressed, the fireplace caught his eye. Instead of dark and empty, it contained a huge bouquet of wildflowers, an odd place for flowers, but it brightened up an otherwise dreary part of the room during the summer when fires rarely burned.

"I don't suppose that's your idea, Wesley?" He indicated the flowers with his chin.

"Lady Averston's touch. They're in every room."

"I see. Rather nice, I'd say." Richard glanced at Wesley. "I can see to myself tonight after dinner. Take yourself off and see to your rheumatism or you'll be no good to me on the morrow."

Wesley offered a stiff bow. "As you wish, my lord."

In the dining room, Elizabeth greeted him with a polite smile. Her gaze darted over his face as if to judge his mood. He missed the dazzling smiles she'd given him in the past but it would be best not to become too attached, either to the smiles, or to the woman who gave them.

"Good evening." He held out her chair for her and took his place at the head of the table.

He tucked into his meal, making mental lists of all the things he needed to accomplish tomorrow, anything to keep his eyes off his wife, and the reminder of how she'd looked at Tristan on their wedding day.

Elizabeth ate in silence, stirred her food with her fork more than eating.

Richard glanced her way. "Dinner not to your liking, my lady?"

She set down her fork without making a noise. "Weren't you asking me to call you Richard rather than my lord only a few weeks ago?"

He paused and then resumed eating. "Of course," he replied between mouthfuls, "how careless of me. Forgive me, Elizabeth."

"There is nothing to forgive, Richard." When he made no further comment, Elizabeth cleared her throat. "Have I done something to offend you, my husband?"

After briefly flicking his gaze her way, Richard

took a drink from his wineglass. "Of course not. I'm pleased with the efficient way you handle the servants. They clearly respect you. The new staff appears be well occupied. The flowers in the fireplaces are a nice touch."

"Then pray, what is it?"

"What is what?"

She moistened her lips. "Why do you avoid me?"

"I do not avoid you. I have dinner with you, and you read to me in the library most evenings."

"That's the only time I see you. I thought we'd be spending more time together."

He drew a breath and stifled the urge to blurt out all his frustrations over her loving Tristan, and that he knew it would only be a matter of time before she left him, and how badly it would hurt even after all the defensive measures he'd taken against her.

He settled for what he hoped would be a convincing excuse. "I have been in London a great deal during the Season and have many tasks that require my attention now that I am home. Surely you must understand this."

"Of course."

Her dejected posture tugged at his heart. He added, "I don't mean to neglect you."

She drew herself up. "You aren't. I'm actually rather relieved you don't hover over me; I have many projects I wish to accomplish."

He bit back a snide comment over whether any of her 'projects' involved his brother. Surely, she wouldn't cheat on him so soon. Surely. "Glad to hear it."

Silence followed.

He searched for a change of topic, torn between

wanting to reach her and terrified to open himself to her. "I understand you've hired some new staff."

"Yes." A spark entered her eyes.

"You can leave that detail to Mrs. Brown, you know."

"I know but I felt strongly inclined to hire from Mrs. Goodfellow's institution."

Richard searched his memory for Goodfellow Institution. It sounded familiar, but he was unable to place it. Probably the name of some staffing agency.

"As you wish." Richard finished his dessert and sat back.

Elizabeth stared out the window with such a faraway look in her eyes that an ache rose up inside him. He longed to tease a smile out of her, to hear her laugh, to make her his wife in truth. If he so much as touched her, though, he'd draw her into his arms and fall under her spell. He'd be vulnerable to any pain she chose to inflict upon him. Such vulnerability would prove his undoing.

He stood lest he be too tempted to give into his desire to touch her. Still, she didn't deserve his cool treatment of her. After all, she hadn't cheated on him. Yet.

He tried to forget how lovely she was, how her lips tempted him to kiss them, how the curve of her cheek begged to be caressed. Eventually he'd need to make her his wife in truth if they were to have the two sons he'd told her in the beginning that he required of her. The idea of sharing such intimacy with a woman who pined for another left him cold. Still, he should at least attempt to make a home life with her; no need for them both to be miserable.

Richard cleared his throat and gentled his tone. "Elizabeth, I hope you know that as the lady of the house, you have full freedom here to make any visits or implement any changes you wish. No room is off limits, and no desire will be rejected." He winced. That last part was poorly worded.

She watched him, bewilderment and hesitation mirrored in her eyes. "Thank you, my lord."

He fisted his hands, craving her smiles, her touch. Was it possible to bask in those pleasures without losing his heart?

She moistened her lips, drawing his gaze. "Would you like me to read to you again tonight?"

The idea of spending time listening to her melodious voice and watching her eyes glow with pleasure as she read the tales of romance and adventure was a sweet torture he didn't know if he could withstand.

"I'd like that very much." Apparently, his mouth had disengaged from his brain.

She offered a tremulous smile. They walked side by side to the library as he mentally shook his head over his lack of sense. Still, listening to her read might be the one pleasure in which he could indulge for the time being. He'd never imagined a celibate marriage, but he refused to become so vulnerable to her probable rejection and desertion.

Though careful not to touch her, he couldn't resist taking a deep breath to draw in her scent, that alluring blend that never failed to paint images best left unexplored if he hoped to retain a particle of his dignity or his heart.

He sketched while she read, the lines under his

pencil shaping into characters and scenes from the tales she read. Sketching kept his eyes off of her and the temptation to make her his wife in every way—a desire he simply could not risk. The clock kept a steady rhythm in the background. When her voice roughened, he reached for a decanter to pour her a drink but her words halted him.

"I suppose I should stop. It's getting late." She stood. "Good night."

"Sleep well, Elizabeth." As she left, he reminded himself he'd be a fool to develop any feelings for her. So much for Tristan's idea to woo her and win her heart. Every idea that came to him toward that end would only leave him more susceptible to the kind of emotions that would leave him helpless against heartbreak.

Chapter Twenty-Three

Early the following morning, Elizabeth wandered through the music room touching the various instruments and wishing for a harp. How she longed to pour her frustrations into her music, but alas, no harp resided here.

Richard had been generous with her pin money and dress allowance, but a harp cost many times that sum. He'd been so distant since their wedding day that she couldn't bear to ask him for any favors. At least they spent a few hours together most evenings.

Perhaps a walk would do. She donned a shawl and bonnet and after leaving the house, she strode through the gardens toward the open fields beyond. Two men, one stooped and aged, and the other a few decades younger, worked together in the gardens talking softly.

As she passed them, she called, "Good morning."

The older man turned. "Oh, yer ladyship." He doffed his hat and bowed.

"I don't believe I know your name."

"Green, m'lady. This is my grandson, Jonah."

A gardener named Mr. Green? She almost laughed out loud at the appropriate name.

The younger man touched the brim of his hat. "Mornin', yer ladyship."

"The garden is looking well."

"Thank ye kindly."

As she passed by them, they returned to their work, kneeling next to a flowerbed. Elizabeth paused, noticing the holes in the bottom of the younger man's boots.

Surely, she could find a pair of boots for the poor man so he wouldn't need to walk about with holes in his soles. Her father often gave older shoes and boots to his staff. She mentally measured his feet, then returned to the house and went to Richard's room. He probably had a dozen pairs or more and wouldn't miss one. She planned to arrange for the man to visit the cobbler, but that would take time, and the gardener might put off a trip to the village, which would leave him in those sad shoes for far too long.

She pushed Richard's bedroom door open like a shameless trespasser, but stood rooted to the floor while all her determination abandoned her. As his wife, she shouldn't fear to enter Richard's chambers. However, they were as much strangers as if they'd just met. The bedroom was an extremely intimate place, a place he hadn't invited her to share with him. Besides, odds were, Richard wouldn't own an old, tattered pair of boots; he was so meticulous about his appearance that his boots and clothing were probably all in pristine condition.

Still, she was here now and curiosity about her husband emboldened her. She knew so little about him. His private chambers might contain clues about the man she married. Summoning her courage, she stepped inside and waited, half expecting some sword of justice to drop from the ceiling. Nothing happened, of course. She chided herself for her childish imagination.

As she expected, bold colors and heavy, antique

furniture adorned the room. She pictured earls of long ago lounging in this room. She glanced at the bed, then looked quickly away, but not before imagining Richard lying tousle-haired and sleepy-eyed amid the pillows. She heaved a sigh. He really hadn't changed; he'd simply reverted to the Richard she'd first met at the house party. Once Richard had done his duty wooing her before they wedded, he'd once again become the stern, aloof lord.

Or had seeing Leticia triggered his return to that persona? The idea that he pined away for another woman left her hollow inside.

After shaking off self-pity, she glanced at the mahogany bureau but found its surface clear of clutter. In fact, the entire room seemed elegant but rather impersonal, as if he never dared let down his guard, even in private. The one incongruity was an armchair drawn up to the fireplace. Draped across the back was a frayed blanket. She fingered the worn, soft blanket, wondering about its origin. Surely, he kept such an old blanket for reasons other than to keep warm.

Next to the armchair stood a small table with a lamp and a stack of papers. Pencil drawings. She picked up the top one and examined it. A lone knight in full armor sat astride a black destrier rearing up to do battle. On the next page, a knight stood alone, his shoulders drooped, his sword tip pointed downward. The third page bore the image of a young jongleur playing a lute, his mouth open as if in song, with tears running down his face. Each page bore a scene from one of the stories she'd read. Each was of a man in sorrow, or in battle. Always alone.

Cleary Richard viewed his life and his future as

bleak without Leticia, the woman he loved.

A sob escaped her throat and she put her hand over her mouth to stifle the sound. They were two lonely people, thrown together, pining for another's love. Stories of star-crossed lovers had seemed so romantic in the pages of a book or a poem, or a song. In truth, it was a miserable, desolate existence.

Tears rolled down her cheeks. If only Richard would allow her into his life, they could at least comfort one another. But he was more closed up than ever.

So be it. They would lead separate lives. She would fill her empty heart with helping the downtrodden and people who others overlooked or abused, like the gardener who needed boots. She dried her tears, replaced the papers, and resumed her search. Off to one side she found the dressing room. Shelves of boots lay directly to her right. She searched for the oldest-looking pair. To her surprise, she found two in the far back corner, scarred and worn, apparently long forgotten. Her father would have discarded any boots that looked so abused.

She picked up one boot and eyed it. It appeared bigger than the boots the young gardener wore, but perhaps he could wear an extra pair of socks. The sole was still intact which would be an improvement over those he currently wore. She paused at the array of overcoats, noticing two that appeared slightly thinning and frayed, but still with plenty of wear. The gardeners could probably make good use of these, as well. Would Richard care if she took them? Would he even notice? She paused, caught in indecision. Her only other choice would be to purchase boots and coats for the gardeners, but she didn't yet have any kind of agreement with the locals outside of the modiste, nor enough money of her own to buy them outright.

Still, as the countess, she had a duty to the villagers and especially to their staff. If Richard had a problem with her gifting his old clothes to the needy, he would have to take it up with her. After another hesitation, she laid both old coats over her arm and picked up the boots.

As she left the dressing room carrying the boots and coats, the door opened and Richard's valet entered.

He stopped short at the sight of her. "My lady."

Shaking off the sensation that she was some kind of thief, she nodded to him. "I don't believe I know your name."

"Wesley, my lady." His gaze fixed on the boots in her hand.

"Wesley. Good day." She strode past him with her head high.

She wasn't sure, but she thought she heard him sputtering something about the master's boots. But that was ridiculous. Richard was always immaculate. No doubt he hadn't worn these boots and coats in years. It was a wonder they were still in his possession.

The young gardener alternately protested and thanked her, and put them on. He preened as he strode around wearing the boots. Both coats were too loose for the men through the shoulders, but they assured her their fit would allow for free movement as they worked. Smiling, she returned to the house.

In the great hall, Richard strode to her. Her heart gave a little leap at his attention until she noticed his fearsome scowl.

"There you are," he said. "Where have you been?"

She went utterly still at his tone as cold fear skittered over her. Her voice hoarse with fright, she managed, "I-in the gardens."

He let out his breath in a sigh of exasperation. "Stop looking at me as if I'm about to pounce on you."

Duchess, too, had hated her signs of weakness, yet she couldn't help but take a step back. "Y-you're angry with me."

"No, of course not. I'm merely a bit frustrated because my boots are missing and I need them. My valet said he saw you with them so I've been looking for you. Where have you taken my boots? And why?"

"Y-your boots?" She shrank from him.

Sadness touched his eyes as he took another breath and visibly quieted his voice. "I'm not going to hurt you, Elizabeth, I vow it. Not now, not ever. Just tell me where you put my boots."

Taking her fear in hand, she drew a steadying breath. "The old brown ones?"

"Yes." His anger faded and humor touched his mouth. "They probably look nothing like an earl should wear."

Emboldened, she shook her head once. "Indeed not."

"So, what have you done with them?"

"I…"

Fear wrapped cold tendrils around her spine. She'd made a terrible mistake in thinking he'd never miss a single pair of boots.

Although Richard's forehead creased in puzzlement, an amused smile tugged at his lips. Amusement?

Finding her courage, she raised her chin. "I gave

them to the gardener's son."

A brow rose. "The gardener?"

"Mr. Green. And his son. I noticed his boots had holes in the sole."

"I see." His gaze searched her face.

"Forgive me. I never dreamed you'd miss them." She chewed on her lip, trying to summon the courage to confess she'd also taken two coats.

"It's quite all right. I only wear them when I want to play laborer with my tenants."

"My lord?"

"Sometimes I enjoy a bit of labor now and then, and I was going to help build a stone fence. I wanted my old boots for that task." He smiled ruefully. "Don't tell anyone or my name will surely be stricken from the guest lists."

She moistened her lips. "Then you aren't angry?"

"No, I'm certain he needed them worse than I. But they were comfortable." He paused, and gave her a sideways glance. "Did they fit him?"

"They were a little large, but he said with an extra pair of socks, they were just right."

"Good." As an afterthought, he added, "That was thoughtful of you."

She shrugged self-consciously, but warmed at his praise. She let out her breath in relief. She should have known better than to be so afraid. Richard had given his word he'd never hurt her and she knew above all else, Richard was a man of honor. He hadn't hit her. Better yet, he'd noticed her absence. Perhaps she should spirit away items from his room more often.

"Er...I hope you don't mind, but I also gave him two of your old coats—one for his son.

He eyed her carefully. "I see. Anything else?"

"No."

"Kindly refrain from raiding my room in the future without warning me, fair enough?"

She nodded. Just as he turned, she thought she spied a hint of a smile crinkling his eyes.

With high hopes for a better evening, she bathed, dressed with care, and asked Maggie to spend extra time on her hair. The effect was an elegant coiffure.

He barely glanced her way at dinner despite her attempts to converse. Instead, he sat engrossed in a ledger with barely a grunt. A ledger? At the dinner table? Her father would never have been so rude.

As dessert was served, he spoke without looking at her, still focused on his ledger. "How was your day?"

She folded her arms and tapped a toe. "Lovely. I had tea with the fairies."

"Mm-hmm."

She ground her teeth. "Tomorrow I plan to drain the lake."

"Hmm." He grunted.

She almost groaned out loud. "Richard."

At last, his gaze met hers.

She took a calming breath. "I wish to speak to you at a time when you are not too busy to listen."

He blinked, then closed the ledger book and pushed it away. "Very well. You have my full and undivided attention." He folded his hands together.

"As the new Countess of Averston, it is my duty to have a ball."

"A ball?" He scrunched his face as if he'd only heard terrible things about such events but had no first-hand account.

"Yes. I'll have to make my bride visits first, of course, which I can't make until after we've been wed a month, and I'll need to provide our guests two weeks' notice, so I think the ball should be in three weeks' time. With your approval, that is."

"As you wish." He returned his focus to his ledger.

"Thank you."

He said nothing as he scribbled in the ledger.

She leaped to her feet. "Good night. I think before I retire, I shall swim naked in the moat."

"Mhmm."

She swallowed her growl of annoyance and told herself his inattention didn't matter. After all, her parents ignored her so often that she should be used to it; she preferred being ignored to having Duchess's attention.

Once their one month anniversary came and went, Elizabeth made her bride visits beginning with the most august persons. With her mind occupied with arrangements for the ball, and her new staff hired from Mrs. Goodfellow, she hummed and worked the days away, trying not to notice whether Richard joined her for dinner—which he often did not—or when he went out of town for days at a time, and pushed back the thought that some of his business might involve a mistress. Surely, a man so honorable wouldn't reject his wife and turn to a mistress. Would he?

It seemed too hypocritical, but he wouldn't be the first man to have such a skewed view of loyalty.

Chapter Twenty-Four

Elizabeth closed the book of poetry Tristan had given her and ran her hand over the title on the leather cover. The book had become a treasure and Elizabeth knew every passage by heart, but this evening, reading failed to soothe her.

How she longed to turn to her harp and immerse herself in the power of music. However, her harp had remained at the ducal estate, and with Richard so distant, she didn't dare ask him to buy her such an expensive item. After all, he could purchase three pianofortes for the price of one harp.

Silence enshrouded the house. Not even the soft footfall of servants could be heard. Though everyone else had been abed hours ago, sleep remained elusive. Perhaps a cup of tea would help.

Taking up a candle, Elizabeth crept down the corridor, descended the stairs, and went toward the kitchen.

A movement out of the corner of her eye caught her attention. Elizabeth paused, eyes and ears straining toward the opposite end of the great hall. A ghostly figure moved toward her.

Chills prickled the back of her neck. She went utterly still as the form continued moving erratically, sometimes pausing, then moving forward again. As it neared, it took on childlike proportions. Elizabeth held up the candle, peering ahead.

A tiny figure came into the circle of light cast by Elizabeth's candle. The small maidservant Elizabeth had hired from Mrs. Goodfellow came to a halt and stood, wavering, as if her legs were nearly too weak to hold her weight. Her thin, nut-brown hair hung down her back against her nightgown and her eyes were wide open, but vacant and staring.

"Janey? Are you well?"

The tiny 'tween stairs maid gave no reply as usual, but her brow settled into a frown.

"It's late, child. You should be abed."

The girl's stare remained empty as she resumed walking—sleep walking, apparently. She padded barefoot through the great hall to the drawing room. Elizabeth followed, watching as the child went through the far end of the drawing room to the library. Inside, Janey stopped at the far wall, staring up at the darkened windows reflecting the light of Elizabeth's candle. The child began crying, great, shoulder-shaking sobs.

"Janey, dear, what is it?"

Elizabeth had heard it was dangerous to awaken sleepwalkers, but wasn't certain why. Moving slowly so as not to alarm her, Elizabeth kneeled by the girl. "All is well, child. You're safe here. Come, you must be cold, let's get you back to bed."

Still weeping, Janey shook her head, and shrank from Elizabeth's touch. Elizabeth waited a moment, then, moving as slowly as possible, took her by the elbow. Since she had no idea which of the servants' rooms was Janey's, she led the girl to a nearby settee, guided her to lie down, and found a blanket to cover her. Janey settled in and closed her eyes.

Elizabeth paused, reluctant to leave her there; she would be disoriented when she awoke in a strange place. Before Elizabeth reached a decision, Janey, stirred, then opened her eyes. She let out a frightened squeak.

Elizabeth hastened to reassure her. "Don't be afraid. You were walking in your sleep."

The girl leaped off of the divan and stood hugging herself.

In the hopes of helping the girl feel less afraid, Elizabeth turned her eyes to the books. Still moving slowly so as not to frighten the child, Elizabeth went to the bookcase. Running her thumb along tomes, she stopped when she found a satisfactory title. "I've come to find a book to read. Would you like to stay and listen to a story?"

Janey blinked, her arms still wrapped around herself.

Elizabeth settled herself upon the divan, opened the illustrated book of fables, and began to read aloud. "Once upon a time, a farmer had three sons…"

As Elizabeth read aloud, Janey crept nearer. By the time she had finished the first fable and began the second, Janey had moved to the settee and was peering over Elizabeth's shoulder at the pictures.

Nearby, a floorboard squeaked. Elizabeth looked up. Richard stood in the room, somehow filling the room with his presence. The child let out a gasp.

Elizabeth put an arm around the girl. "Don't be afraid, Janey, this is my husband, Lord Averston. He's a very kind man. He'd never hurt you."

After taking a few slow steps forward, Richard dropped on one knee and smiled with more gentleness than Elizabeth had ever seen from him. "I'm very pleased to meet you, Miss Janey. I see you're reading one of my favorite picture books."

Her eyes enormous and her breath coming in quick gasps, the girl eyed him as if she feared he'd suddenly attack her.

Elizabeth watched Richard for an entirely different reason, her heart thudding and her mouth dry. Richard's banyan parted over his white shirt, without a cravat and unbuttoned to reveal a small V below his throat. His skin glowed golden in the light of the candle he held. His disheveled hair, so unlike his usual immaculate appearance, made him seem more approachable, revealing latent sensuality she'd never before detected in him. Or perhaps her reaction to him authored that aching awareness singing across her skin. He watched her through unreadable dark eyes. No doubt he thought it unseemly for a countess to read to a 'tween stairs maid.

Elizabeth stood and pulled the girl to her feet. "It's very late, Janey. Perhaps you should return to your bed. Here, let's get you an extra blanket."

Richard stepped aside. Elizabeth offered a smile of apology as she passed him but didn't wait for a reaction. She walked hand in hand with the child toward the servants' stairs and held out the blanket. The girl accepted it with almost a smile, then hurried up the groaning wooden stairs to the servant's level.

Elizabeth turned back and jumped at the sight of Richard standing in the corridor watching her. She drew her dressing gown more tightly around her and waited for his tirade.

He raised a brow. "What in the world possessed

you to read a book to a 'tween stairs maid in the middle of the night?"

"I came across her walking in her sleep. When she awoke, she was disoriented and frightened so I brought out a picture book and read aloud."

In a surprisingly intimate gesture, Richard caressed her cheek, his touch achingly gentle. "You have a very tender heart."

She looked up at him as some nameless longing crept over her. His dark eyes remained unreadable in the semi-darkness, but the lines of his mouth softened. If only she could keep this gentle side of Richard!

As if catching himself, he withdrew his hand, and tightened the sash around his waist, the mask of cool reserve coming between them once more. "Good night." His tone carried a note of finality.

Loss crashed over her and she turned away. "Good night, my lord."

When she returned to her room, she remembered the tea, but had no desire to go back downstairs. She removed her wrapper and crawled into bed. The shadows on the ceiling flitted in the candlelight as if they waged some battle beyond human comprehension. Elizabeth snuggled into the counterpane but the bed remained cold and empty.

Chapter Twenty-Five

When Richard returned home from visiting one of his northern properties, he'd made up his mind about what to do about Elizabeth; he'd wait and watch and allow her the chance to prove herself trustworthy. After all, she'd done nothing wrong and surely, she deserved more trust than he'd given her.

As he strode in through the door, he found the house all a-bustle. He paused, surveying the scene, then, thinking of the correspondence waiting, entered his office. The desk had been cleared.

He rang for Mrs. Brown. "What have you done with all my correspondence?"

"Nothing, my lord. The servants and I know better than to touch your desk. I believe I saw Lady Averston in here."

He heaved a sigh. "Very well. Where is she?"

"I'm sure I don't know, my lord."

Richard dismissed her and stepped out of his office. Hailing a passing maid, he asked, "Where is the countess?"

"I thin' she's in th' drawing room, milor'." She offered a smile he could only describe as flirtatious.

He paused. "Are you new here?"

"Aye, milor'." She gave him a rather brazen perusal.

"You aren't from around here."

"No, milor' I come from Mrs. Goodfellow, an' afore tha' I come from London, I did."

"Mrs. Goodfellow. Yes, I see. Well, carry on."

Apparently, this Mrs. Goodfellow found a good deal of her referrals in Town. He located Elizabeth in the drawing room amid a stack of boxes and a flurry of activity as servants placed candles, polished chandeliers, and hung flower swags.

She made a gesture to the footman who wore a perpetual grin and held a long piece of fabric. "A little looser in the middle, Cooper. Hang it so it drapes down evenly."

The footman, his smile never fading, loosened the swag so it made an arc identical to the previous one.

"Much better." She turned at Richard's entrance. "You're back."

"Indeed. What's all this?"

She smiled. "Doesn't it look lovely? All should be ready for tonight's ball."

Richard choked. "Tonight's ball?"

"Yes, of course." She paused, eying him, her smile fading. "You haven't forgotten, have you?"

"I...no, of course not."

Her face crumpled. "You have forgotten."

"No, no, not at all. I simply had something else on my mind." He made a quick mental note to make sure Wesley brushed and pressed his best superfine. Then again, his clairvoyant valet probably knew Richard's social schedule better than he did.

She nodded but her smile had vanished. "Of course."

He made a gesture. "Can I do anything to help?"

"Not unless you can reassure Mrs. Brown that our

209

new servants from Mrs. Goodfellow won't rob every guest as they arrive."

He cocked his head inquiringly, putting together the clues. "This Mrs. Goodfellow, is she the woman who runs that reform house?"

"Yes, that's right."

"She's the one from whom you've hired all the new staff?"

"That's right."

He nodded, a little disconcerted that an army of London's worst reprobates now filled his house in the role of servants. "How are they working out?"

"Very well. They're eager to please. One of the parlor maids can't seem to stop flirting with every male she sees, and little Janey—the 'tween stairs maid you met a few weeks ago—still hasn't spoken a word, but the others are all settling in." She smiled. "Mrs. Brown counts all the silver and crystal every morning, and nothing has disappeared. The head butler seems to have accepted them."

Richard hesitated. "I didn't realize at first the new staff had come from a reform house."

Her smile returned. "Isn't it wonderful? We're helping them get a new start."

"Er, yes." The thought of the house filling such people sent a shiver through his stomach. While he applauded the theory, having them in his home seemed…well, dangerous. "Be careful, Elizabeth. We mustn't trust them too much until they've proved themselves."

Her smile faded and a mulish glint entered her eyes. "Everyone deserves a second chance."

"Of course." His voice lacked conviction and she

probably heard it.

After a moment she said, "I can't believe you forgot about the ball."

He offered what he hoped would appear a reassuring smile. "Fear not, I will be at your side tonight to greet our guests."

She searched his eyes and nodded, turning away to give directions to the maid standing nearby. "Put this tablecloth on that table, and save the larger one for the table that will hold the punch bowls. Has the chalk artist finished?"

"Almost," called a young man kneeling on the floor putting a flourish on the Averston coat of arms he had drawn on the wooden floor.

Richard called to Elizabeth. "My lady, if you can be spared a moment, I left a stack of correspondence on my desk and now I can't find any of it. Perchance do you know its fate?"

"Oh, yes, I tidied it for you. I didn't think you'd mind. I used to help my father on occasion when his secretary was away. I'll show you." Over her shoulder, she called, "Cooper, finish draping those garlands over the valances; I'll return momentarily."

"Righ', m'lady."

Elizabeth turned to Richard. To his surprise, she took his hand and led him to his study. He looked down at their clasped hands, hers so small in his. He lightly rubbed his thumb over her skin, enjoying the fineness of its texture.

Inside his study, she released him and pulled open a drawer to reveal several files all neatly labeled. "These are invitations, which I took the liberty of answering. These are bills that need to be paid. These are personal letters—no, don't worry, I didn't read any of them—and these are updates from your solicitor, these are your various business ventures—your railroad investment is progressing well—and updates from your stewards for each of your properties."

He stared in amazement. "You've saved me hours of work."

She shrugged. "You've been so busy, I've hardly seen you. I thought I might lessen your load a bit. I also took the liberty of placing an advertisement for a new secretary. So far, only one has responded. His reply is here. His credentials appear to be in order. You might wish to interview him."

For a moment, he didn't know what to say. "Thank you."

She smiled. "You're very welcome." With a brief nod, she returned to the drawing room.

Unable to help himself, he followed. Standing by the door, he watched Elizabeth as she called out orders. The servants scurried to obey, clearly out of a desire to please her, all the while singing or telling outrageous stories and laughing. He should have been annoyed that she'd touched his desk but only vague pleasure resided in his heart.

Between giving away his footwear and coats, hiring reformed criminals, and reading to 'tween stairs maids in the middle of the night, she was turning his house upside down. Yet, the woodwork gleamed, windows sparkled, draperies had been ruthlessly cleaned and aired, pillows plumped, and fabric furniture scrubbed. The servants had scoured and cleaned every surface. As he looked around, he spotted little touches like crystal vases laden with bouquets of fresh cut flowers.

More importantly, happy conversation filled the house, and her smile brightened every room. The old castle began truly to feel like a home. He was beginning to fear he wouldn't be able to live without her.

She caught him watching, and paused, her brows raised inquiringly. He stiffened and left the room, silently swearing if Tristan ever came near her, he'd throttle the blackguard.

Chapter Twenty-Six

At the commencement of the ball, Elizabeth stood in the receiving line wearing a new scarlet gown of sarcenet silk and feeling like a queen. Already, she'd received even more compliments on her gown than she'd dreamed, and her maid had outdone herself on her hair. She touched the strand of pearls around her neck and squelched the thought of how lovely the family rubies would look with the gown. It didn't matter. Tonight she'd have an unforgettable evening and she would let nothing mar her happiness.

She felt poised, confident, and beautiful—unique sensations, to be sure. Better yet, at her side, Richard played the perfect host.

"Welcome," Richard said to a couple that had just arrived. "How is your son? Home yet from Oxford?"

"Yes, and off again on a lark with some of his school chums," the wife replied with an exaggeratedly mournful tone.

Richard laughed. "I remember those days well. I hope he enjoys himself. Thank you both for coming."

Knowing most men despised balls, Elizabeth searched for signs of annoyance as Richard greeted his guests, but he remained gracious and charmed their guests with skill and finesse that surprised her. Clearly, he and Tristan were not as different as she'd first believed.

Everyone invited arrived. The musicians played as fine as Elizabeth had ever heard, the decorations were stunning, and laughter filled the drawing room.

She admired the shine in Richard's black waves, his brilliant smile, the contours of his face. Her eyes moved downward to the perfection of his form and the pleasing way his superfine molded to his chest and shoulders. Again, his subtle masculine sensuality tickled her senses and touched a secret longing inside.

The Wentworths' arrival hit Elizabeth like a bucket of cold water. Elizabeth glanced at Richard, but his expression was too schooled to determine his reaction.

"Welcome," he said. "We're delighted you have come."

Mr. and Mrs. Wentworth replied, but Elizabeth focused only on Leticia, the hitch in her breathing and the shielded hurt in her eyes as she looked at Richard. They stood nearly the same height, betraying Leticia's eyes moving down to Richard's mouth as if she longed to kiss him.

A small place inside Elizabeth cried out in sorrow, and some other dark emotion she could not so easily name let out a less lady-like noise, but she quickly shushed it. The Wentworth family exchanged a few pleasantries before moving away to allow Richard and Elizabeth to greet other guests. Again, Elizabeth watched Richard, searching for signs of loss regarding Leticia. A pursing of his lips and stiffness in his shoulders were her only clues to his distress. He cast a single, long look at Leticia. After taking a quick, sharp breath, he tore his gaze away and greeted the next guest.

Elizabeth found it increasingly difficult to dredge

up a cheerful greeting and hoped at least she managed to look pleasant.

Once the remainder of the guests trickled in, Richard leaned in. "You look stunning tonight."

Surprised, she looked up to find unexpected kindness in his eyes. "As do you."

When they were finished with their reception line, Richard extended a hand and offered an inviting smile. "Will you do me the honor of standing up with me for the first set, my lady?"

Stunned by the brilliance of his smile, and still reeling from his transformation into the perfect host, she could only nod. Warmth seeped from their joined hands through her kidskin gloves and traveled up her arm straight to her heart.

He rested his other palm at the small of her back as they moved onto the dance floor, a gesture both possessive and intimate. Her stomach did odd little flitters at his touch.

"It's unfashionable for a gentleman to dance with his own wife, you know," she teased.

"Perhaps. Nevertheless, we live in the Big House here, so we have the luxury of creating customs."

She only smiled in return, her cheeks heating under his direct gaze.

As others formed a line behind them, Richard took a step nearer. "You've done an outstanding job of putting together this ball, my dear."

My dear? The admiration shining in his face rendered her momentarily mute. Elizabeth swallowed. "I'm gratified it meets with your approval."

The music began, and as they bowed and curtsied to one another, his eyes gleamed with promise. Heat traveled up her neck to her face, yet she could not look away. Richard was without a doubt the most handsome man in the county, and the desire shining in his eyes left her breathless. She admired the strength of his jaw, the shape of his lips, the breadth of his shoulders.

He led her smoothly through the dance steps, and each time she had to release his hand to take the hand of the man beside her, she had the odd sensation of being lost.

Once they made their way to the end of the line and waited for the sequence to repeat before being drawn back into formation, she looked up at him. He smiled down at her. Wonder and delight at his attentiveness mingled within her.

He made a loose gesture toward the windows. "Is it my imagination, or are the draperies new?"

"They're new, but it's the original pattern. I found the mill that produced it and had them make more. I thought they were so lovely and so keeping with the character of the house that I couldn't bear to change them."

His teeth flashed, but his eyes were soft. "You've done an amazing job. Of everything."

Her own lips curved in reply. "I enjoyed myself, actually."

The dance drew them into the pattern again, leaving no more room for conversation.

As the first dance in the set ended, she curtsied. Emboldened by his approachable demeanor, she touched his sleeve. "My lord."

He took her hand and raised it to his lips. "My lady?"

"Thank you for the dance."

"May I be so bold as to ask you to save a waltz for me?"

"A waltz?"

His grin left her weak in the knees. "I know it's quite daring, but considering we're married, I don't think we need permission to engage in such scandalous behavior." His eyes twinkled.

She offered a rueful smile. "I doubt very much a waltz will harm my reputation."

"I'll have words with anyone who dares speak against you." His tone was light, but an intensity touched his eyes that revealed his fervor.

Maybe he was only protecting his own name, but the idea that he would defend her was a heady joy.

The next dance in the set began, preventing further conversation, but Elizabeth's heart lightened and her feet followed suit. At the close of the set, he bowed again over her hand, then brushed his lips over her cheek. The rush of heat spreading over her left her with the desire to fan herself. With great reluctance, she parted from him and moved among her guests. Still, her eyes strayed time and time again to Richard as he played the perfect host.

When the next set began, Richard bowed before Leticia and asked her for a dance. Elizabeth's light heart filled with lead. Trying to stifle feelings best left un-named, she turned away and acknowledged a few late arrivals. As the face of a newcomer became clear, Elizabeth's stomach dropped to her feet. Tristan entered the room looking more handsome and dashing than ever.

He stood across the hall from her speaking to one of the guests, a beautiful young widow with golden hair. The widow tilted her head coquettishly at Tristan, and he threw back his head and laughed. The blonde put a hand on his arm, leaned in, and whispered in his ear. Even at this distance, Elizabeth clearly saw his brows raise and a smile flash. The widow turned and sauntered toward a door leading into the great hall, her hips swaying seductively. At the door, she stopped and looked over her shoulder in a clear invitation. She sashayed out.

Tristan stood leaning against the wall, grinning. In a quick, graceful motion, he pushed off the wall and exited after the widow.

Bracing her hand on the wall, Elizabeth closed her eyes against the sting that Tristan had already begun to woo a new, or perhaps former, conquest so quickly. She thought they had connected in a deeply emotional way. She'd thought he loved her. Clearly, Tristan really was every bit the rake of his reputation. A painful truth stared at her.

He had never loved Elizabeth.

Perhaps she was truly unlovable.

Her breath came in painful little gasps. She needed to escape before someone saw her fall apart, but a crowd stood between her and the way to the great hall. She'd best go out to the terrace. With head high and a smile fixed on her mouth, she moved outside. Finding the terrace occupied with several couples, she followed the steps down to the path and sought refuge underneath a bower of wisteria. She sank down, barely feeling the cold stone bench, and focused on finding her composure.

True, Tristan never loved her. However, she had a good husband. Tonight, Richard's actions encouraged her. One day, they might reach an accord—perhaps even true affection. They might not ever fall in love, but from now on, she would put all her energies into building a friendly relationship with Richard. After all, friendship was almost as good as love between husband and wife. Wasn't it? She sat, inhaling the scents of flowers and growing things, and searched her heart for a way to reach her husband.

Chapter Twenty-Seven

To show the assembly nothing was amiss between his family and the Wentworths, Richard asked Leticia for a dance. Her manner restrained, she accepted. Though she attempted to hide her hurt behind a mask of gaiety and conversation, he knew her too well to miss it. After searching for some words to offer, he decided that saying nothing regarding their situation would be the most prudent course of action.

"The house looks magnificent," Leticia said as they danced together.

Richard followed her gaze. "We have a houseful of staff now. Father let so many go after my mother left that I got accustomed to having very few servants around. I admit, it's been returned to its former splendor."

Nodding, she smiled too brilliantly and the conversation ground to a halt.

A moment later, he said, "How's your sister?"

"Very well. She had her baby, did you know?"

"No, I didn't."

"A girl. They are both fine." She nodded. "Everything is...fine."

"I'm glad to hear it." Richard longed for the dance to end to break the forced conversation, a unique problem between them. Always before, he'd been so comfortable with Leticia and they'd never found dialogue difficult. Now they had resorted to such mundane topics. What next? The weather?

As the music ended, he bowed. "Thank you for standing up with me, Leticia, and thank you again for coming. Your presence here, I'm sure, will help put to rest any lingering rumors about the origin of my…marriage."

Without meeting his gaze, Leticia curtsied. "My pleasure."

He escorted her back to her mother, who smiled politely but didn't quite meet his gaze. After he bowed, he made his escape. Shaking off thoughts that Leticia would have been his wife if all would have gone according plan, Richard mingled with the guests, searching for Elizabeth. He found her dancing with Mr. Drummell.

Exquisite in her red gown, his wife shone like a ruby amid a sea of white. Her hair shimmered and her flushed cheeks and flawless, creamy complexion declared her a true beauty. Then she smiled and his heart nearly stopped. His gaze followed her womanly curves as she moved among the other dancers. Poised and graceful, she couldn't have been a finer countess. Perhaps he'd been too hasty when he'd decided not to consummate their marriage. He could, of course, rectify the situation if she were willing. He hoped very much that Elizabeth was willing.

And yet, that dark little voice that always whispered in his ear spoke again, cautioning him against getting too close to the woman who could ultimately destroy him if he let her into his heart.

"A fine selection of stuffed shirts, you have here, O' brother of mine, but at least you appear to have an equal number of skirts here, too, ripe for the plucking."

Richard turned to Tristan. "Are you really that vulgar, or do you just say that to annoy me?"

"Annoying you is one of my favorite pastimes."

"Right below chasing women?"

Tristan looked wounded. "They chase me."

"Right." Richard scowled. Unfortunately, that appeared to be true, the dog.

Tristan made a point of looking about himself. "The place looks good."

"Elizabeth's doing."

"I knew she'd be a good woman to have around." Something in his tone failed to meet the lighthearted tone he'd no doubt intended. Tristan cleared his throat. "Now if you'll excuse me, I have pretty ladies to meet." Tristan clapped him on the shoulder and moved off to a group of young ladies clustered together.

At least he didn't appear to be hunting Elizabeth. Richard caught sight of Leticia leaning rather heavily against a column, fanning her overly pink face. He threaded through the crowd to her side, searching for Mrs. Wentworth to bring her to her daughter, but did not find the woman. He'd best see to her himself.

"Leticia? Are you faint?"

She startled at his approach. "I think I'm a bit overheated."

"Let's take you out for some air." He guided her through the open doors into the cool night. As they walked in the garden, a breeze cooled his face and seemed to restore her. Their feet crunched in the gravel as they walked underneath Chinese lanterns, and in the distance, a nightingale trilled.

"You're not usually the fainting type," he

commented.

"No. I'm probably just tired. I haven't been sleeping well—" She broke off. "Never mind."

Richard winced. "I'm sorry about everything, Tish. If I'd married you a year ago—"

"Tristan would have dueled with the Marquis of Martindale and been hurt or killed," Leticia finished.

"I would not have allowed that to happen. I would have reached a compromise with Pemberton."

Her breath caught and made an odd hiccupping sound.

Richard glanced at her to see tears trailing down her cheeks. A kick in the stomach would have hurt less, and he nearly groaned out loud. "Leticia…"

Brushing away her tears, she halted and turned to face him. "I'm sorry. I don't mean to be a watering pot."

He wished he could offer a comforting embrace as he had as a child. Instead, he settled for placing a hand on her shoulder and giving it a little squeeze. "You are a fine woman. A jewel. Now that you're not waiting around for me, you can pay attention to all the young bucks who've been pining away for you all along."

She laughed, a soft, sad sound. Then she leaned up and kissed his cheek. It would be, he knew, the last. Her lips lingered as if reluctant to end that final touch. He put a hand on her back, wishing he could enfold her into his arms and squeeze away the hurt as he'd done when she'd come to him as a child, broken hearted that one of her father's horses had trampled her kitten. He couldn't hug her now, of course.

With more passion in her voice than he'd ever heard from her, she declared, "I'll always love you,

Richard. Only you."

Sniffling, she hurried away. Richard stood alone and winded. He fisted his hands. He was, without a doubt, the world's biggest scoundrel—right next to Tristan who'd caused all the trouble.

Chapter Twenty-Eight

With her heart nearly choking her, Elizabeth froze, rooted to the ground, while her husband and his true love stood close together in the moonlit garden underneath a rose bower, close enough for Elizabeth to hear and see them all too well.

Leticia rested one hand on Richard's chest and another on his cheek. She leaned against him, lifted her head, and kissed him, a long, lingering kiss. Richard didn't step away, rather he reached up and put a hand on her back while they kissed in the moonlight. When Leticia stepped away, she stood looking up at him.

Leticia's voice drifted to Elizabeth on the night air. "I'll always love you, Richard. Only you."

Hurt and dismay burned Elizabeth's eyes until she could barely see. Footsteps and the rustling of silk faded away. Elizabeth tried to breathe but the pain in her heart constricted her chest. Alone now, Richard stood unmoving, clenching and unclenching his fists, obviously wrestling with himself over the desire to run after Leticia. No wonder he'd shown no inclination toward Elizabeth. He still loved Leticia.

How long before he took her as a lover? He'd be discreet, of course, yet the thought of his unfaithful affections smote her to the heart. No matter how hard she tried to prove her value to Richard, he still longed for another.

Or perhaps he had already taken Leticia as his mistress. He might have been having an affair with Leticia since before the marriage. It made sense. He'd certainly shown no affection for Elizabeth. Her father had done exactly the same thing with Elizabeth's mother—he'd left an unwanted marriage and returned to the woman he truly loved. Why should Richard be any different?

Immediately she chided herself for such thoughts. Leticia was a gently bred lady who would never behave in such a scandalous manner, nor would she destroy her younger sisters' chance for marriage to respectable men. Besides, Richard would never ruin a lady.

Those facts did not change the bald truth that Richard and Leticia were in love. He would never love Elizabeth and would one day grow to resent her.

Rejection slammed into her, tearing through her heart and leaving behind destruction.

She fled to her bedroom, threw herself onto her bed, and sobbed like a child with a broken heart. How long she wept before she had no tears left to shed, she could not have said. Left only with hopeless sorrow, she lay spent on the counterpane, hiccupping. Her head throbbed with every beat of her wounded heart.

The clock chimed half past eleven. Midnight dinner would be served soon. She had guests and responsibilities she'd neglected while she lapsed into self-pity, and now she must take her place as hostess.

She pushed herself up. A glance in the mirror revealed her swollen face and disheveled hair. Commanding herself to take control over her sensibilities, Elizabeth rang for Maggie and washed her face. Maggie arrived, and after only a briefly startled pause at Elizabeth's appearance, immediately went to work packing her eyes with cold, lavender-scented compresses and restyling her disheveled hair without comment. By the time Maggie had finished working her magic, Elizabeth had regained her composure.

She arrived in the ballroom moments before the supper dance. As the last strains of the music ended, she spotted Tristan, handsome and maddeningly smug, glancing slyly across the room at his coquette. Flush-faced and radiant, she fanned herself,. Did the widow know she would never have possession of Tristan's rakish heart? Did she care?

Tristan swaggered up to Elizabeth and offered a bow, his eyes glittering with mischief. Elizabeth wanted to demand if he'd enjoyed his rendezvous with the widow, but couldn't bring herself to form the words. She didn't want to know. The scoundrel.

"Will you stand up with me for the dinner dance?" Tristan's disarming smile would not be refused.

Accepting would be easier than refusing, and she had no fight left in her. Cursing herself a fool for being civil to such a callous womanizer, she placed her hand in his. He moved with sinewy grace as he led her through the steps. As they danced, he smiled, teased, and laughed. Her heart filled with such heaviness over Richard's sound rejection, and the further proof that she had never meant anything to Tristan, that she could hardly manage a faint upward lift to her mouth.

As they reached the end of the line, waiting for the dance pattern to draw them into the sequence again, Tristan eyed her. "What's troubling you?"

She tried to smile but it probably came out as a grimace. "Nothing worth mentioning."

His dark gaze passed over her but she avoided eye contact and made a point of adjusting her gloves. They began dancing their way back up the line, ending any hope of a serious conversation.

The dance ended and supper began. He led her to the dining room where the midnight dinner, which rivaled their wedding feast, was served. Richard sat at the head with one of the county's *grande dames* at his side. Elizabeth sat at the foot next to Tristan.

Tristan smiled at Elizabeth, his gaze darting over her as if searching her face for answers. "What a fetching sense of style you've developed, Elizabeth. If you'd come to London wearing such a lovely gown, the ladies would copy your designs *en masse*."

Forcing herself to behave with the decorum worthy of a duke's daughter and an earl's wife, she lifted her head higher and coaxed her lips into a more sincere smile. "You're too kind."

"Tell me what you're reading these days, Elizabeth."

She shrugged, unwilling to reveal the few precious, intimate moments that she'd read to Richard and to the little maid. "I haven't had much time to read of late what with running a household—and designing new styles, of course. You?"

"One of my new favorites is Robert Burns, the Scotsman. Goes by Robbie among friends." Tristan leaned back, and with a languishing eye fixed directly upon Elizabeth's face, he began to quote:

"My love is like a red, red rose,
That's newly sprung in June
My love is like the melodie
That's sweetly played in tune.

As fair art thou, my bonnie lass,
So deep in love am I:
And I will love thee still, my dear,
Till a' the seas gang dry."

Elizabeth forced herself to break gaze with him. Tristan seemed to recite those words with such poignancy. He couldn't mean them. He'd never meant them. He only appeared sincere because he was a skilled libertine.

She glanced at Richard at the far end of the table, but he never looked her way. Tristan continued to regale her with his infectious charm, and by the time dinner ended, her heart ached more than ever.

An impenetrable barrier stood between her and the one man who seemed, at least on some level, to want her. Despite Tristan's faults, despite her disillusionment over his affections for her, he still made her laugh, still made her feel important, even desirable, but Tristan no longer made her pulse throb. She'd married a man who didn't desire her, who barely acknowledged her existence, and his signs of disloyalty wounded her so much more deeply than the evidence of Tristan's true colors. She wanted to weep at the injustice.

Chapter Twenty-Nine

Richard made it through dinner without tasting a bite of the food he swallowed. His wife sat at the foot of the table speaking with Tristan as if they were the only two people present.

When she and Tristan had both disappeared within minutes of each other, even using different exits so as to appear innocent, Richard had tried not to jump to conclusions. However, nearly an hour later, when Elizabeth returned with her hair restyled without a strand out of place despite dancing, and Tristan reappeared so smug and swaggering, not to mention their intimate postures at the other end of the table, Richard had to admit it. He'd been betrayed—right under his nose. Whatever guilt had smote him when Leticia kissed his cheek evaporated in the sickening truth of his wife's perfidy.

Each time he thought of it, his anger grew until he thought he'd erupt like a volcano. He must take action. Immediately. He made a quick gesture to a nearby footman.

As the footman leaned over to listen, Richard spoke softly. "Have my brother's carriage prepared to leave as soon as possible."

The footman nodded and left to carry out his orders. At last, the final course was served and consumed. As guests left the table and migrated back into the drawing room, Richard moved to intercept Tristan.

Under his breath so as not to be overheard by his guests, he grabbed Tristan by the arm and said into his ear, "You. Out. Now."

Tristan blinked in surprise but let Richard manhandle him to the front door. "What is it?"

Shaking in rage, Richard literally threw Tristan outside.

Tristan staggered under the force of his shove then, steadying himself, turned back. "Wha…"

His wounded expression almost broke through Richard's cold anger but the thought of Tristan's sin fortified his determination. He'd feared from the beginning that Tristan and Elizabeth would cuckold him, but facing the reality of it left his insides in shreds.

Tristan, of all people. To think his own brother would sink so low, even after vowing he wouldn't…

When Father died, Richard had only his brother and sister. He had almost dared hope he would find a true ally in a wife. Now he had no one. Utter loneliness opened up and swallowed him.

The carriage he'd ordered waited nearby, the tack jingling each time the horses stamped. Two mounted outriders waited ahead, showing no signs of irritation that their master had ordered them to ride in the middle of the night. The coachman and footman also stood by, their gazes fixed discreetly away.

Richard brushed off his hands as if Tristan's coat had sullied them and turned back to his treacherous brother. "Go. Now."

"What is going on?" Tristan looked for all the world as if he had no idea what he'd done to anger

Richard.

Richard glowered. "You come near my wife again and I'll tear off your head. Do not ever step foot in this house." To the coachman he said, "Take him to his flat in London. Then return."

Before anyone could reply, he re-entered the house. His fists clenched, itching to punch a hole through a wall. If only he could and then go for a long run. He paused inside the great hall, drawing deep breaths. He would deal with Elizabeth later, when he wasn't so tempted to throw her out as well. He had promised to take swift action, meaning divorce her, if she'd cheated on him. At the time, he'd meant it as a threat to keep her in line. He hadn't actually intended to do it. What to do now?

The scandal of a divorce would eclipse the scandal of a cheating wife. Nonetheless, to live under the roof with her, knowing what she'd done…

He had guests. He must play the charade until the night's end. Gritting his teeth, he returned reluctantly to the ballroom.

Just inside the doorway, one of the guests approached him. "My lord. I need your help. My bracelet is missing. I fear it's been stolen."

Could this night get any worse? Richard stared in dismay at the lady who stood before him. "Are you sure? Might it have slipped off?"

"I don't know. I only know I had it moments ago. Now it's gone."

Richard pressed his fingers to the center of his forehead where a headache built. Apparently, one of Elizabeth's reformed servants hadn't truly reformed. "Very well. I'll conduct a search."

She nodded. "It's a family jewel, Lord Averston. I'd be most grateful to have it restored."

"Of course."

After she gave him a description of the bracelet, she returned to the ballroom. Discreetly, Richard summoned both the head housekeeper, Mrs. Brown, and Handley, the butler, and informed them of the theft.

Mrs. Brown nodded, her expression smug. "That's what happens when you trust one of *them*."

Handley offered no comment.

Richard fixed a stare upon them each in turn. "Choose a very few trusted servants and have them help you conduct a search. Above all, be discreet. We don't want to alarm any of the guests."

They both went to do as instructed. Richard rested his forehead on the wall.

First Leticia, then Elizabeth and Tristan, and now this. Clearly, this was some kind of punishment for a past misdeed.

After a bracing drink, he stayed visible in the ballroom and hoped no one would see through his façade. He tried to keep his tone light and his smile in place when every nerve in his body urged him to race outside and run until he collapsed.

Only moments later, Mrs. Brown caught his attention. He nodded, then, moving in a casual manner through the crush and speaking with people as he went, met the housekeeper in the passageway leading to the kitchen.

A footman named Foster, and the butler, Handley, held the normally jovial footman, Cooper, by the arms. Cooper's customary grin was replaced by wild panic.

As soon as Richard arrived, Cooper began

sputtering, "'Tain't me, milor'. I didn' even know nuthin' was stole'."

Richard raised a brow at Handley and Mrs. Brown.

Handley cleared his voice. "The bracelet was found in the pocket of a coat underneath his bed."

Cooper interjected, "I didn' pu' it there, milor', I swear it."

Richard eyed him coolly. "Then explain how a stolen bracelet ended up in your pocket under your bed."

"Someone musta pu' it there t' throw off anyone searchin' fer it, then intended to go back fer it when it was safe'. I didn't steal it, milor'. I swear."

"What's amiss?" Elizabeth approached, eyeing them all in unease. "Cooper?"

Cooper turned to her as if she were his only hope of salvation. "M'lady. They think I stole a bracelet but I swear I didn'."

"Well, of course you didn't." She turned to Richard. "I trust Cooper implicitly. He'd never steal, especially not from us."

Richard's temper almost snapped. He rounded on her and fought to keep his voice level, not only for the theft which she indirectly caused, but her indiscretion tonight. "He was a pickpocket before he came here."

She raised her chin. "He has reformed."

Mrs. Brown sniffed. "I always knew that sort couldn't be trusted. Give them enough temptation, and they'll always return to their old ways."

Truer words were never spoken.

Elizabeth's eyes flashed. "Don't you believe people can change? Don't you believe in second chances?"

"Not where valuables are concerned," Mrs. Brown shot back.

Elizabeth drew herself up in indignation. "Your impertinence, Mrs. Brown—"

"She's right and you know it," Richard interjected.

Elizabeth recoiled as if he'd struck her and she stared with her mouth open while the color drained out of her face. Guilt stabbed him. He'd sabotaged her standing with the servants. But what did that matter? He was finished with the lying wretch.

Mrs. Brown nodded to punctuate her point. "Next thing, one of us will wake up with our throats cut."

Richard returned Elizabeth's gaze. "We must summon a constable and turn him over to the magistrate."

Elizabeth practically threw herself in front of Cooper like a shield. "You will do no such thing. He's innocent and I demand time to clear his name."

Behind Elizabeth, Cooper's shoulder hunched and his face crumpled. "I don' wanna cause trouble wi' you and yer man, m'lady."

Elizabeth made no reply. As if daring Richard to go through her, Elizabeth squared her shoulders and stared back at him, her chest heaving in an anger to match his own.

Fisting his hands, Richard turned from her and addressed the servants. "We have guests. Take him to the cellar and lock him up for the night. We'll decide what to do in the morning."

The servants took a defeated Cooper away, leaving Richard and Elizabeth locked in silent battle. Rage simmered in Richard's gut as Elizabeth brazenly stared him down without a trace of the cowed girl he'd agreed to marry.

Her voice shook. "How. Dare. You."

Richard's control shattered. "How dare I? How dare you, madam? How dare you bring pickpockets and cutthroats into this house to endanger our guests? How dare you disregard the advice of a housekeeper who has protected and served my family since before I was born? How dare you have a tryst with my own brother right in front of my nose!"

"What?" She widened her eyes and took a step backward.

She was acting, of course, but certainly played the part convincingly. In what other ways had she deceived him?

Shaking in barely controlled rage, Richard fairly shouted, "Tristan returned strutting like a peacock after your hour together. And you? Did you think I wouldn't notice?" He gazed with disgust upon her freshly coiffed tresses as he tried to regain control of his voice. "Your face flushed, and your hair re-styled. Then you had the audacity to choose him for a dinner companion. Have you no discretion?"

With her eyes enormous and her hair softly framing her face, Elizabeth looked every inch a temptress. Her voice dropped to a whisper. "I can't believe you'd think that of me. I merely—"

"Don't. Do not insult me further by telling me you were out for an innocent stroll with him."

She fixed an unblinking stare upon him, a depth of sadness entering her eyes that gave him pause. "Like your stroll with Leticia Wentworth?"

Elizabeth had seen them together, alone, in a dark garden. As the horrifying realization slapped him in the face, the blood rushed out of his head so fast that the room swam.

Her chest heaved. "I saw you in the garden kissing her, doing the same thing that I was caught doing with Tristan at the house party. You got away with it. I was condemned."

She took a step nearer. "You speak often of honor, and yet easily cast it aside when it pleases you. It's truly ironic that you constantly question my purity but have your own set of morals. Oh, you and Tristan make quite a pair, don't you? You with Leticia, he..." She straightened her spine. "I alone behaved properly this evening and I refuse to stand here and be falsely accused of that which *you* are guilty."

Richard shook his head, trying to keep up with her. Leticia's kiss was as chaste as a childhood friend's, not that of a seductress. He supposed, to a bystander, with her head raised up to his, and his head lowered to hers, it might have appeared much less innocent, especially considering that they were alone in the dark. Whether or not Elizabeth had played him false did not change the fact that he had been caught in a compromising situation. His and Leticia's actions looked bad. Which meant, they were bad. He'd behaved with impropriety.

Stunned by his own hypocrisy, he pressed a hand to his head. In the face of Elizabeth's justified attack on his character, his self-righteous anger dissipated like mist under sunlight. He lowered his hand. "I know what you saw may have looked bad, but we didn't—"

"I saw you two kissing. What else you've done, or plan to do, I can only guess."

Before he could defend himself, she fled, leaving him alone with his thoughts.

The bald truth stared him in the face: he was a hypocrite.

Chapter Thirty

With effort, Elizabeth lifted her head to look at the footman speaking to her—the same footman who'd taken Cooper away and locked him in the cellar.

Richard's accusation that she'd committed adultery repeated over and over in her mind. His rage had left her quaking. At least he hadn't hit her. Yet. She couldn't believe he'd thought she'd been unfaithful. Even after nearly two months of marriage, he didn't know her or trust her enough to know she'd never betray her husband. After all her attempts to prove herself deserving of his affection, he would never develop a fondness for her. Her earlier fears were right; she was unlovable. The thought speared her heart and left an open, bleeding wound.

She thought of him and Leticia kissing in the garden. Then, moments later, he'd dared pass judgment on her and Tristan based on flimsy evidence, hurling at her a terrible accusation without giving her the benefit of the doubt or even a chance to defend herself. His double standard burned in her throat. Anger wove in through her despair. The callous pretender!

The footman who'd taken Cooper trotted to her. "Milady?"

She forced her mouth to move. "What is the problem…er, Foster, isn't it?"

"Yes, milady. Another guest has reported a missing

ring."

She blinked. "When did she notice it missing?"

"Just now, milady. About half an hour ago, she went to the retiring room and is sure she had it on then—another guest admired it. She danced a set, and took some refreshment, and just now saw it gone."

"Has she checked the retiring room?"

Foster nodded. "With the help of a maid."

A glimmer of light cut through the fog in her mind. "So it had to have happened within the last half an hour. Who knows about Cooper?"

"Only me, Handley, Mrs. Brown, you, and the master."

"So no one knows he's been blamed for the theft or confined."

"No, milady."

She drew herself up. At least she might exonerate Cooper, even if she couldn't exonerate herself in Richard's eyes. "Who besides you and the maid knows about the missing lady's ring?"

"No one that I know of." His quizzical glance swept over her.

"Good." She rubbed her forehead, trying to formulate a plan. She dropped her voice. "Did you get a description of the ring?"

"Yes, milady."

"Tell no one this. Search all the footmen and maids. Be discreet."

Foster nodded somberly. "I can do that and they'll never know I'm searching them." At Elizabeth's curiously raised brows, he added, "No one knows this, but five years ago, I, too, was a pickpocket. People *can* change."

Elizabeth laughed weakly, wishing she could throw that tidbit in Mrs. Brown's face. And Richard's.

Foster left to conduct his search. Though tempted to immediately free Cooper, Elizabeth resisted; she didn't dare alert the true perpetrator. She should tell Richard of the new development. Upon searching the room, she found him standing in a circle of men looking as grim and cold as ever. She tossed her head. . She would take care of it herself. However, she'd make sure he learned the outcome and how wrong he was about Cooper. Somehow she'd prove he'd been wrong about all his assumptions tonight.

Moments later, a parlor maid approached. "M'lady. Foster wishes to speak with you in the kitchen."

Elizabeth made a circuitous route to the kitchen where she found Foster standing off to one side to stay out of the way of the chef and his assistants. The chef glowered at them both from underneath his bushy brows, probably put out by the intrusion in his domain.

Foster held up a ring. "I found this underneath Cooper's bed."

"Cooper's?"

"At first I thought he stole it before and that the guest had not yet missed it but I'm sure it wasn't there when I found the bracelet."

"He couldn't have stolen the ring."

"No, milady."

Elizabeth nodded, weary with relief that Cooper's name had been cleared. "Keep your eyes open for anything suspicious, and set Cooper free but have him stay out of sight." Elizabeth returned to the drawing room. Would this night ever end?

The night passed with no further thefts reported.

Finally, the last guests left, and the front door closed with an echoing bang. A hush descended over the house.

Elizabeth glanced at Richard at her side. He stood as if made of iron. Implacable, immovable. He showed no sign of regret for his role in any of the night's events. Bitterness ate through her. She turned away, but halted as Cooper entered the great hall.

Cooper twisted his gloves in his hand. "Thank ye agin, m'lady. I'll ne'er forget yer trust in me."

Ignoring Richard's surprised intake, she replied calmly. "You're welcome, though you have Foster to thank. He discovered the ring that had been stolen long after you were confined." She cast a surreptitious glance at Richard who stared hard at the erstwhile thief.

Cooper touched his forehead. "G'nigh' m'lady."

"Good night, Cooper. Thank you for your continued service. And Cooper?"

"M'lady?"

"Keep your eyes open. We still have a thief and he's trying to blame you."

"Aye, m'lady."

After Cooper's footfalls quieted, Elizabeth turned to make her way to her room.

Richard's voice stopped her. "There was another theft?"

She stiffened and fought to keep her voice level. "A ring. It was stolen after Cooper was detained. Cooper is, and always was, innocent."

A pause. "Then we still haven't caught the thief."

"No." She went to the door, then without turning around, shot over her shoulder, "A great number of false accusations were made tonight, however."

She trudged to her room and collapsed on the bed. Shoulder-wracking sobs overcame her and she bawled like a child, mourning every embarrassment, every lost dream, every dashed hope. She'd been foolish to believe she might ever find happiness with a man so cold and judgmental.

No matter what she did, no matter how hard she tried to please him, or prove herself otherwise, he would only ever see her as a woman of scandal.

Chapter Thirty-One

After the last guest departed, Richard turned away and mounted the stairs, heading for his room. The truth of Elizabeth's infidelity, despite her almost-convincing denial, forced his hand. He'd have to take action as he'd promised.

A maelstrom of thoughts swirled through him—mostly of Elizabeth and Tristan's duplicity. Despite his fears, he hadn't actually thought either of them so disloyal. The searing pain in his heart cut deeper than he'd ever thought possible. He'd been wise to keep himself apart from Elizabeth. If he'd initiated marital intimacy, her betrayal would have wounded him much more.

His own guilty-looking moments a few hours ago with Leticia—who made no secret of her broken heart—rose up in stark accusation. Elizabeth must have assumed the worst, and so would anyone who might have seen them together.

Add to that, a thief had struck, possibly one of his own servants.

Tonight ranked high on the list of worst nights of his life. He rubbed a hand over his face. He had decisions to make. The thought of taking such a heartless stand with Elizabeth either by divorcing her or sending her away to some seldom-visited estate during a permanent separation, thus condemning her to a lifetime of isolation and social condemnation, left a sour taste in his mouth. At the moment, all he wanted to do was pull the covers over his head and sleep for a week.

As Richard headed toward his room, a shadowy figure caught his eye. A feminine figure walked in a rustle of silk near the end of the darkened corridor running the length of the wing. He paused. The woman stepped into the circle of a sconce, illuminating her ball gown and golden hair. He frowned. What was a guest doing in the family wing? The blonde stopped in front of Tristan's empty room, turned the knob, and went in.

More than a little disquieted, Richard followed her. He stood in the doorway and watched the woman as she ran her hands over the cushions of the settee drawn up in front of the fireplace as if she sought something. He couldn't remember her name, only that she was a widow who lived in the area. She turned her head, revealing her youth and beauty. What was she doing here? Could she be tonight's thief?

No, tonight's losses were jewelry, and Tristan kept little more than a few stickpins and cufflinks in his room. Add to that, the widow walked without hesitation past silver candlesticks and valuable vases, clearly focused on some other goal.

After a few moments, she moved to the rumpled bed. She searched the bedclothes and pillows and then let out a small cry of triumph.

He folded his arms and leaned against the wall. "May I help you?" he asked.

She squeaked and whirled around. "L-lord Averston." In the dim candlelight created by a candle left burning on the nightstand, her blush reddened her face. "I…" She bit her lip, then let out a helpless laugh. "I lost one of my earrings so I came back to look for it. I found it." She held out her hand to reveal a pearl glimmering in her palm.

Richard blinked as the truth sank in. "*You* were the woman with Tristan tonight?"

She laughed again, a warm, husky tone. "Yes, I suppose in light of my presence and purpose here, it'd be futile to deny it. Oh, don't worry, I won't require anything of your brother in return. I'm quite happy living as an independent widow enjoying the attentions of healthy young men."

Speechless, Richard stared. Tristan hadn't been with Elizabeth; he'd been with this widow…who was exactly Tristan's type of woman.

The enormity of his error—his unfairness—hit him with hurricane force.

What had he done?

The lady cleared her voice. "Well, goodnight, my lord. Thank you for the ball. I'll see myself out." She slipped passed him in the doorway and disappeared.

Richard cursed, and then cursed again. Pressing both hands over his face, he sank to the floor against the wall and sat curled up.

He'd jumped to conclusions. Elizabeth and Tristan hadn't committed adultery right under his nose as he'd believed. He'd been so sure, but he was wrong.

He'd been so afraid that they would cheat on him that he had assumed the worst. Working under his false belief, he'd treated his wife and his brother like a boorish, judgmental cad. He should have approached them, given them a chance to confirm or explain. Elizabeth's righteous indignation could not have been feigned. The wounded—and apparently sincere—expression lancing Elizabeth's face, and Tristan's when Richard had thrown him out, rose up in harsh accusation. He wanted to cry out in shame. He'd been unforgivably hasty.

He let out his breath in a long exhale. He'd been wrong. He might never make amends.

Still, he had to try. He approached Elizabeth's door, but the bone-deep sobs coming from her room stilled his hand. He paused, aching to apologize, comfort her, help heal the hurt if he could. Yet with her emotions so charged, now was clearly the wrong time.

He'd wait. Perhaps have breakfast with her. Then what? How to truly earn her forgiveness? An apology, certainly, but this kind of mistake required more. Perhaps some kind of gesture. He wracked his brain. She liked to read but the house had a library full of books that he'd already given her leave to peruse.

She liked music. The harp. Of course. She played the harp. She must be missing hers. He made a mental note to buy a harp for her.

What else? Perhaps tomorrow after breakfast he could take her for a ride…provided she agreed to go with him, that is. There he'd make his apologies and spend the day with her showing her around his estate and perhaps enjoying a luncheon *al fresco*. He fell asleep planning the riding route and to whom he would introduce her.

The next morning on his way to the breakfast room, he passed a table holding mail and today's papers. As he caught the headline, he paused.

"Lord Einsburgh has been arrested?" He picked up the paper and read more.

He'd always suspected the man operated slightly above the law, but the arrest outlined a list of charges that stunned Richard. He remembered a day, not so long ago, when he and Tristan and Kensington were together. Tristan had complained that Einsburgh cheated at cards. Kensington had joked that Tristan suspected everyone who beat him cheated. Even then, Richard had believed Tristan and suspected Einsburgh of dishonesty. That his dishonesty stretched to crime didn't surprise Richard as much as it should have. Still, if he received a writ of summons for Einsburgh's trial, Richard would keep his opinions to himself and try to be fair. He tossed the paper aside and turned his attention to courting his countess and repairing his battered marriage.

The breakfast room was alone. As he ate, he deliberated on the best way to approach his wife and beg her to listen to him. Before he'd found the answer, a special messenger delivered an urgent letter addressed to Lady Averston. He waited, but she never came to him. Within moments, the servants began scrambling to obey orders he had yet to hear. Still, Elizabeth sent him no message. What could be amiss? And why was he excluded from it?

Quelling his rising irritation, as well as a touch of concern, he knocked at the door. At her permission, he entered to find her wearing a dressing gown, her tousled hair hanging loose around her back and shoulders. The sight evoked images of her lying with him in bed looking up at him with welcoming eyes.

The image shattered as Elizabeth glanced at him, then turned away dismissively. She selected gowns and threw them on her bed. Her abigail folded everything and placed them in a trunk.

His heart hammered in his ears. She was leaving him?

Richard made a gesture toward the trunk. "Are you going somewhere?"

She never glanced his way. "Father has sent for me. Duchess is gravely ill. I must go to her."

He bit back a sigh relief. She wasn't leaving him. "Duchess? I'm surprised you're so anxious to see her."

She let out a huff that might have been a mocking laugh or a suppressed sob. "I'm very anxious, but not because I want to see her. If she dies…" Her next words came out fast and tripped all over each other. "I have heard of too many people who were estranged and failed to make amends when they could and then the other person dies and the one left behind is wracked with torment because they never reconciled and…" A sob broke through. "Besides, I could have been a better daughter. I disappointed her in so many ways. My parting words to her were hateful. I couldn't bear it if I never had a chance to recant."

He couldn't believe she was defending the woman who belittled and abused her all her life. "You didn't deserve—"

"Father has requested my presence. I really feel I should." The pleading in her eyes would not be denied. "Please."

"Very well. I'll make arrangements."

"I've already made them."

"Oh. Then, I'll ready myself to accompany you."

"No need. I know you are a very busy man. I wouldn't want to drag you away from all your important duties." Her words were biting.

He battled the urge to defend himself. Instead he said to the maid, "Leave us."

Elizabeth opened her mouth, her eyes flashing in irritation. Instead of speaking, she clamped her lips together and opened a clothes press where she selected stockings and gloves.

He waited until the maid left the room before speaking. "Of course I'll accompany you. It's a family emergency. My place is at your side."

She threw him an accusing stare. "Why? So you can ensure I'm not cheating on you?"

He drew a breath and tried to keep his voice even. "No, to be with you should you need me."

"I don't require your presence. I can get along just fine without you. I've been doing so since the day we married. You have made it clear you don't like my company; you can barely bring yourself to dine with me. I don't know why you let me read to you at night."

He opened his mouth to speak, then stopped. He had been neglectful. Unforgivably so. He intended to make it right, now, even at the risk of losing his heart.

Before he could choose the right words, she cut in, her tone mocking and angry. "Don't worry, I haven't invited Tristan so you needn't fear for my fidelity."

He bowed his head under her justified anger. "I'm sorry I assumed the worst about you and Tristan. Please accept my apology."

Ignoring him, she walked back to her dressing room and emerged a moment later with an armload of clothes. "I hear you threw Tristan out last night. Have you apologized to him?"

He let out his breath and decided that was a topic for another time, when she wasn't so angry. "Look.

251

You are about to travel a long distance and I do not wish you to do so alone. I shall accompany you."

"As you wish," she snapped. "My lord."

Richard wanted to shake her by the shoulders. He ground his teeth and left the room. He should be patient with her mood. In addition to being angry over last night, she was no doubt overset about the health of her mother. Although why she would care about that unfeeling monster of a woman, he could not account. Focusing on such uncharitable thoughts, he made arrangements to travel. Within hours, they entered the family coach and began their journey.

Richard settled into the seat and searched for a topic. "Do you know the nature of the illness?"

"No."

He waited but she did not elaborate. He tried again. "Do you wish to travel straight through, or stop for the night?"

"Straight through. Please."

He let out a long exhale at her curtness. "About last night—"

Sharply she interrupted, "I don't wish to discuss it."

"I think we should."

"As you wish, *my lord*." Sarcasm filled the air. She folded her arms and crossed her legs. With her mouth mulishly pressed together, she stared out of the window.

Clearly conversation was pointless, so he kept his peace. All the while, his own irritation grew that his sweet, tractable wife had turned into a dragon. At least she was no longer a timid, quivering creature who feared he'd strike her.

Finally, after nearly an hour of silence, Richard addressed her. "About last night…"

"I don't wish to discuss it," she said crisply.

"I admit that I was wrong. I jumped to conclusions, and for that, I apologize."

The gaze she turned his way, instead of being filled with joy that he'd admitted to his error, pierced him with hostility. "You came to this conclusion, how?"

"I found the woman with whom Tristan had…er, had a dalliance. She admitted it."

"So, with proof, you exonerate me—this time, but before you had proof, you tried and convicted me without giving me a chance to defend myself."

He squirmed.

"The next time you suspect I've done something wrong, you'll jump to the same conclusion."

He had nothing to say. She was right. However, in his defense, she had admitted she still loved Tristan, so the only thing stopping her from falling into Tristan's arms was her own honor. Few women of his acquaintance seemed to possess much honor.

Her voice rose in pitch and volume. "So really, you've made up your mind that I'm an adulteress and you are waiting for me to commit the transgression so you can catch me." She let out a huff. "We have nothing more to discuss."

Richard searched for words to make amends, but she was right; he fully expected her to let him down. He found no answer to their predicament. Which meant they had no way to make amends.

She picked up a book and began reading. They sat in silence until they stopped to change horses. Richard rented a horse and rode outside for the remainder of the day. That night, he rode in the carriage with his silent wife and tried to snatch what little sleep he could, but at daybreak, he resumed the journey on horseback.

Dark storm clouds gathered and the wind whipped to biting speed by the time they arrived at the ducal county seat, an ancient dwelling sprawling over the moors like a ramshackle collection of monolithic stones.

Elizabeth emerged from the carriage pale and drawn. She only glanced once at Richard before climbing the front steps.

The servant who admitted them smiled at Elizabeth. "Welcome home, Lady Elizabeth."

"How is Duchess?"

"The fever broke this morning and she seems to be feeling a little better."

"I must see her at once." Elizabeth peeled off her gloves and hurried up the stairs to the duchess's suite.

Richard followed. It would not do to leave Elizabeth alone with the viper, no matter how ill. The duchess lay in the center of an enormous bed, surrounded by pillows, flowers and an army of servants.

Elizabeth quickened her steps until she nearly trotted to the bed. "Mother," she cried, "I'm so sorry for all the times I've let you down. Please forgive me." She sank next to the bed and threw her arms around her mother's neck.

Looking a little thinner, but hardly on the brink of death, the duchess heaved a sigh. "Faith, child, I always said you were born for the stage. Do show some restraint."

Richard stifled a cry of outrage at the woman's insensitivity. Clearly, no heart beat within that breast.

How could a woman be so cruel to her own daughter?

Hurt and shock overcame Elizabeth's expression. Slowly she drew back and straightened her spine where she sat. As she raised her head, she composed her features. "Forgive me. I was concerned for your wellbeing and tired from the long journey to come to your side."

"You should never use emotion as an excuse to abandon decorum."

In a small voice, Elizabeth nodded once, folding her hands into her lap. "Of course."

Sickened, Richard stepped forward and tried not to grind his teeth. "I am gratified you are looking so well, madam. We had feared to find you in a much more serious condition."

The duchess's cold eyes turned upon him. "I was quite ill, I admit. However, reports of my impending death were exaggerated. There's certainly no cause for such a scene." She made a gesture toward Elizabeth.

Richard clenched his fists. "Your daughter was clearly concerned for your health, and rightly so. We drove straight through to be at your side. Elizabeth and I are fatigued, as you can imagine. Now that we see you are much improved, perhaps we should rest and return later this evening to visit you."

Duchess made an impatient gesture. "Your rooms are prepared, no doubt. Off with you. I must rest."

Her eyes downcast, Elizabeth leaned in and kissed her mother's cheek before arising. The duchess frowned and made a shooing motion.

A surge of protectiveness overcame Richard, and he again vowed to shield his wife from such a creature.

Before they reached their rooms, Elizabeth's sister

Mary came down the corridor the opposite direction.

"Mary!" Elizabeth let out a cry. They threw themselves into each other's arms.

Glad finally to see Elizabeth with someone who truly cared for her, Richard stepped back to allow them time to greet one another.

The younger of the three sisters arrived. Had Joanna lost weight? She looked thinner than usual, and pale. She greeted Elizabeth politely but without her usual energy.

Elizabeth noticed. "Are you well, Joanna?"

Joanna nodded. "Yes, of course."

A footman showed Richard to a suite he would share with Elizabeth. He collapsed onto a chair, grateful it didn't move or bounce like the carriage over rutted roads during their journey. Weary, he rested his head back against the chair and closed his eyes.

He woke to Elizabeth's voice. "Please leave Lord Averston's things in this room and take my trunk to my old room."

"Yes, milady." The footman withdrew.

Richard raised his head. "That's not necessary."

With her hands folded in front of her, she turned to him. In a bitter voice at odds with her serene posture, she retorted, "I assumed you'd be more comfortable in a private room, since you clearly prefer not to sleep with me." She left.

Richard cursed and rubbed a hand over his face. Too tired to find the desire to address the situation at the moment, he went to bed.

The late afternoon sun streamed in through the open windows when Richard awoke, stiff and rumpled from sleeping in his clothes. With Wesley's help, who looked also weary from the journey, Richard washed, shaved, and changed. He ate on the balcony, admiring the view of the lake and distant mountains.

After finishing his meal, he hailed a footman. "Have you seen Lady Averston?"

"No, my lord. I believe she's still resting."

"Show me to her rooms, please."

The footman looked startled but made a brief bow and brought him to the family quarters in the opposite end of the wing. Richard did not miss the implication.

The door stood ajar and swung open on silent hinges at Richard's touch. Richard glanced back, but the footman had disappeared. Elizabeth's room had been decorated in pale green and pink, with Chinese silk wallpaper. It was lovely and feminine, just like Elizabeth.

He found her lying upon the bed, curled up on her side, wearing only her shift. Her face was serene in sleep. Tenderness overcame him as he watched her. He admired the curve of her brows over her closed eyes, the porcelain-like smoothness of her cheek, the fullness of her lips. Her hair lay in a tumbled mass on the pillow, spilling down over the bed sheets. Very lightly, so as not to wake her, Richard smoothed a hand over her cheek, then fingered her silky waves. Struggling against the desire to climb into bed next to her, he turned and left her to rest.

No doubt she needed it after their grueling trip. If only they'd known the situation wasn't as grave as they'd believed, they would have traveled with more comfort. The greeting Elizabeth had received from her mother made Richard want to bid the ducal family a curt farewell and return home, never to darken their doorway again. He couldn't believe Elizabeth had been suffering over that heartless woman, thinking that she had somehow been an unworthy daughter, when all along, the duchess was clearly abusing her.

No wonder Elizabeth had fallen for Tristan's charms. She'd been so hungry for love and acceptance that she'd believed Tristan when he'd poured on a rake's pretty words about her being beautiful and unique and entrancing—all of which was true, of course, but Tristan had probably used the compliments as a means of seduction.

She *was* beautiful and entrancing. She just didn't know it. And that was his fault. Richard had failed to tell her, or to show her.

She probably thought she'd married a man as impossible to please as her mother. He vowed to change that as soon as she awoke. Until then, he'd search for words to apologize and take steps to cross the chasm between them.

Chapter Thirty-Two

Underneath a bright, cloudless sky, Elizabeth walked along the path in the gardens next to Mary, enjoying the song of the birds and the murmur of wind stirring the leaves. Perhaps it had been petty, but she'd ignored Richard's message that he wished to see her as soon as she'd arisen. She couldn't face that kind of tension at the moment. For now, she'd bask in Mary's soothing presence.

"I heard you playing the harp this morning," Mary said. "I've missed that sound."

"I miss playing it." She rubbed sore fingers together. Too much time had lapsed and now her callouses were gone.

"How is married life?"

"Fine," Elizabeth answered automatically.

"Truly?"

Hoping she sounded believable, Elizabeth seized upon any truths she could. "I enjoy being mistress of my own home. I've made my bride visits and have found my neighbors to be pleasant. I also threw my very first ball. It was a triumph."

Mary looked at her curiously as if she found Elizabeth's answer lacking in some way. "You ordered new gowns, I see."

Elizabeth smiled and smoothed a hand over her emerald gown. "Yes."

Mary gestured to Elizabeth's walking dress. "That is very pretty. I've never seen a style quite like that. I shall have to get the name of your modiste."

"It's my own design."

"I miss poring over fashion plates with you. You always had such unique and tasteful ideas. Too bad Mother never allowed us to make our own clothing choices while we were unwed. As soon as I return home, I will send for new gowns made with that tapered-in waist underneath the bust line. And I simply adore how it's lower and gathered at the back."

"A bit more figure-flattering, don't you think?"

"Indeed, I do." They walked in companionable silence a moment before Mary ventured, "You have said nothing about your husband."

Elizabeth paused, choosing her words. "He's polite, dignified, generous, and for the most part, does not interfere with my interests."

Mary stopped walking and turned to her. "Oh, no. What's wrong?"

"I said nothing about anything being wrong."

"That is not the description a new bride gives about her husband if all is well."

Elizabeth examined the ground. "What should I have said?"

"I don't know, how about he's charming, handsome, wonderful, tender?"

"Of course."

Mary led her to a stone bench and sank down upon it.

Elizabeth perched at the edge, unwilling to have this conversation. "My modiste is Madame Prideux and I am persuaded she did a lovely job interpreting my crude drawings. She's—"

"Lizzie, tell me what's happening with Lord Averston."

"Nothing."

Anger tinged Mary's voice. "Is he hurting you?"

"No."

Mary lifted her chin and peered into Elizabeth's eyes. "You never admitted when Mother hurt you, either."

Elizabeth looked her directly in the eye. "Mary, I vow, Richard has never harmed me."

Mary watched her as if determining her truthfulness. "Is he rough with you in intimate matters?"

Elizabeth's face burned. "No." Then, against her better judgment, admitted, "Quite the contrary."

"Then what is it?" Mary put an arm around her.

Her sister's compassion proved her undoing. Keeping so much bottled up inside became too much pressure to contain, and Elizabeth let out a sigh. "Where do I begin?" Tears gathered in her eyes. "How could everything have gone so wrong? He's…" Elizabeth broke off with a sob.

Mary drew her in and embraced her. All Elizabeth's control snapped and she wept. Mary held her without speaking, without moving, simply held her.

When Elizabeth's sobs died down, she leaned against Mary, counting herself blessed to have such a loving sister. Even when Elizabeth had tried so hard to conceal evidence of Duchess's form of punishment, Mary had sensed Elizabeth's need for comfort. Her sister always offered it without prying, without judging, simply extending love.

"Tell me everything," Mary said. "Start with the beginning."

With a candor that surprised them both, Elizabeth poured out the way Richard had suddenly turned so aloof after the wedding, his absence during the day, his lack of attention, seeing him kissing Leticia on the night of the ball, his discrediting her to the servants, and his unjust accusation that she'd been unfaithful to him. It all poured out amidst sobs. Mary listened, her own eyes glistening with sympathetic tears.

Elizabeth blew her nose. "I don't know what's worse; his accusation that I've been unfaithful with Tristan, or knowing that he's still in love with Leticia Wentworth."

"Both are terrible," Mary said quietly.

"We'll end up like Father and Duch—er, Mother, barely able to speak a civil word to one another."

"Not if you prove to him you are faithful. Be patient. You'll have to earn his trust. That will be difficult if he thinks you're still infatuated with his brother."

While Elizabeth chewed on her own guilt, Mary read her expression. "Oh, no, Lizzie. You can't be serious. You cannot truly still harbor a *tendré* for Tristan."

"You don't think I would have gone off alone with him at the house party if I weren't—" She stopped herself before saying the words "in love with him," no longer certain they applied to the state of her heart during the house party. She drew a breath. "I was hoping—"

"Don't say it. You cannot believe that rake had any intention of marrying you."

Elizabeth flinched. "You sound like Duchess."

Mary sighed. "He may have found you attractive, but to a man like that, you were merely an interesting diversion."

Though she'd reached the same conclusion, hearing such a judgment pronounced on Tristan pricked her fading loyalty for him. "I don't trust gossip. Gossip painted me little better than a hussy."

"You cannot entertain thoughts of Tristan Barrett and hope to have a happy marriage with another man—especially his brother. Forget Tristan and turn your attention to your husband. Be there for him, wrap him in comfort and safety."

"He's never home." Misery wore through her, leaving her bone weary. "When he is, he hardly speaks to me unless it's to find fault with me." She let out a huff. "Or with my servants."

"He's here with you now. What did you talk about during the journey?"

"Very little, I'm afraid," Elizabeth said.

He'd tried, on more than one occasion during the carriage ride, to initiate a conversation, but she was too hurt by his accusations, and too anxious over potential lost chances with Duchess, and frantic to be at Father's side if he needed her, to cooperate with Richard.

Mary nodded sagely. "Talk to him while you're here, and during your journey home. Find out what he likes, what he fears, what he hopes. Ask questions. Take this opportunity to get to know him and prove to him you want to make him happy. Don't look back. Focus on your new life. Think about his needs and set your own aside. That's when true happiness occurs."

"In other words, stop being selfish." Elizabeth

twisted her wedding band around her finger.

Mary took her hand. "You are not selfish. You often think of others, usually at the cost of your own happiness. But the man in your thoughts should be your husband, not your first infatuation."

Guiltily, Elizabeth stared down at her hands. "I understand."

Banishing all thoughts of Tristan seemed impossible, though. Perhaps no one ever quite forgot one's first love.

She straightened. Had it been love? Or had it been mere infatuation as Mary suggested? Her growing tenderness for Richard could never find a secure foothold in the face of so much mistrust. Already, it equaled—surpassed, even—her feelings for Tristan. With Richard so closed up and distant, and Tristan so open and charming, it was easy for her heart to choose Tristan. Although, he wasn't the true object of her heart's desire, merely the one who easily pleased her.

Mary was right; she must focus on building a life with Richard, and focusing on his happiness. Richard clearly still loved Leticia. She could not forget seeing him wrapped in Leticia's arms, nor the memory of them kissing. Yet she'd pledged herself to Richard. The only honorable thing to do would be to make the best of their marriage, which must include shutting down her stray yearnings for Tristan.

Chapter Thirty-Three

Dinner passed more pleasantly than Elizabeth had ever remembered. Duchess's absence no doubt had made the difference; she remained too ill to join them at the table. Martindale, Mary and her husband, Father, Joanna, and Richard proved charming dinner companions. Especially Richard. What had gotten into him, she couldn't say, but he was more attentive and complimentary than he'd ever been.

Seated next to her, his eyes shone. "Your gown is beautiful. I like red on you. And you must have your abigail do your hair like that more often. It's even more flattering than your usual style."

She faltered. "Thank you."

Guilt wove through her that she'd made a point of avoiding Richard until dinner. She'd told herself that she was trying to soothe and quiet her anger toward him so they could converse civilly. To be honest, she'd been too upset with his behavior at her ball. It was supposed to be her triumph, and he'd ruined everything. Still, she had vowed to try to be a good wife and make a marriage with him, perhaps even win him away from Leticia. She glanced at him and offered a smile that probably came out tentative, at best.

"It is lovely, Elizabeth," Mary said. "The pearls are pretty with it."

Elizabeth lowered her gaze, thinking how well

rubies would complement the gown, the family wedding rubies with which Richard had not seen fit to trust her.

Richard turned to her family. "You should have seen her put on our first ball. The skill with which my lovely bride carried it off was nothing short of amazing."

At her father's raised brows, she murmured, "It was nothing."

"Without any assistance from me, I might add." Richard smiled wryly. "Unfortunately, estate matters kept me from her side. She handled it all with finesse. All our guests exclaimed over her stunning triumph."

Father listened to Richard's recount with disbelief. Then he turned to Elizabeth. "You surprise me, daughter. Knowing your shyness, I wouldn't have expected it of you."

Mary jumped to her defense. "I'm not surprised. Lizzie has always had a way with people when she manages to overcome her shyness. She's a master at planning."

Joanna looked up. "Really? I must seek your aid when my time comes."

"Elizabeth has proved a delightful surprise in many ways." Richard glanced at her father with what might have been reproof, but she could not be certain.

Why he'd gone from his horrid accusation to suddenly heaping praise upon her, she could not explain. He might be so conscious of his family image that he'd decided to pretend they were the picture of married bliss. Or did he play some other game?

He glanced at her with what she could only describe as a look of apology, mingled with pleading.

She focused on her dinner plate. He had apologized before they left on their journey but she'd been too angry to accept it—what was to stop him from doing it again?

After dinner, the ladies removed themselves to a closed-off portion of the drawing room while Father, Martindale, and Richard remained to enjoy an after-dinner brandy. No doubt Father was taking snuff. Mary sat down to some correspondence and Joanna bent her head over her embroidery. Elizabeth steeled herself and went to look in on Duchess. She was the reason, after all, that Elizabeth had come. Very well, she'd come because Father had asked. Still, she ought to show more concern.

Duchess was her usual disapproving self, but grumbled about her health more than over what a disappointment Elizabeth was in every way.

Only moments later, Richard came in, much to Elizabeth's surprise. "How are you feeling, Duchess?" he asked solicitously.

His polite question sent Duchess off on another tirade about her illness. At least it wasn't about Elizabeth. "I don't like to complain," Duchess ended. "I'm tired. Leave me."

Elizabeth dutifully kissed Duchess's cheek and arose. Richard accompanied her as they left Duchess's exhausting presence.

In the corridor, Richard took her hand and tugged gently as he headed toward the stairs. "A word, if you please."

She hesitated. He was right. They did need to talk.

He led her into the library. Only a single lamp illuminated the room. He closed the door, and for a moment, leaned on it as if borrowing strength. He pushed off, squaring his shoulders as if he were about to deliver a controversial speech to Parliament. "I know I've behaved like a boorish, unfeeling cad. You have every reason to despise me. I jumped to conclusions and treated you unfairly and with great discourtesy."

You treated Tristan discourteously, too, she wanted to say, but thought it better to leave him out of it for the moment.

Richard drew a breath and visibly stiffened his spine. "It's clear to me that you still have feelings for Tristan, but that's to be expected. Emotions cannot be as turned off as we might wish."

She wondered if he spoke of her feelings for Tristan or his love for Letitia.

"I've misjudged you," he continued. "I ask—no, I *beg* your forgiveness. I don't deserve it, but I ask it of you, anyway. I'm sorry. So very sorry. Will you forgive me?" Though he stood with all the commanding aura of a man accustomed to being obeyed, childlike vulnerability entered his eyes. He stood awaiting her words. His eyes narrowed as if in pain. "Please say something."

She moistened her lips. "You hurt me, Richard. Deeply. On more than one occasion."

He winced but kept silent.

Drawing courage from his willingness to let her speak, she continued. "While I confess I have not totally overcome my…feelings…for Tristan, I vow to you that I have been trying to be a good wife. That includes not shaming you. Ever."

He waited, regret and pain shadowing his expression.

Did she dare tell him that she feared this cycle of his mistrust would never end—that he'd always view her with suspicion? That each time he questioned her honor, he wounded her further and gave her greater reason to long for what she thought she'd once shared with Tristan? No. She must give Richard the chance to prove himself, just as she hoped for the chance to prove herself to him.

While she wrestled with her thoughts, he waited, his posture slipping into a much less commanding stance. He drummed his fingers on his thigh and swallowed, the pleading in his eyes growing to desperation.

She couldn't hurt him. She had to offer him her forgiveness. Touching his arm, she leaned in. "Of course I forgive you."

His relief rippled over her in heady waves. "Thank you. I will endeavor to be worthy of your forgiveness." He paused, still searching her eyes. "I sense a condition."

"No, there's no condition."

"What is it, then?"

She folded her arms as if to protect herself from further hurt as a great weariness crept over her. All the memories and emotions of being at her family's ancestral home, her conversation with Mary, dinner, and now her conversation with Richard all left her so tired she could hardly stand. "I will never give you reason to doubt me. I wish you would trust me."

He swallowed as if she'd asked for a piece of the moon. "I don't know if I can just yet. Trust is as fragile as a crystal goblet, and once it's broken, it's almost impossible to repair." He moistened his lips. "You haven't broken my trust; I only thought you did."

She held her breath, sensing a turning point in her tenuous relationship with Richard.

"I find it difficult to trust anyone, but I will try to trust you. As my wife, you deserve at least that."

Hurt at his unwillingness to give her his trust gave way as a new emotion elbowed in—compassion. Someone, or perhaps more than one person, had hurt him so deeply that he assumed everyone would. His lack of faith did not stem from his view of her character, or even his feelings for her. A vulnerable place inside him colored his perceptions.

The new understanding lightened her heart. A desire to wrap her arms around him overcame her so strongly that she had to fold her hands together. Otherwise, she might cause an unseemly display of affection such as what Father and Duchess often chided her for enacting.

She offered him a gentle smile and touched his arm. "Thank you. I vow I will do whatever I must to deserve such a gift."

He inclined his head. "Thank you." He hesitated. "Well, good night."

"Good night, Richard." She left him and went to bed, praying that they'd finally reached some kind of ground upon which to build a relationship.

Over the next few days, Duchess's health improved. They should return home, but Elizabeth couldn't remember when she'd enjoyed a summer at her family's county seat so much. She saw little of Duchess, and a great deal of her sisters. Moreover, the thought of the long trip that lay between them and home held little appeal. During the visit, the tension between her and Richard had eased. Perhaps it was their big talk, or perhaps Richard simply had fewer responsibilities that took his thoughts and his time, but he seemed genuinely relaxed. He and her father and brother-in-law spent time in one another's company and a friendly camaraderie clearly formed between them.

One evening, Duchess joined the family for dinner. Unfortunately, Father and Martindale had been called away on estate matters.

Before the second course arrived, Duchess aimed a poisonous barb at Elizabeth. "Your gown is beyond-the-pale, Elizabeth. Did you design that atrocity yourself or rely on some country bumpkin dressmaker to create it?"

Elizabeth flinched as if she'd been struck and stared at Duchess before quickly dropping her gaze onto her hands. Such a cutting remark made in front of so many others was overly cruel, even for her. "I-I made a few suggestions."

Duchess sniffed. "You really ought to leave fashion to those who are expert in that field. Trying to assert your own limited sense of style in such a clumsy attempt to win approval will only leave you open to further ridicule."

Elizabeth's face burned and she set down her fork, her appetite forgotten. "I'm not attempting to win approval," she ground out. "I know better than that."

"I think her gowns are lovely," Richard said.

Duchess wasn't finished. She had to twist the proverbial knife. "After the shameful way you began your marriage, you ought to keep quiet and focus on producing heirs. If you keep your head down and your mouth shut, by the time your children are old enough to attend school, rumor regarding your shame should have faded."

Would this never end? Anger lent Elizabeth courage and she met her stepmother's gaze boldly. "No one is still interested in our marriage, or its origin. All rumors have been put to rest and my neighbors have been very welcoming."

"How dare you speak to me with such impudence!" Duchess's face mottled red. "Hold your tongue."

Next to her, Joanna was breathing in rapid little gasps. She pressed a napkin to her mouth.

Instead of quailing at the familiar sign of Duchess in a rage, hot indignation burst over Elizabeth. "I'm my own lady now—"

"Remember your place," Duchess snapped.

"Madam," Richard's voice rumbled, "I'll thank you not to speak to my wife in such a manner."

Duchess's mouth dropped open.

"She's right," Richard said. "There have been no further whispers of scandal regarding Elizabeth or our marriage. The gossips have turned their discussion to Lord Byron's latest escapade. Elizabeth is a lovely and proper wife and I am blessed to have her." Richard raised Elizabeth's hand to his lips.

A shocked silence fell over everyone at the table. To her knowledge, no one had ever spoken so forcefully to Duchess.

Gratitude warmed Elizabeth, and tears sprang into her eyes. She looked down lest she reveal her emotion to her family. How kind of Richard to rise to her defense. How noble. How brave. His continued protectiveness must mean he cared, at least at some level.

"That Beau Brummell," Mary said. "Have you heard his latest?"

That prompted a discussion on one of the most fashionable and notorious men in England. Elizabeth sent Mary a silent expression of thanks.

Father joined them and Elizabeth breathed a sigh of relief. Duchess often toned down her poison in front of him. He greeted them all and made a point of nodding to Elizabeth, his mouth softening.

Mary's husband, Lord Brinton spoke. "Speaking of notorious men, I read that the authorities have a lead on that infamous and mysterious criminal, Mr. Black."

Father looked up from his meal. "Have they indeed? That is good news. I hope they shut down all his operations. If half of what I've heard about Mr. Black is true, he deserves to be hanged."

Lord Brinton glanced at Richard. "I'm intrigued by your theory that Mr. Black might be an alias. I wonder where this investigation will lead."

"Merely speculation," Richard said.

"Bow Street is heading up the investigation," Lord Brinton said. "I'm sure they'll uncover the truth."

Father cleared his voice and glanced meaningfully at Elizabeth and her sisters. "Perhaps this is a discussion for another time."

Elizabeth resisted the impulse to roll her eyes and made up her mind to read the paper to learn more.

"Of course, forgive me, ladies," said Lord Brinton.

Father said to Richard, "I regret I will not be able to join you hunting tomorrow, Lord Averston. I have received a writ of summons for a peer trial and must make preparations to return to London."

Richard's fork paused mid-air. "Peer trial?"

"It seems Lord Einsburgh has been arrested."

Elizabeth gasped. The idea of a lord being arrested seemed unbelievable.

Richard nodded. "I read about that in the paper."

Elizabeth made the mistake of glancing at Duchess. Their eyes met. Absolute cold fury poured out of the woman. Her lips curved into a cruel smile, the same expression she'd worn for years each time she'd dragged Elizabeth into her private parlor and punished her. For a moment, Elizabeth recoiled as bewilderment overcame her. Then she understood: Duchess planned to punish Elizabeth for the embarrassment of Richard's words of reprimand. All thought of Lord Einsburgh and a trial fled.

Elizabeth had found some confidence as Richard's countess. Yet that confidence trickled away at the thought of Duchess's retribution. Cold sickness overcame her and she could not eat another bite.

If only she had the courage to wrench that riding crop out of Duchess's hand and refuse to bend to her will. It didn't matter. Duchess would win. In the end, Duchess always won.

Chapter Thirty-Four

After a surprisingly delightful morning of hunting with his brothers-in-law, Richard walked into the house. He removed his hat and stripped off his riding gloves. As he passed Elizabeth in the hall, he halted at her expression. She looked as if she'd seen a ghost.

He touched her arm. "What is it?"

She dropped her gaze. "Nothing. Duchess wishes me to see her in her parlor."

"And?"

"It's nothing. She probably just wants to speak with me," she said faintly as she clasped trembling hands behind her back. "And have...tea."

The hackles on the back of his neck arose. "What are you not telling me?"

Visibly steeling herself, she shook her head without raising her gaze. "It's nothing.."

Concerned by her pallor and the tremor in her voice, he put an arm around her and began to lead her in the opposite direction. "You don't look well. Go lie down. You can speak with your mother another time."

She dug in her heels while a look of absolute terror overcame her face. "No. I must go now. She has summoned me. Putting it off will—er, I will go visit with her now, and lie down afterward. She is, after all, the reason we're here. I should at least visit with her when she wishes to see me."

A sickening suspicion overcame him. "I'll go with you."

She shrank away from him. "No, she wants to see me alone."

"I don't think that's wise."

"Please let me go; she's waiting."

He demanded, "What, exactly, are you expecting to find in her morning parlor?"

"Nothing. She merely wishes to have a word in private." She pushed at his chest, desperation lacing her voice. "You...you need to change. Please go." She wriggled out of his grasp.

"No." The commanding tones in his voice echoed in the corridor.

She flinched.

He softened his voice. "Why are you willing to go to her like a lamb to the slaughter?"

She turned away. "I'm not. We're simply going to have a conversation like two intelligent adults. Stop trying to act like a protective husband when we both know you're not."

Stung by her words, he recoiled. She strode away, her head high and her arms rigid at her side.

Very well. He deserved her anger. For the first two months of their marriage, he'd been neglectful and mistrustful. No longer. He refused to neglect her now when she needed him. Elizabeth did not deserve whatever the duchess had in store for her. If his wife wouldn't defend herself, he would.

Energy flowed through his veins in anticipation of a conflict with the duchess. Richard didn't care who she was or how much power their family wielded, if that woman thought she was going to hurt his wife, she had a lesson to learn.

Elizabeth disappeared into the library, closing the door behind her. He waited until he heard a door on the opposite side of the room open and close before entering the room. He found himself in an empty sitting room with a closed door on the far side. Richard crossed the chamber, listened at the door and pushed it open. It opened onto a sitting room. He spared a thought for English architects who designed so many of the older houses with rooms that opened onto rooms rather than having passageways that connected everything. Voices lead him to the next chamber.

The duchess's shrill tones seeped through the walls. "I will not be spoken to in such a manner! Now turn around."

"No. You will not treat me this way," came Elizabeth's voice. "I am not a frightened child you can bully any longer." Anger and terror laced her passionate words.

There was a thump as if a heavy object had been dropped.

"You are not so grown up as you suppose," the duchess snarled. "And I will not be defied."

Elizabeth let out a cry of alarm. All of Richard's protective instincts sprang into action. He burst through the room. Elizabeth and Duchess stood struggling to control a long, thin riding crop. Richard's heart nearly stopped.

They both froze, their gazes locked on Richard. With rage boiling through him, Richard reached Elizabeth's side in only a few strides. With all the loathing coursing through his body, he stared down the duchess who looked back at him with contempt.

Richard grabbed the riding crop. Elizabeth released her hold on it but the duchess continued to grip it. With a quick twist, Richard wrenched it out of her hand. He glowered at the duchess and pulled Elizabeth against his chest.

He stared at the duchess as rage and disbelief thundered through him. "You were going to hit her with this?"

The duchess didn't have the grace to look ashamed. She made a negligent wave. "I seldom draw blood. She's so wild, she needs correction."

"Correction?" Richard shouted. "How dare you!"

A calculating light glinted in her eyes. "She's not worth it, you know."

Richard drew himself up and poured venom into his voice. "Do not ever touch my wife again. In any manner. For any reason. Is that clear?"

The duchess made a sound of disgust. "Using a light hand on such a hoyden will only lead to your disgrace. She'll turn out just like her mother, the little tramp."

Elizabeth let out a gasp.

Richard stiffened. "What are you talking about? She's nothing like you—" He broke off as a new suspicion sprang into his mind.

After moving to a mirror, Duchess smoothed back her hair. "No, she's nothing like me. I have no doubt she'll be just like the woman who—"

Elizabeth broke in, "Please don't."

Turning away from the mirror, the duchess opened her eyes in mock surprise. "What? You haven't told him? My, you are full of secrets." She smiled like a cat eying a wounded bird.

All of a sudden, everything made sense. Elizabeth often called her mother Duchess instead of Mother, especially in unguarded moments, and the duchess obviously singled out Elizabeth for abuse, criticism, and ridicule.

Richard gently turned Elizabeth around to face him and peered into her misery-filled face. "She's not your mother, is she?"

Hanging her head, Elizabeth let out a ragged exhale and shook her head.

"No," Duchess said triumphantly. "Her true mother was a whore."

Elizabeth visibly wilted. Keeping his hands on her shoulders, Richard drew her in. She stiffened and turned her head away.

"I'm sorry," she whispered. "I should have told you, but I just couldn't."

Richard put a hand under her cheek and raised her face so he could see her expression. "How did you come to be the legal daughter of a duke?"

Her lower lip trembled and she wouldn't look him in the eye.

Before she spoke, the duchess broke in, "She is the child of my husband's mistress. She died a few days after childbirth, fortunately. The duke felt duty-bound to bring home and raise their spawn. He insisted that the world believe she was our daughter. But no birth certificate will change her true parentage."

Richard had never been tempted to strike a woman in all his life. Until now. Turning a venomous glare at the duchess, he snarled. "You sicken me."

With an arm still around Elizabeth, Richard took her out of the room and closed the door. After reaching the outer room, he turned and enfolded her in his arms. "It doesn't matter, Elizabeth."

She let out a cross between a laugh and a sob.

From inside the room where the duchess remained, the sound of breaking glass shattered the silence. Heartsick Elizabeth had been the target of such wrath, he held her and rested his cheek on the top of her head. "It makes no difference to me who your mother was, Elizabeth. Who you are now is all that matters."

Her shoulders shook and she sobbed.

He added, "I very much regret that you've had to grow up with that."

Still silent, she burrowed into his neckcloth. The strength of the protectiveness coursing through him made him almost believe he could overcome anything, even gravity. He vowed always to keep her safe and to treat her as she deserved.

If only he'd proven himself a trustworthy confidant sooner, she might have come to him with her secrets, her fears.

He ran a hand over her hair. "When you said you were feeling poorly and planned to take a tray in your room, you anticipated being injured?"

She let out a sound of distress. "I'd planned to stand up to her, but I feared she'd simply overpower me, or that I lacked the courage to try when the time came."

"I wish I'd met and married you sooner." Although he would have needed to find her as a child in order to have spared her growing up with such hatred and violence.

Not trusting himself to speak, he brushed his fingers across her cheek. Eventually her shaking ceased, yet she remained in his arms as if she had nowhere else she'd rather be. Her heart beat against his chest while her scent curled around him, and the softness of her body felt so very right.

Richard's fierce protectiveness gentled into something warm and tender. He kissed the top of Elizabeth's head.

She looked up at him with such a look of adoration that a lump formed in his throat. Raising up on tiptoe, she kissed his cheek. "Thank you."

He cleared his throat. "'Tis merely my duty, my little bride."

He skimmed one hand across her back, immeasurably grateful that he'd arrived in time to prevent her from suffering violence today. She shivered and made a tiny sound of pleasure. Wishing he could find a place of privacy, he tamped his desires and opened the outer door for her, allowing her to pass through ahead of him. She slipped her hand into his. Everything inside him warmed.

Richard glanced at her. "If you have no objection, I'd like to return home. Immediately."

"I have no objection."

"Excellent. Can you leave within the hour?"

"Of course. But are you sure you wish to begin so late in the day? It's almost time for luncheon."

"I think it's best to remove you from the duchess's presence as soon as possible. We'll stop this evening at a posting inn."

Her lower lip quivered and she squeezed his hand. "You do care."

"Of course I care." His face heated in shame that she'd seemed surprised. "I'm sorry I haven't shown you."

Vowing to make sure she understood how much she'd grown to mean to him, he escorted her to her room and rang for her maid. The moment Maggie entered, he barked out commands for their imminent departure ending with, "If the duchess comes near Lady Averston, send for me immediately."

Maggie bobbed a curtsy. "Yes, milord."

An hour later, they said their goodbyes, a somewhat tearful and hastily whispered conversation occurred between Mary and Elizabeth, and then they were off. The duchess made no appearance but the others appeared perplexed by their sudden departure.

As they climbed inside their carriage, a rider appeared. "I have a message for Lord Averston."

Richard halted. "I am he."

"It's marked urgent, my lord. I went to your estate, and they sent me here."

"You must have been riding for days." Richard paid the messenger, broke the seal, and read. He looked up at Elizabeth. "It's a writ of summons. I'm to go to London for a parliamentary trial. We must make all haste. This message is nearly a week old and I'm to report by Tuesday next. I had been wondering why I hadn't received one when the duke had." He drummed his fingers on his thigh. "We'll go home first since it's not far out of the way. Then I will on to London from there."

Richard glanced at Elizabeth, musing over the wisdom of leaving her alone at home. London was miserable in the summer, but he hated to leave her behind now when their relationship had turned a corner. As the coach rolled along, Elizabeth smiled almost shyly at him. Then as if catching herself, she looked out the window.

He took one of her hands. Her fingers curled around his, a welcoming response. For a moment, he sat enjoying the simple contact. If only they could make this trip pleasurable instead of rushed.

"I feel I must apologize in advance for the journey," Richard said. "I had meant to enjoy the ride and stop for food and lodgings. I fear we must travel with as much haste as possible."

"I understand." Her hands tightened around his. After a moment, she spoke. "I can't tell you how relieved I am that you aren't upset about the truth of my birth."

He lifted her hand to his lips and kissed it. "Not one whit. Who was she? Do you know anything about her?"

"Not much, just that she was a beautiful, auburn-haired actress before my father became her protector, and that he loved her so much that he almost married her instead of Duchess."

Richard nodded. Such an act would have been an affront to the duke's family, but with his own burgeoning feelings for Elizabeth, he could understand the temptation to fly in the face of society's strictures.

Her expression turned wistful. "I also know that she died shortly after childbirth. About that time, Duchess gave birth to a stillborn. My mother had no family, no one to care for me, so Father took me home and presented me to the world as his legitimate child."

"And the duchess hated you for it."

Elizabeth shrugged. "At least I had a home with food and clothing, and I got an education. If he hadn't taken me home, who knows what might have happened to me. I might have died as a baby. I'm grateful to him."

Growing admiration for this woman warmed him all over. How could he have doubted such a pure soul?

As the afternoon waned, the conversation did, too. Yet, a more comfortable silence than they had ever known prevailed. She leaned back and stretched out her legs but after a few minutes, her head nodded. Smiling, he guided her head to his shoulder. She snuggled in against him. Peace and wellbeing stole over him. He dared hope that with a little luck, they just might find a measure of happiness together after all.

Chapter Thirty-Five

The carriage hit a bump, waking Elizabeth. Outside the windows, sunset spread a golden glow over the landscape. Stretching, she glanced at Richard sketching in a notebook.

She yawned and sat up. "What are you drawing?"

A corner of his mouth lifted. "A cottage we passed by a few miles ago."

She admired his detailed sketch of a stone cottage with a fence almost bending under the weight of wild roses intertwined in it. The tone of the drawing seemed peaceful rather than the lonely sketches he'd drawn of the knights. "You have a remarkable talent."

He shrugged. "Father thought it a great waste of time, but Mother enjoyed my sketches. I hope I've improved since then."

"You seldom speak of your parents. I understand you lost them both at a young age."

He paused. "My mother left us when I was eleven."

"How did she die?"

"She didn't die. Not then. She left." He gripped the pencil with white fingers.

Elizabeth studied his face. Intuition whispered that she hovered on the edge of an important discovery. "Where did she go?"

He said nothing for so long that she thought he'd decided not to tell her. Finally, he drew a breath. "She and my father had problems. They quarreled. Almost constantly. When they weren't fighting, they ignored one another. Then one day a strange man came to the house while Father was away. He paid her many calls over the next few months."

Realization overcame Elizabeth. "She was having an a*ffair de coeur*?"

His jaw tensed and his lips pressed together in a thin line. "I'll never forget the day she came to my nursery and told me I was a good boy and that she was proud of me. She said I should always strive to uphold the family honor and to be just like Father. She kissed me. Then she left. She never came back."

Elizabeth touched his hand, silently weeping for the abandoned child. *'Frailty, thy name is woman'* she silently recited from Shakespeare. No wonder Richard kept expecting her to betray him. He probably assumed every woman had a faithless heart. Or perhaps, like her, he felt deep in his heart that he was undeserving of love and faithfulness. Of course, she'd been unfaithful in her heart when she continued pining for Tristan even after she'd married Richard.

"I'm sorry, Richard. I'm so very sorry."

"Father took it well, never showed any outward signs of grief. Nonetheless, he never smiled after that. He let go most of the staff and closed up all but a few rooms in the house."

"He must have been heartsick." The old earl's grief must have been terrible for a child to witness.

He stared at the carriage wall. "The gossip columnists learned somehow and had a heyday with it. They badgered him whenever he left the house. He finally sent word that he was too ill to sit at the House of Lords. He sequestered himself in our county seat and never visited any of the other properties. Tristan and I bore the brunt of it in school." His white-lipped expression revealed to Elizabeth what he could not tell her.

She gave his hand a gentle squeeze.

His fingers curled around hers. "A year later, we received word she'd been in a fatal accident on the continent."

"Oh, how terrible."

"She was already dead to us," he said flatly, but pain shadowed his eyes and his hand gripped hers as if it alone prevented him from a fall.

"Then your father died?"

"When I was eighteen."

"You were young to assume the role of earl."

"I'd already been doing it for the last few years. Father had begun turning more and more of the affairs of all the estates to me, and I'd been trying all my life to keep Tristan out of trouble."

She smiled sadly. "You love him well."

Some of the tension left his brow and his mouth pulled up on one side. "He always knows how to make me smile. He reminds me not to take myself too seriously."

"You are a good and honorable man, Richard Barrett, twelfth Earl of Averston."

He huffed a wry chuckle. "I try to give that impression."

"You succeed." She hoped he heard the sincerity in her words.

As much as she still missed Tristan's infectious charm, Richard possessed admirable strength, his own moments of charm—less obvious and less gregarious, but he was, nevertheless, an amazing man in his own way. He'd even stood up to Duchess in a manner Tristan probably never would have. If only he'd let his brother back into his life. Brothers needed each other.

She hesitated. "May I ask something of you?"

"Anything."

She knew she trod on dangerous ground, but had to speak her thoughts. "When you get to London, won't you please call upon Tristan? You need to make peace with your brother."

He let his breath out in a long exhale. "I plan to. I wrote to him but have not received word back. After the way I threw him out in the middle of the night, without even telling him his crime—much less giving him a chance to defend himself—he will be slow to forgive. I wouldn't blame him if he refused to ever speak with me."

"I am confident you will make amends someday."

Richard nodded, his posture resigned.

Darkness fell, and Elizabeth rested her head on Richard's shoulder. He put an arm around her. Being nestled in his arms created a sense of wellbeing.

"Elizabeth." He paused, growing solemn. "If you feel threatened by anyone, at any time, you must tell me. Do you understand? I cannot protect you if I do not know you are in danger."

She drew a shuddering breath and nodded.

"Is there anything else you wish to tell me? Anyone else who frightens you?"

"No." She drew a breath. "Except you when you accused me of being with Tristan at the ball. I was frightened then."

He winced. "Oh, sweet Elizabeth! Will you ever forgive me?"

She studied her hands. "You hurt me, Richard."

"I was wrong to make assumptions. I should have asked you about it, given you the opportunity to explain. Instead, I passed judgment on you both. I'm so sorry."

She watched his expression, finding sincerity and regret etched in every line of his face. "I cannot change the feelings I had for Tristan, nor can I vow that I have purged them entirely from my heart—but I'm trying. I promise I will never dishonor you." She sighed. "I wish I could convince you of that."

He tightened his arm around her shoulder. "I will try to be fair, and not always look for evidence of your potential to become the same kind of wife my mother was to my father." He raised her hand to his lips and kissed it. "In time, I am certain I can give you my complete trust. In time, I hope to earn your forgiveness."

She smiled. "I have already forgiven you, Richard."

For now that was enough.

As the carriage bumped along the road, Richard touched Elizabeth's smooth cheek, traced his fingers over her mouth and lifted her chin. She willingly moved her head under his touch, bringing her lips upward toward him. He leaned in and brushed his lips over hers. Tingles spread across his mouth at the simple touch and warmed his whole being. He kissed her more fully and the tingles intensified. Her lips moved with his, so soft, so willing.

With a groan, he pressed his mouth more firmly

against hers, tugging, pulling, tasting. Her mouth was warm and sweet as she responded with more eagerness than skill. A small part of his brain registered her inexperience. A surge of triumph raced through him at the sign that she had not been kissed often. He claimed her lips again. She rested a hand on his chest, its heat soaking through his clothes. Pulling her in closer, he kissed her over and over, deepening the connection as she opened to him.

She learned the art of kissing before long and soon matched him in ardor. Pressing herself against him, she slipped her hands behind his neck as her mouth devoured him as hungrily as he devoured her. His control slipped. The urge to lay her down and take her in the carriage nearly overwhelmed him.

A carriage was no place to seduce a lady, least of all his new bride. Her first time should be in her marriage bed, surrounded by candles. He must proceed slowly. But oh, she was soft and desirable. And so willing. Enthusiastic, even. Shivering as lust battered his control, he ordered his hands to remain on her back rather than explore the curves tempting him, and simply kissed her. He moved his mouth to her forehead and her nose. She tilted her head back, lifting her lush mouth toward him. With her moist, pink lips and flushed cheeks, she looked blatantly desirable. He captured her lips once more, taking his time to taste their sweetness, inhale her subtle scent of violets and roses and that musky sweet tang of angelica, and drinking in her softness.

Her chest heaved with each breath she took. Satisfaction curled inside Richard. She wanted him. She was simply too naïve to recognize her passion. Again, relief that she was innocent flowed over him like cool water. An inner longing arose, a longing which he'd always denied, a longing to love and be loved. She would be the one to meet that longing, to give and receive as he'd always dreamed. He'd lived his whole life to reach this moment. After their lips parted, he pulled her against him. She nestled into his embrace. An utter sense of peace crept over him. He belonged to Elizabeth. Had always belonged to her. As she belonged to him.

Was this love?

For once, he had the sense not to fight it and instead surrendered his heart to her.

Chapter Thirty-Six

Richard and Elizabeth arrived home early in the evening the following day, exhausted from the trip. Richard gave orders to prepare to depart for London and began making arrangements. Too tired to be of assistance, Elizabeth ate a hasty meal and went to bed. As she sank into the feather mattress, she let out a sigh. How delicious to lie in a comfortable, motionless bed instead of the moving carriage. Yet, she missed Richard's presence.

As she dozed off, she thought she heard him enter the room, but by the time she roused herself enough to open her eyes, no one was there. Perhaps her wistful thinking had taken over her imagination.

The following morning, Richard joined her for breakfast. She beamed at him in elation at this unprecedented event. "Good morning."

He kissed her cheek. "Good morning. Did you sleep well?"

"My bed is decidedly more comfortable than the carriage for sleeping." Feeling almost flirtatious, she glanced at him through her lashes. "Although your shoulder was very nice as well. Perhaps you'll lend it to me again in the near future."

He lifted a brow and turned to her. "As you wish, my lady. I was rather hoping you might wish for my...er, shoulder last night after we arrived home.

However, you seemed rather fatigued."

"I admit I was extremely sleepy." The words *but I wanted you anyway* sprang to her lips but her courage failed her and she couldn't form the words. Surely it wasn't a lady's place to make such overt suggestions, even to her husband.

They spoke of unimportant matters in an easy, natural manner that warmed Elizabeth and gave her hope that they'd at last reached a comfortable friendship. Perhaps, love would follow. She clung to that hope.

After finishing his meal, Richard arose. "I'd best catch up on my correspondence before I depart."

"When shall you leave?"

"By noon, if possible."

She nodded, disappointed that he'd be going so soon. After an hour of alternating between trying to stay out of the way and hoping to be helpful, she gave in to her desire to be with him and she peeked into his study where he sat going through an assortment of papers.

"May I help?"

His teeth flashed. "Please. I have been corresponding with the applicant for a secretary. He will meet me in London."

"I hope you find someone to suit. Until then, I can assist you if you wish."

"I welcome your aid."

He handed her a stack and she sorted the papers as she had once before. They worked side by side, not speaking, except for her to receive clarification on a paper or him to ask her to pen a reply on some estate matters, but the silence enfolded them in comfort.

As they had luncheon together, Richard received a

Donna Hatch

note from his steward. As he read, he pursed his lips. "It appears I will have to delay my trip. I must attend to a matter on the estate."

She smiled. "That gives me more time with you before you must leave."

He lowered the note, his dark eyes looking her over, all solemnity except for a tiny smile tugged at one corner of his mouth. "Does that please you, my lady?"

"Well, the fairy queen cancelled tea with me, so I suppose you'll do for a substitute."

He chuckled, kissed her cheek, and rose. "In that case, I'll try not to be too long."

During his absence, she spent time in the gardens. Her own little garden had been lovingly tended in her absence. As she stood admiring it, almost wishing it needed her care, a footman appeared.

"Milady, are you at home to a Miss Wentworth?"

Elizabeth swallowed against a dry mouth. Memories arose of how she had come between lovers, of how Richard may forever compare Elizabeth to Leticia and find her lacking. That kiss in the garden. Still, Leticia had been kind when she could have been bitter and angry. Elizabeth owed it to Leticia to receive her graciously when she called.

Elizabeth smoothed a shaking palm over her hair, wishing she could as easily smooth the knots in her stomach. "Please show her to the front parlor and bring the tea service and cakes."

Elizabeth squared her shoulders and donned a plum-colored velvet spencer to dress up her simple white muslin frock. Pushing back her doubts, Elizabeth drew a breath and entered the parlor. "Miss Wentworth, how lovely to see you."

294

Leticia Wentworth sat composed, her hands folded, the picture of absolutely serenity. She arose and took Elizabeth by the hands. "Please call me Leticia."

"How kind of you to visit."

"You look absolutely radiant, and what stunning gowns you wear. I simply must have the name of your modiste."

"You're very kind. I used Madame Prideaux."

"No! Then they must be your designs."

"I made a few suggestions."

As they sipped tea and sampled scones and biscuits, talking about innocuous village news, Elizabeth's qualms quieted. Perhaps Leticia could not help loving Richard any more than Elizabeth could help her own feelings for Tristan…although the thought of Tristan no longer sent her pulse pounding. Richard consumed her thoughts and a great deal of her heart. She only wished she could claim all of his heart. At least he'd vowed to try to trust her.

Leticia leaned forward. "I wanted to invite you to our sewing group. We meet at my home every Wednesday at noon for luncheon. Some of us sew, but many of us prefer to visit. Often we discuss books we've read. Won't you join us?"

"Thank you, I would be delighted. I do love to read, but I'm afraid my sewing isn't much to recommend me." A fault that had earned her many of Duchess's beatings. Elizabeth shivered and pushed away the thought.

Leticia's attention focused on something behind Elizabeth's shoulder. Her smile faded and she seemed to have trouble breathing.

Elizabeth turned her head to see what had captured

her attention. Richard stood in the doorway, his gaze locked with Leticia's.

Elizabeth's heartbeat ground to a halt.

Richard recovered first. "Forgive me for interrupting. Good afternoon, Miss Wentworth."

Leticia's voice grew faint. "Good afternoon, Lord Averston."

The formality of their speech proved they still held feelings for one another. Were they denying them, or trying to put on a show for her?

Richard turned to Elizabeth. "I didn't realize you still had a guest. When you've finished, please see me in my study."

Only able to manage a whisper, Elizabeth said, "Of course."

With a brief incline of his head, Richard said, "Lovely to see you, Miss Wentworth. Please pay my respects to your parents."

Leticia offered a wobbly smile. "Of course."

With a slight bow to them both, he left.

Her mouth dry, Elizabeth watched Leticia as she shuddered in a breath. Then, gathering herself, she raised her chin. The memory of Leticia kissing Richard hit Elizabeth with the force of a hurricane.

Leticia turned tortured eyes on Elizabeth. As she probably witnessed Elizabeth's distress, her eyes widened in clear understanding and she held up a hand. "Forgive me, I did not expect to see him. I vow I have no designs upon Richard."

"None?" She spoke more harshly than she intended but really, how could she believe a woman who'd kissed another woman's husband?

Leticia shook her head, her shoulders slumping. "I

loved him as a child, but I have driven out all those childish feelings and I only have the kindest regard for you both." She spoke with the conviction of a woman who wanted desperately to believe her own words.

Elizabeth studied her, trying to believe her but still fearful to hope.

Leaning forward in her seat, Leticia looked her in the eye, her expression earnest. "Truly, I bear you no ill will. Seeing you both so well has been good for my soul. You belong together and I wish you every happiness."

"Thank you," Elizabeth managed.

"I am certain that if I were in your position, I'd worry about my husband's fidelity. I assure you, however, I have never been with him in an improper way." She blushed. "I did kiss his cheek in a sort of farewell at your ball, but I vow that was the only time I have ever touched him. I will never touch him in the future at all. Ever."

Elizabeth stared. The cheek? Leticia expected Elizabeth to believe the kiss she'd witnessed had only been on the cheek? As she reviewed in her memory the exact details of that night, she had to admit, taking into account the darkness and the distance, the kiss might have been on his cheek rather than his lips. Perhaps she was as guilty at jumping to conclusions as she'd accused Richard of doing.

Leticia's voice broke into Elizabeth's thoughts. "I truly wish you both every happiness."

Elizabeth watched her with dreadful hope. "Thank you, Leticia. Your grace is to be commended, and—"

Leticia held up her hand. "Please. Say nothing further. I am trying very hard to do and say everything that I ought. The truth is, there were days when I thought terrible things about you, especially in the beginning. For that, I am sorry. I will try to be a good friend to you both and stop wishing for what might have been. But do not make the mistake of thinking I am some kind of saint because I am far from it."

Tears of sympathy welled up in Elizabeth's eyes. "I wish…"

"I do, as well. You are a better match for him, however. At least, that's what I keep telling myself. Maybe someday I'll believe it." Leticia's voice grew hoarse. She stood, blinking quickly and pulling on her gloves. "Thank you for a lovely afternoon. And I hope you'll join our sewing circle."

Elizabeth arose on unsteady legs. "Thank you for calling."

They parted and Elizabeth sank back on the settee. Leticia was one of the kindest most gracious and lovely ladies of Elizabeth's acquaintance. Richard would be a fool not to love her. He probably compared Elizabeth to Leticia. He was just too much a gentleman to show it. At least there was no longer any look of disapproval in his eyes.

After seeing Leticia again, no doubt his regard for her would be awakened. Then he would find Elizabeth a poor substitute.

Chapter Thirty-Seven

Leaning one shoulder against the window of the upper story, Richard watched Leticia's carriage disappear down the drive. Seeing her again had been...odd. Unexpected.

He had dreaded facing her again—had feared he would remember all the reasons he'd decided to pursue a betrothal with her in the first place, and that all those reasons would awaken old feelings, thus eclipsing his growing affection for Elizabeth.

Instead, he'd felt almost nothing. Surprise. A moment of discomfort. Then, except for a bit of awkwardness, only comfortable friendship stirred in his heart, mingled with a touch of sadness that she'd been hurt by events out of her control.

Perhaps he'd never really loved Leticia—not the kind of adult love one should have for a woman one hopes to wed. If someone had asked him a few months ago, he would have declared he'd loved Leticia. Yet in retrospect, his love had been brotherly. He remembered her as the saucy little girl who always seemed to have skinned knees and who tried to bridge the gap between wanting to swim in the river with the boys, and ride side saddle like a demure young lady. She'd been a friend. He'd never, not even when he'd planned to marry her, imagined her as a lover. She'd been comfortable. Familiar. Safe. He'd always trusted her.

He'd never doubted her ability for monogamy, due in part that she, unlike every other woman under the age of a hundred, had never fallen for Tristan's wild and rakish charm. Or abandoned her family.

That was it, then; he'd never actually loved Leticia. More importantly, he was happy with Elizabeth. His wife stirred in him a depth of tenderness he'd never experienced.

With an unexpected peace, he returned to his work, ordering the modifications his steward had recommended, listening for Elizabeth's lively step, and anticipating taking her into his arms.

He sent a footman with a message for Elizabeth, informing her he would not depart for London until the morrow, hoping she'd appear. He received no response.

He strode to his chambers and stripped off his cravat in preparation to change into his evening attire for dinner, passing Elizabeth's opened door. He paused, backed up, and looked in. Elizabeth sat wearing a dressing gown and brushing her hair, staring straight ahead as if lost in thought.

He paused at the entrance to her room. "Did you enjoy your visit with Miss Wentworth?"

"Leticia," she corrected in an subdued voice. "She asked me to call her by her Christian name."

"Ah, good. Glad to see you getting along so famously with her."

She stopped moving, simply gripped her hairbrush with white fingers.

Richard leaned against the doorframe. "You aren't getting dressed for dinner." Then he winced. Stating the obvious was never a brilliant way to begin a conversation.

"No."

He moved to stand behind her and touched her shoulder. "What is it?"

She tensed under his hand. "I'm not feeling well. I believe I'll take a tray and go to bed early."

He touched her forehead but it was cool. "Headache?"

She hesitated briefly. "Yes."

Perplexed, he waited, but she volunteered nothing. "Elizabeth, is something amiss?"

"No, I merely have the headache and I wish to retire early."

What the devil was wrong? At luncheon, everything seemed perfect.

She arose, and after drawing her dressing robe more tightly about her, folded her arms. "Good night."

Suspicion trickled through his mind. "Elizabeth, are you overset by Leticia's visit?"

She stared down at the floor. "Why do you ask?"

"Did she say something to upset you?"

"No…" She pressed her lips together and lifted one shoulder in a shrug.

He placed a hand on each of her shoulders and turned her so she faced him. "Did I give you the impression that I desire her over you?"

She flinched. Her lower lip quivered. So, at last the truth. "When I saw you in the garden during our ball, it looked to me…" She trailed off, moistened her lips, and drew a breath as if steeling herself. "…as if you and she were kissing…on the lips."

He recoiled. "No. No, not at all. She kissed my cheek. That is all."

She fixed her gaze upon him, her expression two

301

parts hope and one part hurt. "She told me that today. I can't help wondering if you wish you'd married her instead of me."

He brushed a finger across her cheek. "No. I don't love Leticia. And I never kissed her."

She searched his face, her eyes filled with longing and fear and a vulnerability that chipped away a little more at that now-crumbling wall he'd built around his heart.

Taking a step closer, he cupped her cheek. "I don't wish I'd married her instead of you."

She let out a half breath, half sob. "You were all but betrothed."

"Yes, but not because I was in love with her—I know that now. When I see her, I feel nothing beyond friendship. I've known her all my life. I never loved her the way a husband should love his wife."

Fearful hope brightened her eyes but a glimmer of doubt remained. How else to convince her? He remembered the stories of King Arthur's knights. "I never loved her the way Prince Erec loved Enid, or the way Lancelot loved Guinevere."

A tiny smile lifted the corners of her lush mouth, that tempting, lovely mouth. He bent his head to kiss her, to show her just how much she'd grown to mean to him. She kissed him hesitantly at first, but with increasing passion.

A servant's voice broke through the tide of desire washing over him. "My lord. A rather large box has just been delivered." Annoyed, Richard lifted his head to bark a sharp *go away* but he'd left the door open, so he had no reason to snap at the servant.

Then the servant's words sank in. A large box? Ah.

"Excellent." He smiled at Elizabeth and smoothed her hair away from your face. "Something has arrived for you."

He took her by the hand and led her out of the room. When they arrived in the main hall, Elizabeth let out a squeal of delight. The box must have given itself away. It had to be either a harp or a very large coffin. Richard's chest swelled at the sheer happiness in her eyes.

As they pried the boards off, revealing a case, she squeaked little sounds of joy, her smile brighter than fireworks. Working together, they opened the case revealing a gleaming mahogany harp nestled in a thick bed of straw. Richly carved garland streamers of leaves and flowers twisted around the column all the way to the base. The soundboard had been painted to match the column, generously touched with gold paint. From the graceful curve of the top where the strings wound around pegs, to the claw feet, the instrument was exquisite. The rapture in Elizabeth's expression was more exquisite, still.

She plucked a few strings. They were badly out of tune, even to Richard's untrained ear, but she smiled as if they were melodious. With her eyes shining, she practically leaped toward him. Then, as if checking herself, she halted, rose up on tiptoe, and kissed his cheek. He wished she'd thrown her arms around him. But her initiation of contact encouraged him.

"Thank you, Richard. Thank you so much." She clasped her hands together.

Well worth the price, indeed.

Chapter Thirty-Eight

Very early the next morning, Elizabeth fairly raced to the music room. She half expected the harp to have been the figment of a dream. There it stood as if it waited for her. She caressed the graceful curve, the carvings on the column.

Richard's gift had been unexpected and very generous. Why would he spend so much money, and go to so much trouble to buy her a harp, and not give her the wedding rubies? Did he mean it as a friendship gesture, but wasn't certain he was willing to accept her as his wife?

The significance seemed almost cruel. Still, the harp was a wonderful gift, and she planned to enjoy every minute of it. Besides, Richard's kisses had grown more frequent, and increasingly filled with tenderness and passion. His declaration that he'd never loved Leticia gave her hope that they'd find true happiness together.

After laboriously tuning it with fingers sore from last night's playing, she sat and plucked out a melody. Moments later, Mrs. Brown's voice boomed through the house, penetrating the dulcet harp tones. Irritated, Elizabeth growled. She should have closed the door in the music room so she could enjoy her music in peace. She'd spent nearly half an hour tuning the harp and since it was new, its strings wouldn't hold their pitch for long. She'd have to retune the harp all over again when she returned.

"Janey! Answer me!" Mrs. Brown's voice intruded again.

Alarmed that the silent little 'tween stairs maid was being bullied, Elizabeth settled her harp on its feet and arose.

She found Mrs. Brown in the landing of the servant's stairs wagging her finger at Janey. "Speak up. What do you know?"

Wide-eyed with fear, the mute child shrank from the housekeeper.

Elizabeth flew to the child's defense. "Mrs. Brown, leave off. You know she cannot speak."

With a growl of impatience, Mrs. Brown waved her hand. "She's just stubborn and uncooperative. The case of silver is missing and she knows where it is but she won't tell me."

Elizabeth positioned her body between the housekeeper and the quivering child. "You have no idea what she's gone through or the abuse she's endured. Have a little compassion. I told you when I first brought her here that you were to treat her with extra kindness."

The housekeeper folded her arms. "Your compassion, madam, has led to two guests being robbed and now the silver stolen."

Elizabeth drew herself up. "You are in danger of insubordination."

Mrs. Brown sneered. "It's clear you have no authority here. I'll not stand by while shameful creatures, including the one who calls herself lady of the house, bring ruin to the family."

"Mrs. Brown," Richard's voice carried across the

corridor. "You have been a trusted member of this household since before my birth. It would grieve me to dismiss you for being impudent to my countess."

Mrs. Brown paled. She looked first to Richard, then to Elizabeth, her mouth working a moment. Then, "My apologies, my lord. My lady. When I discovered the silver missing, I became distressed. Forgive me. I should not have forgotten myself."

Elizabeth hoped her gratitude to Richard showed as she looked at him. With all the chivalry of a knight of old, he'd restored her position of the lady of the house in Mrs. Brown's eyes, and in the eyes of all the servants. Richard nodded to the housekeeper. Elizabeth held a hand out to Janey, who slipped her small hand into Elizabeth's.

Hoping resentment for the woman's disrespect didn't color her voice or show on her expression, she asked Mrs. Brown, "What makes you think Janey knows where it is?"

"She was running out of the room when I entered and found it missing."

Elizabeth frowned. "She couldn't have taken it. You and Handley are the only ones with the keys to the butlery where the silver is kept."

"They must have picked the lock then, because it's gone."

Elizabeth crouched to meet the child's gaze. "Do you know where the silver is?"

Janey nodded.

"Will you show me?"

Again a nod. Janey led Elizabeth, Richard, and Mrs. Brown to the kitchen where two footmen, trading jests and stories, busily polished the silver. At the sight of their lord and lady, they leaped to their feet.

Mrs. Brown cleared her throat. "Oh, of course. My apologies." She turned on her heel and strode away.

Elizabeth wasn't sure if the apology was directed at Richard, Janey, or her. She nodded to the footmen. "Carry on." She looked down at Janey. "A story tonight?"

The child nodded, almost smiled, then slipped away.

Richard raised a brow in amusement. "Are you still reading to her?"

"A few nights a week. I'm teaching her to read, too. I think. She doesn't repeat anything, of course, but she seems very interested."

Richard chuckled. "A 'tween stairs maid who reads." He shook his head in amusement.

"The ability to read will be of great benefit to her."

"Of course. By the way, my departure has been delayed another day."

"Will that put you too late in London?"

"No, merely give me less time to rest before I must report in." His gaze slid to hers and something deeper than his words settled in there.

They walked side-by-side back to the morning parlor. "How long will you be gone?" she asked.

"One never knows with these things."

She nodded, her lips compressing, her heart growing empty at the thought of him leaving her behind for possibly weeks.

He drummed his fingers on his thigh in a sign she'd learned to recognize as unease. "You could accompany me if you wish."

She lifted her gaze to his. "You would have me go

with you?"

His mouth quirked. "I know London is terrible this time of year, but the shops are always open, and there's the theater and the opera and the museums—"

"I'd love to," she interjected in a breathless voice.

He paused. "In truth?"

"More than anything, I wish to go with you."

He chuckled. "Then by all means tell your maid to pack, Countess."

Smiling, she hurried to instruct Maggie to pack. Tension she hadn't realized she'd been carrying loosened. If only he'd totally accept her as his wife.

Chapter Thirty-Nine

The rest of the day, Elizabeth prepared for their trip to London, packing for every possible occasion.

Richard checked on her twice. The second time, he laughed. "My dear. Should some event arise for which you haven't brought proper attire, we will pay a call at the modiste and have her rush an order."

She smiled. "Very well. I'd like to bring the harp."

"It is, at this moment, being packed and crated with utmost care." He winked and left her and Maggie to the packing.

How thoughtful he was!

Mrs. Brown came to Elizabeth. "My lady, I request that the new staff from Mrs. Goodfellow's house come with us to London."

Surprised both by her tone of respect and her request, Elizabeth paused. "You want to bring them?"

"Since I am to accompany you to London, there will be no one here to keep any eye on them."

Elizabeth wondered if the new servants would ever earn Mrs. Brown's trust. Wearily, she nodded. "Very well, since there's only a skeleton staff in Averston House in London this time of year, you may bring whomever you see fit."

Mrs. Brown bowed stiffly. "Thank you, my lady."

The following morning, as they were about to leave, Elizabeth noticed Janey hovering in the far side of the great hall. Something about her posture caught Elizabeth's attention. She went to the child. Janey looked up at her with tears shimmering in her eyes.

"Janey, dear what is it? Has someone been unkind to you?"

The girl shook her head and reached out to grab the hem of Elizabeth's traveling gown, while Elizabeth wracked her brain to figure out what had upset the child.

"Are you upset that I'm leaving?"

Janey nodded, then buried her face in Elizabeth's skirts.

With a hurried glance over her shoulder at the child's unseemly behavior, Elizabeth crouched to meet the girl's eyes. "Do you wish to go with us?"

Richard appeared at her side and went down on a knee. Janey eyed him with uncertainty. Richard's tone and expression exuded gentleness. "Will you come with us to London for a few days? No one places coal in my grate as quietly as you."

Janey blinked and for a long moment made no reaction, then she nodded.

"Very well," he said. "Pack your things and you can ride in the carriage with the other servants. I'll instruct them to wait for you."

Janey let out a tiny gasp of pleasure, then turned and dashed up the servants' staircase.

Elizabeth turned to him with a smile. "You are a good man."

Chuckling, he tapped her nose. "I must come up with more ways to win your approval."

Elizabeth smiled, hoping she'd begun to gain *his* approval.

After an uneventful trip with easy conversation and comfortable silences, not to mention Richard's sketchbook filled with peaceful drawings, they arrived in London. The sweltering heat only thickened the stench of soot and sewers, but the gardens surrounding Averston House in Mayfair helped clear the air inside.

Elizabeth busied herself with setting the household to order, reveling in her role as hostess and the new, tentative friendship springing up between her and her husband. She also spent a great deal of time at the harp.

A few days after their arrival, a few wives of peers gathered in the drawing room of Averston House; one of her guests noticed her harp standing in the corner.

"Oh, how lovely. Do you play, or is that a family heirloom?"

Elizabeth stuffed down thoughts about the family heirloom Richard hadn't given her. Obviously, he thought the harp would be more treasured than a necklace and she should be content.

"It was a gift from my husband."

"Do play for us," urged another.

The thought of playing for an audience made her break out into a cold sweat. "I don't really play well enough to perform."

"How modest you are, Lady Averston."

"My wife is an accomplished harpist," rang out Richard's voice.

Elizabeth admired her husband as he entered the room. How handsome he was, especially when he smiled as he did at that moment.

He paused at the threshold. "I wish you could hear her play, but alas, she can never be persuaded to perform. I am sure angels in heaven take notice and

311

follow her example on their golden harps."

Elizabeth blushed at the praise and a collective sigh from the ladies settled in the silence. One of them stood, the others quickly following. "Goodness me, how late it grows. Thank you, Lady Averston, for your graciousness."

Other words of thanks and farewell rang out until they were left alone.

"My hero." She rose up on tiptoe and kissed his cheek. Catching herself, she stepped back. Perhaps he didn't wish contact. Her father always discouraged acts of affection.

Richard's expression, however, remained pleasant and he brushed a finger across her cheek. "My pleasure, my lady."

Too afraid to hope, she pulled away. "I ought to dress for dinner."

Richard was quiet throughout the meal. Elizabeth watched Richard from across the table searching for a safe subject. "How is the trial progressing?"

He kept his focus on his plate. "I'm persuaded he's guilty, but some of the members of the jury are not so sure."

"Is the evidence so convincing?"

"That, and Lord Einsburgh is in possession of some indefinable darkness that always made me uncomfortable."

"Of what is he accused?"

"There's evidence he's been involved in smuggling during the war, and that he's the owner of several flash houses, and worse things."

"Flash houses?"

Grimly, he explained, "Thieves sell stolen goods to

flash houses and they, in turn, sell them elsewhere. Many of the thieves work for him. He's been running a crime operation for years."

Elizabeth remembered his harshness with a servant during the house party. Still, that didn't make one a criminal. "I never would have believed a peer would involve himself in illegal activity."

"I'm not surprised, considering what I know of him, but I really ought not discuss the case further." He glanced at the clock. "I must be leaving. I'm meeting with Kensington at White's, so I'll probably be late. Good evening." He stood, rounded the table and kissed her cheek before heading toward the dining room door.

She might be imagining it, but he seemed to initiate contact more lately than before. Perhaps he was, at last, developing affection for her.

She thought, too, of Richard's estrangement from Tristan. Now that they were here, Richard could try to make amends. Perhaps personal contact would be more effective than a note.

Shoring up her courage, she called him before he left the room. "Richard."

He turned back, a soft smile touching his mouth.

"Now that we're in London, are you going to reconcile with Tristan?"

His expression fell. "When I have time. I'll be back late."

Elizabeth rested her forehead on her hand. She should have left well enough alone and not brought up his brother. Now that she'd mentioned Tristan's name, would Richard revert back to accusations and suspicions, despite all the progress she thought they'd made? Would she truly earn his trust?

313

Chapter Forty

Richard trudged through White's Gentlemen's Club and went upstairs to a private room. He sank into a chair. Despite himself, he was developing a true attachment to his wife. No matter how much he wanted to dismiss her, he could only remember the brilliance of her smile, the sunlight shimmering in her hair, the softness of her touch. Though at first he'd vowed not to form an attachment for her, and had even refrained from initiating consummation, he'd grown to care for her. He'd even dared hope that she might, in time, grow to love him.

But she kept bringing up Tristan's name, which meant, at least on some level, that she often thought of him. Perhaps a part of her heart would always belong to his brother.

At first, Richard deluded himself into believing that he didn't aspire to win her love, that all he needed was a wife who would remain with him and not shame him by running off with another man. That was no longer enough. He wanted her to love him, but as long as Tristan inhabited a portion of her heart, she would never give it to Richard.

Even if she never left him, she might never truly love him. A terrible dread of abandonment and rejection sank into his soul so deeply that the sensation of drowning swept over him.

A knock sounded at the door but Richard ignored it. When it came again, he muttered, "Go away."

The door opened and a rueful chuckle greeted him. "When a man looks that bad, the only sure cause is a woman." Rhys Kensington's voice pierced his melancholy.

Richard sighed.

Rhys made a tsking sound. "Is that the way to greet your old friend? Here I've come to join you in your misery and you order me away?"

"You've only come for brandy."

"Well, there is that." He crossed the room and poured a snifter. He handed Richard a second glass and stood sipping his. "Madam LeFrontier's girls are very good at cheering a man who's feeling low."

Richard lifted his gaze, taking in Kensington's disheveled hair and mussed cravat. He might be mussed from riding, but the smug and wicked gleam in his eye suggested otherwise. "You look as though you've already cheered your spirits this eve."

Kensington grinned. "Oh, aye, but I'm always game for another romp. I'll introduce you to Estelle. She's magical."

Richard made a sound of impatience. "I never went for loose women in my bachelor days, what makes you think I would now?"

"Something about your expression tells me you haven't had a woman in your arms for a while, which, in your case as a married man, is a tragedy."

"That's none of your concern."

"Ah. It is that bad." Kensington fell into an armchair nearby. "Your problem is that you let your heart get involved."

Richard leaned back against the chair. "A mistake I had hoped to avoid."

"Forget her. There are plenty of ladies. Take your pick. You're young, rich, titled, and the women seem to find you reasonably good looking. Take my lead and enjoy yourself with—"

"Enough!" snapped Richard. "Debauchery isn't the answer."

"Then you aren't asking the right question."

"When did you become so much like Tristan?" He finished his glass and set it down.

Despite ladies' obvious attraction for Kensington, he never seemed the type to take advantage, or pay for a woman's attention. But people changed, and not always in good ways.

Kensington made a negligent wave. "If the thought of bedding a prostitute doesn't appeal, take a mistress. Or find a lonely young widow."

Richard shuddered at the thought of buying a woman's favor. He let out his breath in frustration and shook his head.

Kensington cocked his head to one side. "Then divorce the lying wench and remarry. Wed a beautiful woman with ample charms."

"Divorce." Richard choked on the word. Then, "Lying wench? What gives you leave to speak about my wife in such a way?"

Kensington raised a brow. "She's still infatuated with Tristan, right? Probably going to cuckold you any moment. So throw her out. 'Tisn't so bad for a man of your means and standing to get a divorce. All the ladies will pity you for your faithless wife and fall all over themselves to prove they can do better."

Richard leaped to his feet and began pacing. "I can't believe you'd even suggest such a thing. She'd be ruined. And her parents...no telling what her mother might do."

Besides, he didn't want to divorce her. He didn't want a mistress, or a lover, or another wife. He wanted Elizabeth. He wanted her exclusively, not while even the smallest part of her pined for Tristan.

Trying to sort out the root of the problem, Richard drummed his fingers on his thigh. "She's not having an affair with Tristan or anyone, I'm sure of it; she's too innocent and too honorable. Yet she frequently thinks of him—she's made that clear. I will never have possession of her heart."

"Does she have possession of yours?"

He recalled her smile, her warmth, her compassion for the downtrodden, the courageous way she'd championed Cooper and Janey. His life would be austere without her. He wanted her near him always and ached for her welcoming smile.

"I do...care for her, deeply."

A satisfied gleam entered Kensington's eye. His friend had been goading him all along. The scoundrel was probably lying about the women, as well, just to get him angry. "It's about time you admitted that. Does she know?"

"Of cour..." Richard trailed off and considered. He'd never told her in so many words. He had yet to initiate much in the way of physical contact. "Perhaps not."

Kensington shook his head. "Then what's to keep her with you? You've accused her of cheating on you, and you've given her no reason to believe you love her.

Why do you think you deserve her?" He leaned forward and stared into Richard's eyes with an intensity he had never seen. "If I had the love of a woman half as fine, I would throw myself at her feet and beg her to have pity on my worthless self and let me try to prove myself to her."

Richard stared as the truth of Kensington's words sank into his heart. "I've been a terrible husband. I've impugned her honor, questioned her motives, and rejected her in every way. But I do...love...her." Oddly, that word wasn't as hard to say as he'd feared. "I'm not throwing her over."

"Then you'd better spend every moment of every day making sure she knows how you feel and that you're fortunate to have her."

"You're right. I need to stop being suspicious. I need to trust." He gulped. Could he?

Kensington pinned him with a fierce stare. "If she does love Tristan, then your task is to win her away from him, not turn into a statue and let her think you don't care."

"I didn't mean to, but when I thought she and Tristan..."

"He told me the whole story a few weeks ago when he first arrived in London," Kensington said. "He swore he'd never touched her after that first kiss in the garden at the house party. He's angry and hurt you'd think he'd sink so low as to bed your wife. What you did isn't easily forgiven."

Richard snorted. "He'd have to have a heart to be hurt."

Kensington leveled a stare upon him that made Richard shift uneasily. Kensington was right.

Regardless of Tristan's faults, he wouldn't betray Richard. Throughout their lives, they'd always been there for one another. His brother had been his staunchest supporter, his truest friend..

Though he'd never admit it out loud, Richard missed Tristan. Tristan made him laugh. He knew when Richard was overwhelmed with responsibility and needed a diversion. At those times, they'd gone swimming in the lake, steeple-chased, and climbed the cliffs. After a day of hard and usually dangerous play with his brother, Richard always felt shored up and ready to face the rigors of the title. Tristan would fade into the background until Richard needed him again.

Richard dropped his head into his hands. "I've been such a fool."

"You're not a fool for loving your wife—just for assuming she'd betray you, and for assuming it of your brother. I'm not sure why, but you seem to have this notion everyone will abandon you."

Richard raised his head inquiringly.

Kensington nodded, staring at some far off scene only visible to himself. "You said that to me once. Do you remember the fight we got into after your father died?"

"The one outside the hall?"

"No, the one by the lake. I can't even remember what it was about, but I remember you blackened my eye."

"I don't remember what that was about either, except that you were annoying."

After a brief smile, Kensington continued. "After I picked myself up off the ground, I said you were a lout and I turned and walked away. You shouted at me to go

319

ahead and leave just like everyone else in your life."

Like Mama. And Father. The same desolation that had gnawed at him as a child returned with brutal force. Richard rested his head in his hands so Kensington wouldn't see the tears stinging his eyes.

Kensington's voice hushed. "Now you think your wife will cheat on you or leave you. If she does, it will be because you drove her away."

Panic arose at the thought of losing her—not because of the scandal or the shame, but because of the emptiness that would consume him if the woman he loved were gone. Richard drew himself up. "I will not lose her. I will not let her go."

Kensington made a shooing motion. "Then go get her."

Richard left immediately to win his wife's heart.

Fog swirled around Richard's feet as he descended the front steps of White's Gentlemen's Club and headed toward the waiting carriage. What offering could he make to Elizabeth? Jewelry? Clothes? A book of poetry? None of those seemed heartfelt enough. The harp had been his ace and he was out of cards.

The lamplighters had already come, the streetlamps casting ghostly glow as darkness mingled with fog. His carriage materialized out of the darkness and Richard got in.

Then, it came to him. The ruby necklace. She'd even asked about it once after seeing his ancestors' portraits.

Upon reaching home, he gave the orders to a trusted servant to have the ruby and diamond necklace brought from Averston Castle. "I know I'm asking a lot from you," he said to the servant, "but I'd appreciate it if you'd go immediately. Take at least two other armed riders."

Elizabeth had already retired by the time he went to check on her, and the following morning had not yet arisen by the time he had to leave for the trial. He only hoped his offer of the necklace wasn't too late. The servants must have ridden straight through, for the necklace arrived the next evening.

After giving the men his thanks and a bag of coins for their trouble, Richard found Elizabeth playing the harp. He smiled over the crease of concentration in her brow as she played what was no doubt a particularly difficult piece of the music. Then as the music slowed, her face relaxed into absolute serenity. She completed the piece and glanced up. Her cheeks bloomed and she fluttered her hands.

He held up a hand. "No need to be embarrassed. Your playing is lovely."

"I made a mistake—"

"It was perfect." He went to her. "I have something I've been meaning to give to you." Confessing that he didn't want to give it to her until he was certain she'd proved faithful sounded terribly harsh. So he kept his reasons for the delay to himself. After opening the velvet bag, he inverted it into her outstretched hand.

She drew in her breath. Then, in a rather wooden voice, said, "Oh, Richard, it's lovely."

Something he could not name touched her expression, but it certainly wasn't the same joy she'd expressed when he'd given her the harp. "I am honored. Thank you." Her voice cracked.

She turned her head, made a sound in her throat, then gave him a quick kiss on the cheek before turning and practically running out of the room.

Richard stared after her with absolutely no idea what to make of her reaction, but it hadn't been the one he'd expected. Was it too little, too late?

Chapter Forty-One

Elizabeth stood in front of her mirror admiring the ruby necklace and wiping the tears trailing down her cheeks. She barely managed to control her impulse to throw her arms around him and kiss him. Instead, she'd fled the room to avoid revealing too much of her emotions. He'd probably think her mad for making such a fuss over a few old jewels. Her pride still stung that he'd waited so long to give her a traditional wedding gift, but he'd given it now. That meant the world to her.

He'd given the rubies to her as a symbol that he accepted her as his wife. Mrs. Brown had implied that the necklace had been given as a gift when the wedding was a love match. Yet she feared to read too much into the gesture. There was a difference between loving her, and merely accepting her. Still, his acceptance brought a rush of heady pleasure.

After fingering the necklace, Elizabeth placed it in a jewel case on her dressing table. Tomorrow, she'd instruct Maggie to have it locked in the family safe until she could wear it the next time they had dinner together. Tonight, she'd keep it near, knowing it symbolized how far she and Richard had come in their relationship and vowing to keep it safe always.

That night, she fell asleep dreaming of lying in Richard's arms.

In the morning, her necklace had vanished.

Elizabeth stared in disbelief. When Maggie entered, Elizabeth turned urgently to her abigail. "Maggie, did you put my necklace in the family safe?"

Maggie's brow furrowed in puzzlement. "No, milady."

Elizabeth pressed her hands to either side of her face. "Oh, no. This cannot be. I left it here last night when I went to bed and now it's gone."

Maggie was all business. "Perhaps it fell off. I'll look for it."

They pulled the furniture away from the walls, scoured the floors, and then searched the pockets of everything Elizabeth owned in case she'd simply misplaced it. Nothing.

"It's gone." Elizabeth slumped onto the counterpane on the bed and threw an arm over her eyes. "What will I ever tell Lord Averston? I lost a priceless family heirloom only hours after he entrusted it to me."

Even worse, he'd see the loss as a slight to his offering.

A new, more sinister, thought struck her: a thief had been in her room as she slept. The violation left her decidedly unsettled. She rubbed her hands over her arms and cast a glance in every direction.

Jittery at the thought of an intruder, and loath to face Richard and confess the news, she dawdled over her morning toiletry. By the time she forced herself to go to breakfast, Richard had already left for the trial.

Elizabeth summoned Cooper. "I need your help most urgently."

"Anythin' m'lady."

"My husband has given me a diamond and ruby

necklace. You can see it in many family portraits here and at the country estate. I left it in my room last night, and this morning it disappeared. I need your help recovering it."

He paused. "I don' recall noticing no necklace in no portraits, m'lady."

She led him to the drawing room and found a painting of the sixth Countess Averston wearing the necklace.

He peered at it, whistled in appreciation and nodded. "Leave it' to me, m'lady. I'll find it for ye."

That evening, Elizabeth wore a pale blue gown and her favorite pearls, hoping Richard wouldn't notice. He came home late, but found her in the library curled up with a book.

"Good evening, my lady." His gaze fell to her neck as he bent to kiss her cheek. "I'd hoped to see you wearing the rubies."

Elizabeth nearly stammered, "My red gown needed cleaning, and I didn't feel the rubies would do with a blue gown. Besides, I dined alone tonight; it didn't seem appropriate to get so dressed up."

He paused a heartbeat, then, "I see."

Her face burned at her deception.

"You might be interested to know I tried to contact Tristan today," Richard said. "His valet informed me he was out, but I had just seen him enter only moments before I arrived. He clearly does not wish to see me. Reconciliation may be difficult for the time being."

Compassion edged through her discomfort and Elizabeth put a hand over his. "I'm sorry. Mayhap he just needs time."

"He's an irresponsible whelp. I'm better off not

knowing of his escapades." His curtness did not quite conceal the pain of rejection in his eyes. As if to protect himself from revealing too much, he stood and bade her good night.

Elizabeth sat alone in the room, torn between wanting to help heal the rift between brothers, and not wishing to do anything that might endanger Richard's fragile trust. The loss of the rubies already stood between them; if she were to contact Tristan and beg him to allow Richard to make amends, she might add another wedge in her relationship. Yet how could she do nothing?

Cooper entered. "M'lady, I thin' I know who stole the rubies, but I can't prove it."

"Did you find them?"

"No. He might have already sold them."

She pressed her hand over her eyes. "Keep trying. Sooner or later, my husband will learn they are missing. He might blame you or one of the others who are reformed."

She briefly entertained the idea of having a copy made, but couldn't bring herself to commit such a deception. How long could she keep making up excuses before Richard learned the truth? When that happened, she would completely lose his trust.

Chapter Forty-Two

Richard left House of the Lords with Jenison and headed toward the street to their waiting carriages. "I don't see how the others can be so uncertain," Richard said. "The evidence against Einsburgh is convincing."

"I agree. With any luck, they'll come around." As they waited for their carriages, Jenison patted his chest. "Time to make peace with the lady."

"Make peace? Is something amiss?"

"She's unhappy with me. It's gone on too long, and I'd rather have her smile at me than prove I'm right."

Richard nodded at the wise words. "What do you plan to do?"

"Apologize, tell her she's a gem, and give her these." He withdrew a bag from a breast pocket and opened it up into his hand.

Richard's jaw dropped. The Averston rubies lay in Lord Jenison's palm. Richard blinked, certain he was seeing wrong.

Jenison held them so they caught the light. "Magnificent, aren't they?"

Richard made a strangled noise.

Lord Jenison gripped his shoulder. "What is it? You look the very devil."

"That necklace," he said hoarsely. "Where did you get it?"

"Well, don't tell her, but I found it at a pawn shop.

Got a good price on it. Why?"

"I vow that necklace has been in my family for generations."

Lord Jenison frowned. "Are you certain?"

Refusing to voice the fear that Elizabeth had simply sold it, he managed, "I have no doubt."

"I guess you were robbed and they pawned it. Hmm. Puts me in a bad spot. No matter. It's yours. Here." He handed them to Richard.

"I will, of course, reimburse you for the purchase price. I'll send you a bank draft first thing in the morning."

Jenison ran a hand over his thinning hair. "Seems bad form to make you buy back your own jewels. No, don't pay me for them. That will teach me to buy from a pawn. Should have gone to my regular jeweler. Hmm. I need something to take to my wife as an offering." He bid Richard a good night and stepped into his coach.

Richard stood waiting for his own carriage, heedless of the mist that gathered into a fine rain. He sorted through many possible explanations. The most obvious was that she'd sold his gift. If she'd needed money, surely she would have come to him. Then again, she kept so many secrets from him—her mother's abuse, her uncommon friendship with the 'tween stairs maid, her servants' backgrounds—she probably had other secrets he hadn't begun to suspect. He'd be foolish to think she would suddenly begin confiding in him.

Regardless, her simply pawning a priceless family heirloom that had symbolized love for centuries, proclaimed her disregard for its significance, or perhaps her disregard for him. Surely she knew he would miss it.

He stopped that line of thought. He needed to start trusting her. After all, she'd never given him any reason to suspect she'd pawned it. Perhaps it had been stolen. They never caught the thief at the ball. Mrs. Brown mentioned some missing silver. Elizabeth might be reluctant to tell Richard of the missing jewels for fear that he'd blame her servants, based on his reaction of thefts during the ball.

He couldn't miss the obvious implication that she didn't trust Richard. The thought made his heart sink. His carriage arrived and he climbed in on weighted feet, feeling as if someone had punched him in the stomach. He stared without seeing out the window at the gathering fog. Loss, so stark that his breathing became arduous, crept over him with insidious tentacles. He didn't deserve her trust. He had much to do to win such a difficult and precious gift. He could start by giving her his trust.

"My lord?"

Richard realized they'd reached Averston House and that the footman was standing with the door open, waiting for him to exit. Gathering himself, Richard entered the house, shed his overcoat and gloves, and headed for his room just as Elizabeth emerged from her bedchambers. Her white silk evening gown clung to her lovely figure.

Her brows raised. "Richard. I'm surprised you're home in time for dinner."

With a heavy heart, he took her hand and kissed it. "I would like nothing better than to have dinner with my lovely wife."

She blinked rapidly. "Oh…"

"Can't a man have dinner with his wife?"

"Of course. It's just that you haven't done it much."

She was right. He'd been neglectful. He'd been so absorbed in the trial, and his estrangement with Tristan, and his fears about his wife…in other words, he'd been a self-absorbed fool.

"Then it's high time I made a change. I vow to make an effort to be home to have dinner with you more often."

"I'd enjoy that."

He paused, trying to decide how to broach the subject of the rubies. He snatched the first idea that seemed to make sense. "Elizabeth, now that we're in Town, you may, of course do any shopping you desire. If you need more money—for anything at all—you have only to ask, or charge it and have the bill sent to me."

Her face pinked and her words came out in a rush. "Oh, that's not necessary. My pin money and dress allowance was most generous and I have not yet exhausted that. I thank you."

He rubbed his forehead. What had gone wrong? The only two people he truly cared about wanted no part of him in their lives. And now his wife was keeping secrets.

It was probably his own fault. He should just tell her how he found the rubies and listen to her explanation, if she had one. How did he broach the subject without sounding judgmental and accusing? At worst, she would probably fear he was blaming her for dishonesty, or at best, for accusing her servants. Every phrase that leapt into his head sounded worse than the last. If Richard had been abandoned upon an uninhabited island, his sense of isolation could not have been more profound. Or left him so lost.

He agonized over the subject during dinner. Elizabeth seemed quiet as well. By the time she bade him goodnight and went to bed, he'd completely lost his nerve. Blasted fool! When did he become such a coward?

Perhaps making amends with Tristan would give him the courage to speak to Elizabeth. He took a hansom to Tristan's bachelor flat. Unable to find him at home, Richard searched for him at a number of clubs but to no avail. His carriage finally stopped at White's. Though Tristan seldom went to such a respectable gentlemen's club, Richard had to try.

Someone reported seeing Tristan earlier, but he'd left already. Richard cursed. It was so unlike his brother to hold on to a grudge. They'd always forgiven each other. Had he truly gone too far and left no room for making amends?

Finding the reading room at White's empty, Richard collapsed into a chair and scrubbed a hand over his face. He'd made a complete mess of everything. Now it might be too late.

"Lord Averston." Someone slipped into a chair next to him.

Glancing up, he nodded at his father-in-law, the Duke of Pemberton. "Evening, Duke."

"What do you think of Lord Einsburgh?"

"I'm surprised it's taken this long for him to be accused of something."

Pemberton paused. "Then you are convinced of his guilt?"

"Without a doubt. Aren't you?" The duke's expression was so bland that Richard took a closer look.

"I admit the evidence is damning but it seems too neatly stacked. I think we're accusing the wrong man."

Richard froze, shocked to hear such words from the duke. "What are you saying? Do you think someone is framing him?"

"Perhaps." Pemberton nodded. "Doesn't it all appear too neat? Lord Einsburgh is no fool. He wouldn't have left a way to trace all these crimes back to him."

"I believe he's involved in more illegal activity than we know. Tip of the iceberg, so to speak. I have no doubt he's guilty."

The duke held up a hand. "Don't be too hasty. I urge you to reconsider. After all, we're considering the fate of a marquis. We would do well to err on the side of caution."

Richard stared. "He is involved in illegal activity."

"Perhaps. Perhaps not. There's no way to know for sure. Even if he is, who is he hurting, really?" Pemberton's tone reached a feverish pitch and Richard glanced around to reassure himself that they were alone.

For a moment, Richard could find no words around his shock. "Are you telling me I should vote for his innocence even though I'm convinced of his guilt?"

An almost fanatical light entered the duke's eyes. "The consequences are bigger than you may suspect."

"I can't believe I'm hearing this from you."

The duke stood. "He's innocent, and I hope you, as my son-in-law, will follow my lead in the vote tomorrow." He wrenched open the door and strode away.

Richard stared after the duke's retreating back but could find no explanation for his sudden conviction. A few days ago, the duke had expressed an opposite viewpoint. Odd that he would so passionately plead this new and suddenly different position.

With a mental shrug, Richard turned his thoughts to another path. Tomorrow, they would vote. Then he would be free to turn his attention to salvaging his relationship with his brother and search for a way to reach Elizabeth and earn her trust. Maybe someday, he would earn her love.

Chapter Forty-Three

With her heart pounding, Elizabeth folded her hands together as she stood in the library and waited for Cooper to give her his news.

Cooper shook his head. "Got good news and bad news. Th' good is, I figured out who it was what stole yer rubies and the jewels at th' ball."

"You did?"

"'e'd been avoidin' me ever since that ball. I forced a confession from 'im. 'E said 'e pawned yer rubies. I went t' th' shop where 'e said 'e took 'em but some lord bought th' rubies. That's the bad news. I don' think we'll never get 'em back."

Elizabeth closed her eyes to hold back the tears. She'd failed Richard!

"I'm sorry, m'lady."

"Who was the thief?"

"One o' th' footmen."

"Reformed?"

"No, one of the new staff Mrs. Brown hired."

A childish victory rose up inside Elizabeth that one of Mrs. Brown's servants—and not the reformed staff—had been the cause.

"I found out 'e works for Mr. Black."

She opened her eyes. "Mr. Black? The scoundrel who runs a theft operation?"

"The same."

"You did very well, Cooper."

"Wish I coulda got yer rubies back."

"I do, too. Well, never mind, that can't be helped."

Reformed thieves were one thing, but a current thief who struck again and again was something else entirely. "Send for the nearest constable, and when he arrives, bring the footman to me."

Cooper nodded. Elizabeth braced herself for the unpleasantness.

An hour later, she'd glared at the footman until he confessed, and turned him over to the constable who hauled him off to face justice. Afterward, she sat thinking about her next battle.

Richard already asked about the rubies. She must confide in him. At least, she could tell him now that she knew the thief's identity. She didn't fear his anger; he wouldn't hurt her, but he might still view her as ungrateful for having been so careless as to leave them laying around. Richard was already hurting because of the silence between him and his brother. She had to do something to ease his pain. Perhaps if he and Tristan reconciled, the blow of losing the rubies would be less painful.

She scribbled a message and handed it to Cooper. "Please see that this is delivered immediately. If his valet tells you he's sleeping, insist upon waking him."

He touched his forelock. "Yes, m'lady."

Elizabeth changed into a riding habit and ordered her horse be ready. She paced until the footman returned.

Grinning, Cooper handed her a letter. "For ye, m'lady."

She smiled. "Thank you. Mr. Cooper, it's

considered impertinent to grin at your employer. Here in London, propriety is more important than in the country."

"Ah. O'course. Miz Goodfellow warned me 'bout tha' un. Don't know why. Everywhere else, it's al'righ' t' smile a' folks."

"I don't mind, but others might." To soften the reprimand, she changed the subject. "Did you wear that old suit of Lord Averston's I gave you to court your girl?"

"Miss Jeannie." A smile spread over his face. "Aye. I never had nuthin' so fine. An' Miss Jeannie, she liked it."

"I'm sure you looked quite the thing."

He nodded, then seemed to remember his role as a servant and ducked out of the room.

Unfolding the note, she read

Meet me at Hyde Park just north of Rotten Row at ten o'clock today.

Your servant,
Tristan

Tristan had signed it with a flourish, as flamboyant in his handwriting as he was in his flirting.

"See that my horse is saddled, Cooper," she called. "I'm going for a ride to Hyde Park."

He reappeared. "I'll go with you, my lady, to insure your protection."

She smiled. It was rather sweet, actually, to be fussed over. "As you wish."

Dressed in her riding habit and boots, Elizabeth rode to Hyde Park while Cooper and a groom named March rode behind her. To give herself time to enjoy a ride, she arrived before her appointed meeting time with Tristan. She cantered down the path, ignoring other equestrians around her and breathing the cool morning air. After a brisk canter, she slowed her mount to a walk, moving leisurely in the direction of the location where Tristan had agreed to meet her.

A beautiful black Andalusian trotted toward her. The rider raised his hand in greeting and Tristan's smile flashed as he reached her. He rode as beautifully as he did everything, cutting a dash everywhere he went. Yet, his face was not nearly as dear as Richard's.

Cooper and March melted back into the scenery to provide her some privacy with Tristan.

"Well met, sister-in-law," he called. "I hope you have a very good reason for dragging me out of bed at this unholy hour of the day." His lopsided smile and red-rimmed eyes bore testament to his late night.

"I hope you weren't too indisposed to arise from your bed," she chided.

"Dreadfully. Fortunately, my overpaid valet proved his worth today with one of his famous concoctions to wake the dead, as it were."

"Difficult night?" she asked in mock sweetness.

"Horrid. I won four hundred pounds and spent the remainder of the evening in celebration." With the same grin that had stolen her heart—was it only a few months ago?—he dismounted with all the grace of a practiced rider. As his hands closed around her waist to help her dismount, she looked into his face, so like Richard's and yet, not nearly so beloved. His touch failed to evoke even a flicker of desire.

She went still inside, stunned by the realization that her infatuation for Tristan had ended.

Her feelings for Richard were so much stronger

than any *tendré* she'd ever nurtured for his brother. Was it love?

Tristan released her and stepped back, gesturing to a bench. "Shall we?"

They tied up their horses and sat together. A cool breeze stirred the leaves, and songbirds flitted in the branches.

Elizabeth waited until a pair of riders rode past before speaking. "Thank you for meeting with me."

"How may I be of service?"

"It's about Richard." She toyed with her riding crop.

His eyes narrowed. "Is he making you unhappy?" No sign of teasing revealed itself in his expression, only concern and a suggestion that he'd happily rise to her defense. Such gallantry must be in the Barrett blood.

She shook her head. "No, that's not it at all. Richard misses you and he regrets throwing you out."

"Yes, well, I regret that as well." Tristan stared out over the landscape. "In truth, he's never turned on me like that. We've had our differences, but he's always been there for me. He wouldn't have done that if not for you." His dark eyes took on a faraway look. "He must love you a great deal to be so hurt and jealous by what he thought he saw."

Elizabeth hoped Richard's jealousy sprang from affection and not just possessiveness or a desire to avoid scandal.

Tristan's smile turned soft. All signs of the dangerous seducer vanished, and in that moment, she saw him as she'd seen him during the house party, a thoughtful man who was deeper than he appeared.

Boldly, she asked, "Was I really just another

flirtation?"

He paused. "At first, you were a challenge—trying to get you to talk to me, smile at me. Then I felt a...connection with you. I truly liked you."

She looked away, afraid of what she might find in his eyes. "Your behavior did not indicate you respected me."

"No, my behavior was, indeed, untoward. I apologize for misusing you. I was acting instinctively, and selfishly, when I should have been more concerned with both your feelings and your reputation."

He'd already apologized the morning after their garden encounter at the Einsburgh's house party, but hearing it again had a healing quality. She offered him a smile. "Perhaps it worked out as it should."

He leaned back. "You are much better suited for Richard. I'm not ready to settle down. Maybe I'll find someone like you someday...in twenty or thirty years." Again came that slightly lopsided quirk of the mouth.

As her thoughts tumbled, she stared out over the park, idly noticing others who rode or walked. "You need to make amends with him, Tristan. He loves you well. This animosity between you hurts him. Hurts you both."

Tristan looked away, but not before she caught the look of pain in his eyes. "What would you have me do? When he threw me out, he forbade me from entering Averston House."

"He said you didn't reply to his message, and he was turned away when he came to your apartment."

Tristan paused. "I wasn't ready to see him just yet. I feared I'd say something I'd later regret. It won't hurt him to writhe a little."

"Tristan, please, don't let him leave London without making amends. He's your brother. You need each other."

Wearing a pensive expression, Tristan nodded. "He's all I have. At least he has you." His mouth twitched into a rueful smile. "He does care about you, you know. He might be too stubborn—or afraid—to admit it, but he does."

She toyed with the fingers of her gloves, wishing it were true. "Talk to him."

"Very well. I'll reply to his message and agree to listen to what he has to say."

"He's a proud man. Don't make him grovel."

He leveled a surprisingly intense stare upon her. "He isn't the only one in the family with pride. Farewell, sister-in-law." He mounted and rode away.

Elizabeth remained on the bench for several moments, enjoying the birdsong and the whisper of the trees. Even the usual crowd that frequented the park was absent, or at least at a distance for the moment, leaving her in peaceful solitude. After breathing in the scent of flowers, she gathered her skirts and moved to a rock she could use as a mounting block.

A figure approached from the side. Before she recognized any danger, a man grabbed her by the shoulders.

Fear shot icy fragments through her body. She screamed and hit him with her riding crop. Swearing, he wrenched her riding crop out of her hand and raised it to strike her. Terror swept over her.

Cooper appeared, sailing through the air. He knocked her attacker to the ground. They landed heavily, grappling and punching each other.

March pulled her out of the shock that had frozen her in place. "Onto your horse now, my lady."

The groom boosted her up and glanced back at the fray, but Cooper had already subdued Elizabeth's attacker. The man lay unconscious on the ground. Cooper stood and spun around, searching the area for further signs of danger. When he found none, he took off his belt and bound the attacker's hands.

Cooper looked at Elizabeth. "Ye all righ' m'lady?"

She nodded, clutching the reins with trembling hands. A couple from a distance stood watching as if uncertain what, if any, action they should take. She tried to smile and waved to let them know she didn't require their aid. Her hands shook and her knees knocked together.

Cooper spoke again. "Bow Street will want to take a statement from you."

Mute with the fear over what had happened, she nodded again. "Wh-who… Why?"

Her loyal servants exchanged glances. "Could be jest a thug, but I thin' 'e's one o' Mr. Black's men," Cooper said finally.

"What would he want with me?"

"I 'ope we nev'r find out. Tell th' staff you're in danger. Don't let anyone in the 'ouse."

"Could be just a random attack," said March.

"Could be." Cooper nodded, clearly unconvinced. "Take 'er home and don' stop fer nothin'. I'm taking him in to the magistrate." He toed the unconscious assailant. "I'll return as soon as I can."

Elizabeth rode home with March keeping a careful watch over her. Richard hadn't arrived home yet. After a hot bath and a cup of tea, Elizabeth's shaking stopped but she longed for a comforting embrace. She longed for Richard.

Chapter Forty-Four

By the time Richard returned home, Elizabeth had gained control over her emotions. Though she longed to unburden herself regarding the attack, Richard seemed more tense than normal and she didn't dare tell him she'd been to the park to see Tristan nor about the attack, so she kept her peace.

After dinner, they sat together in the study, she attempting to read silently, and he writing a letter. Silence settled heavily between them. Richard fairly bristled with tension.

He finally laid down his pen. His voice was quiet, controlled, but tension underlined every word. "I owe you an apology. I have not been approachable. For that I'm sorry." He paused and his mouth worked as if he could not form the words in his mind. "You can tell me anything. Please don't keep secrets."

Secrets? Oh, heavens, had he seen her with Tristan and jumped to the wrong conclusion again? He stared at her for so long that she wanted to squirm. Fighting the urge to ask if he knew she'd sought out Tristan, she waited. Perspiration trickled down between her shoulders.

"I…" He drummed his fingers on the desk, and started again. "Is there something you need to tell me?"

She swallowed. How would she tell him without it sounding as if she and Tristan had met at the park to

have a tryst?

Even more softly, he added, "About the ruby necklace?"

The necklace. Another confession she'd have to make, but hopefully not as serious as if he suspected her of disloyalty with Tristan. "The rubies?" Her voice squeaked and she had to swallow, suddenly terrified he'd fly into a rage. Steadying herself, she forced calm into her voice, determined not to reveal her fear. Such weakness had only ever earned her a more severe punishment from Duchess.

He waited patiently.

She forged ahead, and come what may, but at least she'd have a clear conscience. Her words came out in a breathless stream. "I…lost the necklace. I put it in a case on my dressing table and I lost it…or at first I thought I had, but my maid and I searched everywhere, and it was nowhere to be found and I thought it might have been stolen, so I asked Cooper to help me and he found out it was a footman Mrs. Brown hired before we were married and that he sold it to a pawnshop. I'm sorry." She tried, unsuccessfully, to swallow the lump in her throat. "I should have told you but I kept hoping I could recover it. It was only this morning that Cooper traced it to the pawnshop, and learned it had been purchased so I couldn't go and buy it back. It's gone. I'm so sorry." She lost her control and a sob forced its way out of her. She withdrew a handkerchief and blew her nose. She snuck a peek at Richard, but he didn't look angry.

Pain mirrored in his eyes. "I see." He looked down with his shoulders slumped, as forlorn as a rejected child. She'd hurt him. Oh, merciful heavens, that was worse than a beating.

"Where is the footman now?" he asked.

"After he confessed, I turned him over to the law." Utterly wretched, Elizabeth tried to pull herself together but tears continued to leak from her eyes. "I'm sorry, Richard. I know the gift wasn't only an heirloom but a traditional gift from husband to wife. And I lost it. I should have told you sooner but I couldn't bear the thought of disappointing you. I kept hoping we'd recover it." She wiped her cheeks with her handkerchief and blew her nose.

After a long pause, Richard leaned forward. "What made Cooper think it was that particular footman?"

"I'm not certain, but when he confessed to Cooper, he told him about the pawnshop. He confessed to everything and showed me the receipt. So I called the constable and had the footman taken away. The necklace was purchased by a lord."

"Lord Jenison. I know."

She lowered her handkerchief. "How did you know?"

He reached into his coat pocket and withdrew the ruby and diamond necklace.

She stood. "How—"

"Lord Jenison gave them to me." With a surprisingly tender expression, Richard stood and moved to her side. Gently, he turned her and placed the necklace around her neck. His lips brushed over her shoulder. "I should have given it to you sooner. I didn't know how to tell you I'd seen Lord Jenison with the Averston rubies and I wasn't sure I wanted to hear the explanation. I'm so sorry. I should have had more faith in you. In many ways."

She sniffled and looked up at him. "Will you forgive me for not telling you?"

"If you'll forgive me for doubting you, and more importantly, for not earning your trust. I've jumped to the wrong conclusion about you at every turn. Forgive me."

"Of course I forgive you."

He caressed her cheek before he kissed her. So gentle. So tender. His lips moved against hers in a familiar dance of offering and accepting genuine affection. Her nerve endings sprang to life and sang with all the joy of harp strings creating a melody—new and fresh, yet as old as the earth itself. His lips still on hers, he enfolded her into his arms. Her heart thudded and a pleasant buzz of dizziness hummed through her body.

She wrapped her arms around him and melted against him. She kissed him as if this one moment would forever shape her future. He slanted his mouth over hers, kissing her so deeply that he gathered in a little bit more of her heart, a little bit more of her soul with every motion. Her blood roared until it drowned out every sound. She leaped into a river of pleasure, aching for more, burning, longing. Deep beneath her urgent hunger for him, something quieted deep in her heart. All her loss, her pain, her fear, all the roiling tumult of her past stilled, quieted by his healing kiss. Their lips parted only long enough for her to catch a breath before kissing over and over again. Their feverish passion blotted out everything except the fire sizzling every nerve. The press of his body against hers only fanned the embers of her fire.

This must be the beginning of that unity of which

Mary had spoken, the pleasure and bonding that husbands and wives should share. Still, she wanted more, knew more awaited her, and trusted Richard to reveal it.

In her fervor, she didn't realize they had moved until the edge of the divan bumped against her legs. She fell backwards. Their fall seemed to shake some of the instinctive hunger from Richard. He slowed, ended the kiss and pressed a gentle hand to the side of her face.

"Elizabeth—"

She cut him off with another kiss. Whatever he had to say, it could wait. She needed—they needed—whatever came next, whatever would fuse them together mind and body. He let out a groan, and for a moment, seemed to surrender. Once again, he pulled back. Clarity dulled the bright hunger in his eyes.

"Elizabeth," his voice sounded hoarse. "I have much for which to beg your forgiveness, and I vow to be a better husband to you in every way. We shouldn't do this here where the servants might see. Come. Let's go upstairs and love each other freely."

Not trusting herself to speak, she nodded. He arose and pulled her to her feet, then with his arm around her, they walked together toward the stairs.

"My lord," came the voice of the butler. "Forgive the intrusion, but there's a matter I must discuss with you." His gaze flitted to Elizabeth but returned to Richard.

Richard's brow creased in obvious irritation. "Can't it wait?"

"No, my lord, but I promise to make it brief."

Richard glanced at Elizabeth.

She smiled. "I'll wait for you upstairs."

Richard smiled, his eyes burning with such heat that a new level of warmth shot through her. Another smoldering look came her way before Richard disappeared with the butler into the room beyond.

As she passed the drawing room where the harp stood, she paused. Something about the solitude of the harp called to her, despite her hunger. Besides she'd forgotten to cover it. Before reaching for the protective dust cover to pull over her harp, she caressed the wood, thinking of the man who'd given the instrument to her, his thoughtfulness and generosity. He'd given her the rubies. Again. She touched the rubies around her neck, the symbol of a husband's love. Now he wanted to make her his wife in every way. She let out a breath as pure joy infused her.

With a dreamy sigh, Elizabeth pulled on the dust cover, tied off the flaps, and blew out the lamps. A cool breeze drifted in through the opened French doors leading out to the terrace, caressing her skin like a lover's touch. As she went to close them, out of the corner of her eye, she caught a shadowy movement. She took a second glance at the terrace but saw nothing unusual. Seconds later, a soft scraping noise drew her attention. A dark figure slipped in.

A man wearing all black entered. Elizabeth froze, too startled to make a sound. The intruder made a lunge for her. She screamed and stumbled backward. He grabbed her by the arms and clamped a hand over her mouth. Smelling of cheap wine and cigars, the man pulled her against him, and dragged her toward the open doors.

Elizabeth kicked and struggled but she had no effect upon the man. Wild terror poured through her and sent her into a frenzied struggle.

"Release my wife!" Richard's voice rang out.

Still holding Elizabeth in an unyielding grip, her assailant went still. Only Elizabeth's frightened breathing broke the silence. Behind her, the man's muscles tensed and she braced herself against him. Instead of making a dash for the door, he threw her into Richard's arms. The attacker disappeared outside.

Shaking, Elizabeth collapsed against her husband while servants poured into the room. Richard wrapped a steadying arm around her.

Cooper dashed in. "Wot happen' milor'?"

"An intruder assaulted my wife! He ran out that way."

Cooper ran out the French doors into the night.

The other servants exclaimed over the incident. "What was he after? The rubies?"

Another mused. "Surely he wouldn't attack the lady if he were a mere burglar."

"Mr. Black's men would."

Elizabeth buried her face into Richard's neck cloth. The men who'd broken into Mary's house had attacked the servants; perhaps they were ruthless enough to attack ladies as well. Richard wrapped both arms around her. As the shock receded, true fear stepped in, and she shook.

Richard rubbed circles on her back. "All is well, now. You're safe."

"What is happening?" she gasped. "Why do people keep trying to hurt me?"

Richard's hand halted. "Has something like this happened before?"

"Earlier today. I went to Hyde Park and someone

Donna Hatch

tried to grab me. Cooper and the groom, Mr. March, fought him off."

His breathing became ragged. "Why didn't you tell me?"

"I couldn't. I-I was so worried about the rubies, and then you came home looking so overset…"

He whispered into her hair. "Oh, sweet Elizabeth. Forgive me. I trust you. Let me be there for you. Please tell me your concerns. Give me your trust."

"You have it now. I vow it."

"Do I? No more secrets?"

She hesitated. "I do have one confession." She drew a breath. "When I went to the park, it was to meet Tristan to try to convince him to see you—to reconcile with you. That's all, I vow. We are not involved in any way."

"Shhh. All is well. I believe you. Anything else?"

"No."

"You can tell me anything. I'm through with playing the jealous husband. You can give away all my worldly possessions, but please do not give away my heart."

She drew in her breath. Was that a declaration of love—that she was already in possession of his heart?

Cooper returned, locking and barricading the door behind him. "'E went over th' wall and I lost 'im in th' streets, but I got a glimpse o' 'im. I know 'im. He's one of Mr. Black's men, same as th' one in th' park."

Richard's voice turned grim. "Arm every able-bodied man. This is their second try for her. We're going to turn this house into a fortress."

He released Elizabeth long enough to scribble two messages and order them delivered. Then he led her to her bedchambers with Cooper and Foster trailing behind.

Richard cupped her cheek with a gentle hand. "I'm staying with you tonight. I doubt anyone would try to scale the wall three stories up, but I'm taking no chances."

At his show of fierce concern and protectiveness, Elizabeth wiped a new onslaught of tears, but couldn't tell him how much his concern meant to her.

Richard pulled her in close and nodded at Cooper. "Take position by the door."

"Aye, m'lord. Foster's pretty handy with a gun, too."

The unlikely footman hovered nearby, already armed. Richard nodded to him. Foster glanced at Elizabeth, offered a reassuring, albeit tight smile, and sat on the floor with his back resting against the doorjamb, a rifle in his hand.

Richard glanced uneasily at the windows. After making eye contact with Cooper, he gestured to an armchair. Cooper took up post in the chair, his gun resting easily across his knee.

After removing the rubies and placing them into her jewelry box, Elizabeth removed her shoes and crawled into bed fully clothed while Richard set a pistol on the nightstand next to the bed. The bed sank under his weight. He rolled onto his side and scooted next to her, fitting his body behind her, and wrapped an arm around her waist, pulling her in close. She marveled at the quiet joy of lying in his arms. His body heat soaked into her. His heart beat a steady cadence against her back, each beat reassuring. As she nestled against him, she let out a sigh of contentment. If only they were alone…

He cradled her close with one hand, and with the other, he stroked her hair, slowly, gently. One by one, he removed the pins in her hair and resumed stroking from her head down to the end of each lock. Nestled with her back against his chest, Elizabeth's fears abated and a new sense of wellbeing crept over her.

He lifted his head and whispered in her ear, "I want you." His lips brushed against the hollow underneath her ear, and trailed warmth down her neck. Reaching behind her, she caressed his face and ran her fingers through his thick hair. He let out a ragged sigh and tightened his arm around her waist.

He breathed in her ear, "As soon as this confounded trial is over, we're going home where you'll be safe. Then, my love…I will *love* you."

My love. Was that a mere term of endearment, or a true declaration? At the moment, it didn't matter. His affection was apparent. For now, it was enough.

Yet, the very real threat of danger hung over them like a loaded gun with a hair trigger.

Chapter Forty-Five

Tristan arrived early in the morning, alert and wide-awake, which was something of a miracle. Richard eyed him, uncertain of what to say. At least Tristan didn't look hostile. Instead, his expression seemed, if anything, expectant.

Tearing down his own barriers of pride and embarrassment, Richard pulled him into a rough hug before stepping back. "Thank you for coming."

Tristan quirked a grin. "How could I resist such an urgent plea for help from my older and wiser brother?"

"I owe you an apology, and though I don't deserve it, I hope you'll forgive me." Richard cleared his throat and toed the carpet.

"What is it you need?" Tristan asked.

The relief that Tristan had come despite Richard wronging him so egregiously left him half-weak with relief, half-light enough to fly.

The two people who mattered the most were back in his life; Elizabeth had trusted him with the truth, and Tristan had come back.

However, these were grave conditions and they must act without delay. "Elizabeth is in danger. Twice yesterday someone made an attempt to carry her off."

Tristan's expression turned to alarm. "Why? Who? Is she hurt?"

"She's unharmed. I'm not certain who is behind the

attacks, or why. One of our servants said he thought the assailants work for Mr. Black, the head of a crime ring, but I can't imagine why he would be after Elizabeth." He paused. "I wonder at the coincidence that this tie to the crime ring occurs at the same time that I get called to a trial involving crime connections…"

"Using her to force your vote?"

"Perhaps. Maybe they are confederates. I must leave soon to vote in the trial, but I don't wish to leave Elizabeth alone. The servants are guarding her, but I need someone I can trust."

Tristan raised his brows. "You're telling me that you trust me, and me alone, to guard your wife, the woman only weeks ago you accused me of seducing?"

Leveling a sober stare upon his brother, Richard nodded. "That's exactly what I'm saying." How would he ever gain Tristan's forgiveness? Maybe he wouldn't. Maybe Richard's plea came too little too late. He scrubbed a hand over his face. "I was wrong. I'm sorry." He'd certainly been making the lion's share of apologies lately. "I hope you will forgive me someday…even though I don't deserve it. For now, for her sake, please protect her."

"What makes you so certain I won't seduce her now?" Tristan lifted his chin in defiance.

"You'd never betray me. You have more honor than to betray me. I should have known that from the beginning. All I could see is how much you cared for one another. I…appear to have an aversion to trusting anyone, especially those closest to me."

"Yes, well, you're right—you should have known." Tristan looked away and raked his fingers through his hair. "I suppose you know it now. Of course I'll watch over her."

They gripped hands. A sniffling noise came from behind him and Richard turned. Elizabeth stood in the doorway of the room. With tears shimmering in her eyes, she slid an arm through Richard's bent elbow and reached a hand toward Tristan.

"Thank you for coming, Tristan." They clasped hands.

Solemn, Tristan said, "I'll protect you."

"I know you will, but my thanks are for making amends with Richard."

Tristan's irreverent smile slipped back into place. "Brothers, and all that."

Richard kissed Elizabeth's forehead when he wanted to kiss her lips. Her sweet mouth beckoned to him with the promise of so much more. "I must go. We vote. I hope to return shortly, but I can never predict how long deliberations will take."

She stood on tiptoe and kissed his cheek.

Grinning, he headed for his waiting carriage, anxious to finish his duty and return home to Elizabeth. He entered the carriage, and as the footman closed the door, Richard noticed, too late, two large men already inside. One pointed a pistol at him.

"Don' make a sound, guv."

Richard froze.

The second man moved quickly and pain exploded in the back of Richard's head. Dazed, he struggled against his assailants but they wrestled him down. After another stunning blow to his head, he collapsed. His last thought was of Elizabeth left under Tristan's protection.

Chapter Forty-Six

As Elizabeth penned a letter to Mary, a commotion in the foyer caught her attention. She lowered her pen and raised her head.

"Milady!"

Nearby, Tristan leaped to his feet, his gun at the ready. Cooper burst into the sitting room with the silent Janey on his heels. The normally grinning footman's face was white and his eyes were wide and alarmed.

"Tell 'er, Janey. Tell 'er wot you told me."

Perplexed, Elizabeth arose, glanced at the little girl, then back to Cooper.

He nodded. "She's talking. Never seen 'er do it afore."

Elizabeth returned her gaze to Janey whose eyes were enormous, and her face streaked with dirt and tears. "Janey?"

Janey sniffled. "They took 'im. They took milor' Averston."

Elizabeth gaped that the child had spoken. She gathered her thoughts. "Who took Lord Averston?"

She whispered, "Th' ones what work fer *him*."

"Mr. Black's men," Cooper supplied.

Elizabeth processed this, a cold sinking feeling opening up in the center of her stomach. "Are you certain?"

"She saw 'em do it," Cooper said.

"Why would they capture him?" Tristan interjected.

"Don' know, not 'less Lord Averston's made an enemy of 'em. 'E don't usually bother wi' the upper classes. Don' know why he's after you an' yer 'usband."

She sank back into her chair and folded her shaking hands together. Pain lanced her heart as if a barb had pierced it. To lose him now, just when they'd finally reached understanding and planted the seeds of love, would be utterly unbearable.

Tristan moved to Cooper. "Where did they take him?"

Janey shook her head. "I couldn' run fast enou' t' follow th' coach."

Elizabeth turned to Cooper. "Do you know where they've taken him?"

"No, but I could put word ou' on th' streets."

"Please do. I'll offer a reward if you think it'll help."

He nodded. "I'll go change. Won' ge' nowhere all trussed up in these fancy togs." He disappeared.

Tristan shouted orders to the staff as Elizabeth paced the floor, her fear mounting. She imagined Richard beaten and bound, at the mercy of unscrupulous men. Profound loss overcame her as she considered the void of her life without Richard. She'd never told him how much she cared…that she loved him.

She loved him! Why hadn't she seen it?

She recalled his compassion, his fury when he faced down Duchess, his tenderness when he held her last night. It could all vanish. The first opportunity she got, she'd tell him she loved him. She'd make sure he had no doubts. And she'd do it as soon as he returned. If he returned.

As she stood staring out of the window, a tiny hand slipped into hers. Janey's solemn eyes looked up at her.

Again, the child spoke. "Scared?"

"Yes, Janey. I'm very scared."

"Story?"

Elizabeth laughed weakly and wiped her eyes. "Yes. I think a story is exactly what I need. Go choose a story and we'll read."

While the child was gone, Elizabeth spared a thought to marvel that it was Janey's concern over Richard that had finally coaxed her to speak.

Three maids, the footman called Foster, and a stable boy appeared before her.

Foster spoke first, "We found the coachman and a footman beaten and tied up in the mews. Their livery has been stolen, so we can only assume their attackers took their place to capture Lord Averston."

A maid spoke. "Ma'am...er, m'lady, we want t' 'elp find 'is lordship. But Mrs. Brown says if we leave, we canna come back."

Elizabeth made a dismissive wave. "If you think you can help find my husband, by all means go, and of course you may resume your posts when you return, I'll see to it. I'll pay you each extra for trying, and I'm offering a reward for his safe return. If you hear anything—anything at all—return and report to me."

They nodded, made awkward bows and curtsies, and left as Janey returned with a book held reverently in front of her. Tristan hovered in the room, his eyes alert and darting. He kept a firm grip on his gun.

With Janey on her lap, and the book open in front of her, Elizabeth tried to focus on the stories, but read mindlessly. Her thoughts centered on Richard and his immediate danger. A sob burst out of her and she placed a hand over her mouth.

Tristan touched her shoulder in a gesture that fortified her courage, then he resumed his position by a window. Unbearably grim, he gripped his gun as if it held the key to the answers they sought.

Mrs. Brown swept into the room. "My lady, I know it isn't my place to say, but surely you do not intend to place your trust in those people."

"Those people?"

She waved her hand. "The ones you hired form the reform house. They may be lying about Lord Averston. Or they may be the ones holding him captive."

Elizabeth drew herself up. "Mrs. Brown, if you ever question my judgment or my decision again you will be dismissed. Is that clear?"

Mrs. Brown sniffed. "Perfectly, Countess." She made a curtsy and left.

Janey wriggled and got out of her lap. Elizabeth stood and resumed her pacing, her stomach twisted into a ball of nerves.

Tristan returned to her side and took her hand. Though his grip felt steady and sure, his eyes mirrored his concern.

His sympathy was her undoing. Sobbing, she sank into him. "He's in danger. What can I do? What if they hurt him, or…" She couldn't speak. Her legs gave out.

He swung her into his arms and carried her to the settee. "Here now, they're not going to hurt him. They want something or they would have killed him outright." He gave her a handkerchief. "It may be all over once the trial ends."

Cooper and the others arrived, dressed so shabbily and with so much dirt and grime smeared on their faces that she hardly recognized them.

"Milady?"

Elizabeth pulled herself together. "What news do you have?"

Before Cooper could reply, a harried-looking footman came to the door. "Captain Kensington to see you, mum."

The captain pushed his way in looking first at Elizabeth and then focusing on Tristan. "I got your message."

Tristan nodded. "One of the servants saw some men assault Richard and him take away."

Captain Kensington paled but a new alertness brightened his eyes, and he straightened, visibly alert, every inch a soldier.

Elizabeth nodded at Cooper standing nearby. "You learned something?"

"We found th' coach. Lord Averston was transferred to a 'ackney and taken t' a swell's house— er, I mean a lord's house—righ' 'ere in Mayfair."

She stood. "Take me to him."

"No," a chorus of voices practically shouted. Tristan, Captain Kensington, and the footmen all glared at her with set jaws and firm stances.

She squared her shoulders. "My husband is in danger."

"Tha' will be no place fer a lady," Cooper said.

A murderous glint entered Tristan's eye as he checked a second gun that seemed to appear in his hand. "We'll bring him home safely."

Captain Kensington touched her arm. "Stay here, Lady Averston. Richard would never forgive us if we let you go anywhere dangerous."

"You cannot expect me to simply sit idly by while—"

Tristan made a sharp gesture. "That's exactly what you're going to do. They may still be after you, too."

Elizabeth put her hands on her hips. Janey's hand slipped into hers again, wiggling its way underneath her planted palm and tugging it down toward her. "Stay." She pled. "Don' git 'urt by th' bad men."

Two maids folded their arms, looking for all the world as if they'd been promoted from maids to guards. "She's right m'ldy," the parlor maid said. "You don' know 'ow bad those men are. You let th' men folk 'andle it."

Tristan put an arm around her shoulder and gave her a sideways hug. "I will not let them hurt my brother. You can count on that." He glanced at Cooper and the other reformed servants standing with him. "Take us to him."

Cooper nodded. "We must 'urry."

Tristan squeezed her shoulder. "Stay here. We'll bring him back."

She nodded as tears in her eyes blurred her vision. The men, servant and upper class alike, checked their weapons and left together, their voices echoing in the main hall.

Elizabeth pressed her hands over her cheeks, utterly helpless and angry, but mostly afraid.

Afraid Richard would be hurt.

Afraid she'd never see him again.

Afraid of the looming emptiness of a life without him.

Chapter Forty-Seven

Lying on his side upon a hard bed, Richard tried to breathe without becoming ill. Every motion sent shockwaves of pain rippling over him and his head felt like he'd been kicked by a horse. When he felt strong enough to try again, he tested his bindings with stiffening limbs.

Blindfolded, gagged, and bound, he had no clues as to his whereabouts. He detected noises of the streets: children at play, vendors calling, the rattle of carriages, and horse hooves clattering. From outside his room came footsteps, doors closing, and muffled voices. He wasn't even certain of the time of day, nor how long he'd been unconscious.

Each time he turned his head, he stirred the scent of old linen. Moving his bound hands also tugged on the ropes around his legs; he'd been trussed like an animal. His captors had not visited him, nor given any clue as to their intent. Surely if they planned to kill him, he'd already be dead. No doubt his abduction directly related to the trial. The lords would be voting today, so if he weren't present to cast a guilty vote, Lord Einsburgh might not receive a conviction, especially if other lords failed to appear because they'd been taken captive or otherwise coerced.

He wondered if Elizabeth were safe, or if she'd also been captured. The thought of her in the hands of dangerous men made him cold with fear. She'd stepped with grace into the role of countess and proven herself a caring woman. Yet he'd never tried to reciprocate, not really. He might never see her again, never have the chance to tell her he loved her.

And Tristan. He'd wronged his brother. Horribly. He'd thrown Tristan out of the house without even stating an accusation or giving his brother the opportunity to defend himself. He'd rejected his own brother. At least he'd tried to make amends with Tristan. If nothing else, he'd done all he could to set things right with his brother.

Uncertainty swirled in his heart around his sister. Had he done all he could for Selene? At the time, he'd thought encouraging her to paint in Italy would be the best solution for her. Perhaps it had only been an easy solution. Did she know he loved her? Or had she felt cast off by her family?

Most of all, his heart ached for Elizabeth, sweet Elizabeth…lost opportunities rose up and mocked him in all their cruel accuracy.

The metallic clink of a key in a lock reached his ears, but the key failed to turn the tumbler on the first attempt. Whispers mingled with scraping noises. Richard strained for clues of friend or foe. The door opened on creaking hinges. He tensed. What resistance he could offer, he did not know, but he would fight.

"Richard!" came a frantic whisper.

A rescue? Richard tried to reply, but the gag muffled his voice.

"He's alive," said a hushed voice.

"Richard? Can you hear me?" Tristan's quiet words bordered on panic.

Richard let out his breath in relief. In reply to Tristan's anxious call, Richard moved his head. Hands tugged at his blindfold and gag, while someone sawed at his bindings. The blindfold fell away first, and Richard squinted in the candlelight at his brother who looked as if he'd seen a ghost. Beside him stood Rhys Kensington and Cooper, as grim as a soldier in battle.

While Kensington continued sawing at the ropes binding Richard's hands and feet, Tristan let out a strangled breath. "Are you all right?"

Richard whispered, "Remind me to have more sympathy next time you tell me your head feels as if it's been used for target practice."

Tristan dragged his fingers through his hair. "I earn my headaches having fun, not getting clobbered by ruffians."

"I think I'll try it your way next time," Richard rasped.

"I'll buy," Kensington said in a low voice.

Moments later, his bindings snapped and Tristan helped him sit up. The motion sent pain spiraling out from his midsection. Richard gently probed his ribs. They hurt, but not badly. He touched the back of his throbbing head and hissed in his breath. As he realized the danger in which Tristan had placed himself by coming here, he grabbed his brother's arm.

"What are you doing here? These men are dangerous. You shouldn't have come."

"I'm here to save your pathetic hide." Tristan said. "And I'm looking for a way to prove my superior shooting skills."

Richard snorted. "How did you find me?"

"Your wife's disreputable staff proved surprisingly

useful." Tristan glanced at the footman. "Cooper here tracked you down."

"Wot I won' do fer a good suit," the footman said. "But we're no' ou' o' danger jest yet."

Alarmed by the ramifications, Richard stared at Tristan, aghast. "If you're here, who's protecting Elizabeth?"

"A veritable army, I assure you. She's safe, I give you my word." Tristan held out a hand. "Can you stand?"

Richard got to his feet but the room spun. His legs wobbled and he had to sit again until he could see straight.

"Easy, now." Tristan wrapped an arm around his waist and put one of Richard's arms over his shoulders.

"How long have I been here?"

"You've been missing for four hours."

With a gun in his hand, Kensington opened the door and flattened himself against the wall. After, peering around the corner, he gestured to them to come.

They moved down the narrow passageway, past other doors. Someone moaned on the other side of one.

"Wait," Kensington whispered tersely. He gestured to the door.

Cooper picked the lock and they found Elizabeth's brother, the Marquis of Martindale, also bound, blindfolded, and gagged.

When they freed him, he looked at them through bleary eyes. With cracked and swollen lips, Martindale croaked, "You."

No wonder the duke had been so frantic to get Richard to change his vote; his son had been held hostage.

Cooper broke in. "M'lord, we must go now."

"There may be other hostages," Richard said. "We need to search all the rooms."

Two more rooms contained prisoners, relatives of peers taking part in the trial. As a group, they crept down the corridor to a narrow staircase. Footsteps coming the other way gave them warning. A burly man came up the stairs, treading as if his feet were leaden, and staring at the floor. With a quick uppercut to the chin, Cooper knocked him out and caught the limp form before it hit the floor. Cautiously stealing down the stairs, Richard strained his ears for any sound. All remained quiet.

They reached the next floor but their luck ran out. Three men built like professional pugilists came from the opposite direction.

"You there. Stop!" The thugs pulled out pistols.

Cooper and Kensington were faster. They opened fire. Both thugs crumpled, but the gunshots set off shouting and the pounding of feet.

Richard yelled, "Tristan, give me a gun!"

Tristan tossed a pistol to Richard, and hefted a second one. Kensington pulled out two more guns and cocked them.

"This way," Cooper yelled.

They charged down the corridor toward the main staircase, away from the footsteps pounding up the servants' stairs. A gunshot roared from behind them. The wall near Richard's head splintered where the bullet struck.

"They're shooting to kill!" Kensington turned and shot at their pursuer.

The stairs ended and they burst out of the narrow

staircase into a foyer. A dozen armed men ran in from two different directions. They were surrounded.

As the guards fired, Richard dove for cover behind a nearby chair. He glanced back at Tristan who launched himself behind a large planter next to a sideboard table. A lamp above his head exploded. Another gunshot sounded. Tristan let out a grunt and crumpled.

"Tristan!" Richard shouted.

Dropping onto his stomach, he crawled toward his brother. Bullets rained all around him. How many men were there? How many guns must they have? The pauses for loading time took almost no time. One bullet whistled past his nose as Richard pulled himself to his brother. Smoke stung his eyes and his heart thudded in his ears. He reached Tristan who lay moaning. Blood seeped through his coat. He grabbed Tristan's coat, and dragged him behind a chair.

Kensington and Cooper used up their shots and could only take cover while the other men continued to fire. With more shouts and a cacophony of noise, a group of men wearing scarlet waistcoats poured into the room.

"Drop your weapons," shouted the red-clad one in the lead.

"The Bow Street Runners," Kensington said with a breath of relief. "Tristan sent for them before we came in to get you."

Outnumbered, the gunmen surrendered to the Bow Street Runners.

Richard turned his attention to his brother, shaking him gently to rouse him. "Tristan? Open your eyes..." He shook him a little harder.

If Tristan died, Richard would never forgive himself. He'd treated his brother dreadfully, always censuring him, always calling into question his motives—his only brother, that happy, irascible boy who brought mischief and sunshine, who forgave him more than he deserved, who appeared when needed most.

It was Richard's role to save Tristan, not the other way around. Tristan should never have played the hero. Yet he'd done it admirably. He'd been there for Richard just as he had always been there.

His brother lay unmoving, all the color seeping out of his face.

Chapter Forty-Eight

Elizabeth paced the floor of the front parlor under the watchful gaze of her servants-turned-guards. Worry ate a hole through her stomach. What if something happened to Richard? What a fool she'd been to waste the time they had together. How blind to think her girlish infatuation for Tristan was love. Now that she knew love, real love, with Richard, there was no comparison. Now she might never have the chance to be the wife to Richard she wanted to be, the kind of wife he deserved. Aching helplessness opened a wide chasm inside her soul. The clock in the hall chimed, mocking her inaction.

Elizabeth twisted her hands. "I have to do something. I can't just wait here."

The maids exchanged glances with the footman. "You mustn't leave th' 'ouse, m'lady. It's not safe. Mr. Black's no one to trifle wi'."

With a groan of frustration, Elizabeth paced the length of the parlor and then out to the great hall.

The footman by the front door sprang to his feet, a gun in his hand, and peered out the window by the door as if he heard something outside. The maids each grabbed nearby objects to use as weapons and took up defensive positions next to Elizabeth. Through her fear, she had the presence of mind to admire her loyal staff. Who would have thought former criminals would become such staunch defenders?

The footman watched, then let out a sigh of relief. "It's them, m'lady." He opened the door as three figures mounted the outside steps.

Richard and Captain Kensington entered, half dragging Tristan who had an arm around each of their shoulders. He leaned heavily on them as if he lacked the strength to stand.

Richard, disheveled and haggard, eyed her the way a child gazes at a desired toy in a shop. Except for a bruise on his cheek and a slight stiffness in his walk, he looked whole and well.

"You're back." With a sob, she launched herself at Richard and fell against him.

Elizabeth clung to him, pressing her cheek to his neck and inhaling his scent. He wrapped his free arm around her and pulled her close to his side.

"I have him." Kensington lifted Tristan's body away from Richard. "Hug your wife."

She burrowed in closer against her husband as he wrapped both arms around her. His shoulders began shaking. "I am beginning to suspect you're glad they didn't put a bullet in my head."

"I was so frightened for you." She drew back as she realized he was laughing. "Richard?"

Smiling, he smoothed her hair away from her face. "I can't tell you how relieved I am that you're so happy to see me." He kissed her with utmost tenderness.

She sank into him, sighing and returned the kiss with equal affection. With love.

"Ahem. If you two love birds are finished mooning over each other, I'd like to lie down now," Tristan's voice broke in.

Elizabeth's face warmed. "Sorry." She stepped back and eyed Tristan whose eyes were bright despite his pallid skin. "What happened?"

Tristan waved a hand. "A mere trifle. I only got shot rescuing your husband from certain death."

Richard and Captain Kensington let out snorts. Richard gestured to one of the servants, whose numbers had grown since their arrival. "Send for a surgeon." He cleared his voice, "Thank you all for your aid, and especially for watching over my wife in my absence."

As two of the larger footmen came forward and eased Tristan's arms around their shoulders, Elizabeth took Tristan's hand. "Thank you for helping him. You were very brave."

He grinned. "I owed him a few."

"We're even," Richard said. "Don't do anything like that again."

Tristan made a strangled noise. "Not on your life. I did the hero thing and you got the girl. Where's the justice in that?" He turned and leered at the pretty parlor maid who gave him a sultry look.

Elizabeth coughed delicately to catch the parlor maid's attention, then shook her head. "Reformed, remember?"

The parlor maid nodded. All the servants dispersed. Tristan groaned as the footman carried him upstairs.

Elizabeth put her arm around Richard and snuggled against his side. "Will he be all right?"

Kensington answered, "The ball went clean through the shoulder. He'll be fine in no time."

Elizabeth hoped her gratitude showed in her expression. "Thank you for your assistance, Captain. I am in your debt."

"Anything for a friend, my lady. Take care of him." Kensington gripped Richard's shoulder and left.

"What do you need?" she asked as she tightened her hold around Richard's waist.

"Just you. And something to eat."

After ordering a meal, she kissed him again, long and tenderly, basking in the feel of him. When their lips parted, she said, "Tell me what happened."

He led her into the library where he poured himself a brandy. Watching him lest he suddenly vanish, she sank into a chair. After sipping his drink, he seated himself next to her, close enough that their thighs touched.

"I was convinced of Lord Einsburgh's guilt and had made up my mind to cast a vote guilty. Einsburgh's men captured me and held me prisoner in Lord Drummell's house to prevent me from voting. Three other prisoners were there, too—your brother, and family members of other peers involved in the trial."

"Martindale?" Alarm shot through her that her brother had also been in danger.

"He's safe. We freed him and the others." Richard fingered his glass. "Yesterday, your father tried to convince me to vote Lord Einsburgh innocent. I thought the conversation seemed odd. Now I know he was doing it to save his son. Why this Mr. Black fellow was helping Einsburgh is anyone's guess."

Elizabeth tapped her finger against her lip, thinking. "So when they failed to capture me, they went after you."

Richard closed his eyes and drew a shaking breath. Then another. He put an arm around her and squeezed her so hard that she nearly squeaked. "I'm so grateful they didn't capture you." His husky voice touched a tender place in her heart.

They sat together, content to be in each other's arms, until Elizabeth asked, "How did you get out of there?"

"While we were trying to escape the house, some servants acting as guards came. There were some shots fired, and then the Bow Street Runners arrived and arrested everyone involved. Tristan was hit and I don't mind telling you I was terrified he'd been killed." He shook his head. "I nearly went out of my mind."

She put her hand on his chest and rubbed it, hoping to comfort him.

Mrs. Brown arrived with a tray of food for Richard. "My lord, I am gratified to see your safe return."

"Thank you, Mrs. Brown." Richard tucked into his meal.

Mrs. Brown turned to Elizabeth looking as if she were about to face the gallows. "My lady. I was wrong to doubt you and your choice in hiring the servants from Mrs. Goodfellow."

Elizabeth nodded. "I am sure you only had our best interests at heart."

"I did, but I was rude to you. As the lady of the house, you deserve my loyalty and respect. I failed to give it to you. I do most humbly apologize." She stood with her hands at her sides, her head bowed, looking so contrite that Elizabeth didn't have the heart to bear a grudge.

"You are unfailingly loyal to the Barrett family and have served them well for many years. I'm willing to let bygones be bygones if you're willing to accept me as the mistress."

She kept her head lowered. "Of course. Thank you, my lady." The woman made a brief, respectful curtsy and left them alone.

Richard squeezed her hand. "Well done. I, too, vow to honor you and your wishes…with all my heart."

Before Elizabeth could fully immerse herself in his words, a footman said, "A Bow Street constable here to see you, sir."

"Show him in."

The constable entered with his hat in his hands. "I know you gave us a statement at the scene, my lord, but I need to get more details, if I may."

"Of course. Have a seat."

Richard related all the day's happenings while the constable nodded, asking occasional questions and scribbling in his small book. Then he asked Elizabeth about the attacks on her.

When they were finished, Elizabeth spoke, "There's one thing I still don't understand."

Richard brushed a hand across her cheek, smiling tenderly. "What is that, love?"

She smiled at his term of endearment but directed her words to the constable. "The servants were convinced my husband had been taken by men who worked for someone named Mr. Black. Cooper thought that man in the park worked for Mr. Black, too. Now it appears that Lord Einsburgh was behind it?"

The Bow Street investigator tapped his pencil against his pad. "Mr. Black is a fictional name at the head of the crime organization. We've been after him for a long time. We just learned that Mr. Black is actually two men—Lord Einsburgh and Mr. Drummell."

Richard nodded. "Clever. Very clever."

"They both made fortunes smuggling and dealing in the black market during the war," the Runner said. "Now that the war has ended, they focused their attention on London where they already had a strong presence. We didn't know Drummell and Einsburgh were connected to Mr. Black, only that Einsburgh was reportedly associated with flash houses and a theft ring." The constable stood. "Thank you for your statement, my lord, my lady. I'll let you know if we need further testimony."

When they were alone, Elizabeth wrapped her arms around him and rested her head on his chest. "I'm so glad you're safe."

"I owe that to your reformed servants as much as to Tristan and Kensington."

She tried to lighten the mood. "It's fortunate for you that I have such good instincts about servants."

"Indeed."

His heart thumped a reassuring rhythm underneath her cheek, and she blessed each beat. Gratitude for his safe return warmed her and eased aside the last of her anxiety over the day's events.

After a moment, she said, "You sounded a little surprised by my greeting when you first arrived."

He said nothing for a long moment. "To be honest, I thought you might have been more worried for Tristan's well-being than my own." He flashed a sheepish smile. "I said I trust you and I meant it, but I wasn't sure where your heart lay. You seemed so much in love with him."

"It was mere girlish infatuation. I assure you, my feelings for you have far surpassed what I felt for him."

He grinned as if she'd handed him the finest gift ever. "I can't tell you how happy I am to hear that." He pulled back just enough to kiss her, lingering and gentle. Then his lips grew more possessive and his arms tightened around her.

With lips that tremble, and with glistening eye
All the soft luxury
That nestled in his arms.

She'd always loved that scene from "Calidore" by Keats when the knight saw his lady love. Now she truly knew what that meant.

She touched Richard's face, returning his kisses with equal ardor. "All yours. Forever. I love you, Richard, only you."

He let out his breath. "I love you, and you alone." A determined glint entered his eye and he scooped her up.

With decisive steps, he carried her to his room where his outpouring of gentleness and passion proved to her just how much he loved her. No knight of old could have surpassed Richard's fierce, tender love. No poet had adequately penned the bubbling joy she found in his touch.

Her thoughts from the house party came back to her, only filled with Richard: Lady Elizabeth had never dared hope she would find the kind of joy that inspired poets and musicians…until she met the incomparable Richard Barrett

Enfolded in his arms, she faded into a sweet slumber, safer and more blissfully happy than she'd ever dreamed.

A word about the author...

A hopeless romantic and adventurer at heart, Donna Hatch discovered her writing passion at the tender age of eight and has been listening to those voices ever since. She is a sought-after workshop presenter and juggles freelance editing, multiple volunteer positions, and most of all, her six children. A native of Arizona who recently transplanted to the Pacific Northwest, she and her husband of over twenty years are living proof that there really is a happily ever after.

www.donnahatch.com

Thank you for purchasing
this publication of The Wild Rose Press, Inc.

If you enjoyed the story, we would appreciate your
letting others know by leaving a review.

For other wonderful stories,
please visit our on-line bookstore at
www.thewildrosepress.com.

For questions or more information
contact us at
info@thewildrosepress.com.

The Wild Rose Press, Inc.
www.thewildrosepress.com

Stay current with The Wild Rose Press, Inc.

Like us on Facebook

https://www.facebook.com/TheWildRosePress

And Follow us on Twitter
https://twitter.com/WildRosePress